Gray Fisher #2

Tabula Rasa

by
Debbie McGowan

I0640444

Beaten Track
www.beatentrackpublishing.com

Tabula Rasa

First published 2018 by Beaten Track Publishing
Copyright © 2018 Debbie McGowan

ISBN: 978 1 78645 217 7

Beaten Track Publishing,
Burscough, Lancashire.
www.beatentrackpublishing.com

For Julie, Bill and Kirsty:

You worked miracles.

Acknowledgements

Much gratitude to David, Bob, Amy, Nige, Al, Andrea and Jor for (respectively and respectfully) crit-partnering, alpha-reading, beta-reading, editing and proofreading, and catching me when I fail/flail/fall.

Acknowledgements

Contents

"*The hero surviving his own murder, his own suicide, his own addiction, surviving his own disappearance from the scene...*"

Allen Ginsberg
The Fall of America:
Poems of These States 1965-1971

Prologue

The rich mixed aroma of chargrilled meats and beer began its daily takeover as the evening rush hour petered away, such as it ever did in London. Gray turned the corner into the street where the restaurant was located, observant, alert, briefly assessing the pedestrians ahead, every vehicle along the short stretch of wet tarmac. No agenda, no motive; habit reinforced by more than a decade of service.

A motorbike roared past, horn tooting a second later to announce the arrival of the guest of honour: former Constable Rob Simpson-Stone. The right indicator flashed, and the bike turned into what Gray knew to be a dead-end alley, an access-and-delivery point for the restaurant and hotel between which it fell. Less than a minute later, when he arrived at the neck of the alley and peered down it, he saw the bike parked at the far end, but no sign of Rob.

Must've missed him. It was no big deal. Gray wasn't concerned about walking in on his own. There was a good chance he'd know most of those in attendance—one that increased in likelihood when he stepped through the doors and discovered the restaurant had been entirely taken over by the Metropolitan Police for the evening. A few heads turned, eyebrows rose here and there in recognition, before they returned to their drinks and conversations. Laughter erupted to Gray's left; another new arrival excused their way past; a hand raised in a wave at the bar—Martina Hedley, standing alone. Gray went over to join her.

"Evening, Ma'am. How are you?"

She'd never been his superior and laughed at his formal address. "Evening, Gray. I'm well, thanks. You?"

"Fine." He squinted, his eyes struggling to adjust to the bar's blue LEDs. "Do we order drinks or wait for them to come to us?"

"I gave up waiting and ordered mine. I'm surprised Rob isn't here yet."

"He passed me on his bike about three minutes ago."

"Oh? He hasn't come in."

Gray saw the bartender heading his way and stepped up, ready to order. "He'll be making sure his pride and joy is secure for the duration."

Martina's eyebrow arched doubtfully. Irrespective of Rob's apathy for the evening's frivolities, both knew he was a stickler for punctuality.

"He'll get here sooner or later, I'm sure," Gray said.

"I'd bloody well hope so, seeing as it's his leaving do."

***

Rob barely got his helmet off when the bag came down over his head and he was dragged forcibly to the ground. Before the panic had a chance to set in, he was up on his feet again. His back slammed against the wall, a heavy weight across his chest forcing him to take shallow breaths and pinning him in place. One of his assailants—he could hear two sets of boots—gave a warning *shhhh* and then nothing else happened.

A minute later, someone said, "Clear." The pressure on Rob's chest eased, exchanged for a strong grip around his upper arms as he was marched back along the alley to the street and manhandled into what he assumed—from the height he had to step up and the heavy sliding door—to be a van. The door screeched shut, and with a painful jolt, Rob was thrown onto his side as they took off into the early evening city traffic.

30 Minutes Earlier

1: Jock

Leathers over slacks and shirt, helmet in hand, Rob was at the door and ready to leave when his phone buzzed against his chest.

Leave it, answer it, leave it... If it was important, whoever it was would call back. It stopped. Rob opened the front door a couple of inches at most before it started up again. With a grunt, he pushed the door shut and partially unzipped his jacket. There was a time when he could've ignored a ringing phone—the number onscreen was unfamiliar to both him and his address book, cold caller, more than likely—but he wasn't prepared to take the chance.

"Hello?"

"Hello, Shaz?"

"Sorry, mate, you've got the wrong number."

"Nah. I don't think so."

"There's no-one here by... Ah, hold up. Jock?"

"Yeah. Alright?"

"Bloody hell. It's been a while. How did you get this number?"

"Rang your landline. Your missus gave me your mobile."

"Fair enough." It wasn't like Zoë to give out his number without checking with him first, but he'd worry about that later. "How're you doing, man?"

Rob caught the microsecond pause before Jock—aka Corporal Harry 'Jocky' Wilson—answered, "Yeah, I'm doing all right. You?"

"I'm doing great. I thought you were still OS."

Jock barked out a laugh. "Where the hell have you been? I've been back five years. Forty-five and retired. Not bad, eh? Bought a gaff down Brighton way. The kids hate it, of course."

"Still just the two?" Rob remembered only because he'd heard Jock's second kid had been born the day after Lucas, seven years ago. He'd never met Jock's family—had hardly spoken to the guy since leaving the army.

"Yeah. You had any more?" Jock asked.

"No, unfortunately. Zoë and I are divorced."

"Sorry to hear that."

"Cheers." Rob braced, hoping Jock wouldn't ask him what happened. Most people didn't, but Jock wasn't most people.

"So…still got flat feet?"

Rob chuckled, relieved to be let off the hook so easily. "Ask me again in five hours. I'm just heading out for my leaving do."

"Bollocks. My timing's good as ever, eh?"

"Why? What's up?"

"There's a few of us getting together this evening for a pint and catch-up."

"Crap. If there was a way I could get out of it…" There wasn't, or Rob would've taken it. He hadn't wanted a leaving do to start with, and much as he and Jock weren't exactly on friendly terms, he was well up for a couple of pints with his old army mates. "How long are you gonna be out, d'you reckon?"

"Not sure. Depends who's got wives and kiddies to get home to."

"Right." Presumably, Jock had left his down in Brighton for the weekend.

"We're meeting at Euston. Are you anywhere nearby?"

"Yeah, at the Quarterhouse. Five minutes away."

"How about this, then? I'll text you where we are. If you make it, all well and good. If not, I'll call back tomorrow and we can sort something else."

"Perfect," Rob said. "Have a good one."

"You too, mate. Bye." Jock ended the call.

Rob saved the number and put his phone back in his pocket, this time making it out of the door and onto his bike, but his thoughts were still on the conversation as he rode into the city. He hadn't heard from any of his old army mates in over five years, because he'd been off the grid, and even before that, when they did meet up, it was with some reluctance that they invited Jock. He was one sadistic bastard and a racist to boot, but they'd had to work together, so they'd got on with it, although Jock's attitude was one of the reasons Rob had come out of the army when he did.

Given the way things were between them, there had to be an ulterior motive for the call or someone else would've made it, and Rob's curiosity was threatening to get the better of him. For the time being, he put it out of mind and focused on his riding.

Even though it was past rush hour, the roads were chaos, and he was beginning to regret not getting the train, but the bike would stop people buying him drinks all night. He needed a clear head; he was off up north first thing. He hadn't been home since Christmas, and in the three months that had elapsed, he'd become a great-uncle. Never mind that he'd had no idea his youngest niece was pregnant.

Traffic was backed up from the junction, and Rob could've got past it, but instead, he settled behind a bus and let his mind drift again. With the prospect of a couple of weeks of proper holiday, he was well up for some quality family time and a bit of R and R before he set the wheels in motion for his new venture. Of course, there was no guarantee it would take off, or, if it did, how long it would take to get fully established, and he was prepared for the possibility of failure. So long as it was moving in the right direction, he'd stick with it, but he had a backup plan just the same. As soon as he got back from his mum's, he was going to sign on with an agency as a security officer, pick up a few hours of paid work, maybe get up to speed on mechanics.

But first, this leaving do he'd said he didn't want. A sit-down meal and a restaurant to themselves was not Rob's first choice for a decent night out—but that he'd been given a choice at all. A couple of pints and a curry, he'd have been happy, and he'd planned an early exit strategy, which was pretty pointless now he was expected elsewhere.

What it is to be popular. Except popularity didn't come into it. True, Rob wasn't short of friends, some of them amongst his colleagues—or former colleagues—and his army mates, but there was always a performance to getting together—who could drink the most, stay conscious the longest, come up with the best bullshit for how perfectly bloody wonderful their life was. Most of them were single and made out it was their choice to be so, or saw nothing wrong with acting as if they were. What happens on a night out…

Rob wasn't a fuddy-duddy, however much Travis—Zoë's fiancé—made him feel like he was old enough for the hill to be a distant blur in his mirrors. Difficult as it had been for Rob to accept it, Travis was good for Zoë and Lucas. The guy seemed to have endless energy and time to burn it off on family outings—a luxury Rob's work could never afford, or, at least, one he had never permitted himself to take. Nonetheless, if he heard 'we went there with Travis, didn't we, Mum?' one more time…well, he'd grin and bear it, for Lu's sake, just as he'd done every time before.

Finally, Rob made it through the junction and put his foot down. A few hours of socialising, a good night's kip, then he could forget about posturing coppers and *Stepdad of the Year* in favour of a few nights out with his old mates, a few nights in watching telly with his mum, and if he could be arsed, he'd catch up with Jock and the others when he got back.

2. Not Leaving Yet

"Do you want me to come with you?" Will yawned the question.

Gray put down the iron and flipped to the next section of shirt, briefly glancing at Will's face onscreen. "You, in a room full of police officers?" He picked up the iron again.

"I've done it before."

"Have you?"

"Well…it was a courtroom. But I was quite civil."

Gray looked up and had to laugh. Will's grin glowed white in his stubble-darkened, mud-streaked face. He looked anything but civil. He was also very obviously knackered.

"You should go shower before you nod off," Gray advised.

"I'm all right yet. Tie's picking up food on his way home. Which means hummus again."

"There's nothing wrong with hummus."

"Every now and then, but we've had it every night this week."

"You know what you could do? It's a bit radical." Gray checked his shirt to make sure he'd pressed all of it, switched off the iron and tugged his t-shirt over his head.

"Get the train to your place and wait for you to come home from your party?" Will's tone was decidedly sultry.

Gray emerged from inside his t-shirt and covered the camera with his hand.

"Rotter."

Laughing, Gray successfully got his shirt most of the way on with his hand still covering the camera, only moving it when he had to in order to fasten his buttons.

Will scowled. "I was enjoying the view."

"I'm sure you were. But I need to go or I'll be late."

"Yeah, OK. What were you gonna suggest?"

"Suggest…oh. That you go shopping instead of sending Tie?"

"Think I'll put up with hummus. I'll leave you to it. Don't forget to enjoy yourself."

"Forget in the next half an hour? Unlikely. I'll give you all the gory details tomorrow."

"OK. Later." Will ended the call, leaving Gray free to finish getting dressed and ruminate over turning down Will's offer.

He hadn't set out to mislead Will, but somewhere along the line, he'd had a bit of a wobble and implied going to Rob's leaving party was a chore he could do without—hence Will's offer to go with him. It would've been a first for them—accompanying each other to an official function—but that wasn't why he'd put Will off. Plus-ones were rarely welcome at police socials, and even though this one was being held in a restaurant with a nightclub attached, the culture would be rife. Gray remembered it far too well—the all-consuming nature of the job that made it difficult to switch off.

Hopefully, tonight would be different because Rob had never been a typical copper. Work or play, no mixing the two unless he was under orders, and he was leaving because he'd had enough. He'd tried going back in uniform and a stint in CID, but he couldn't settle in his old job. So, he'd resigned to set up a private investigation agency…and asked Gray to go in with him.

It sounded far more thrilling than it would no doubt prove to be, and that suited Gray just fine. Only thirty-five and he'd already had his lifetime's worth of excitement. It wasn't so long since he'd been out every night of the week, getting drunk, getting high… it hadn't been fun. But he was past all that now and dealing with his problems like a functioning adult instead of an out-of-control lunatic with a death wish. If it were anyone other than Rob, Gray would've given tonight a miss in favour of lounging on his couch.

Or Will's, along with at least one dog. The image popped into his mind of Will flopped full length of the sofa at the bottom of a dog pile, pitta bread in one hand, hummus in the other. It was a surprisingly alluring vision.

In the hallway, putting on his jacket, the *should I, shouldn't I?* debate started up again. Gray would've liked to have taken Will along, but no. He wanted the company, worried he'd be left standing alone at the bar all night—selfish reasons, in other words, none of them valid when Will would need to get a cab home and be up early for work. Another time.

Finally settled to the decision, Gray checked he had his phone and wallet, and set off for the Underground station. It was a bit lazy, seeing as it was only two stops, and he could almost have walked it in the time it took for the journey and getting through the stations at both ends. An eternal lift ride at Russell Square was followed by the realisation that Rob's leaving card was still on the coffee table, along with Gray's packet of gum. The card could wait till he saw Rob next; the gum couldn't, not that Gray was planning on getting up close and personal with anyone tonight, but garlic and conversation was not a good combination and he did like his garlic—Jean's legacy.

There was a metro supermarket just around the corner from the station, which Gray had shopped in a few times, although, as usual, the powers-that-be had taken it upon themselves to switch all of the stock around, and Gray found tins of soup and baked beans in the aisle where the confectionery had previously been shelved. Rice and pasta now resided where the tinned goods used to be, and he eventually found the chewing gum—not even in the same place as the chocolate and sweets—on the top shelf in an aisle he couldn't ever recall walking down before, which meant it was probably once the home-baking aisle.

Typically, his usual brand presented an empty box, and as he considered the alternatives, a woman passed behind him, her trolley brushing his hip. She didn't notice, too absorbed in the heated discussion she was having via a headset.

"Yeah, I mean he's literally dropped off the face of the planet."

Literally? Flat Earth member?

The woman rounded the end of the aisle and disappeared from view, but continued talking at a volume Gray could hear.

"We were together for eleven years, for Christ sakes, John. I can't just let it go."

Intrigued for no reason other than his enquiring mind had yet to break the habit of latching on to snippets of potentially useful information, Gray moved slowly along the aisle and eavesdropped the entire conversation.

"No forwarding address, no new number—nothing… Nope. Passport's still there… Oh, yeah, I know his Facebook profile is still live, but he hasn't logged into it since—of course he's not been kidnapped! … It's not in the least comforting. Yes! … No, I really would rather he'd upped sticks and found someone else. I don't hate him *that* much. I still…"

The woman stopped talking as they emerged simultaneously from the other end of their respective aisles. She gave Gray a self-conscious smile and, dropping her volume to almost a whisper, said, "I miss him."

Gray could've gone straight through the self-service but it would've meant ditching the free entertainment—it was turning into a real tearjerker—so he queued at the checkout behind the woman, and turned side on, his eyes on the activity of other shoppers, his ears still trained to her conversation. 'Kidnapped' was an attention grabber, although it didn't sound like a kidnapping. If anything, it sounded like a good deal of the cases he'd worked undercover—fraudsters and embezzlers who changed their identity and ditched their old life for a fresh start, with the sole intention of doing it all over again. The social networks were littered with ghost profiles that made it easy to pinpoint when someone 'went missing', but if they knew what they were doing, the trail ended there.

Of course, the more likely scenario was that the woman's partner had, as she said, found someone new. Without his passport, he couldn't have gone far, and leaving it behind indicated he intended to return at some point—unless he couldn't.

The woman continued her phone call all the way through loading her shopping onto the conveyor belt, packing it back into the trolley and paying for her purchases, but by then it had moved on to gossip, and Gray tuned out, wondering how it was he so often made the subconscious slip back into his old way of thinking. He'd been out of the police for almost a year; with his PhD well underway, his teaching, and weekends with Will, he had more than enough to occupy his mind. Yet at the mere hint of 'a case', off it went, sifting information for vital clues, which wasn't necessarily a bad thing when he'd be needing those skills soon enough, although not to find missing spouses. He and Rob still had to hone the fine print, but they were in agreement about limiting their commissions to corporate and commercial investigations.

Twenty minutes later, Gray made it out of the store, shoved a piece of gum in his mouth and the overheard conversation out of his mind, and set off for the restaurant. It was less than a ten-minute walk from his current location, and as he walked, the streetlights switched on, bleaching out the blue-grey late-March dusk. Gray squinted painfully; his eyes were hyper-sensitive to light and took a long time to adjust, if they adjusted at all. The surgeon had been optimistic it was temporary, but almost four years on, he'd concluded he was stuck with it.

It was one of the more minor but no less inconvenient consequences of the crash—not too bad if he planned in advance. A cinema trip meant wearing prescribed tinted glasses or prosthetic lenses for 3D, and he always wore his glasses when driving—even at night. Sunlight didn't cause any problems; his 'photophobia' was specific to artificial light, and fluorescent and LED lighting was the worst.

Thus, Gray wasn't one hundred percent sure it was Rob's bike that passed him as he arrived. The horn toot suggested it was, but judging by the way Martina was searching the restaurant, she was concerned her would-have-been protégé wasn't going to show.

"Are you all right for a drink?" Gray asked.

Martina held up her glass, which contained about an inch of dark liquid. "Double brandy and Coke," she said, reaching into her pocket. Gray raised his hand to stop her.

"I'll get these. Ice?"

"Please."

"Who's next?" the bartender asked and homed in on Gray. "Yes, sir?"

"A pint of Guinness with blackcurrant and a double brandy and Coke with ice, please."

"Guinness and blackcurrant?" Martina queried.

"It's my tipple of choice these days," Gray said, distracted by the murmurs of conversation across the room. A few other people had noticed Rob arrive on his bike, and the question kept cropping up of where he'd got to.

Martina wrinkled her nose. "To each their own."

Gray had to recap to figure out she meant his drink. "They wouldn't have pulled a stunt, would they?"

"For a leaving do?" Martina's tone implied she thought that was a ridiculous suggestion. "I'm not sure they'd pull one on Rob even if he was getting hitched. He doesn't take practical jokes well."

"Really? That surprises me." Gray somehow kept his face straight. It wasn't so much that Rob had no sense of humour. OK, it was. Even away from work, he was serious and intense, and when he did crack a joke, it was hard to gauge whether it was appropriate to laugh. Gray had always assumed it was because he hated the undercover work, but from what Martina was saying, it was a personality trait.

The bartender set their drinks on the counter, and Gray handed over Martina's.

"Thanks," she said, a little contrite. "Sorry to snatch and run, but I need to catch up with my boss while he's in a good mood."

Gray laughed, understanding all too well. "No problem. See you later."

Martina edged past a group of men standing a few feet away and disappeared into the growing crowd. Gray paid for their drinks and took up residence on a barstool. Perhaps his worries about spending the evening alone hadn't been unfounded after all.

As he'd predicted, there were a few other familiar faces, all engaged in conversation, but he was quite happy watching for the time being. And it was just ordinary watching, he was relieved to find, not the obsessive vigilance that had contributed—possibly on a par with Jean's death—to his craving for mind-altering substances as a means of shutting off. But he didn't do that anymore—ten months clean and counting. Just like anyone else, he had bad days when it was harder to resist, but on the whole, it was getting easier every day.

The evening moved swiftly along, and after another half an hour, the staff had no choice but to ask everyone to take their seats, still with no sign of the guest of honour. Gray took out his phone and started typing a message, but he abandoned it, unsent. Rob would be inundated by now—or not. No-one seemed overly concerned by his continuing absence. However, Rob was never late without just cause.

"Sir?" A waiter smiled at Gray and pointed him towards the tables.

"Yes, of course." Gray moved away from the bar, but rather than find a seat, he headed for the exit, phone held out in front of him as if he were going out to receive a call.

"Gray! Over here!"

He mouthed, "Won't be a sec," at Martina and dodged outside. It had gone completely dark, but his eyes had barely adjusted to the light inside, so he continued unencumbered to the mouth of the alley and squinted into the gloom, making out a few dark objects of various shapes and sizes—bins and boxes. But no bike.

3: Hostage

As soon as the van's inertia would let him, Rob pushed himself upright, resting his back against the chilly side panel.

"You fuckers," he muttered. He could've taken the sack off his head himself—he wasn't cuffed—but he waited for someone else to do the deed, and grabbed them by the wrist, twisting their arm the wrong way.

"Ow, you bastard." John 'Bish' Garvey shook his hand and flexed his fingers. "My good arm, that."

"Aw, mate." Rob was loving the familiar banter already, even if they had, effectively, kidnapped him. "What the hell is this?"

"Rescue mission," someone called from the cab—Tonka, or 2nd Lieutenant Yvette Parker if you fancied losing your balls.

"Correct," Bish corroborated. "Jock told us you were looking for a get-out from this police do."

Rob sighed, long and loud. "Attendance isn't optional."

"I disagree," Tonka said.

"You realise they'll have half the Met out looking for me within the hour?"

"Only if they notice you're missing."

Rob smirked, taking the insult on the chin. This was madness, but he wasn't kidding about the search party. "Where are we off, Ma'am?"

"That's on a need-to-know." Tonka's reply was half-masked by the crunch of gears. "Christ, Bish, this is a bag of shit." More crunching ensued. Bish cringed and thumbed towards the driver's seat, mouthing, "Women drivers."

Rob shook his head and laughed. "Where is Jock, by the way?"

17

Tonka eyed the rear-view mirror. "Behind us."

Rob leaned forward and peered through a small crack in the paint covering the back window. "You haven't let him ride my bike?"

"It was him or me." Bish grinned and waggled the stump that was all that remained of his right arm.

"If he trashes it, I'll rip off the other one and beat you with the soggy end."

"You and whose army, Shaz?" Pre-empting the smack around the head, Bish ducked, and Rob's fingers spliced thin air.

"All right, I'll come willingly, but—"

"Like you've got a choice."

"*But* I'm only staying for one. I need to at least put in an appearance tonight."

"We get the picture. Your police mates are more important. We're not offended, are we, Ma'am?"

"Not in the least."

"You soft gets." Rob took another glance out the back window; they were in Camden, heading for Hampstead Heath, Rob guessed—Tonka came from over that way—with the Cyclops eye of the bike's headlamp still on their tail. It was a forty-minute round trip; if he stayed for a pint and chinwag, he could be at his leaving do a little after nine. True, he'd be over an hour late, but with any luck, they'd only just have realised he was missing by then.

The sketchy view, front and rear, changed from lit roads to dark trees, and Rob caught sight of light reflecting off water—one of the bathing ponds, he thought—before the van veered right. Half a minute later, they stopped. Tonka got out and slid the side door open. It was the first decent look at her Rob had got, and he wasn't quick enough to hide his shock. From the state of her, she hadn't slept in months.

Tonka faked a cheery grin. "You getting out, or what?"

"Or what," Rob said but shuffled on his backside until he could jump down onto the tarmac beside her. "Good to see you, Ma'am."

She hauled him in for a hug. "You too, Rob." As she released him, she murmured, "Need your help."

He gave a subtle nod to confirm he'd heard and turned his attention to Jock, who was fighting to get the kickstand down on the bike. Rob went over and had it sorted in a matter of seconds.

"There's a knack," he explained in answer to Jock's grunt and held out his hand for his helmet and keys. Jock compliantly handed both over. "And my phone?"

"Ain't got it."

"For real?"

"Yeah, for real. You calling me a liar?"

"Come in, lads," Tonka called, already on the move. "That heap of scrap can stay out on the road. Maybe a neighbour'll get it towed for you, Bish."

"They bloody well won't," Bish muttered as the three of them followed Tonka, pausing for her to open wide double gates, beyond those a significant detached house that shone blinding white in the near-daylight illumination. While they waited for her to unlock the door and turn off the alarm, Rob sized up the property. Tonka must've been in her late-fifties by now and hadn't long retired. She'd been in thirty years, so she'd have been on a damned good pension, although Rob doubted it would be enough to afford a house like this on her own.

He continued his surveillance as she beckoned them inside. Sometimes he wished he'd stayed in the army, or stayed single, at least, then he wouldn't be living in a crappy one-bedroom flat and handing over seventy-five percent of his salary. He honestly didn't regret marrying Zoë or having Lucas, but he had to wonder at the injustice of it when all his mates seemed to be so much better off than he was.

For all that Tonka's house was impressive, it wasn't his kind of place. It was one of the Scandinavian-style 1970s builds with an open-plan ground floor, and too much pine and bare brickwork. Windows like a department store front ran the length of one wall; two oversize white sofas at right angles squared off the living area; beyond those were the dining area and kitchen, with a steep, open-step, spiral staircase tucked away in the corner.

Tonka strode across to the kitchen and opened the fridge, saying, "Beer?" as she withdrew four bottles, popped them open on the lip of the countertop, and distributed them.

"Cheers," Rob said. He swigged from the bottle and rotated on the spot to take another look at the place. The other two men carried their beers over to the living area and sat, one on each sofa. "You live here alone?" Rob asked.

"More or less. My brother lives here too, officially...but he's away at present. You're not impressed, are you?"

"Well..." Rob frowned. He hadn't realised he was being that obvious.

Tonka laughed. "Don't worry about it. It's not to everyone's tastes—it was our aunt's place, and I'm not that attached myself—but it's a nice area and it's too much hassle to move."

"I know what you mean." Rob was in much the same situation, or not as regards living in a nice area. He'd seen a couple of better flats in the paper for the same rent, which was going to be a stretch without a regular salary coming in. Ideally, he wanted something a bit bigger so he could have Lucas over more often, but on his income, he'd have to move so far out of the city he might as well go back up north.

"Shall we sit?" Tonka suggested.

"Sure," Rob agreed. This was nothing like he'd expected when Jock said they were meeting for a reunion, but he wasn't going anywhere until Tonka told him what was going on.

Seeing as Jock had parked himself smack bang in the middle of one sofa, Rob opted for the other one, sitting at the opposite end to Bish.

Tonka perched on the arm next to Rob. "You're leaving the police, then?"

"Yeah. I've had enough—not of the job itself. I still like the work, but I'm done taking orders."

Tonka spluttered air into the neck of her beer bottle. Rob scowled, but he had to admit, he'd been a defiant little shit when he first joined up. He soon learnt.

"Have you got something else lined up?"

"Pretty much. I'm going self-employed. Private investigations."

"Told you he was a dick," Jock said—predictably.

"Actually, you said I was a black c—"

"All right, lads," Tonka warned, though it was more a command, which they obeyed without hesitation.

"Sorry, Ma'am," Rob said. He knew better than to let Jock get under his skin.

Tonka nodded her acceptance of his apology and stood up. "You haven't seen my new car, have you?"

"Not that I know of." Ignoring the lewd remarks from the other two men about the two of them going for a quickie—it was never going to happen, but that didn't stop the wind-up—Rob trailed Tonka across the room to the staircase, behind which was a door leading to the garage. She flicked a light switch and stepped aside for Rob to come in far enough that she could close the door behind him.

"Whoa! You finally got one?" Rob edged along the garage wall, eyeing up the gleaming white paintwork and sleek curves. He wasn't into cars, but who wouldn't get a bit hot under the collar for a Lamborghini Aventador? "You get out in it much?"

"From time to time. You remember Siggy?"

"Yeah. Course I do." He remembered her very well, seeing as she'd been a constant presence when their unit was stationed in Germany. She owned a hotel a few miles from the base; they'd spent many evenings there. "You're still in touch?"

Tonka nodded, an uncharacteristically sappy expression softening the lines of age and sleep deprivation. "It's a good excuse to give the car a run out," she reasoned.

Rob smiled. "Couldn't agree more." He walked back to Tonka and checked the door to the house was closed. "You said you needed my help."

"Yeah." Tonka's eyes strayed briefly to the car and then met Rob's gaze. "You know Ethan's being discharged?"

"I didn't." He felt the effect of the adrenaline surge brought on by Tonka's question at the same moment she sensed it in him. Her jaw tensed, and her pupils, already dilated to compensate for the dimness of the garage, almost filled her irises. Rob turned away and stared at the far wall.

"It's been a long time," she said.

"I'm aware of that, Ma'am."

"They can't keep him locked up indefinitely."

"Why not? If he was a civilian—"

"It would've made no difference."

"Of course it fucking would!" Rob's shout echoed back at him in the bare-brick box; he quickly got his temper in check. "That Marine in Afghanistan who went down for murder—first case of its kind, they said, but we both know that's not true."

"What Ethan did—"

"Wasn't a mindless execution?"

Tonka tugged her hair back in frustration. "It was mindless, I'll give you that, which is why he's spent the last eighteen years locked up, but it's not in the same league as torturing an enemy soldier for fun."

"No, it's worse."

"I've got to say, I expected you to be more sympathetic, Rob."

He laughed in disbelief. "Sorry, Ma'am, I've got no sympathy for wife beaters."

"You know it wasn't like that." Tonka's tone had changed, trying to plead with his common sense, but he'd heard it all before. Sergeant Ethan McGrath had gone home on leave and caught his wife in bed with another man. He'd battered his wife and killed the bit on the side. He was charged with manslaughter and admitted to Brookhurst secure hospital. The official diagnosis was PTSD, but Ethan's anger issues had been there long before he saw action.

Rob cut to the chase. "What do you need?" Before Tonka's relieved smile had fully formed, he added, "I'm not agreeing to anything."

"Just hear me out, OK?"

He shrugged and nodded; he could agree to that much.

"We all know how hard it is to adjust to civilian life, and that's without a criminal record and a mental illness. If Ethan stands any chance of surviving in the outside world, he needs a fresh start."

"You're talking about a new identity."

Tonka unblinkingly held Rob's gaze but didn't answer.

"Much as I hate to disappoint you—"

Her short, brutal 'ha' cut him off.

"I've never let you down before," Rob said, hurt by her insinuation.

Tonka patted his shoulder. "You're right. I'm sorry."

"Even if I was still in the police—and willing—it's well outside my jurisdiction. In any case, it's there to protect victims and witnesses, not to hide madmen in plain sight."

"And to rehabilitate young offenders," Tonka argued. "Those lads who killed that kiddie up in Liverpool, for instance—"

"In very special circumstances, yeah. I'll give you that. But they were no more than kids themselves, and whether they've been successfully rehabilitated or not, the public are on a witch hunt."

"We're getting a bit off track, here, Rob. I'm not asking you to pull strings—"

"I wouldn't have done it anyway."

Tonka's eyebrows rose and her lips thinned in annoyance. "Ethan's not a common criminal. He's got a mental illness, but it's under control."

"Until the next time he loses it and batters someone to death. Mental illness or not, he's dangerous—"

"Now, look," Tonka shouted him down. "With respect, you haven't seen him recently, Rob. He's a different man, trust me, or go visit him and see for yourself. If he wasn't, I wouldn't be doing this, but if we don't do something…well, they might as well throw away the key now. He's got to live with the consequences of what he did, which would be hard enough without being a veteran with a criminal record and a psych diagnosis. All we're doing is giving him a chance at a normal life."

Tonka waited for Rob's response, but she'd only given him the 'why', not the 'what'.

"Go on," he said.

"I know someone who'll give him a new identity."

"Ma'am…"

"You're going to tell me it's against the law? I know. Incredible how that same law doesn't apply to child killers who tortured for their own entertainment, eh?"

"It's a whole other situation."

"Ethan lost his temper for good reason, and he handed himself in."

"Because he wanted out of the army."

Tonka threw out her hands in a wide, angry shrug. "You know what, Rob? You've changed. I mean, you always were a stickler for the rules, but this?"

"Of course I've changed. The shit I've seen…" A few choice images flashed across Rob's mind and he quashed them like always. Since Bosnia, nightmares were par for the course, and working undercover had done little more than add some variety, a bit like his own personal Freeview horror channel, but he'd never lost control, never taken a civilian life. "Out in the field, you tell yourself it's because there's a war going on, that people wouldn't do those kinds of things in a normal situation, but it's all lies."

"Money," Tonka said. "That's all I'm asking for."

"How much?"

"We need to raise another hundred and twenty-five grand. We've already got three hundred and seventy-five—"

"Half a million? Fucking hell. I might need to rethink my exit strategy."

"We're running out of time, Rob. Can you help or not?"

Rob ran his palm over his scalp; he was under immense pressure, because he could raise the money, but it wasn't going spare. While Hedley and Petridis had wrangled him a decent settlement from the Met, that was all he had until the business started paying. If it started paying.

"What about compensation? Has he put in a claim? And he's got his disablement pension, hasn't he?"

"When he's discharged, yeah, but only if he's still Ethan McGrath, former REME…"

"Sorry, Ma'am. I've spent the last four years digging through the dregs of society, and I'm not prepared to play a part in you joining their midst. Because it will come back to get you later. You know that as well as I do."

"Not if we get it right."

So complacent, but she had no idea the resources the likes of the Special Investigations Unit had at their disposal.

"I've just resigned from the police. I've got no income." Rather than risk further conflict, Rob opted for an emotional appeal, but she was giving him the silent treatment and wouldn't even look at him. He could imagine what she was thinking: he had the luxury of walking away from a well-paid career while Ethan would be lucky to get a job paying minimum wage. If she was that bothered, she had half a million sitting in her garage. "I really am sorry, Ma'am."

"So am I, but I understand."

"What're you gonna do?"

"Doesn't matter." She stepped around him to reach the door to the house, paused and gave the Lamborghini a longing look.

"Yeah, cheers for the guilt trip," Rob muttered. She didn't take it back. He followed her inside, where he downed his beer and picked up his helmet and keys. "Who's got my phone?"

Bish and Jock looked at each other and shook their heads. They were sticking to their story.

"Crap. I must've dropped it. Ah, well. At least..." He was going to say 'I'm getting my money's worth on my insurance' but thought better of it, although he wouldn't have put it past either of them to have nicked it for a laugh. He'd have to wait and see if any practical jokes were in store. "I'd best get off."

"All right, mate," Bish said. "Good to see you again."

"And you. Jock, behave yourself."

"Always do." He stayed facing forward, his focus on the label he was peeling from the empty bottle in his hands.

Rob drew breath to suggest they arrange a proper get-together sometime soon, but there was no point. He'd let them down, and it would be a long time before they forgave and forgot, if they ever did.

4: Guest of Goner

It was difficult to raise the alarm…without raising the alarm. Gray had tried to collar Martina on her own, but instead she'd insisted he join her table and introduced him to her tablemates: six other senior officers, one of whom was Martina's wife: Chief Superintendent Erica Dunleavey. It went without saying that Erica was one of those people who took command in every situation, and it was some fifteen minutes later, after he'd answered her questions pertaining to who he was and how he knew Rob, before Gray got a chance to tell Martina that both bike and owner were nowhere to be found.

It was when Martina said, "He's a sod," as if she were describing an errant kitten clawing at the curtains that Gray realised he needed to up the urgency factor a notch or two.

"Ma'am, I'm not convinced he left of his own volition."

"Ma'am?" Martina repeated in amusement. "We're the same rank, Gray. Or we were."

And that she'd had quite a bit to drink.

"Sorry, old habits," Gray excused, though he'd done it on purpose, hoping to tap into some far corner of her brain that still recalled she was a police officer.

"We'd best go and investigate, then," she suggested and pushed her chair from the table at the same moment as a waiter arrived with the starters.

"It's all right, Martina. You stay there. I'll go and have a poke around and report back."

"OK, Gray, you do that." She pulled her chair in again and picked up her glass but didn't drink from it, momentarily lost in a daze; her wife raised an eyebrow in Gray's direction. Martina was evidently taking Rob's leaving pretty hard.

A couple of officers were outside, having a smoke, both pausing to eye Gray in suspicion. He gave them a swift smile as he passed them and rounded the building, slowing as he moved along the dark alley that stank of piss, as they always did, a make-do public convenience for late-night revellers caught short and nocturnal animals alike. At the halfway point, Gray tripped over a box and skidded on something he didn't want to think about. He took out his phone and activated the LED, blocking the dazzle with raised hand and squinting at the mute blue patch on the ground ahead of him. Flattened cardboard pulp, ring pulls, cigarette ends, a couple of used condoms, bins… He reached the end of the alley and turned to look back towards the street.

He could see tyre tread in the mush of muck and rubbish, and a few boot prints, potentially from more than one type of boot, but there was nothing to indicate a struggle had taken place. Switching off the LED briefly, he brought up Rob's number to try calling him again, but the signal was sketchy and his phone abandoned the call. Gray moved back along the alley, watching his screen all the while, cursing when he tripped over the same box as before. He kicked it hard in revenge, sending it three feet into the air, and watched in satisfaction as it collapsed on impact. There was a sudden and bright blue glow in the gloom. A dropped phone? Gray was almost certain it was and backtracked to investigate.

The screen was locked, but displayed multiple missed calls. By this point, it wasn't really necessary to establish ownership; nonetheless, when Gray reached the street and the signal picked up, he called Rob's number again, sighing in resignation when his name appeared, attached to the incoming call on the phone from the alley. Maybe he was wrong about the absence of a struggle—that or Rob had dropped it intentionally as a clue. Or he'd just dropped it making his getaway and Gray's imagination was running amok. Whichever of those it was, he returned to the restaurant and made a beeline for Erica.

"Can I have a word?"

She set her cutlery and napkin aside and edged around the table to reach him. "What's up?"

Gray turned so he was facing the window and away from the guests. "I think something's happened to Rob, Ma'am. He drove past me at approximately 1950 hours and I saw him turn into the alley to the side of this building. When I got here, his bike was there, but he wasn't, or not that I could see, and I assumed he'd already come in. He hadn't, as you know, and when I went to check again at around 2010 hours, his bike was gone. I wondered if he'd popped to the shop or something…"

Erica looked doubtful.

"Yeah, I know," Gray said. Rob didn't smoke, and he didn't drink much, either, so it was a silly theory to start with. He held out the phone. "I found this in the alley."

"Rob's?"

"Yep."

"Ah. That's worrying." Erica took the phone from him and activated the screen. It asked for the PIN number. "That's not a lot of use, is it?" She handed it back. "Right. Let's see…who looks sober?" She scanned the room and spotted her target. "Theo?" She beckoned him over.

"Yes, Ma'am?"

"Do you know each other?"

Gray and Theo Petridis did a kind of mixed nod and shrug. They'd both been Rob's boss at some point, so they'd corresponded, but that was the limit of their familiarity.

"Gray, can you tell Theo what you've just told me?"

"Sure."

"Great." Delegating done, Erica returned to her wife's side.

"Must be nice up there, huh?" Theo muttered.

"Yeah," Gray agreed with a chuckle. He thought it was wise not to mention he'd been on his way to the upper echelons before he met Jean. He'd left ambition behind when he'd fallen in love and hadn't been tempted to pursue it a second time, not even when he found himself single again. "All right. Short version: Rob's gone missing, along with his bike."

"What makes you think he's missing and hasn't just ditched the party?"

"Why would he have rode all the way here to ditch the party?"

"To cover up that he was going to?"

Gray couldn't decide if Petridis was being facetious or the guy really thought Rob would pull a stunt like that, although… "It's a possibility," Gray admitted reluctantly. In a gathering of this size, Rob could claim to have been there all the time and they'd be none the wiser. "But wouldn't he at least have put in an appearance so he had eyewitnesses to corroborate he was here?"

"Or one ultra-reliable eyewitness."

"Hmm…" Gray wasn't buying it.

"Do you have any reason to believe he's in danger?" Petridis asked, looking Gray in the eye—the left one—as if by doing so he could telepathically glean what that reason might be.

"If you mean, is Rob's involved in any undercover cases at the moment, I wouldn't know. I left the police last summer."

"Lucky bastard. I've got another five years before I can afford to go."

Gray grimaced sympathetically. There was real envy there, as was always the case with officers in their forties or fifties who discovered Gray had got out at the tender age of thirty-four—unless they knew what he'd been through prior to penning his resignation.

"I could get the patrols to keep a look out," Petridis offered. "Will that do you?"

Gray checked the time: coming up on nine o'clock. "He could be well out of the area by now."

"Or sitting it out in a wine bar down the street."

Am I overreacting? Rob had put away some bad people over the years and hadn't exactly been 'undercover' on the last case they'd worked together. If he'd been recognised... "All right, let's give it another thirty minutes."

"If you're sure." Petridis was already moving away.

Gray nodded. Half an hour would make little difference. He returned to Martina Hedley's table, where his starter—mushroom paté and pain rustica, which, thankfully, was cold to begin with—had been covered with a napkin while everyone else was almost finished with their main course. He speed-ate one slice of the yeasty bread and caught the attention of their waiter.

"Your main course, sir?"

"Please."

The waiter nodded and strode away.

"What's happening?" Martina asked.

"We're giving it a bit longer to see if Rob turns up."

"I'm sure he will."

"Yeah," Gray agreed dubiously. Martina patted his hand. She'd switched to drinking water and seemed a little less intoxicated than earlier. The waiter returned and exchanged Gray's half-eaten paté for his main course: a mock-fish Thai curry with beautifully fragrant rice that set his mouth watering before the plate touched down. "Thanks." Gray sniffed deeply, filling his nose with the scent of spicy coconut and citrus.

"That smells incredible," Martina said. "What fish is it?"

"It's not. It's made from soy beans and seaweed."

"Are you vegetarian?"

"No, but I eat a lot of veggie stuff."

"It's a healthier diet."

"It is," Gray agreed.

"So, you're going in with Rob on this investigating business, I hear."

Gray was kind of relieved she hadn't passed further comment on his choice of meal, although the change of subject was unexpected. It wasn't a secret as such, but Rob generally kept his cards close to his chest. "He told you?"

"I think I interrogated it out of him. I wanted him back on my team. He could've made DI by now."

"Yeah, it's the paperwork he doesn't like. Luckily, I do."

"A perfect match!" Martina picked up her glass and raised it.

Gray passed on drinking the last of his pint—still his first, thus tepid and stale—and poured some water into his wine glass. "Cheers," he said.

The desserts arrived, and the half-hour mark came...and went. Petridis was involved in a loud political debate which Gray didn't want to interrupt, although that conversation sounded a lot more interesting than the one at Gray's table. Senior police officers seemed incapable of talking about anything other than targets and cutbacks. He quietly excused himself and took a detour to the Gents' on his way outside for a breather, and to further contemplate the possibility he was making a mountain out of molehill.

The traffic had dwindled to the usual nightly array of buses, cabs and pedestrians; they paid Gray no heed. That was London: a city crammed with nine million people, all of whom ignored each other. It was part of what had drawn him to buy a house there, the anonymity. That and the awful hours he kept, although even in London, it could be tricky to find a decent cappuccino at three in the morning.

"You all right there, mate?" One of the officers he'd seen earlier had come out for another smoke.

"Yeah, thanks." Gray offered half a smile and returned to staring across the road. A black cab stopped to let out its passengers and pulled away again. Smoke drifted in front of Gray's face; he held his breath until it had passed, yet still inhaled some.

"How d'you know Rob?" the smoker asked.

"We worked together on a couple of cases a while back."

The smoker nodded slowly and took another draw on his cigarette. "He's a good bloke."

"Yeah, he is. No idea where he's got to tonight, though."

"I expect he's caught in traffic." The smoker checked his watch. "Blimey, it's getting on. Didn't realise." He stubbed the half-smoked cigarette out on the bin, saying, "See you," on his way back to the door. The noise of chatter bloomed briefly and the door closed again.

Two hours to get from Kilburn to Euston? It should've taken half an hour, tops, and in any case, Rob had arrived on time. There had to have been an emergency of some sort, and Gray had Zoë's number saved, but he was reluctant to call when all it might achieve was to have two of them fretting.

The door opened again, and the other smoker gave Gray a nod as he passed, stopping a few yards away to light up and take out his phone. Gray watched him and made a decision: he'd call Zoë when the guy went back inside.

Two cigarettes later, by which point Gray had realised it wasn't a particularly warm evening, the other officer left at last, and Gray made the call.

"Damn it." Voicemail. "Hi, Zoë, it's Gray Fisher. If you happen to hear from Rob, can you let him know he left his phone behind? Take care." Gray ended the call, hoping he'd been cryptic enough to not worry her, and returned inside, on a collision course with Theo Petridis, who raised his thick silver eyebrows in query. Gray shook his head. Theo squeezed Gray's shoulder as if to say 'there, there' and then, with phone clamped to ear, he strode back to his table.

"Gray, come and sit," Martina called. With nothing more he could do for the time being, he obliged. "Do you need another drink?"

"No, I'm fine, thanks." Gray topped up the water in his wine glass and sipped absently, casting his mind back to the Strang investigation. It had begun in London, when Gray's preliminary research into a corrupt legal firm tied them to a larger scheme to defraud will beneficiaries of their inheritance; Strang, Folden and the other lawyers involved were now in prison. However, the corruption extended upwards through the criminal justice system—the SIU investigation was ongoing—and Rob's infiltration had relied on his pre-existing association with Lambert—one of the lawyers—who was dead, but her friends on high were not.

"You think something's happened to him." Martina's observation broke into Gray's thoughts. Now he'd worried her too.

"I'm missing a perfectly decent night in for no reason here," he complained, trying to make light, though it was true enough, and if Rob had just decided to give it a miss, he'd be hearing about it later.

Martina's laughter was a little forced. "Had a better offer, did you? Who's the lucky man?"

"Nobody you know," Gray said evasively. "How long have you and Erica been together?"

"Twelve years."

"Fifteen," Erica corrected, barely breaking from the conversation she was having and to which she immediately returned.

"That's what I said, fifteen years." Martina winked at Gray. "Sometimes it seems like only yesterday. Other times, it feels like forever."

Erica glanced witheringly at her wife.

Gray smiled, appreciating the glimpse into their relationship. He and Jean had barely reached the point where infatuation evolved into easy familiarity, but even in the darkest months after Jean's death, Gray hadn't coveted or envied others for having that.

Rather, he celebrated it, hoping that one day it might be within his reach again.

"Will Richards," he said.

"Will Richards…" Martina frowned in thought. "Is he on the job?"

"No, he's not."

"Why do I know that name?" She shook her head. "Too much alcohol."

Gray hoped his smile covered his astonishment. She'd seen the two of them together at Freddie Berringer's apartment the night the Berringers were arrested, and she was taking over from Rob in handling the witnesses. She had to be seriously tanked up to have not made the connection.

She shrugged. "Oh, well. It'll come to me."

Gray really hoped it didn't, or not until the party was over. "Think I fancy a drink after all. You want one?"

"God, no—thank you."

Gray confirmed no-one else needed a refill and went to the bar. He sent Will a text message: *Rob was a no-show.*

Another customer arrived and stopped next to him. "Alright?"

Gray nodded. "Yes, thanks. You?"

"Yeah."

"Who's next, please?"

Gray's phone buzzed. He gestured for the other guy to queue-jump and read Will's reply: *Bummer. Any idea why?* Gray responded: *Your guess is as good as mine.*

The bartender served the other guy's drink, the price of which made him mutter, "How much? Fucking hell." He paid anyway and picked up his glass but stayed where he was, surveying the restaurant, then homed in on Gray. "Dave Miller," he said and held out his hand.

"Gray Fisher."

"So *you're* the one Petridis is moaning about."

"Quite possibly."

"Whatever you said, it worked. He's got Traffic keeping an eye out for Rob."

"Good to know."

"Yes, sir?" the bartender prompted.

"Pint of Guinness and black, please." And this time, Gray was determined to finish it. The bartender poured the beer and left it to settle while he served someone else.

Miller sipped his Scotch and sniffed. "Waste of time, if you ask me."

Gray was fed up with hearing that—or words to that effect. He turned Miller's way, noting the confident pose, the ingrained arrogance. "I'm asking," he said.

"Rob told Hedley he was doing a flit after shift."

"You heard him, did you?"

"One of my colleagues did, yeah."

Hearsay, then. Gray would be asking Martina to substantiate what Miller was telling him, although it did sound like something Rob would say.

Gray's drink arrived in front of him. He paid—on that point he agreed with Miller, the prices were extortionate—and picked it up, already moving off. "Nice talking to you."

"Yeah, likewise."

Gray glanced back at Miller, who'd already downed his Scotch and was ordering another. Heavy drinking was an occupational hazard, one which Gray had side-stepped only to pursue another, so he was judging no-one. He returned to Martina. "Dave Miller's one of yours, isn't he?"

She nodded. "He's a DS. Why?"

"No reason. I was talking to him at the bar. Do you get on all right?"

"Mostly. He can be a bit of a wanker at times."

"Can't we all?" Gray asked rhetorically.

"What's he said?"

"That someone heard Rob tell you he wasn't coming tonight."

Martina leaned sideways and glared past Gray at Miller. "Where the hell did he get that from?" When Gray didn't answer, Martina homed in on him, her eyes narrow and dangerous. "Rob didn't say anything of the sort."

Gray held up his free hand. "Look, I'm merely trying to figure out whether Miller's spreading gossip or if there's some fire to go with that smoke. I'm worried about Rob, yet nobody else seems bothered. Is there something I'm missing?"

Martina pursed her lips, contemplating Gray for a moment and, in the process, confirming his suspicions weren't without merit. She sighed. "All right. You want the truth? I'll tell you, but you're not going to like it."

"Go on," Gray invited.

"Most of us would've been more surprised if he'd turned up tonight. Every social, it's the same—he says he'll try and make it, but he never does. We still invite him, because we enjoy his company, and…he wasn't always like that."

"It's since he worked for the SIU," Gray cut in before Martina could say it.

"Yes," she confirmed.

The food and beer in Gray's belly turned to concrete. It was like being told a friend had only months to live.

"In all other ways, he's no different," Martina said—for Gray's benefit, he was sure. "He gets on with everyone and has a laugh… well, he's always been a cool operator, and he's a bit more serious than he used to be, but he's still the same Rob on the job." She chuckled at her accidental poetry, and Gray managed a smile.

"But he doesn't socialise anymore, is what you're saying."

"Exactly. Did you know he started our footy team and coached them?"

"I didn't."

"Yeah, and they were bloody good, too. And he used to organise trips to the TT Races, the Grand Prix…"

"Why bother putting tonight on if you were all so sure he wouldn't make it?"

"Because he promised me he'd be here." Martina turned away to reach her glass. She was unsteady, but Gray didn't think it was the alcohol. Her pride had taken a hit.

"He wouldn't have let you down on purpose," he consoled. Martina stopped mid-sip, eyebrows arched like a silhouetted seagull flying above her glass. "He arrived here. I saw him."

She swallowed her emotions and nursed her glass. "Then where is he?"

"On the M40." Petridis appeared at Gray's side. "Traffic spotted his bike at High Wycombe, northbound carriageway."

***

"Dom, me ol' mucker. How's it going?" It was the worst Cockney accent ever, and it made Dom Hooper cackle.

"Bloody hell, Gray, don't give up the day job, will you?"

"Damn cheek! I don't know...you think someone's your friend..." Gray grumbled against Dom's continued throaty chuckle. He was smoking again—not surprising. Laid-back as Dom Hooper was, leading the SIU was unbelievably stressful, as Gray knew all too well.

"Aside from speaking with a dodgy accent—"

"When in London..."

"—how are you doing?"

"Very well, thanks, although this isn't a social call."

"Yeah, you've never called me socially."

"I have," Gray protested and searched his memory for an example. He didn't find one.

"Don't worry about it. I know you love me anyway. So, how can I help you this fine Friday evening?"

Gray was still reeling from the revelation. Fourteen years, he and Dom had known each other as colleagues and friends, but Dom was right. Gray had never called 'just for a chat' or to see how he was. It was a poor show on his part, but he'd deal with that later. There were more pressing matters to attend to. "Don't suppose you've still got access to that insurance underwriter? The one who does all the mobile devices?"

"Aspects, you mean?"

"That's the one."

"Let's have a look."

"It can wait," Gray said.

"If it could, you'd be all tucked up in bed by now instead of calling me."

Gray had no defence, so he stayed quiet, the silence punctuated by noises from Dom's end of the call—clicks and taps of a keyboard, the flick of a cigarette lighter, a long inhalation and then, "Yep. I'm in."

"Excellent. Can you look to see if there's anything for Rob Simpson-Stone?"

"That's ominous."

"We'll see."

"OK. Simpson, Simpson, Simpson, Simpson-Atkins, Simpson-Pettigrew—why would you bother? Ah, here we go. Simpson-Stone, L. Damage claim last year. His niece?"

"Possibly."

"And another... Yep. Simpson-Stone, R. Phone reported as lost or stolen at 21:26. Phone and SIM blocked. Why? What's happened?"

"Rob's leaving do was tonight," Gray said. "I saw him arrive but he didn't make it inside. Traffic cameras picked up his bike heading north on the M40, and they were going to pull it, to make sure it was Rob, but lost sight of it in Oxford. I guess he could've stopped off somewhere...Stratford, maybe." Gray was speculating aloud. "Anyway, I found his phone in the alley where I'd seen his bike, but if he's reported it..."

"It's logged as reported by the owner."

"Does it say whether a replacement handset's going out?"

"One's been approved. No shipping info, though. It must be on a separate system for the courier."

"That makes sense. At least I know he's alive. Thanks, Dom."

"Anytime, mate."

"Listen, I'll do better."

"Ha. Yeah, all right."

"I'll give you a call next week—socially," Gray promised, which set Dom off laughing again. "And stop smoking."

"No problem, boss. Catch you later."

"Bye." Gray hung up, undecided whether the use of 'boss' was out of habit or sarcasm. Either way, he *would* do better.

5: Dodgy

Rob's guilt rode pillion all the way to Stratford-upon-Avon. He'd been on his way back to Euston, following a diversion around roadworks that took him within five minutes of the flat. At the junction where he should've turned left with the rest of the diverted traffic, he'd turned right and gone home. He'd stayed long enough to call his mobile phone company and leave Hedley a voicemail to say he was safe and would explain everything later, then he'd packed his panniers and hit the road.

He didn't stop in Stratford, but the brief detour off the slow-moving motorway went a long way towards clearing his head. It was quiet for a Friday late evening, not too cold, though not yet warm enough for people to sit outside. As Rob neared the river, moisture in the air hit him like hard rain, and the drop in temperature made him shiver in spite of his leathers. He slowed down and breathed deeply, intoxicated by the smoky mix of moss and new leaves that filled his nose while memories of Zoë filled his mind. They were so powerful that, for a moment, he felt her warmth pressed to his back, her arms gripped around his waist. Alluring and no longer painful, the sensation tempted him to circle back so he could feel it all over again, but he was ready to move on.

His route out of town took him past where his life as a beat bobby began: Stratford-upon-Avon Police Station. It somehow felt more fitting to revisit his time there than to spend his last night on the job with relative strangers in a soulless restaurant in a soulless city. His colleagues at the Quarterhouse would have finished eating long ago—Rob hadn't eaten since lunch—and the serious drinking would be underway. He realised, now it was too late, that he should've gone back if only for one pint. He'd let everyone down, not least Martina Hedley, and there would be no opportunity to make amends.

Rob was pleased, in a way, that he'd lost his phone—he still wasn't ruling out a prank—not that he expected a shedload of missed calls. At most, he anticipated a couple from Hedley, maybe a voicemail to tell him he was a let-down. Gray Fisher would no doubt also call at some point to give him grief for inviting him and not bothering to turn up. He'd apologise; he owed them that much, and he was sorry for wasting their time, but he wasn't sorry he'd missed his leaving do. Most of the people he'd worked with before he joined the SIU had moved on, and those in attendance were only there for a night out. It made no odds to them whether Rob showed or not.

The self-pity faded, along with his bad mood, as he headed away from Stratford towards the open road, and disappeared entirely after his pit stop for overpriced fast food. He was big enough to admit that the issue was him, not everyone else. After so long working alone or in the limited and exhausting company of false acquaintances, Rob was out of practice with socialising and still sore about the divorce. Almost eighteen months down the line, he needed to get his shit together, but he didn't—couldn't—think about that now.

With a bit more throttle, his worries were instantly wiped out, lost to the all-consuming joy of the ride. The new tyres bit into the tarmac as Rob leaned low around bends, zipping past cars on his side of the road, headlights approaching on the other side a short-lived blur sucked into the darkness as quickly as they'd appeared. He'd needed this: a few hours of just him and the bike.

As always, the journey was over more quickly than Rob would've liked, although it had started to rain, so it was no bad thing that he was almost home—or his mum's place, at least. She'd moved there after he'd joined the army, yet it still felt like home.

It was coming up on two a.m. as he turned into the road, keeping his speed down and the revs low so as not to disturb the neighbours. His mum would hear him regardless of how quiet his approach and whether she was asleep—he wasn't ruling out the same kind of parental telepathy that had got him up to Lucas the night he'd vomited in his sleep.

Rob parked up and let himself in with the key his mum kept in a planter, against his advice, though only a fool would risk running the gauntlet with Linford the giant—even for his breed—Rottweiler that belonged to his mum's partner, Harvey. Both dog and owner were fierce-looking softies, and the dog greeted Rob at the door—no barking, but he was snorting in his excitement and couldn't have wagged any harder if he'd tried. Working around the slobbery loving, Rob unzipped his jacket and just about got his boots off before the light came on.

"It's me, Mum," he called as she appeared in silhouette at the top of the stairs.

"I know. I heard the bike." She was on her way down. "I wasn't expecting you until the morning." She arrived in front of him and hugged him while his hands were still inside his jacket sleeves. He wriggled out of them, letting the jacket fall to the floor, and hugged her back.

"I missed you," he said.

"Hmm." She released him and turned towards the kitchen. "Didn't want to miss out on breakfast, you mean?"

"Added bonus." He'd have picked up his jacket, but Linford was in the process of turning it into a makeshift bed. That jacket had been through far greater trials, so Rob left the dog to his scuffing and circling and went to join his mum, who had already filled a pan with milk and set it on the lit stove. Rob collected the cocoa and sugar from the cupboard and then stood by, watching her expertly mix the sweet paste. The adrenaline was wearing off, leaving him at the mercy of the aches and pains of the ride and the aftermath of three months of working without a break. He yawned and stretched, catching the tail end of her question.

"…be at a work's night out?"

"I didn't make it—I was abducted," he said, hoping his weary tone conveyed that it wasn't a serious attempt, although if his mum had known half of what he'd been involved in over the past ten years, he wouldn't have used the word at all, not even in jest.

"Oh?"

"By the REMEs. An impromptu get-together." He wasn't covering for his mum's sake, or even for his ego. There was little point in staging an abduction simply to get at Rob's very limited funds, and Tonka hadn't tried that hard to persuade him. Surely she'd have realised he'd refuse to help Ethan, which meant either she was desperate and Rob was a last resort—the Lamborghini said otherwise—or there was more to it than she'd told him. Either way, he couldn't see her parting with the car when it had been her lifelong dream to own one.

Chocolatey steam warmed his face as a mug appeared in front of him and his mum ruffled his hair, bringing him back from his thoughts.

"Thanks, Mum." Cupping his drink with both hands, he sipped carefully and sighed in contentment, feeling all the stress and strain ebb away.

"Go on to bed." She pointed towards the stairs.

"I will in a minute. I just need to get my gear in—"

"Where are your keys?" She held out her hand for them.

Rob put his mug down and went out to the hallway, where Linford was curled up into a surprisingly small ball, and was snoring and drooling all over his jacket. Rob tugged a corner out from under the dog and fished his keys from the pocket, both his hand and the keys drenched in slimy dog spit. With a grimace, he dried off on his t-shirt and took one step towards the front door before the keys were snatched from him.

"Bed, now!" his mum commanded as she disappeared outside. It was a direct order, and Rob knew better than to disobey. He retrieved his cocoa from the kitchen and went upstairs, to the spare room, set his drink on the bedside table, stripped to his boxers and made a quick trip to the bathroom. By the time his mum came up, he was under the duvet and fighting to keep his eyes open.

She put his panniers in the corner of the room. "Don't spill that on the bed," she warned without looking his way. Rob downed the warm cocoa in one. His mum took the empty mug from him and turned off the light on her way out.

"Night, Mum."

"Night-night, sleep tight." The door clicked shut behind her.

Rob slid down the bed and rolled onto his side, smiling at the way his mum still bossed him around like he was an eight-year-old flouting bedtime. He turned forty-one in a few months, but he'd never be too old to appreciate her pampering—it wasn't so long ago he'd feared he might have lost it forever.

His niece Lois had graduated from law school during the Strang case and started working for Jess Lambert, which was a good career move, on the surface. Lois wanted to specialise in family law—Jess's area of expertise—and she knew Rob and Jess were old friends, but it also meant Rob's investigation started with snooping on his niece to see if she was involved in the fraud scheme. He'd thanked God she wasn't; however, it put her at greater risk of getting caught in the crossfire.

To guarantee Lois's safety, Rob had kept his cover with his family, on the premise that if they didn't know anything, they couldn't accidentally let something slip. Then came the sting operation—a fake reunion to draw Jess and her associates out into the open—but Lois was too close to the target. She'd seen her Uncle Rob cosying up with her boss when he'd claimed he was trying to save his marriage, and when she called him on it, his choice was to either come clean—and blow the entire investigation—or dig himself in deeper.

Deeper he went. No training could've prepared him for dealing with his mum's sense of betrayal, and it had been an enormous relief to own up once the investigation was over even if some of his family—his sister, mainly—thought he'd stayed quiet because he didn't trust them. Everything he'd done was to make it easier for them, which had made it a lot harder for him.

More than a year on, his sister was still keeping her emotional distance, and Amber—Lois's younger sister—wasn't talking to him at all, which was why no-one had told him Amber was pregnant. He knew not to force it. Maybe, in time, they'd get back some of the closeness they used to have. For now, he'd settle for being allowed to call in and see her while he was home.

***

"Quarter to one? What the hell?"

Rob had expected to wake up the following morning to an empty house. Well, he got the empty house right.

Laughing in disbelief that he'd slept for ten-plus hours and felt bloody awesome for it, he wandered down to the kitchen to raid the fridge, noting the package—complete with a handwritten note addressed to him—on the counter on his way past, but his requirement for fluid was more urgent. He opened the fridge and contemplated which of the milk and OJ he'd get in the least trouble for swigging straight from the container. He opted for OJ and gulped down half the two-litre carton in one go. "I'll get some more later," he thought aloud and went to attend to the package.

The note was brief—*Something you're not telling me? Mum x*— but it made sense once he'd examined the printed label on the box: his replacement handset and SIM. Now he'd find out what had—or hadn't—happened to the old one.

Downloading the data didn't take long; Rob wasn't big on social networking and mostly used his phone for texts and calls. Those were the first things he checked—no outgoing calls or messages after 7:30 the previous evening. If Bish and Jock had it, they'd have cracked his PIN, so he could safely conclude he'd dropped it in the scuffle in the alley.

It took a bit longer for the incoming messages and voicemails to arrive; while he waited, he considered all the data that would need to be rewritten or wiped to give someone a fresh start. The half-a-million fee Tonka had spoken of sounded a bit steep, but now he thought about it, there was a lot of work involved— hacking into government databases, credit companies, amending medical records, or those that had been computerised.

It would need someone like Aaron Tanner, with the know-how but with fewer scruples—and there was the other thing: Tonka had a good upbringing, came from a respectable, fairly well-to-do family. What was she doing, getting mixed up with organised criminals? How had she established contact? Rob contemplated calling Aaron-Naomi on the off-chance Aaron could give him a lead on who Tonka might be dealing with, while also aware it was an excuse. Since the remand hearing, Naomi had been on Rob's mind more than she should've been.

His messages finally finished downloading and were much as he'd predicted: quite a few missed calls, mostly from Martina and Gray. He sent both a text message to confirm he was alive and would explain in full when he got back from his mum's. Gray replied with a simple *OK - thanks for letting me know.* Martina, on the other hand…

"Afternoon, Ma'am."

"Where the hell did you get to?"

"Something came up."

"An emergency?"

"Of sorts. It was out of my hands."

"I can't believe you sometimes, Rob."

"I know. I'm sorry, Ma'am."

She didn't say anything else for a while, then, "Is everything all right?"

"Yeah. Everything's fine."

"And Lucas and Zoë? They're OK?"

"As far as I'm aware."

She paused, waiting for him to say more. When he didn't, she asked, "Are you at your mum's now?"

"Yeah. For two weeks."

"Right."

"Anyway, I'd best—"

"You're really not going to tell me?"

"It's a long story."

"I've got time."

Rob laughed. "I haven't. I promised my niece a visit today and I overslept."

"Then I'll let you go. Just tell me this much. Are you in trouble?"

"No, Ma'am."

"You realise I'm not your boss anymore?"

"I dunno about that."

She chuckled, but Rob realised from her questions that she'd moved past being angry to worried. He was going to have to give her something to put her mind at rest.

"It's to do with an old army buddy," he said.

"Gray saw you arrive at the restaurant."

"Yeah. I got called away."

"If there's anything I can do to help…"

"I doubt it, Ma'am. Martina. But cheers, anyway. Listen, how d'you fancy going for a pint when I get back?"

"Will you show up?"

"Scout's honour."

"Yeah, OK." She didn't sound like she believed him. "I'm going. Have a good rest."

"I'll try."

"Take care, Rob."

"And you. Bye."

The call ended, and Rob realised he was smiling to himself, no longer worried that leaving the police had cost him Martina's friendship. On with the next mission: repairing his previous balls-up.

He called Amber's number, wondering what excuse she'd give him this time, assuming she answered at all. After a few rings, it went to voicemail. Rob hung up and tried again, deciding if she didn't pick up, he'd leave it, but as he moved his phone away from his ear, he heard the call connect.

"Hello?"

"Amber. It's Uncle Rob. Alright?"

"Oh, hi. Yeah, I'm good. How are you?"

"I'm good too. What are you up to?"

"Just putting the shopping away. Can I call you back?"

"It's only a quickie. Will you be in later if I pop round?"

"What time?"

"Whenever suits."

"Erm…" She tailed off, and Rob heard quiet rattles and bangs and cupboard doors closing. "We're having dinner with Kyle's parents."

Rob bent so he could read the clock on the microwave—almost half past one—not that it mattered. He'd got the message. "Never mind. I'll give you a ring during the week, yeah?"

"I come over to Nan's on Wednesday anyway."

"OK. I'll see you then." He was gutted, but he kept his tone light.

"Yeah. Bye…Rob."

"Catch you later, turtle." The pet name tumbled out of his mouth before he could stop it, and the few seconds of silence before she hung up were like waiting for a retaliative punch that didn't land. If she ever spoke to him again, he'd tell her he was sorry, promise not to call her that anymore—he shouldn't anyway, now she was twenty-four. And a mum.

It was hard to get his head around; his baby nieces were both grown women with family—in Amber's case—and careers of their own, but he still missed being part of their lives. He'd always been closer to Lois than he was to Amber; he was just a kid himself when Lois was born—well, an impressionable teenager—but the first time he'd held her, he'd known he wanted to be a dad someday. She was so tiny and beautiful, all long lashes and soft, dark curls, and the smell of her… Baby talc and milk—he could've got high on it, although he'd been happy to take his sister's word for it that Lois didn't smell too clever at WTF-o'clock in the morning with a full nappy.

Apart from that particular privilege, which he'd got to experience firsthand with his own son, Rob was one hundred percent the besotted uncle, unlike his brother, who'd only shown off his nieces to impress girls. According to JJ, being 'dad material' was a surefire route to getting a girlfriend, but JJ hadn't been pursuing Jess Lambert, who'd had no interest in babies—or being a girlfriend—then or ever. It was a pity that infatuation couldn't be knocked on the head by common sense, not that Rob had had much of that, either.

Amber had always been the more affected of the two girls, but he could bide his time with that one. With the other...

"Alright, Lois?"

"Uncle Rob? I was just thinking about you! What are you up to?"

"I was going to ask you the same thing."

6: Saturday Skirmish

The train journey to Croxley had become routine to Gray, so much so that, regardless of how absorbed he was in his music or reading, he could gauge, by the distance between stations, the variations in speed, the curves and the number of passengers embarking and disembarking, when it was time to get up from his seat—assuming he got one at some point.

His choice of entertainment for today's trip was an eclectic selection beginning with *Bolero*, detouring into a couple of dance anthems he'd fallen in love with in his formative years, and culminating in *Rhapsody in Blue*, to which he quickly abandoned his reading material—an academic paper that was all the more droll against the soundscape of musical acrobatics. Gray leaned back with eyes closed, imagining his journey as one and the same as that which had inspired Gershwin's busy composition. In what seemed like no time at all, he sensed the familiar pattern—the rock from side to side when they passed over the points, the slight bend to the right, the brief dulling of light caused by an overhead bridge, deceleration… The piece ended a few seconds after the doors opened.

Gray popped the earbuds from his ears and left them dangling from his coat front until he was out of the station. It had been raining when he'd left home, heavily enough to have warranted forking out for a cab had it still been raining. For the time being, the downpour was holding off, although the sky was thick with dark clouds; Gray decided to chance it anyway.

It was a lovely walk—in appropriate footwear, which he now owned—a twenty-minute amble through woodlands and along the canal bank, and he was early, as per usual. He was also past justifying his perpetual punctuality as a hangover from the job. Admittedly, he hated being late, but between Will's early morning rounds and Gray's midnight-oil burning, they rarely saw each other during the week, and by Saturday lunchtime, Gray was embarrassingly eager for their time together.

Of course, it would have been far less embarrassing if, when pressed, he hadn't attempted a long-winded explanation about timetables and delays. In the face of Will's obvious amusement, Gray had given up without reaching his point, because he didn't have one…aside from the truth, though he suspected Will had been fully aware of that from the outset.

Pausing to tuck his trousers into his socks, and to marvel at how little he cared if he looked ridiculous, Gray stepped through the kissing gate into the woods and greedily inhaled the rich, moist air. Spring had arrived in its full verdant glory, a sensory overload of colours and scents to the accompaniment of blackbirds' songs and the drumbeat of accumulated rainwater, released by the canopy to nourish the tight furls of newborn bracken far below. Gray tucked his earbuds into his inside pocket in favour of listening to nature's overture; human music had no place here.

He was surprised to see so many people out walking their dogs and envisaged, being the only one without a dog at his side and in spite of his walking boots, he stuck out like a sore thumb. He smiled politely at everyone he passed whilst fastidiously ignoring their four-legged companions. Granted, he was much less nervous around dogs these days, but even with Will's mutts, there were moments when he was certain one of them was set to rip a chunk out of him, apart from Kenny—the biggest and, allegedly, least friendly of the six—who had taken an instant shine to Gray, and he to Kenny.

"Ouch! What…" A sharp bang on the calves made Gray's knees buckle, and he tumbled forward, grabbing a tree trunk to steady himself. When he turned back to see what had hit him, he laughed in amazement.

"Hello, mate!" Almost as if his thoughts had conjured him into being, there was Kenny. Hobbling a little, Gray greeted the big dog on wheels and glanced through the trees, spotting the rest of the pack heading their way, with Will, in his postie's uniform and wellies, trailing behind, his focus on his phone.

Gray sent him a text message—*nice togs!*—stifling his laughter at Will's confused frown, but as always, he caught on quickly, and looked up and smiled. Gray smiled back, blushing at the fluttery feeling Will's presence evoked.

"You're early," Will said when they met at the midpoint.

"So are you," Gray observed and fell into step at Will's side.

"There was hardly anything to go out. What's your excuse?"

"Do I need one?"

Will shrugged with overplayed nonchalance. "You created an expectation. I'm merely offering you the opportunity to fulfil it."

"Oh, you know how it is." Gray played along. "No margin for error with the later train…"

"Leaves on the track?"

Gray's laughter almost concealed the catch in his breath when Will's hand found his, interlocking their fingers. "Leaves, twigs… entire trees in places…"

"Same every March."

"Terrible service," Gray agreed. He glanced sideways at Will's delighted grin. "What?"

"It's still a nice surprise. I like this."

"Me too," Gray admitted, to himself as much as to Will. He sighed, contented. No, more than that. Happy. Hand in hand in the woods with this unconventional man and the company of his motley canine crew, it was easy to let go. Their relationship was still new, the bond still flexible enough for Gray to walk away, not that he intended to. The strengthening emotional connection between them delivered blissful moments that Gray had to consciously grasp to avoid poisoning them by association.

He could fall in love with Will if he let himself. He thought he wanted to, but it was hard to push aside his fear.

Perhaps he should follow Kenny's example. Run over by a car and paralysed, wheel-dependent...and utterly fearless; the big mixed-breed dog romped ahead of the rest of the pack, weaving at speed between trees, tongue lolling in joy. He paused to sniff at a tree trunk and manoeuvred closer, in his mind cocking his leg and making his mark before he bounded off again.

"Did you figure out what happened to Rob?" Will asked.

"Not exactly."

Kenny hit a raised root and flipped upside down, wheels spinning in the air. Without a second thought, Gray dashed to his aid and got no thanks at all from the dog, who raced off as soon as he was upright. Gray supposed that was thanks enough.

"Remember when that used to freak you out?" Will murmured, his chin heavy on Gray's shoulder.

He smiled at the reminder. At the start, everything Kenny did freaked Gray out—the shuffling around the house and thadumping down the stairs with his back legs dragging behind him, capsizing in the woods, falling into the canal—even his hydrotherapy sessions in a doggy lifejacket with a therapist standing by gave Gray palpitations. And while he was caught up in all that worry for nothing, that big old dog had thadumped his way right into Gray's heart.

"We've made good progress, haven't we?" he said.

"For a dog who doesn't like people, and a people who doesn't like dogs, I'd call it outstanding progress."

"Outstanding..." Gray side-stepped, laughing when Will jolted forward at the sudden loss of chin rest. He caught Will's hand and they moved on.

"What did you mean by 'not exactly'?" Will asked.

"With Rob? I got a text from him on the way here—he's at his mum's, which I'd already guessed. He said he'd explain when he gets back."

"You undercover cops and your secretive ways."

"Hmm. Says he with the mysterious bruises on his knees."

"And leet observational skills…"

"You never did explain why you were covered in mud when I called yesterday."

"Fell down a rabbit hole."

"See, this is what happens if you follow rabbits."

Will coughed the word, "Cats."

"A cat hole, then, surely," Gray argued.

"You know absolutely nothing about small mammals, do you?"

"Not true! I can name at least—" Gray tallied in his head "—five different species."

"Prove it."

Gray laughed, no intention of further making a fool of himself when it was a cover for his probing to see how much Will would tell him—no malice intended; just simple curiosity. Will was a risk-taker who often acted with little regard for his own safety if the life of another—animal or human—was at stake. That was who he was, and whilst Gray had no desire to change him, it would take time and significant effort to come to terms with that aspect of their relationship. In the five months they'd been seeing each other, they'd established a good level of trust, and they talked quite freely, although Will omitted the more dangerous elements, and for Gray's benefit. He'd already lost too many people he loved, but he also acknowledged that his future happiness depended on his own willingness to take risks—emotionally as opposed to with his mortality.

Still, exercising a little caution couldn't be a bad thing, particularly as he wasn't the only one doing so; Will's two newest pack members had hung back while the four old paws went tearing off through the trees in pursuit of unseen quarry.

"Damn it." Will let go of Gray's hand. "I bet it's that fox again." He strode away in the direction the dogs had taken, calling back a command to, "Stay there," which could have been for the two newbies or Gray, or both. In any case, the dogs were so close they were leaning against Gray's legs, and Will was no longer in sight.

"Good dogs," Gray said, trying to sound firm and assertive. The larger of the two—an Irish-cream-coloured bull terrier of some kind—gave a brief wag of its tail in response. The other was a scruffy little brown thing with its ears back and its tail curled between its legs; it looked at least as nervous as Gray felt being left in charge. Assuming he had been left in charge, of course; the bull terrier—called Bailey, possibly—was standing guard, square and alert with its nose in the air.

Gray listened hard, trying to interpret the rustling sounds coming from within the trees. The rustling got louder and Kenny reappeared, bouncing his wheels through the undergrowth as he made a beeline for Gray at the same time as another dog materialised from nowhere. For a few seconds, the three big dogs circled each other, the two that weren't Kenny with tails held high, wagging stiffly. Gray noticed Kenny's hackles go up, and then it all kicked off.

"Shit!"

The little dog bolted off down the path—Gray saw it from the corner of his eye, but his attention was on the frenzy of teeth and spit and a racket like hell hounds baying for souls that had him frozen to the spot. He wasn't a dog person; these weren't his dogs, but he had to do something. The question was what.

"Kenny, here!" he shouted, wishing rather than believing that the dog would obey, and he didn't, or not exactly. The command made him pause, and in that split second, the other two locked onto each other in a horrible tumbling, yowling mess. "Kenny!" Gray yelled again. This time he meant it, and the dog got close enough for Gray to grab his collar. He dragged Kenny a few feet away from the other two in case he changed his mind and re-joined the fracas.

It seemed forever before Will arrived, along with someone else, and the pair of them waded straight into the scrap and somehow broke it up. There was blood and a whole lot of foamy saliva, and Gray was shaking so much he could barely keep hold of Kenny.

"Sorry about that," the woman holding the unknown dog panted breathlessly. She'd already clipped a short lead to its collar.

"Not your fault," Will said. It was a relief to see the fight had left even the chilled Will Richards a little ruffled. "Is he OK?"

"I think so. Are yours?"

Will was still checking Bailey over. "He seems to be. How's Kenny?"

It took Gray several seconds to process the question, and several more to act on it. He lightly ran his hand over Kenny's back and visually inspected his head. "His ear's torn."

"Badly?"

Gray shrugged. "I don't think so." The tear was about a quarter of an inch in length and there was very little blood.

Keeping hold of Bailey, Will checked the injury. "Just a nick. A clean with saltwater and he'll be right as rain." He straightened up, still holding Bailey, and made eye contact with the other dog's owner. "I'll give you my mobile number, just in case."

"I'm sure he'll be fine, but I'll give you mine too."

The rest of the dogs had returned from their adventure and were milling around but keeping their distance. In the background, Gray half heard the conversation over his 100-decibel racing pulse. He'd never witnessed a dog fight at close range before, and he hoped he'd never have to again. It was terrifying. Unfortunately, committing to a relationship with a man who insisted on taking in every stray, friendly or otherwise, meant this was probably the first of many, which left Gray with only one option, and his heart would've sank at the prospect, had it not been bouncing around his chest like a rubber ball.

Soon after, the woman and her dog departed in the opposite direction to Will's house, and Will rounded up the renegades.

"I hope Holly knows her way home," he said breezily, though Gray saw the worried frown. "Poor little girl got used for bait."

That was more than Gray wanted to know.

"At least she got out of the way," Will mused. Understandably, his attention was on getting his dogs home safely—Gray was eager to get there himself—but the silent walk along the canal bank stretched on and on. It was only when they reached the gate to the farmhouse—where Holly was scratching to be let in—that Will looked directly at Gray and did a double-take. "Are you all right? Did you get bitten?"

"No, no. I'm all right." Gray nodded and smiled to back up his mostly true claim.

"You're shaking," Will observed, his worried frown renewed.

"Adrenaline does that," Gray dismissed. He followed Will and the dogs through the gate, closing it behind him, which wasn't easy with his hands so unsteady, but he did it and floated, lightheaded, past Tie's caravan and into the very welcome sanctuary of Will's kitchen.

"Sit down," Will instructed.

"Do you need a hand with Ken—"

"Sit!"

Gray raised his hands in surrender but quickly lowered them to his sides and went to sit at the kitchen table.

"All right. Kettle first…" Will filled it and switched it on, then beckoned to Kenny, who complied immediately. Will's voice dropped to a comforting murmur as he explained what he was doing and why, as if the dog understood every word.

Gray's concentration drifted. He hadn't felt this spaced out since he'd stopped taking drugs, but he caught the phrase 'sweet tea' and it made him smile. It was his mum's cure-all for everything from a bumped knee to that time a car clipped his back wheel and threw him off his bike. He was obviously made of tough stuff, because he'd escaped serious injury then, too, and the sweet tea had seen off the shock. If his mum had been there after Jean's accident…

"Here you go." A cup of tea appeared in front of him. "I've put sugar in it, OK?"

"Thanks." Gray tried his luck with gripping the handle, but he was still too shaky. He left it for the time being. "I need to talk to you," he said. Will was already on his way out of the room.

"Hold on. Just taking my wellies off."

Gray glanced down at his muddy boots. There was no way he'd manage those laces.

Will returned, made it halfway to the table—"Wheels"—and backtracked to free Kenny from his harness. He gave the rest of the dogs a visual once-over before he sat down with his tea opposite Gray. "Holly and Monster are holed up in the living room," he explained. "I'm a bit worried."

"It must've given them both quite a fright," Gray reasoned.

"They'll be fine—you know how Monster is. I meant about you needing to talk to me."

"Oh! It's nothing bad. Sorry."

"Phew!" Will rolled his eyes, but his dramatics did little to conceal his genuine relief. He was so laid-back and confident in general, it was easy to overlook his insecurity when it came to interpersonal relationships. Whenever they talked about previous loves, Will was mostly open and honest, until it came to the breaking-up part, which he'd gloss over with humour or change the subject. He'd been hurt badly, more than once, and part of Gray's reluctance at the beginning came from needing to be sure he wouldn't add to that tally.

"We're good," he said. His words prompted a smile from Will that was gratitude and happiness rolled into one and did strange things to Gray's gut. Will had the most gorgeous smile, wide and heartfelt, all sparkly eyes and dimples. Between his looks and his gift of the gab, the investors Will used to sweet-talk would've stood no chance.

Those sparkly eyes widened, the smile became a grin, and Gray realised he was staring with his mouth hanging open. He cleared his throat self-consciously but didn't look away.

"So, what did you need to talk about?" Will asked.

"It might be wise for you to clue me in on how to stop a dog fight."

Will laughed. "Yeah. I wish I knew."

"You did it."

"I took a chance, stuck my leg between them, which was stupid, especially in shorts, but I'd rather I get hurt than the dogs. Anyway, you were awesome, getting Kenny out of the way."

"That was luck."

"I disagree. You intervened at exactly the right moment—your training kicking in?"

"Training?"

"Police—stopping a dog fight's no different to breaking up a Saturday-night pub brawl."

"A riot more like…" Gray tried his drink again. He was still dithering a bit, but it was wearing off, and he managed to swallow a mouthful without spilling it or dribbling.

"The other dog wasn't neutered," Will said. "That won't have helped." He sipped his tea and stared into space—no doubt figuring out how to persuade the woman to get her dog seen to. He zoned back in and smiled at Gray. "Any better?"

"Getting there." He blew out a long, quivery breath and diverted his attention to the dogs, all snoozing and none the worse for their adventures.

"So, now the excitement's over, what do you fancy doing today?"

"Sleep?" Gray suggested. He was kidding, although it might take more than a few teaspoons of sugar to keep him conscious once the adrenaline rush had passed.

"We can do that if you like. We've got the place to ourselves." Will's wicked grin made it clear sleep was low on his list of priorities. "Why don't you have a lie-down?" he suggested. "I'll join you after my shower."

7: Reconnecting

"I'm not sure how I feel, coming second to my sister." Lois gave Rob a tight hug and kissed his cheek. "Love the aftershave. What is it?"

"The stuff you bought me for Christmas." Rob hadn't paid any attention to the name.

"Oh, well, that explains it. I have excellent taste."

Rob laughed at Lois's boast, but he had to agree. She was dressed down for the weekend—long baggy sweatshirt, leggings and flat pumps—but Beyoncé had got nothing on her. OK, he was a bit biased. "What d'you fancy doing?" he asked. "We could go to the park…"

"Feed the ducks and play on the swings?" Lois grinned as she looped her arm through his. "I don't mind. It's so nice to see you, Uncle Rob. I've missed you."

He gently squeezed her arm against his side. "Missed you more."

"Have not."

"You don't know that."

"I know everything." Lois strutted, pointing her toes like a proper little madam—the way she used to when she was a five-year-old who really did think she knew everything and would throw the biggest wobbler if she was proved wrong, not that she often was. No tantrums today, though. Just a big beaming smile—Rob imagined he had one to match.

"I'm gonna take you out somewhere special while I'm here," he said. "Belated birthday treat—"

"You don't have to," Lois interjected.

"I want to. Not tonight, though."

"Why? What are you up to tonight?"

"Only the pub. You can tag along if you like."

"On one of your lads' nights out? Think I'll give it a miss, thanks."

"Your loss."

"Dodgy lager and pool followed by an even dodgier kebab…"

"How can you possibly refuse?"

"Like this: no, thank you, Uncle Rob. I'm washing my hair. But you can have one for me."

"I'll hold you to that," Rob said sincerely. His relationship with Lois was back to how it used to be, and that was definitely worthy of celebration.

While they hadn't consciously made the decision to go to the park, they ended up there anyway, bypassing the playground, which was teeming with kids. Another bunch were playing football—Rob and Lois stopped abruptly when the ball flew past their faces. A boy of around seven or eight sprinted after it, puffing and panting, and then back again with the ball tucked under his arm.

"He reminds me of Lu," Lois mused. "How's he doing with his footy?"

"Not bad. His coordination's still all over the place, but he's getting there."

Lois unlinked arms to buy 'duck food' from the vending machine. "I'm surprised you didn't bring him with you."

"He's in school."

She tutted. "Of course. I keep forgetting how old he is. He'll always be four in my head."

"I used to do that with you and Amber. I still tell people you're twenty-one."

"You won't hear me complaining."

"When you're nearly thirty…" Rob teased.

"Hey! I've got another three years yet!" Lois went to bop him on the head with the bag of grubs, but he successfully dodged out of the way—the first time. The second, she hit the target. The bag popped. "Oops!" Giggling, she stretched on tiptoes. "One there," she said and rubbed his head vigorously with her knuckles.

"Watch it, you," Rob warned—not seriously. He was having too much fun to worry whether a few dried grubs had landed in his hair. To be on the safe side, he confiscated the bag and only gave it back when they reached the pond. "Incredible," he said. He'd been coming to this park for thirty-five years, and the pond had always been exactly the same: murky green with a few flowerless water lily plants, a fair bit of rubbish and way too many ducks.

"D'you remember the last time we did this?" Lois asked.

Rob nodded. He remembered it vividly, but he stayed quiet, hoping she'd tell the tale.

"You were home on leave... I used to love that—sitting on the windowsill and watching for your bike. We could hear it from miles away." She smiled up at him. "And then you'd bring us here and let us play for ages, but we always knew—once we'd fed the ducks, it was time to go home." She threw some grubs to the three young drakes paddling patiently, awaiting their reward. "Amber always sobbed her heart out when you went back."

"Did she?" Rob hadn't known that.

"Yeah. Mum had to turn the news off if there was anything about soldiers dying, because Amber would freak. It was weird. She was so little, she shouldn't have understood stuff about war and fighting, but she did, and she was scared you'd be killed."

"Your mum never told me."

"No. She swore me to secrecy, said it would upset you if you knew. But now you're out of the army *and* the police, I guess it doesn't matter anymore." Lois turned to face him and held his gaze. She wasn't breaking the secret; she was sharing it so he could see Amber's perspective.

"Thank you," he said, but the words only half sounded. It felt like there was hot food stuck in his gullet—his guilt for Amber's suffering—and he was pissed off Tanya had kept it from him, but what good would it have done to tell him? Short of entirely changing his career path, he couldn't have made it any easier for Amber. Still, he was hopeful he could fix things with her now he knew where she was coming from.

"So, anyway," Lois turned back to the ducks and threw the rest of the grubs into the water, "you met up with Jess—the last time we came here."

"Yeah." Rob glance over his shoulder at the bench where he and Jess had sat and talked while Lois and Amber had played on the slide. He'd had to abandon the conversation to go and push the girls on the swings. Then they'd fed the ducks, he'd dropped the girls home and gone back to Jess's place for the night.

"She didn't like us much, did she?" Lois asked with a coy smile.

Rob laughed. "She wasn't a fan of kids at all. There was this one time, I reckon you were only about a year old, and I'd promised your mum I'd babysit. It was a couple of weeks after I'd got up the nerve to ask Jess out. Of course, I forgot about the babysitting, so I asked her to come with me. She ditched me for the night—went to the pictures with Andy Jeffries."

"What a cow!"

"I dunno about that. I mean, with Daisy dying and everything, it was a bit insensitive of me to ask in the first place, and we were all right afterwards. Well…" He shrugged. "Sort of all right. We were never girlfriend and boyfriend as far as she was concerned. Are we ready to move on?" He wasn't trying to change the subject. The ducks didn't seem to believe they were out of food, and quite a crowd had gathered on the bank.

"Yeah, we might as well."

Lois linked arms with him again, and they strolled back the long way, past the tennis courts and flowerbeds, pausing to visit the animals. There was no way they were the same ones as had been there when Rob was a kid, or even when Lois was little, yet there had always been the same combination of rabbits, guinea pigs, finches and peacocks, and they watched for a long time, hoping the peacock would display his tail. He wasn't in a showing-off mood, though, and all too soon, they were passing the playground once more.

"Guess I'm too big for the swings now," Lois said with an airy sigh. "Being *nearly thirty* and all."

"You took that to heart, eh?" Rob glanced sideways at her, and she turned her nose up. "How old d'you think it makes me feel?"

"You're not old," Lois argued.

"Hmm. You haven't met Travis, have you?"

"Zoë's fiancé?"

"Yeah. Nice guy."

"But you don't like him."

Rob weighed it up, as he'd been doing ever since Zoë and Travis got together. "I don't *not* like him. It's tricky, you know?"

"Yeah, it must be." Lois frowned, briefly lost in her thoughts. "You still get to see Lu a lot, though?"

"Not as much as I'd like, but I think that'll change now I'm my own boss. I'm a bit of a dope, really. If I'd thought about it, I could've left it a couple of weeks, come up for the spring break and brought Lu—assuming the mighty Travis isn't jetting them off to the Maldives." Postponing his trip hadn't even occurred to Rob, because he was still in the salaried job mindset of 'being on leave'. "I'm up again in three weeks, anyway, for Josh and George's party."

"You could bring Lucas with you then," Lois suggested.

"And get your nan to babysit?"

"Or me."

"You?" Rob asked in disbelief.

"Yes, me! Don't you trust me?"

"Of course I trust you. I just figured you weren't really...the babysitting kind."

"I babysit Leila every week while Amber's at salsa."

"I stand corrected."

"Too right. Just because I'm a career woman..." Lois grumbled.

Rob was pretty sure she was faking her disgruntlement. In case she wasn't, he said, "Sorry. I shouldn't have assumed."

Lois held her scowl a little longer but then relented. "No, it was a logical assumption to make. Jess thought I was nuts when I told her I wanted kids at some point—most of my uni mates thought so too—and now Amber's got Leila…"

"You're broody," Rob said with a grin.

Lois shook her head, laughing at herself. "Just you wait—you'll see. Guaranteed, within the year, you'll be remarried and giving Lucas a baby brother or sister."

"I doubt it, unless you've got someone in mind for me."

"You're not seeing anyone?"

"Nope."

"Have you been looking?"

"Not really." He'd been cramming in the overtime to get a bit of extra money in the bank, which hadn't left much opportunity for looking, but since the divorce, he wasn't interested. Apart from Naomi Silvestri; he'd found her attractive the first time they'd met, but she was a witness for the prosecution against the Berringers, so it was a no-go, or it had been. Whatever, he hadn't seen or heard from her since Frederick Berringer's remand hearing.

"I think you were right about Jess, by the way," Lois said. Rob sensed a consolation coming.

"In what way?"

"Her being anti-kids—it was as much about losing her little sister as being a career woman." Lois leaned her head on Rob's arm and sighed. "I miss her."

"Yeah, me too."

"She was fun to work with—I learnt so much. And she used her contacts to find me a job—the legit ones, I should point out."

Rob didn't comment. There was no need for Lois to know the SIU had continued watching her after Jess had died, but he wouldn't lie to her if she asked.

"Do you still love her?"

That was marginally better, he supposed, and he'd been expecting it. "Yeah, but not like when I was younger and an idiot."

"An idiot? Not my Uncle Rob?" Lois's tone was jokey but also a bit defensive.

"Oh, yeah, your Uncle Rob. Mind you, I wasn't the only one. Most of us lads had a crush on her at some point or another, although she was pretty intimidating."

"How do you mean?"

"How to explain... She was a bit snobby and sarcastic. I didn't blame her, with a bunch of spotty morons ogling her all the time. She was just stunning, Lo, and clever—unobtainable, really—so, when she said yes, she'd go out with me, it was like getting pole position on the starting grid."

Lois shoved him in the side. "A woman isn't a prize to be won!"

"Fair comment." He'd deserved that and decided to nip the conversation in the bud before he dug himself a deeper hole by admitting that when Jess had 'dumped' him, he'd accused her of leading him on. It was only when Josh had given him an earful—which was brutal but what he'd needed to hear—that he'd accepted he'd misread the signals and concocted more than was there.

After that, Rob and Jess hardly saw each other from one year to the next, but the chemistry had stayed as powerful as ever—even that last time, when Rob had been laying the foundations for the sting operation. Of course he'd still cared, and he'd hated the deception, but the infatuation, his belief he'd been in love, was a thing of the past.

"What about you?" he asked. "Any romance in your life?"

Lois laughed. "No, and I intend to keep it that way."

Rob patted her hand. "Wise girl. I mean woman," he corrected all by himself, although it wasn't sexism this time. She'd always be his little niece, and he'd kill to protect her. Amber too.

They reached Lois's apartment block, and she stepped around him to open the door. "Are you coming in for a coffee?"

"No, thanks, but can we take a rain check?"

"Sure."

"Cheers. I'm gonna head back, give your nan a hand with whatever's on her list of tasks for the day."

"Saturday…" Lois pursed her lips in contemplation. "Beds and bathroom."

Rob laughed. "I'll report back—let you know if you're right."

"I am," Lois asserted smugly. "I'd lay money on it."

"Yeah? How much?"

"Let's see… Loser buys the next bag of duck food?"

"You're on," Rob said. They shook on it and hugged again. "Thanks for this afternoon."

"No, thank you. It's been fun, plus you saved me from the huge pile of paperwork hogging my sofa."

"It's the weekend."

"Hypocrite much?"

"Right, that's it. I don't have to stay here and take your insults." Rob moved off backwards. "Let me know what evenings you're free and we'll go for dinner or something."

"Will do." She waved, and he waved back, watching to make sure she was safely inside before he jogged to his mum's place, chuckling to himself at the line full of bed linen wafting in the back garden and almost choking on his laughter when his mum appeared at the top of the stairs with a spray bottle of bathroom cleaner in her pink-rubber-gloved hands.

She frowned suspiciously. "What's funny?"

"Nothing, Mum. I'll do that for you if you like."

"For me?"

"You know what I mean."

"Hmm. Well, anyway, you're too late." She disappeared from view.

"Will that washing be dry?"

"Not yet. A cup of coffee would be nice, though."

"OK." Rob went through to the kitchen and prepared the coffee maker, waving at Harvey through the back window. He was planting bulbs, with Linford's 'assistance', which involved a lot of pouncing and dashing around in circles, followed by a bit of digging, a telling-off, and more dashing around in circles.

Rob's regret for not bringing Lucas resurfaced. Lucas loved dogs and had been pestering for one for a while. Zoë refused on the basis there was no-one home during the day, except that wasn't true. Travis worked from home more often than not, but for once, Rob wasn't going to hold it against him. A dog was a big responsibility and would put an end to Travis's impromptu family weekends away.

On second thoughts, a bit of gentle encouragement... He took a couple of photos with his phone and emailed them to Zoë. She wouldn't thank him for it.

It was only after he'd sent the email that Rob noticed he'd missed a few calls while he'd been at the park. He hadn't felt his phone vibrate.

"Yeah, that might help." He'd forgotten to turn on notifications when he'd run through the setup; he did so before checking the call log: three missed calls and a voicemail. Rob deleted the voicemail without listening to it. Whatever Jock had to say, he wasn't interested.

8: Feasting

Gray managed to swallow a few more mouthfuls of tea before the sweetness made him shudder; he tipped the rest down the sink. On the plus side, he was no longer shaking and got his boots off with relative ease. Leaving them in the hallway, next to Will's wellies, he went upstairs to the bedroom. He was not alone.

"Pick a side, Benj." Gray tentatively shuffled across the mattress, under the false premise that he could claim the space, and instead ended up lying diagonally with his legs on the bed and his body hanging off the edge. Through the open door, he saw Will emerge from the bathroom with towels wrapped around his lower body and his head, the rest of him shimmering with water droplets. He stopped in the bedroom doorway and smiled.

"You made it."

"I did. There's a rabbit in your bed."

Will bent forward, letting the towel drop from his head into his hands, and rubbed briskly at his hair. "You're not talking about sex toys again, are you?"

Gray laughed. "A rabbit, Will. Really?"

Will straightened up with a grin. "I'm told they're very satisfying."

"I'm sure they are," Gray agreed distractedly. Will had dispensed with both towels and held his arms out in a wide, unavoidably naked shrug. "What?" Gray asked.

"Am I getting dressed, or are you stripping off?"

"You choose," Gray suggested breezily. From where he was lying, Will's preference was perfectly clear—getting clearer by the second—but there was still a large white lop-eared bunny in the way.

"Come on, Benj, off you get." Will knelt on the edge of the bed, scooped the poor creature up from his comfy resting place and set him down on the floor.

"Aw. We could've worked around him," Gray said, although his guilt for Benjy's eviction was short-lived, lasting only as long as it took to get his fingers in Will's tea-tree-scented tangle of blonde-brown hair. The warmth of Will's damp skin permeating Gray's clothes was an instant trip switch for his arousal.

"I'm going to the barber's this week," Will murmured against Gray's lips.

"So you keep saying."

"Just a trim."

"Hmm-hmm…"

"You're not stripping off."

"No hands."

Will moved away, or tried to, but Gray grabbed his head and pulled him back in, taking control of the kisses. Will didn't resist, instead changing tactics. He unfastened Gray's jeans and pushed them down as far as he could. Gray kicked them off the rest of the way, sat up briefly to remove his socks and then whipped his shirt over his head.

"Better?" He hardly got the word out before his yelp of surprise at the coldness of Will's wet hair against his chest. He braced in preparation for what he knew would follow. Will's teeth clamped onto Gray's nipple and tugged lightly, pulling the surrounding skin taut while Gray held his breath so he didn't vocalise his response; he'd not yet decided if it was one of pain or pleasure.

That was only the beginning; Will attended to Gray's body as if it were a multi-course feast—a lick here, a nibble there—leaving virtually no spot untouched by lips, teeth or tongue. It always progressed the same way, and more than once, Gray had quipped, 'I thought you didn't eat meat,' but he wasn't feeling playful today. Will's touch, combined with the post-adrenaline comedown, left him both hyper-sensitive and in a state of deep relaxation; the paradox was like jet fuel to his libido.

"Can you, err…" Gray formed the phrase *cut to the chase* in his mind. He couldn't say that.

"Get on with it?" Will guessed. He reached Gray's belly button and circled it with the tip of his tongue.

"Well…yeah, basically."

"Not a problem."

Gray clamped his lips between his teeth and studied the ceiling. There were times Will's perpetual agreeableness irritated him. Like now.

"Don't you care?" he asked. It was an excellent example of cutting one's nose off to spite one's face, or one's penis to spite one's groin, seeing as Will had acted decisively but had to release him to answer.

"About?"

"Me hurrying you along."

Will shrugged and went back to it, although really, he'd only skipped a few courses. He was certainly making the most of the dessert, so to speak, interspersing long, slow sucks with licks and nips, nudging Gray closer to the edge but not quite close enough for him to go over.

"It's not an ice cream," Gray muttered.

"Nope. It's better," Will mumbled with his mouth mostly full. Gray drew breath to protest further, but changed his mind. Two could play at that game.

Without warning, he rolled sideways, taking Will by surprise, and pushed him onto his back. "Your turn," he said.

"OK."

"No. Not OK."

"It's not?"

"No."

Will looked hurt, and Gray partly rescinded. "I mean, it is... normally."

"You're bored," Will stated.

"I'm not. But I'm craving a bit more...something today."

"You're jonesing for adrenaline."

Gray raised his eyebrows. "Did you make that up?"

"Nope. I get it all the time when I'm surfing, especially if I screw up. What you want is something...a bit more...like this?" In a flash, Gray was flat on his back again, and Will was on top of him, kissing him so hard his head submerged into the pillows. He tugged the corner of one and threw it on the floor—remembering Benjy after the event. Lifting, with the intention of checking he hadn't accidentally suffocated a rabbit, Gray gasped and stopped breathing. Will's mouth clamped to his neck. *I'm too old for hickies...oh, so what? I own polo necks.*

The weight of Will's body, coupled with his hard rutting, made it virtually impossible for Gray to move, which was for the best. He was teetering on the edge again, and he still wanted more. With difficulty, he slid his knee up between Will's thighs, which gave him enough leverage to roll them onto their sides. They both reached down at the same time, firmly grasping each other.

"Don't you want a turn?" Gray asked.

"Yeah, but..." Will's breathing juddered.

"Next time..." Gray increased his speed, smiling as Will's body went rigid, his erection swelling in Gray's fist as ejaculate like rapid-cool lava hit Gray's abdomen, triggering his own orgasm that left him jolting with aftershocks for several minutes after. It had definitely been worth the risk to speak up, not that it was much of one when Will was so easy-going—about most things. Certainly worth pushing a bit further...

"Can we go out for dinner?"

Will opened his mouth to respond. It would've been a refusal, Gray knew, so he pressed on while he had the advantage.

"The food last night was excellent, but I didn't exactly get a chance to appreciate it."

"I'm skint, Gray."

"I'll pay."

"But—"

"I'd be happy to."

Will propped up on one elbow and studied him awhile. "You're changing it *all* up today, huh?" His tone had switched from defensive to amenable, neutralising potential dissent. It was an impressive tool in his professional negotiation skill set, but Gray was growing wise to it. Next would come the redirect. "What did you have to eat?"

"Mock-fish Thai curry and jasmine rice. I know what you're doing."

"Not steak?"

"I don't always have steak," Gray argued. In fact, he couldn't remember the last time he'd eaten steak. It had become a bit of a hobby, trying to find restaurants that served good vegetarian, or better still, vegan food, for future dates, such as he and Will went any further afield than the local pub. Between what Will sent to Suzannah's mum and however much he 'donated to animal welfare', he rarely had funds to spare, whereas Gray was in the privileged position of being able to say 'it's only money'. He didn't care if it was always on him—there were so many other things Will contributed to their relationship—but Will did care.

"What's the occasion?"

"I just want to take you out to dinner."

"For no reason?"

"It's my mum's birthday."

"Is it?" Will asked doubtfully.

"On Monday." And not really an 'occasion'.

"Did you send a card?"

"Yeah, and a gift voucher." For cruelty-free cosmetics—not the gift he'd have chosen before he met Will. "I almost didn't bother."

"Do you usually?"

"Every year. And every year, I go through the same argument in my head. It's not as if I expect her undying gratitude. I'd settle for knowing my cards get there, but she doesn't even mention them to Becky. She could put them straight in the bin for all I know."

Will bent to kiss Gray's shoulder. "You're a good son."

"Debatable," Gray said. He appreciated the support, even if there was an ulterior motive, but he hadn't lost sight of his objective. He shuffled closer—so close their noses were touching. "I want to buy you dinner. Is that so bad?"

Will kept his poker face, but the emotions played out in and around his eyes—amusement, a little bit of admiration—"I need to get me some new tactics."

Gray laughed. "You really do."

—finally settling on submission. "OK."

"And for you to be happy about it," Gray added.

"So many demands..." Will lamented with an overly weary sigh. Gray gave him a shove, and he fell back, laughing. "I can do that."

"Good." Gray closed his eyes, wondering how long he could bear to lie there, naked and sullied. It was such a peaceful afternoon, not that it would've mattered if the dogs were going loopy, or Tie was trooping in and out. The farmhouse was one big, rustic chill-out zone. Even so... "Are you planning on washing those towels?"

"I wasn't. Why? Ah, I'll get some tissue. Be right back."

Will sprang up from the bed far too energetically for one in a post-coital state and padded away to the bathroom. A moment later, the toilet flushed, but Gray didn't hear him coming back over the din of several sets of paws thumping their way up the stairs. A length of loo roll fluttered down onto Gray's belly; he did the fastest clean-up ever and yanked the duvet over him in the nick of time, grunting as Fido landed on his midriff.

"God, you're heavy," he spluttered, rolling his head from side to side in an effort to avoid Doris's tongue-based display of adoration. Meanwhile, Kenny yapped at the bottom of the stairs.

"At least they waited until we were done," Will said. "Are we staying up here for now?"

With no other body movement capability, Gray stuck up a thumb. Will left again, returning a moment later with Kenny. He set him down on the bed and slid in next to Gray.

"Did you just carry him up here naked?"

"He's always naked."

"I meant you, you…"

Will grinned.

"And if Tie had come in?"

"He's not here. Anyway, he's seen it all before."

"Thanks for the reminder."

"He wouldn't care. We could be watching TV starkers and he wouldn't notice."

"I'll take your word for it. Where is he, by the way? Releasing goldfish into a river somewhere?" Will and Tie's most recent campaign had brought down a guy selling goldfish and other animals as live food.

"We didn't release them into a river. They went to—"

"A safe tank?" Gray suggested, already chuckling at his own joke. "You know? Like a safe house."

Will turned his face away. "I'm not telling you anything anymore."

"The piscine witness protection programme…"

"Mock all you like. We put the guy away, didn't we?"

"You did," Gray agreed. In the continued absence of mobility, he sought out Will's hand and lifted it to kiss it.

"Watch it or I'll start thinking you approve."

"I do, most of the time. I just don't much fancy the idea of spending every Monday afternoon visiting you in prison."

"Why Monday?"

"Whatever day. You know what I mean."

"You worry too much, Gray. Most of what we do is legal."

"Such as?"

Will flashed him a grin and winked. "So, what time are we heading out for dinner?"

"Give me one example."

"Do I need to dress up?"

"Just one."

Will rubbed his chin. "I should shave…"

"Where did you say Tie was again?"

"Community service. I'm gonna go shave." Will was gone before Gray could claim the victory. Kenny immediately shifted into Will's space and rested his chin on Gray's chest, peering at him with sad brown eyes.

"Don't worry," Gray whispered, stroking Kenny with one hand and Fido with the other—and pretending he hadn't noticed Will come back into the room. "If it comes to it, we can all look after one another."

Will left again with the towels and without a word.

Gray's legs were going to sleep, and the rest of him wasn't far behind. He let his eyes close and his thoughts take over. They went straight to his mum and, by extension, Will's mum. On Mothering Sunday, he'd gone with Will to visit his mum's grave and somehow—the tears had a lot to answer for—agreed to reciprocate the visit at some yet-to-be-determined point in the future. That was two weeks ago, and he'd been waiting ever since for Will to bring it up again. He'd half hoped the conversation would veer that way earlier, because unless Will pushed for it—which was only slightly more likely than him turning carnivore—it wouldn't happen.

Unfortunately, thinking about his mum had Gray so worked up that he was able to truthfully answer no, he hadn't fallen asleep, when Will returned from the bathroom clean-shaven and with his hair neatly tied back.

"I take it you're not getting back in?"

Will eyed the abundance of dogs.

"Your own fault for letting them on the bed in the first place." Gray attempted to extract himself from under Fido, getting one foot on the floor.

"Don't hear you complaining."

"Err…"

"Usually," Will amended. He collected boxers from a drawer, socks from another. "What time do you want to leave?"

Gray shuffled on his bottom, freeing his other leg, and sat up. He checked the time, surprised to discover it was almost half past four. Saturdays always went far too fast. "When we're ready?" he suggested. The sooner they left, the sooner they could get back for a pint in the local pub, or even have an early night.

"Works for me." Will perched on the end of the bed to put on his socks. Gray gathered his clothes from the floor and got dressed, watching out of the corner of his eye as Will did the same—the watching and the dressing—both fighting a smile and then giving up when their paths crossed. Will put his arms around Gray's waist. "I could get used to this."

"I already am." Gray kissed him and edged past to collect the pair of ordinary boots he'd stowed in the wardrobe.

"I'll go sort dinner for this lot," Will said on his way out of the room.

"OK. You want me to bring Kenny down?"

"If you don't mind."

"Not a problem," Gray called after him.

"Hush, you."

Laughing, Gray beckoned Kenny to the edge of the bed and scooped him up—one arm around his chest, the other around his back end—the way Will had shown him months ago and which was now second nature. He carried Kenny downstairs to the kitchen, where the rest of the dogs were already eating. Will was at the hutch, filling the guinea pigs' food bowls. Gray lowered Kenny to the floor; the dog shot off as soon as his front legs touched down, his back end landing with a thump that made Gray cringe.

Will closed the hutch and frowned, nose wrinkled in thought as he stared out of the window. "I'll leave the chickens. Tie should be back before it goes dark. Are you ready?"

"Yep."

9: Call of Duty

Rob was almost grinding his teeth in anticipation by the time he and his mum were done in the kitchen. He carried the pan of curry chicken over to the table and put it down as he sat. His mum arrived with the flat breads, shouted Harvey and moved the curry out of Rob's reach.

"Aw, Mum…"

"It's not all for you."

"But it's too far away."

"You've got long arms. *Harvey!*"

"I heard you the first time." Harvey closed the back door on his way in and made a speedy stop at the kitchen sink to wash his hands.

"The dog, Harvey…" The poor guy barely got his bum on the seat. With a gruff grunt, he pushed his chair back and glared under the table. Linford got up and skulked off to his bed. Harvey pulled his chair in again and looked over the array of food appreciatively.

Rob watched on, hawk-like, vaguely aware of his phone vibrating in his pocket and with no intention of answering. It was a definite no-no at mealtimes in his mum's house, and in any case was probably only Jock. Right at that moment, all Rob cared about was his mum's curry chicken.

"Most of the seedlings are in now," Harvey said. He carefully scooped with the ladle and waited for it to stop dripping before he moved it to Rob's mum's plate. "If the weather holds, I'll get the rest out tomorrow."

"Did you remember the canes for the sweet peas?"

Rob followed the empty ladle's progress back to the bowl.

"I'll do those tomorrow."

Down it went, scoop, up...

"You forgot, you mean?"

"I wanted to get everything into the ground first."

A piece of chicken tumbled over the edge and landed with a splat. Harvey frowned at it.

"Come on, I'm starving here, man," Rob complained, to which Harvey chuckled and dragged it out a *little bit* longer.

At last, a mound of hot, spicy chicken and chick peas landed dead centre of Rob's plate; he had to sit on his hands to stop himself from digging straight in. He was virtually drowning on his own saliva, but Harvey didn't have any food on his plate yet. Fond as Rob was of the guy, if he didn't get a move on...

"For goodness' sake, Robert, turn off that phone."

"Sorry, Mum." He took it out, switched it to silent, noted the most recent missed call was from Zoë, not Jock, and put it back in his pocket. Nothing was coming between him and that curry, and as soon as Harvey was loaded up, Rob impolitely grabbed a couple of flat breads, scooped up as much curry as he could and crammed it into his mouth without blowing on it or even checking whether it needed to be blown on. It was so hot it made his eyes water. He put up with it, groaning in pleasure at the delicious sweet-spicy flavours mingling in his mouth.

"Could you pass the bread, please, Harvey?" Rob's mum requested with a stern glare in Rob's direction, the impact of which was diluted by her obvious delight that he was enjoying her cooking so much. As if that would ever change.

"Delicious," he mumbled, holding his hand in front of his mouth. She raised an eyebrow in disapproval. He reloaded his bread, greedily eyeing the pan to check there was plenty left for a second helping. After that, he ate and half listened to the conversation about bedding plants, quite sure if he keeled over right then, he'd die the happiest man alive. Certainly the fullest.

"No leftovers for supper tonight," his mum laughed, removing the scraped-empty pan after Rob's third helping. "You want dessert, too, I suppose?"

"I wouldn't say no," he answered with a grin. He got up to help, but she shooed him back to the table. Harvey gave him a knowing nod.

"So, how's life treating you these days, young Robert?"

"Not bad, thanks, Harvey. How about you? You're looking well."

"Ah, you know…" Harvey nodded, but his usual wide smile was missing. He leaned closer and said, "Prostate, you know?"

Rob frowned, not sure if he'd interpreted correctly and hoping he hadn't.

"Cancer," Harvey confirmed.

Rob's pulse rate shot up. "Sorry to hear that." His voice didn't sound like it was coming from him.

"It's common in men of my age. And they can treat it."

"Yeah?" Rob poured a glass of juice, avoiding eye contact. He was lucky; he'd known relatively few people who'd been diagnosed with cancer. Not so luckily, all of them had died from the disease, but that didn't mean it was a guaranteed death sentence. Rob just needed to keep it in perspective.

"Lois has a copy of my will," Harvey finished as Rob's mum returned with three dishes topped by mounds of white fluff. Lemon meringue pie—Rob's favourite—which seemed a bit frivolous in the aftermath of Harvey's news.

"You haven't been telling scare stories again, have you?" She winked at Rob and scowled at Harvey.

"Cancer is scary," Harvey argued.

"Ignore his rubbish." Rob's mum set his dessert dish in front of him and kissed his head. He smiled up at her, appreciating her attempt to make light of Harvey's doom and gloom. The man was right. Cancer was terrifying, but, as Rob's mum had pointed out the night he'd broken down over Jess, so was riding a motorbike and he did that voluntarily.

"I made that especially for you…"

"Sorry, I was miles away." Rob put a road block on his trip to Miseryville and tucked in; within two spoonfuls, he was well on his way back to normal operations, the only trouble being it went down too quickly. "That was spot on, Mum."

"There's more."

Rob rubbed his bloated belly. "Can I save it till later? I'm stuffed."

"If I don't get to it first," Harvey said.

"Don't you dare!" Rob's mum admonished. "I'll cover it and leave it in the fridge for you, Rob."

"Favouritism…"

"If you want it—"

"No, no. It's all yours." With a firm pat, more of a lean, on Rob's shoulder, Harvey heaved to his feet and left the room, whistling Linford on his way to the front door.

"Thanks, Mum," Rob said.

"Always a pleasure cooking for you."

Between them, they cleared the table, and Rob got a good start on washing the dishes before his mum noticed. She kept shoving him with her hip, but he refused to surrender his position in front of the sink, and she eventually gave up in favour of making a pot of coffee. With all the dishes dried and put away, Rob stepped out onto the patio; his mum frowned at him by way of asking what he was up to.

"Returning Zoë's call. That's who phoned before."

"I hope everything's all right."

"She'll have forgotten I'm up here. I'm sure it's fine." In case it wasn't, Rob pulled the door to and moved a few feet away before he made the call. "Alright, Zo?"

"Hey, Rob. Having a good break?"

"Give me a couple more days and I'll let you know."

Zoë laughed. "Like that, is it?"

"I haven't had much chance to chill yet. Anyway, you called?"

"I did. Someone came to the house asking for you."

"Who?"

"No idea. He didn't say."

"Didn't or wouldn't?"

"I'm not sure I asked."

"OK." Rob always asked, but then he was a copper. Ex-copper. "Did he say anything else?"

"He asked if you were in. I told him you weren't but I'd pass on a message. He said to let you know he was disappointed you weren't in."

"Not a debt collector, then," Rob thought aloud.

"I didn't realise you were struggling."

"I'm not. I'm running through the possibilities."

"If we need to rethink the maintenance payments..."

"I'd tell you, I promise, but thanks. Did you get a good look at him?"

"I did. He had scars—a lot of them—all over his face, wide cheeks, broken nose... I know it's stereotyping, but he looked like a squaddie."

She was bang on the money with both the description and the career. It was Jock again, which lent a different meaning to 'disappointed you weren't in'. Rob wasn't happy Jock had involved Zoë.

"Who is he?" she asked.

"REME. Same bloke as rang you yesterday."

"Sorry?" The second syllable was a high-pitched squeak. She didn't know what he was talking about.

"He called me last night, said he got my number from you."

"Err, no!" And now she was pissed off. "The only call I received yesterday was from Gray to say you'd left your phone behind. I take it you've spoken to him?"

"I ordered a replacement. I didn't realise he'd picked it up."

"Apart from that, no-one called. Even if they had, I wouldn't give out your number."

"I did think that."

"Yet you believed the guy?"

"No—I'm sorry, Zo. He caught me on my way out, so I didn't give it much thought—I didn't get to my leaving do, by the way."

"Because of Moonface?"

"Ha, yeah." Funny she'd called him that—it was the same name Rob had used whenever Jock gave him shit—and in fact, he wasn't surprised Jock had gone this far. But it was Tonka's show, and he hadn't expected heavy-handed tactics from her. "I'll give him a call now. I wouldn't mind but he knows we're divorced. He's a pain in the arse."

"Rob, if there's something going on—"

"Nothing you need to worry about." He hoped. "I'll let you go. Love to Lu."

"Yeah, same to you and yours."

"Take care, Zo." Rob hung up. "Might as well get this over with." He found Jock's number and made the call. It was answered right away. "Jock. It's Rob."

"About fucking time. Been calling you all day."

"Yeah, I've been busy. Listen—"

"You told her to do one, didn't you?"

"Who?"

"Tonka."

"Never mind that. How did you get my number?"

"I told you, your missus—"

"No, she didn't. Who gave it to you?"

"A copper at your nick. He mistook me for one of your colleagues. I wasn't going to correct him."

Rob clenched his free hand into a fist and pressed his knuckles to the brick wall until he felt it. "And Zoë's address? He gave you that, too, did he?"

"Nah. It's on your army record."

Of course it was, because Rob hadn't updated it.

Jock pressed on. "What happened with Tonka?"

"I told her I couldn't help."

"Help?"

"With Ethan."

"What the fuck are you talking about?"

"He's being released, isn't he?"

"Not that I've heard. Is that what she told you?"

"She said…" Rob paused, only for a second. He hated Jock, and for good reason, but when they were serving together, Rob had trusted him as much as he'd trusted Tonka or Bish, or even Ethan, to have his back. And he still trusted him. "She said she'd found someone who could clear Ethan's record before his release date—no medical or criminal history, give him a clean slate."

"Aww, what a lovely bedtime story," Jock said, sickly sweet. "I've got another one to tell you if you're into fairy tales. You didn't fall for it, did you, Shaz?"

"Fuck you," Rob muttered, but there was no venom behind it. "Right, your turn."

"Yeah. Well, as it happens, me and Bish went down to see Ethan a few weeks back. He didn't mention anything about a new identity or whatever blag Tonka gave you."

"She might not have told him," Rob speculated. "Didn't want to get his hopes up."

"No offence, mate, but that's bollocks. Ethan's been on lockdown. He attacked a nurse or guard or something, so unless they decide he's sane and transfer him to a prison—there's more chance of Bish's arm growing back, in my not-so-humble opinion—that mad bastard's going nowhere."

"Is this a wind-up?"

"Not this time, I swear."

Rob ran his hand over his head, pressing on the tension spots forming. His holiday was quickly turning to shit. "What's going on, Jock?"

"Ain't a clue, mate."

"Did she ask you and Bish for money?"

"Yeah, but without the bull about Ethan, because we'd have seen straight through it. She told us she'd had a tip about a sure investment and wanted to share the good fortune—some property company that buys derelict houses in Eastern Europe, does them up and flogs them for four times what they paid out. They were looking for capital in return for stocks and shares."

"She's not involved in investment, is she?"

"No, but her brother is, which is why me and Bish were ready to hand over our hard-earned dough."

It made less sense the more Rob heard. Tonka was trying to get a large amount of cash together, that much seemed clear, but why hadn't she given him the same spiel as the others? Of course, if she'd known he'd worked for the SIU, it was reasonable she'd assume he knew a thing or two about investment. The fact he knew next to bugger all was by the by. But *none* of his army mates knew about the SIU—he hadn't seen them to tell them and wouldn't have done so, anyway—which meant either she'd found out through other means, or she hadn't wanted him to part with his money in the first place and the whole setup was…what? A means to scam Bish and Jock?

"How much did you give her?" Rob asked.

"Nothing in the end. After you left, she ripped up our cheques, said it wasn't enough without your share and she'd go in on her own."

"She was planning to go through a fund manager," Rob thought aloud.

"What's one of them?"

"Someone who invests on your behalf to spread the risk." And he'd already said too much. "What's your gut feeling?"

"All is not as it seems, Shaz. All is not as it seems."

He could almost see Jock's hideous moon-faced grin. "Yeah, I got that. Do you think she was trying to rip us off?"

"I dunno. Maybe she wants to buy a Lambo for the Kraut—hers and hers matching pair?"

"It's a possibility."

"See, now that *was* a wind-up."

"Likewise," Rob said dryly. He obviously needed to turn down the sarcasm dial on his sense of humour.

"I think she's in bother," Jock said.

"Agreed."

"Looks like you've got your first PI case, then, eh?"

"Yeah, once I'm on my feet, I might consider mates' rates."

"We'll pay you," Jock cut in quickly.

"Jock—"

"Me and Bish already talked it over last night. Well…as long as you're cheaper than two hundred and fifty grand." Jock laughed, and Rob joined in. It wouldn't cost them even a tenth of that, and while it was nice to know money was no object, Rob wasn't sure he wanted to be at Jock's beck and call.

"Before we jump the gun, I need to do some preliminary work—"

"Already one step ahead of you, Shaz. She's gone. The neighbours heard the car—they reckon it was about four, four-fifteen this morning."

"We don't know she's gone for good, though. Let me try talking to her first."

"Yeah, good luck with that."

"Number not recognised?" Rob guessed.

"I can see why you became a dick now. You catch on quick, considering."

"Considering what? That you need my help so it's in your best interests to stop being a knob?" Rob would normally have let it go, but he was stalling for thinking time. He'd heard enough to believe Tonka was having the kind of money trouble that came with threats to life and limb, and he'd have done some digging around with or without the incentive. However, he and Gray had timed the official launch—when the website, phone line and advertising went live—for Rob's scheduled return, and while he'd be a fool to turn down the money, if he agreed to do this, he'd have to cut his holiday short, and he'd miss the opportunity to sort things out with Amber. That was more important to him than getting his business off to a good start. There again, it wasn't just his business.

"Right, Jock, I'm gonna talk to my partner. If he thinks we're ready to take a case, it's a goer. Fifty percent of the fee up front—"

"If it's not a goer?"

"I'll point you towards someone else who might be able to help, which would be a better option for you—a cheaper one, for sure."

"Don't worry about that. You know me and Bish run a security firm, I take it?"

"I didn't."

"Yeah. We've got some big contracts—a couple with pharma companies. And you know how Bish is. He's always had a soft spot for Tonka. Me, I don't give a toss, but Bish is the brains behind this operation, so if it keeps him sweet…"

Jock was worried about Tonka, whatever he said, but he'd never admit it, certainly not to Rob. "OK. I'll be in touch in a couple of days, let you know our decision. How's that?"

"I look forward to it."

10: For Dessert

Gray and Will made it through the starters on mundane small talk, with nothing more contentious than Gray pointing out hummus was among the vegan menu options and then mercilessly mocking Will for choosing it after everything he'd said. For the main course, Will opted for the three-bean chilli with soft tacos and rice while Gray made a second attempt at the mock-fish Thai curry—now he stood some chance of tasting it on the way down. That was when the conversation took a slight nosedive.

"Aaron wants me to go with him to visit Freddie Berringer." Will put it out there like a 'nice wine' bland statement.

Gray stopped mid-chew. Will remained relaxed, or appeared as such, but it was hard to tell. Maybe he believed what he'd said was inconsequential.

"Why?" Gray asked.

Will bobbed his fork from side to side, weighing up. "I say Aaron. It might be Naomi. But if it's Aaron on the day, he won't cope with the security frisk."

"That only explains why they want you there."

"They have unfinished business."

"Berringer's remanded in custody precisely because he'll interfere with witnesses."

"I'm sure Aaron and Naomi are aware of that."

Gray wasn't being intentionally obstructive, or he was a bit. He had yet to fathom the dynamics of Will's relationship—past and present—with Aaron-Naomi. "You'll be monitored," he pointed out.

Will smiled placidly. "You're telling the wrong person. My lips will be firmly sealed for the duration."

"This could jeopardise the prosecution's case."

"Only if we...*they* talk about it. How's the soya and seaweed?"

Message received. Gray cut a piece from his mock-fish, lifting it to his mouth with an unnecessary flourish. He chewed and hummed in pleasure, perhaps more than his meal warranted. "Delicious. How's the chilli?"

"Almost as good as my mum's." Will looked around him, his gaze slowly passing over the wall décor, the paintings, the lighting sconces, and flitting past Gray to take in the same on the other side of the restaurant. "Very upmarket. Expensive?"

"Not overly so." The absence of prices on the menu suggested otherwise, but unless they switched to drinking Champagne, the bill wouldn't be extortionate. "So you're definitely going, then?"

"I told Aaron I would. Are you advising me not to?"

"It's not my place."

"In your professional opinion," Will pushed.

"I would be very concerned if my key witness visited the defendant in prison. Not only for the witness's safety, but for how the jury will perceive it."

"Like you said, we won't be alone."

"You won't. You need to be really careful, Will. Both of you. All of you. When is it?"

"Well, funny thing...I thought you already knew."

"How would I?"

"Friends on the inside?"

"I haven't got..." Gray stopped short of finishing the automatic lie. "I didn't know. Why did you think I did?"

"It's a week on Monday."

"Ah. What I said earlier. Pure coincidence, believe it or not."

"Or an unconscious tell?"

"From you? Unlikely. But if it came to it, I'd spend every Monday afternoon visiting you."

Will grinned. "You say the sweetest things."

"You're easily pleased." Gray tried to keep a straight face against Will's suggestive taco nibbling, then closed his eyes and shook the image from his mind. "On a serious note..." He opened his eyes again; Will gave his full attention. "Don't lay a finger on Berringer—don't even shake the man's hand."

"Not a prob—" Gray raised his eyebrows. Will sighed and stopped being flippant. "Understood," he said.

"Everything all right?" the waiter asked.

"Yes, thanks," Gray responded. The waiter bowed and continued on his way.

Will leaned closer and whispered, "Are we being too loud?"

"I don't think so. They're just giving us our money's worth."

"Do they offer a personal massage with the dessert course?"

Gray laughed. "Now, there's an idea."

"You know...I've never been comfortable with these kinds of places. I'd say it was down to social class, but our backgrounds aren't that different. Or they weren't when we were kids."

"We didn't go out for dinner much," Gray agreed, "unless you count fish and chips at the seaside."

"Fish and chips..." Will's expression took on a nostalgic quality. "My uncle used to get them for us after we'd been to the football. We didn't tell my mum."

"Would she have been mad?"

"No. But she'd have felt guilty on our behalf and given Uncle Jim an earful."

"I've always assumed he's veggie too."

"He's pescetarian, which is pointless. If you're going to eat one dead animal, you might as well eat them all."

They'd had this conversation several times before, the most recent being when Gray had brought a selection of goat's cheeses for their Saturday supper and hadn't thought to check whether his choices were from humane farms, never mind whether the rennet was vegetarian. It was a foolish mistake, but he only made it the once. He wasn't sure when it had happened, because it was more than simple respect for Will's values. Somehow they'd become Gray's values too. Or perhaps, on an unconscious level, he'd always shared them.

He also understood Will's discomfort with living it up at someone else's expense. It wasn't so long ago it had been beyond Gray's means to dine out whenever he felt like it, when top-class restaurants and hotels were hostile territories where the language and culture were entirely alien.

Thinking back to the night Will had confronted Freddie Berringer, he'd slipped into his former merchant banker role with far greater ease than Gray had ever managed with any of his assumed identities because, contrary to Will's claim, their backgrounds weren't that similar. Will's parents were politically minded, educated people who fully supported their son's endeavours. Gray's parents had essentially left him to fend for himself, and whilst he hadn't earned his wealth, nor asked for it, he sure as hell wasn't going to squirrel it away in favour of living a humble existence of deferred gratification. But it was losing its appeal.

"I shouldn't have made you come here tonight."

"You didn't make me do anything."

"I hit you with it at the optimum moment."

"Yes, you did do that, but I'm enjoying it—the food, the company—it's all good."

"I'm sorry, Will."

"Hey, where's this come from all of a sudden?"

"I was thinking about money. Jean's money. I don't know what to do with it."

"In relation to investment?"

"Some of it is invested, but it's not that. It's...I don't know. Like a poisoned chalice that never empties. I bought a house that feels nothing like home. I've got all these gadgets I use once and put back in their boxes. I get cabs when I could use public transport, eat out instead of cook, force you to come along with me—for what purpose?"

"Because you can?"

"That doesn't mean I should. I could put it to better use, invest in a worthy cause. Look at all the good things you do with your money."

"I've got a daughter and moral obligations. I don't have any choice. But if you'd seen me when I was younger…it was like water running through my fingers. I didn't mean to put you on a guilt trip."

"You didn't. You got me thinking. Do you want dessert or… can we just go and drink good old working-class beer?"

Will laughed, a deep chuckle laced with amusement and so much more. It was like savouring a bite of a rich chocolate torte, and it was all the dessert Gray needed.

"Waiter, can I have the bill, please?"

***

They'd been at Will's local less than half an hour when Gray's phone rang. He frowned at the display. "That's unexpected," he said and hit the green button. "Evening, Rob."

"Alright, Gray? Haven't caught you at a bad time, have I?"

"No…" Gray made eye contact with Will. "You've caught me at a great time, actually. I'm in the pub."

"Fair enough. I won't keep you long, then. We might have our first case."

"Do you know the meaning of the word holiday, Rob?"

"It came looking for me not the other way round. A sort-of mate of mine. Ex-forces. That's why I didn't make it last night— I'll give you the full gory details when I see you—but if you're up for it, we'll be starting this week."

"Shouldn't be too much of a stretch. Is there anything you need me to do now?"

"I don't think so. I only called to check you were OK with it before I said yes."

"I am if you are."

"Good stuff. I'll let you go—I'm off to play pool with the lads."

"Dan and Aitch?"

"Yep. And Josh'll be there to kick my arse again."

"Is he any good?"

"I'll give you a tip—if he ever challenges you to a game, insist he's designated driver."

Gray laughed. "Noted. I'll see you when you get back."

"You will. It'll be less than two weeks, unfortunately, but I need to take care of a couple of things first. Enjoy your evening."

"You too, Rob. Bye." Gray ended the call and put his phone down on the table.

"Is who any good?" Will asked.

"Sorry?" Gray picked up his drink, exhaling against the beery air and wishing it was cooler. If he'd answered instead of being evasive...in fact, he wasn't sure why he was being evasive, other than that Will had asked a direct question which implied he'd thought the matter was of no consequence. Thanks to Gray's response and the terrific blush accompanying it, Will now knew otherwise, although he wasn't pushing for more information, but it was time Gray actively demonstrated his commitment to their future together.

"Josh," he said.

"OK." Will shrugged. "I didn't realise you had history with the guy, but you don't have to explain."

"It's more than that. Or less... Or maybe it isn't. I'm not in the best place to judge."

"Or making much sense," Will teased lightly. He finished the last inch of his pint and got up. "Another?"

"Please." Gray glugged the rest of his ale—a fair bit more than an inch—and handed the empty glass over.

Warm fuzzies. The beer, on top of a couple of glasses of wine earlier, multiplied Gray's gratitude for the brief reprieve. Will was giving him a choice: change the subject, knowing he wouldn't be pushed for an explanation, or continue his confession.

He watched Will at the bar, chatting with the other punters, smiling, laughing, light touches of palm to forearm or shoulder, such easy interaction, such a charmer... Gray still had moments of uncertainty—was Will stringing him along? Would his honesty be reciprocated? It was impossible to ever know for sure, but it was a gamble Gray was prepared to take. He wanted to tell this man the whole truth and nothing but the truth...so help him.

The bartender beckoned for Will's attention, indicating the logos on the counter mounts. Will pointed at the yellow one, second from the left; the bartender collected a pint glass and began pulling the pump. Will glanced back at Gray and mouthed, "Wheat beer?" Gray nodded his approval. He'd yet to see Will choose a dud.

A couple of minutes later, Will returned to their table, deposited the beer, said, "Little boys' room," and walked off.

"Don't leave me to think about this too long," Gray muttered under his breath, worried he'd lose his nerve before Will came back. Dragging one of the pint glasses closer, he gazed into the cloudy pale liquid. He was partial to *weissbier*. Very partial. As in drink-too-much-too-fast partial. He took a tentative sip and pushed the glass away. Then picked it up again.

"They're keeping at least one wheat beer on permanently," Will said, sliding back into his seat.

"That's dangerous." And great news that had Gray grinning.

Will chuckled. "I thought you'd be pleased."

"You might have to ration it unless you fancy carrying me back to your place every Saturday night."

Will looked him up and down with a smirk. "The idea has a certain appeal."

"Stop it!" Gray ordered, not seriously. Being mentally undressed was not helping his alcohol blush at all. Conversely, it wasn't making it any worse. "I was going to tell you something, remember?"

"Yes, you were. Like I said, you don't have to."

"I'd like to." Perhaps 'like' was the wrong word, but it was right for where they were up to in their relationship. "As long as you're not going to get jealous."

"Me?" Will looked a little affronted.

"Well, the way you are about Naomi and Freddie..."

"Jealousy has nothing to do with it. Anyway, you were saying?"

For all that Gray was curious, he didn't push it. They had plenty of time ahead of them for discovering all of each other's dirty little secrets. "I told you I had Josh under surveillance, didn't I?"

Will nodded and grinned. "While he was on his honeymoon."

"Right, and for a long time before, but that was, err…" Gray fidgeted, rubbing his hands together and then clasping them tightly. "OK, promise you won't laugh."

"Hey, you laughed at me."

"Did I?"

"When I told you I had a crush on him."

"I'm pretty sure I didn't. I was stunned."

"Stunned? I…" Briefly, Will lost focus—replaying events, Gray envisaged. "I thought you were trying not to laugh."

"If I laughed at all, it was at the sheer audacity of him pushing us together when we both…" The heat in his cheeks notched up a couple of degrees.

Will's eyes narrowed. "You too?"

Gray sighed. "Me too, and it wasn't just a crush."

Judging by Will's careful attentiveness, Gray could have skipped past the confession to the explanation, but in for a penny…

"It started out innocently enough, or in relation to Josh, at least. I picked up a fraud case involving a company in his hometown—not because of him, I should add. I had no idea he existed at that point. I'd found out George was my brother years before and never done anything about it. Yes, I'd planned to track him down while I was there, but that would've been the extent of abusing my position. I'd already done the preliminary work on the case and had Josh's name on my persons-of-interest list—he was a friend of one of our targets—but I wasn't aware he and George knew each other.

"I also had no idea how big the fraud operation was, which was foolish at best. I put together a small team to conduct surveillance, go in undercover, and I…" Gray's throat tightened. This was a harder admission than the one he'd set out to make. "It was after the accident, and I was a mess—mentally and physically. I went back to work too soon, and I insisted I was fine, but I wasn't. I was reckless. I didn't protect my team the way I should have, and they were incredible, faultless. Especially Rob. He hated the case... hated me...I don't blame him. But he did the job, saw it through right to the bitter bloody end."

Gray paused to drink some of his beer and gather his thoughts, all the while aware of Will watching him and waiting. The guy had seemingly infinite patience—one of his greatest yet most frustrating qualities—and would leave Gray to reach his point in his own sweet time. However, he hadn't intentionally sidetracked. He re-centred and forged on.

"It took nearly three years to nail our targets, and I should've been elated the case was over. We could all go home...but home to what? In those three years, I'd lost Jean, grieved for him, and—at the risk of vomiting poetic cliché—discovered my heart wasn't broken beyond repair. I'd developed feelings for Josh, and while I was cut up over never seeing him again, it was also liberating."

"You were healing," Will said.

Gray nodded but didn't answer, caught up in reliving the emotional resurgence of those last few weeks of the case. The nod became a self-conscious headshake and laugh. "I was so relieved the numbness had passed, I was like a kestrel on an updraft, observing without examining too deeply what I was doing."

"Very poetic," Will complimented.

"Not clichéd?" Gray prompted optimistically.

"You're the literature professor. You tell me."

Gray's confession was on the horizon, and he felt OK making it, but sensed Will was trying to divert the conversation. He decided to cut to the chase.

"I was in love with Josh, but, of course, he wasn't in love with me, mostly because he didn't know he had an admirer. Actually, that's not true. It wouldn't have made any difference if he had known. I fell in love with him from afar, which sounds crazy. But when you watch someone's every move, hour after hour, day after day…in company, alone… Like you said, there's something about him."

"Blonde hair, blue eyes…"

Perhaps he'd been wrong about Will feeling uncomfortable, because his expression had turned positively dreamy. Gray dipped a finger in his beer and flicked it at Will's face, making him blink.

"Cheers for that." Laughing, Will dried off on his sleeve. "I can't believe you'd waste an extremely decent wheat beer to make your point."

"Hmm. I could always invest in hair bleach and blue contact lenses," Gray muttered. Will was still laughing. "That wasn't what I meant. I'm not that shallow."

"Shallow?"

"Yes, shallow. There's more to the man than his blonde hair and blue eyes." Gray huffed at Will's continuing amusement at his expense. "OK, I'll admit I find him physically attractive, but it goes beyond that. He's complicated, intelligent, funny, quick-witted, honest—fascinating. *I* was fascinated. I wanted to uncover the real Josh Sandison, get inside his head, pin down his motivations. I *needed* to know if he was involved in the fraud scheme, and that was all it was, at first. But over time, my fascination transformed. It was no longer professional, and I didn't notice it happening. Not until it was too late."

"At least you realised eventually," Will comforted. Gray averted his eyes. "Huh. You kept watching?"

"Worse. I made a move on him."

"Gray!" Will was aghast, and hamming it up, which went some way towards easing Gray's embarrassment, but he wasn't proud of what he'd done. Nor could he honestly blame it on bereavement or the drugs. He had no excuse.

"Obviously, I couldn't just ask him out on a date. He was with George—married even—and he'd have dismissed it as a joke. He'd probably have told me to fuck off. In fact, he did tell me to fuck off on a regular basis, but that was after I…asked him to come and work with my unit as a profiler."

"Very cunning," Will said with way too much admiration.

"Low, is what it was, Will. Low. I'm ashamed."

"Did he fall for it?"

"Hook, line and sinker. He was a damned good profiler too. Anyway, I did own up in the end, and for his benefit. I guess I always knew, deep down, that I didn't stand a chance. It just took a while for my heart to get with the programme. When I told Josh how I felt, he was surprised, which I didn't expect, because he'd already figured out everything else about me. The first time he made me, I was talking to George—a completely innocent conversation, I hasten to add. George intervened in a dog fight, funnily enough, or not funny at all, but interesting it's come up today. He beat up a guy who'd set his dog on someone else's. My colleague went with the ambulance and I arrested George—he wasn't charged. But that was what we were talking about when Josh saw us."

"What happened to the dogs?"

"The one that did the attacking had to be destroyed—it was very aggressive. The other dog lost a leg, I think, but it made a full recovery."

"Nice one, George."

"Yeah, I've got to say, I prefer your rescue methods to his."

Will sat back and puffed out his chest. He couldn't have looked more proud if he'd tried.

Gray shook his head. "I really shouldn't have told you that."

Will grinned and relaxed again. "I ruined your flow. Please, continue."

"So bossy," Gray muttered playfully. This had been nowhere near as difficult as he'd anticipated. His feelings for Josh hadn't seemed like a burden, yet he felt so much lighter for sharing. "How are we doing on the jealousy front?"

"All clear so far," Will confirmed with a smile of reassurance that appeared to be the genuine article.

"Good because that's not why I wanted to tell you."

"I know. It's the same as me telling you about Shelley and Suzannah. Josh is an important part of your journey."

"Yeah, he is." Gray met Will's gaze and for a moment was lost in it and the wonder of being with someone who understood where he was coming from. "Where was I?"

"The dog fight…"

"Right. A few months after that—you can fill in the blank—"

"Gray Fisher, licensed to stalk?"

Gray sniffed sharply but continued. "This is what I mean about Josh being clever. He noticed a tiny discrepancy in Lambert's will—she was our target and a very close friend of his—and he started poking around. He was interfering with our investigation, so I went to warn him off, and he almost blew my cover. He had me completely sussed from minute one—where I was from, that I was a widower with one sibling—I have no idea how he does it."

"Yet he fell for your con?" Will was right to question it.

"He was suspicious of my intent. He just didn't see it for what it was, and…well, I can't really explain without betraying confidences—"

"Then don't." Will cut him off, and Gray was grateful to be saved from his dilemma. He wanted to share and felt comfortable doing so, but it wasn't his place.

"In conclusion, Josh is a very skilled pool player, according to Rob."

"But can he play poker?"

"It wouldn't surprise me. His poker face is almost as impenetrable as yours—perhaps you could take him on sometime."

Will looked Gray over with the same sultry, bordering on predatory, expression as before. His fingers walked up Gray's thigh. "There's only one man I'm interested in taking on."

Gray caught Will's hand before it crept any closer to places it shouldn't be in public, and grinned. "You say the sweetest things."

"I'm a professional," Will murmured. "Luckily, because you're really not that easy to please."

11: Eight-Ball

"Centre pocket." With the cue extended behind him, Rob leaned back and gave it a measured jolt with his left hand, tapping the white ball into the black. Down it went.

Aitch puffed air loudly and handed his cue to Dan. "This calls for some serious commiseration."

"Agreed. Your round, I believe." Dan grinned. It was Aitch's second defeat in a row, and they'd only played two frames.

"Yeah, all right. Same again?"

"Nothing for me, thanks," Josh said.

"Are you driving?"

"No, but I've got work to do when I get home."

"Fair enough." Aitch collected the empty glasses on his way to the bar.

"You're up next," Dan said, chalking the cue and holding it out to Josh, who waved his hand in dismissal.

"I'm useless at pool when I'm sober."

"Aitch, mate, buy this man another pint."

"Dan!" Josh protested, but Aitch was already ordering it. Josh blinked helplessly at Rob.

"Don't bring me into this," Rob said. "They're sods for it, but while they're getting you hammered—"

"They're leaving you alone," Josh finished, and then shouted, "Rob needs one too, Aitch."

"Oy! I've got to be up at the crack of dawn."

"For?"

"Footy." Rob gave Dan a glib grin and got one back.

"Are you playing?" Josh asked.

"Apparently."

"Oh, well, we're all in the same boat, then."

"You don't play, do you?"

"Not even drunk."

Dan offered Josh the cue again; reluctantly, he took it and gestured to Rob to break. "Who are we playing tomorrow?"

"The Vets," Dan said.

"What kind of vets?" Rob asked. He took the break, leaving a ball in prime potting position.

"Not your kind. Vets and veterinary nurses from all different surgeries, and they're a decent side—mixed."

Josh paused from lining up his cue and glared at Dan. "Was it necessary to qualify?"

"Huh?"

"They're a decent side *in spite of* having players who aren't men."

"That's not what I said," Dan protested.

"You implied it."

"No, I—"

Josh took his shot with a little too much vigour, which shut Dan up, although the ball rebounded off the pocket. Josh sighed and retreated to his seat.

"I thought George was coming," Dan tried as a neutraliser.

"He is. Actually…" Josh checked his phone. "I wonder where he's got to? He was only dropping Libby off at a friend's. I'll give him a call. Won't be long." Josh went outside.

Rob circled the table, trying to find a decent shot. Josh had left the cue ball against the cushion and touching both a stripe and a solid. Whichever way he went, he was going to foul. "Charlie Davenport still plays for the Lions, I'm guessing?" he asked and took the shot.

"She does," Dan confirmed, the 's' merging with his sharp intake of breath as the cue ball went down. "I reckon you'd get away with taking another." He tilted his head in the direction Josh had gone.

Rob laughed, pretty sure Dan was joking. In the thirty years they'd been friends—and before that when they were sporting enemies—he'd never known the guy to cheat, which begged the question, even though Josh had just come back in, "How d'you get away with having a woman on the team?"

"Short answer: we don't. The FA told us if we didn't lose Charlie from the squad, we'd be disqualified. She offered to leave, but we'd be crap without her. So, we were gonna quit, disband the senior team and just continue with the youth team—under-18s mixed-gender is allowed—but the rest of the league took our side against the FA."

"Including the Anchors." Aitch delivered Josh's and Rob's pints. Both mumbled less than heartfelt thanks.

"Blimey. Who'd've thunk it?" Rob said. The Blue Anchor was a notoriously rough pub that attracted all kinds of rogues, including those from the police station directly opposite—Aitch's station.

"Yeah, we're an independent league now." Dan nodded at Josh. "It's your shot, by the way."

Josh glanced around the pub, insinuating the question 'what's the rush?' and he had a point. It was dead for a Saturday evening, or maybe it wasn't. Pubs in London were always chock-a-block, and Rob was out of touch. Nonetheless, Josh got on with it and potted the first ball of the game. He didn't have the same luck with his second and extra shots.

"Still sober, then?" The question came from behind Rob and startled him.

"Alright, George?"

"Rob." They shared a very businesslike handshake. "Everyone OK for a drink?"

"My shout," Aitch said. "What're you having?"

"I'll get…" George started to protest, but Aitch stared at him until he backed down. "Lager, thanks."

Aitch clapped him on the shoulder on his way to the bar.

Rob bent over the table, lining up his next shot as George edged past to reach Josh. He could see them in his peripheral vision, and hear them talking—more interrogation than conversation.

"Did you get caught in traffic?" That was definitely an accusation on Josh's part. Rob gently tapped the cue ball, sending it on a slow roll across the table.

"Roadworks on Moss Lane."

One down. Rob changed position. *Far-left pocket.*

"Why didn't you go through town?"

"I thought the back roads would be quicker."

Two down. *Far-right.*

"OK. If you say so."

Three down...and snookered. Rob tried for a rebound, but hit nothing. "Josh, you're up, mate."

Josh nodded to show he'd heard. "You can tell me later," he said to George.

"Tell you what?" George had the puzzled frown to a tee, but he wasn't fooling Rob or Josh, and as soon as Josh's concentration shifted to the pool table, George made eye contact with Rob. It was either beseeching or threatening, the former, hopefully, although it was tricky to tell with George. Outside of Rob's field of vision, a ball dropped and rolled back to the reservoir.

"Damn it."

Josh's cuss gave Rob a welcome excuse to divert his attention back to their game and his opponent's predicament. "Trick shot?"

"If this were a magic wand." Josh waved his cue and then crouched, putting him eye level with the felt. "Impossible." The white teetered on the edge of the pocket, a hair's breadth from the black, with two stripes forming a curved wall.

"Forfeit?" Dan suggested.

Rob pressed his lips together, trying not to laugh at Josh, whose flared nostrils, just visible over the lip of the table, made him look like a basking hippo.

Josh straightened up again and held out his hand for his drink, which George duly delivered and Josh downed more or less in one go. He handed the empty glass back and moved in for the kill. He was right; it was an impossible shot. Still, Rob prepared for defeat. Josh and Dan's one-upmanship was a reassuring constant that had reared its head at every social event, every night out, since the start of high school. Losing a game of pool to their point-scoring was a small price to pay for the privilege of a night in the pub with his best buds.

The loud clack of balls signified, for all of his determination, Josh had failed to clear the wall. The white flew upwards, hit the table lip, bounced, and landed some six feet away, directly in Aitch's path. Pints in both hands, he drew to a sudden halt and peered down at the ball. Josh went to retrieve it, mumbling an apology.

"No worries." Aitch followed him back to the pool room.

Josh set the cue ball in the D and stepped away from the table. The remaining three striped balls—he must've potted one by accident—were well spaced, and within minutes, Rob had cleared the table under Josh's watchful scowl.

"Rematch when we've had a couple more pints?" Rob suggested. He heard Dan mutter 'hypocrites'. Josh glowered at him.

"You're on," he said. He handed his cue to George and set off for the Gents', while Rob gave his cue to Dan and went over to join Aitch on the barstools at the end of the room.

"Where's Tash tonight?" Rob asked.

"Working till ten. She's gonna join us after her shift. Overtime—honeymoon spends, she says."

"Good stuff. And are you all set for the wedding?"

"Yeah." Aitch picked up his pint and frowned into it. "I think so." His frown deepened. "I dunno, mate, to be honest."

Rob laughed. "Leaving it to the expert, are you?"

"Yep. We both are."

"Oh?"

"Adele's new company."

Both men looked over at Dan, as if he were accountable for his fiancée's business. He didn't even notice.

"She's a wedding planner?" Rob guessed.

"Weddings, bar mitzvahs, conferences, psychic nights—you name it, she'll event-plan it."

"Shall I break?" Dan suggested.

"Yeah, sure," George answered. He was on his way over and stopped next to Rob, leaning in to speak and keeping his voice low. "Can you do me a favour? Don't mention the party to Gray."

"Err...sure." It wouldn't have crossed Rob's mind to mention it, although it could've slipped out in conversation.

"Josh didn't invite him and Will," George explained. "It's a long story."

Rob nodded. "Fair enough."

"Thanks." George darted back to the table in the nick of time and quickly eyed up his shot. Josh returned from the Gents' and joined Rob and Aitch in watching the game. No shots wasted, it was a very efficient frame that lasted less than ten minutes. Dan won and for once kept his gloating to a minimum as he thrust the cue in Josh's direction.

"Someone else can play," Josh said.

"We've all had two games already," Dan argued. "Plus the pool Mafia's just arrived."

Rob glanced over at the bar, where a group of younger men were supping and keeping watch on the pool table.

"In that case, another game it is." Josh took the cue from Dan and strode over to the table, which George had already set up. Josh chalked his cue, his expression dead solemn, whilst George's morphed into a grin. He moved the triangle out of the way and, as Josh was about to break, said, "Go easy on me."

The balls scattered. "Go easy on you... Pfft! You always beat me at pool."

"Not true," George claimed and went on to pot four balls in a row. He missed the fifth and groaned in disappointment. Josh immediately swooped in and systematically potted one ball after another until only four solids and the eight-ball remained.

"Victory is mine!" The wide grin that accompanied Josh's pre-emptive gloat gave Rob a flashback—of the good kind—to nights at the snooker hall with Zoë, before they had Lucas. They were evenly matched, but it was never about winning; it was about doing stuff together. Somewhere down the line, they'd stopped or forgotten how, and they'd blamed each other, or Rob's job, or Zoë being stuck at home with a baby, when maybe it was because neither of them was prepared to put the effort into their relationship. Or maybe they just weren't compatible anymore.

When Josh and George's game was over—Josh scraped a win in the end—the five of them moved to a table in the main room. Dan bought the next round and came back with a box of dominoes.

"How old are you? Seventy?" Aitch ribbed him but still accepted his tiles. Three games later, he was so set on beating Dan he didn't notice Tash arrive—nor did anyone else, for that matter—until she pushed her way into the space between Aitch and Rob.

"Alright, mate?" Rob greeted her.

"I will be," she said and held her pint aloft. "Cheers." She took a good, long swig and sagged on her stool. "God, that was the shift from hell."

"Yeah?"

"Oh, nothing out of the ordinary," Tash dismissed. "How's your holiday going? Getting plenty of time to relax?"

"Ha, I wish!" Given he'd slept the first ten of the twenty or so hours since he'd arrived, Rob couldn't grumble. He'd spent time with Lois, and he was having a great evening, but it was all the messing around in between that had worn him down and rose to the forefront of his mind whenever his concentration drifted.

"What d'you reckon? Curry? Kebab?" Dan asked, stashing the dominoes away and ignoring Aitch's pleas for 'best of five'.

"We could go to the Turkish place on the high street," Tash suggested. "Aitch has been promising to take me there ever since it opened."

"It opened two years ago," Josh said.

"Yep."

"We're never off at the same time," Aitch justified.

"We are."

"All right. Never off at the same time *and* free of obligatory nights with the family."

"We're not *obliged*, Aitch."

"My vote's with Turkish." George neatly cut off Aitch's wade into hot water.

"Mine too," Josh said.

Dan nodded. "That's four votes. OK with you, Rob?"

"Absolutely." He wasn't going to let on he'd already eaten before he came out.

"Turkish it is. I'll—"

"Oy!" Aitch interrupted. "Don't I get a say?" He made a grab for the dominoes, but Dan whipped the box out of his way and got up to return it to the bar staff. Aitch stuck out his bottom lip. "I was gonna suggest we stay for another, give you a chance to catch up." He blinked, martyr-like, at Tash, who took it as a prompt to guzzle the rest of her beer. She set the empty glass down firmly.

"I'm done," she said and rose to her feet. The others followed suit.

"Fine. Whatever..." Aitch muttered, shuffling after them.

"Watch it or I'll bench you for unsportsmanlike behaviour," Dan warned. Aitch curled his lip, but there was no real hostility from either man, and as the six of them left the pub and walked into the town centre, Aitch and Tash put their arms around each other. Ahead of them, Josh and George walked hand in hand; Dan and Rob strolled a few yards behind the two couples.

They chatted casually about business and football; it was easy, comfortable, just as Rob had imagined. Selfishly, he was glad Adele didn't come on lads' nights out, and that Andy had cried off. If either had been with them, Rob would've been walking on his own and playing the sad, single mate when that wasn't how he felt. Seeing his friends' strong relationships right in front of him, on top of his earlier epiphany about where it had gone wrong with Zoë, he was confident he had a handle on getting it right the next time around. Now all he needed to do was put himself out there.

***

The restaurant was intimate yet buzzing at the same time. The minimal light from patterned lamps and candles was mostly absorbed by the dark walls. Up-tempo Turkish pop music competed with conversation, laughter and the sizzle of the open grill. Every table was taken, and they had to wait at the bar for one to become free, which happened as soon as they ordered drinks. They took them over, and once they were settled into their seats, the waiter gave them menus and recommended the shared-platter starter: calamari, grilled halloumi, wings of fire and garlic mushrooms.

"Something for everyone on there," Aitch asserted.

"Except Josh," Dan said loudly enough for him to hear.

Rob made a point of examining the lamps suspended from the ceiling. On this occasion, Josh didn't take the bait, claiming he liked all of the things on the platter—a statement that led to George snorting his drink out of his nose. His eyes were still watering when the waiter returned for their orders, and then again ten minutes later with an accomplice who assisted in filling every spare inch of the table with food.

It was, allegedly, a platter for six and could've fed twice that, but the beer and pool had given them an appetite, and they cleared the lot. Unfortunately, all that food on top of four pints of lager, on top of three servings of curry chicken plus lemon meringue pie, left Rob with zero space for his main course. He could hear his mum's voice in his head—*eyes bigger than your belly*—as he shoved the delicious-looking, mouth-wateringly aromatic chunks of chargrilled lamb around his plate.

"Are you OK, Rob?" Josh asked. He was watching him intently, and Rob suspected he'd been doing so for some time.

"Yeah, just stuffed. You?"

"Yes. It's delicious, but…" He put his fork down and picked up his napkin. "Too spicy for me." He wiped his hands and discarded the napkin, his attention back on Rob. "So…what's troubling you?"

The conversations with Jock and Zoë earlier were niggling, but Rob didn't feel overly troubled by them, or he hadn't until Josh mentioned it, and considered fobbing him off.

"Sorry." Josh grimaced. "You can't take me anywhere."

Rob laughed. "No worries. To be honest, I think I'm making something out of nothing. One of the blokes I was in the army with went to see Zoë earlier. He was looking for me, he said, but we spoke yesterday, so he knows Zo and I aren't together anymore. There's a situation involving our old CO—no idea why they've involved me in it—but that's why he was trying to get hold of me."

"Your detecting is obviously legendary."

"Ha, yeah. I did wonder if it was because I'm a copper—*was* a copper—and they thought I could pull some strings. What I can't figure is why he hassled Zoë, but I've spoken to him now, so hopefully, he'll leave well alone."

Josh's eyebrows rose, only for a fraction of a second—an unspoken invitation for Rob to elaborate.

"I dunno, Josh. There's something off, but I can't put my finger on what. Still…not much point worrying. I can't do anything from up here."

"Why don't you ask Gray to keep an eye on Zoë?" Josh suggested. "Treat it as a trial surveillance run for the new business."

Rob was doubtful. "He's not gonna agree to that."

"Oh, he will."

"For real?"

"It's like the sniff of the barmaid's apron to an alcoholic. He can't help himself. As soon as he gets a hint of a case…"

"I probably shouldn't feed his addiction."

"I'd say it's more a…passion." Josh grinned. "Joking aside, if he can't help, he'll tell you, but I think he'll be happy to, and it'd put your mind at rest, give you a chance to enjoy your holiday."

Rob considered his plans for the coming days—the morning's football match, sorting stuff with Amber, meeting his great-niece, dinner with Lois—and all the 'take it as it comes' down time he'd been looking forward to for months. He'd already had to cut it short—the last thing he needed was to be stressing over Jock and ruin what time he had.

"Yeah, all right," he said. "I'll ask him tomorrow."

12: Sunday Love

As Gray came to, he rolled and stretched his arm above his face, hitting something solid yet soft. At the grunt, he opened one eye and squinted up at Will, standing beside the bed. "What are you doing?"

"Taking the dogs out."

"You woke me up."

"Not on purpose. I was trying to figure out if you were already awake. Then you hit me."

"I didn't hit you. I stretched."

"The net result's the same." Will rubbed his chin and looked pained.

"And it wasn't that hard."

"Are you coming with us?"

Gray's eyes closed again. "Depends. Are you planning on getting back into bed afterwards?"

Will chuckled. "If you want me to."

"Mmm."

"OK. See you in a little while."

Gray rolled onto his other side, flipped the pillows and sank into them. A Sunday morning lie-in was *the* manifestation of heaven on earth—sleep-warmed bed, duvet-muted mumblings of activity familiar and comforting, and nothing Gray needed to worry about. The curtains wafted as the external door opened and closed behind Will and the dogs. An hour of glorious, peaceful sleep and then maybe some sex, cuddles, a bit of breakfast—any or all of the above. Gray wasn't fussy. With the bed all to himself, he scissored his legs, breathed deeply, let go…

"Huh?" He jolted awake again. "Tie?"

"Sorry, mate. I'm just checking to see if Benjy's in here." Tie's dreadlocked head bobbed out of sight. "I think he might've followed the dogs out." His voice resonated against the side of the bed. "Nope, not under here."

Gray skimmed his hand across the mattress, up to the pillows and back down again, in search of furry obstacles. "Yeah, he's here." The cunning little chap had burrowed under the duvet and snuggled up against Gray's thigh, and he hadn't felt a thing.

"Thank fuck for that." Tie popped back into view. "Last time he escaped, he was gone overnight. I didn't think we'd see him again. Here, I'll get him out of your way."

Gray pulled back the duvet, bracing against the cool draught. One-handed, Tie scooped up his bunny, said, "Cheers," and stalked out of the room. Gray released the duvet and rolled onto his front, hiding his sudden blush in the pillows, not that anyone was there to see it. Will was right; Tie didn't actually care if they were naked.

***

"Alright, Rob? We're in here." Dan's head poked out of a double doorway in the middle of the vast red and grey back wall of the stadium's stand.

Rob slung his bag on his shoulder and walked over. "I was expecting a kick-about in a muddy park."

"We've gone up in the world, though for the time being, we've only got access to the bar, one shower room and the pitch. The rest of the building's being renovated."

Rob followed Dan into a dark, windy passage with the football pitch ahead of them, to the left and right the closed doors of the changing rooms. The smell of sand and salt gave away the building work taking place.

"Didn't this belong to Comco Glass?" Rob asked.

"Yep. Till last year. It's part of Campion Community Trust now."

"And the Lions' home ground?"

"Got it in one. I'll give you a quick tour if you like."

"Great."

At the end of the passage, Dan veered to the left and took Rob clockwise around the perimeter of the lush green pitch.

"Astroturf?"

"Nope. The groundsman's worked here for years and he's top notch."

"No kidding. You could play cricket on that."

"You don't play cricket, do you?"

"Now and again."

"Well, you might get a match here at some point. Once the work's done, it'll be a multi-purpose stadium."

They reached the end of the pitch, and Rob stopped to take in the view through the net. "It's bigger than I thought."

"Yeah. It's got a 6,000 capacity, which is madness, or it was when Comco owned it, but the trust's got ambitious plans. Concerts, farmers' markets, car auctions…it'll have a retractable roof by this time next year. And there's a conference suite, too, or there will be."

"Nice." They continued on their circuit. "So Campion's son's doing all right?"

"Very well," Dan said. "He's a funny kid, doesn't say much outside of discussing Trust business. I must admit, after what happened at Black Hole, I expected him to throw in the towel, but it had the opposite effect."

"That's good to hear." In a way, Rob wasn't surprised. The SIU had kept tabs on Jason—Campion's estranged son—as soon as it was known he'd inherited his father's millions, because he shouldn't have, and the fraudsters had been livid. It would have pissed them off less if Jason had blown the lot on sex, drugs and rock 'n' roll because in the end, it wasn't Rob's closeness to Jess that had got the SIU their win. It was that Anders Folden—Campion's murderer—couldn't stand to see all of *his* money wasted on 'childish pet projects', and he would've killed Jason, too, to get his hands on it.

They had arrived back at the tunnel, and Dan turned to face Rob, stepping closer so he could keep his voice low. "Are you still involved in the investigation?"

Rob frowned, caught short by Dan's apparent insightfulness. "The fraud ring? No. Why d'you ask?"

Dan tugged at his chin as he scrutinised Rob. "Daft question, really. You wouldn't tell me if you were. Why I asked… Comco originally put the stadium up for auction, and an undercover officer approached me and Andy about making a joint bid. We didn't know who or what he was at the time, of course. The auctioneers were bent—did a lot of business with Jess's cronies—and your lot shut them down."

"Who told you they were connected to Jess?"

"Not to Jess, her mate Angie Sharston and a few other crooks in high places. Andy reckons they're all still out there."

"Well, I can tell you the ones we caught are locked up," Rob said evasively.

"And the rest of them?" Dan pushed.

Rob shrugged. "You know more than I do, by the sounds of it." Dan gave him a smug grin. Rob laughed. "No, I'm not involved in the investigation. I bowed out after Black Hole. A year playing best mates with a psychopath…" He still had nightmares where he was trapped in a doorless room like a giant lead box with Folden. He couldn't escape and no-one could hear him banging on the walls, and all the while Folden was laughing like the lunatic he was. "I was ready to quit the police then."

"Fair enough," Dan said. "Right, we're in here." He pulled a door open, and warm, beery air spilled out, the voices and laughter carrying with it.

Rob peered in at the players from both teams, all getting changed together in the fully kitted and stocked bar. "That's got to have helped win over the rest of the league, eh?"

"Put it this way, it didn't hurt."

***

"I bet you didn't even miss the bacon," Tie said as he picked up the empty plates and took them to the sink.

Full English breakfast, veggie style. It wasn't too shabby, and no, Gray hadn't missed the bacon. He didn't really like it. Black pudding, however... "You're right, Tie, I didn't. Hey, I'll do the washing up." He took over at the sink.

"OK. Thanks. I'll be off, then. Only another forty-four hours to go..."

"Have fun," Gray said.

Tie offered a grim smile and left by the back door.

"That's gone quick, hasn't it?"

"Which?" Will asked.

"Tie's community service."

"Not for him." Will came over and picked up a tea towel. He stood by, waiting for something to dry, and fidgeting. "Can I ask you something?"

"What?"

"Have you actually gone veggie?"

"More or less." Gray tried to think when he'd last eaten meat; he couldn't remember.

"Is that *for* me, or *because of* me?"

"Both, I suppose." Gray glanced sideways at him. "I'd hate to contaminate you."

"I can see where you're coming from," Will leaned close. "You get it stuck in your teeth..." Closer still. "And then we kiss..."

Gray nodded seriously, going cross-eyed in his attempt to stay focused on Will's face, then grimaced. "That's disgusting."

Will left a slow kiss on Gray's lips. "We don't need to worry about it…now you're veggie."

Gray smiled. "Very true." The decision was easy yet as momentous as his admission the previous night—a long-term commitment to change his lifestyle for Will. It was unconditional, but at the same time, he couldn't help but wonder what Will would do for him in return.

***

"Not a bad result, that," Dan congratulated the men on his team—Charlie had gone for a shower with the other women players. They'd drawn 2:2 against The Vets, who'd played a lot dirtier than Rob expected of those involved in the care of sick animals. He'd been fouled several times, and George got a boot in the shin from his own vet—the opposition's goalkeeper. For all of that, there were no sour grapes as the men from both teams bundled into the showers once the women were done.

"You're coming to The Red Lion, Rob, aren't you?" Josh asked when they all made it out to the car park a little after one p.m.

"Yeah, I'll come and have a quick pint."

"A quick pint?" Aitch repeated as if Rob were suggesting the impossible.

"My mum's making roast beef and Yorkshire pudding."

"I think I'll come round to yours," George said.

His teammates stared at him in horror.

"They put on an excellent roast dinner at The Lion," Josh contended. The lads all nodded and murmured their agreement.

"All right, I'll come," Rob said. "I'll drop the bike home and let her know." Somebody made the sound of a whip being flicked; Rob didn't catch who.

"D'you want a lift back?" Dan and Andy asked at the same time.

"Yeah, cheers," Rob accepted and left them to figure out which was giving it while he put on his helmet. A flip of a coin selected

Andy, who followed Rob to his mum's. As if the neighbours didn't stare enough at the bike already, now they had a 1960s red Mustang to ogle. Rob popped inside, dumped his bag in his room and told his mum he wouldn't be there for dinner on the way back out. Yes, it was cowardly, and he hoped she'd save him some for teatime, but he didn't dare ask.

"Top motor," he said as he climbed in beside Andy.

"It's not bad, is it?" Andy checked his mirror and pulled out. "But look at this." As they stopped at the end of the road, Andy rocked the steering wheel from side to side.

"There's quite a bit of play on that."

"Yep. I've checked everything and adjusted the gear box. I'm at a loss what else to try. Any ideas?"

This was good—quite possibly the longest conversation they'd ever had and a decent neutral subject for breaking the thirty-five years of ice between them. "It could be the ball joint on the control valve," Rob suggested.

"Where would I find that?"

"You have to get underneath the car. I can have a look when we stop."

"Nah, you can't be lying on the floor in a pub car park."

Rob laughed. "I've done worse."

When they reached the pub, Rob made his offer again, and Andy rejected it again.

"I'll take it in to Len's mechanic."

"Len's your mum's husband, isn't he?" Rob said without thinking.

"Yep. He imports classic American cars. But you probably know that."

"I think Dan told me." It was better Andy didn't know how much his privacy had been compromised during the Strang case. Rob held the pub door open for him and then for another guy who'd followed them into the car park. The guy nodded in thanks and edged past the other players all standing around the bar.

"Not a supporter, then," Rob muttered under his breath.

"Rob!" Dan shouted. "What're you drinking?"

"Just a lager, cheers." He watched the guy dodge into the Gents' and glanced back out of the doors to the car park.

"Did you leave something in the car?" Andy asked.

"Hmm?" Rob zoned back in. "No, sorry. Old habits…" He hoped.

13: Spyware

"Well, well, I didn't think I'd be seeing you again, especially not this bright and breezy of a Monday morning."

Gray scanned the building's outer wall and around the aluminium roller door, searching for a means by which he'd been 'seen'. The last time he'd come here, over two years ago, the camera had been disguised as a power box under the alarm, but neither of those items were present this time around.

The raucous chuckle coming through the intercom cut off suddenly, and the door began to rise. Gray stared dead ahead into the gloom gradually revealed by the shutter, along with a waft of stale cigarette smoke and warm electronic components. The shutter clanged home, and Gray stepped inside.

"Morning, Paddy."

"Good morning, yourself, Mr. Fisher. Come on through. Cup of tea?"

"I'd love one, thanks." Guided only by the dark silhouette against the square of yellow light twenty feet ahead of him, Gray walked blindly along the windowless corridor, his breaths shortened by the sense of history that struck him every time he visited Paddy's store. The building was a WWII gunnery partly repurposed into warehouses in the 1950s with many of the structural relics—long wooden workbenches and tables scarred by the heavy metal-cutting machinery they once bore—left in place.

"Milk no sugar?" Paddy asked as soon as Gray set foot in the tiny room that doubled as an office and, by the looks of it, these days, a bedsit.

"Yes, thanks." *Tobacco and feet.* He resorted to breathing through his mouth and focused on the custard-colour paint flaking off the brick wall beyond where Paddy toiled with skeletal back turned. When Gray had taken up position as leader of the Special Investigations Unit, DI Paddy Stewart was his antagonistic second-in-command—a pallid-skinned, chain-smoking stick of a man who'd worked undercover in Northern Ireland during the late 1980s and had been on a final written warning for the majority of his long career. He'd done plenty to get him summarily dismissed, had anyone been fool enough to follow through with further disciplinary action. What Paddy didn't know about surveillance wasn't worth knowing.

In the end, it was poor health that had got the better of him, and he'd finally retired to concentrate full-time on the 'hobby' that had subsidised his smoking and gambling—and at least three ex-wives plus assorted children—leaving the way clear for Gray to bring in Dom Hooper as his 2-IC. It had also subsidised the SIU's overstretched budget on a regular basis. Paddy's wares were cheaper than the official suppliers and probably knock-offs, but Gray didn't ask questions, then or now.

Given the overall grubbiness of Paddy's cell, Gray was pleasantly surprised by the clean, chip-free mug he was handed, three-quarters full with muscular-looking tea.

"Sit down, sit down." Paddy led the way over to a pair of threadbare office chairs, pale blue with rusted tubular chrome legs. Gray wasn't heavy, but perched carefully just the same. Paddy retrieved a tobacco tin from his breast pocket. He flipped the lid open and liberally sprinkled leaf onto a crumpled cigarette paper. "How's life treating you, Mr. Fisher?"

"Better." A smile slipped out with the word.

Paddy glanced up from his rolling and nodded his understanding. They'd never had a conversation about Paddy's fiancée who was killed in The Troubles, nor about Jean's death, yet each was aware of what the other had lost—the uncommon bonded by the common.

"And you, Paddy?"

"Fair to middling. You know how it is." He held the rolled cigarette lengthways to his mouth and licked as he looked up and around him. "Third wife got the house, so this is me." He picked up his lighter and flicked it open, paused as if to consider asking Gray if he minded the smoking, then lit up anyway and disappeared, like CancerMan the Magnifico, in a cloud of dirty-blue smoke.

The cloud drifted towards Gray, and he held his breath until it had dissipated to a slightly less noxious density. He exhaled into his mug and then inhaled the steam under some half-conceived notion that it might be safer than the cooler yet equally damp air in the room. All it did was make his eyes water.

"Down to business, then." Paddy propped the cigarette in the corner of his mouth and stretched sideways, snagging a notebook from his desk. "Unless I'm mistaken and this is a social visit?"

The words resurrected the pang of guilt. After speaking to Rob yesterday—a call which had stopped Gray languishing on Will's sofa for the entire day—it looked increasingly likely that Gray's next call to Dom would not be social after all. "No, it's not," he said. "I'm going into the PI business."

"Aye. You can leave the job, but it never leaves you."

Gray covered a sigh with a slurp of the tea and almost coughed it back out. It was even stronger than he'd anticipated.

Paddy hacked out a laugh. "Put hairs on your chest, so it will."

How that could possibly be construed as a good thing, Gray didn't know. Since he'd turned thirty, he'd had no problem in that regard. Keeping the hair on his head? Now that would be a boon. In every photo he'd seen of his dad, his shaved scalp showed male-pattern baldness, likewise for George. It didn't bode well. His eyes strayed to Paddy's full head of fuzz like nicotine-stained grey candy floss. Perhaps going bald wouldn't be so bad.

Paddy frowned and ran his hand over his hair, flattening it in places. "Right, so, what d'you need?"

"For now, enough kit for twenty-four-hour street surveillance—a couple of static cameras, sound-activated recorder that can be left in situ—I'll be back when I've finalised the rest with my business partner."

Paddy nodded as he scribbled, brushing aside the ash that dropped onto the page. "That's easy enough." Leaving his cigarette balanced on the edge of the desk, lit end outwards, he groaned his way to his feet. "You might as well have a peruse while you're here, see what else takes your fancy. Bring your tea with you, why don't you?"

Gray left the tea and followed Paddy from the room, halfway back along the dark corridor, where Paddy expertly unlocked by touch a reinforced steel door. With a creak worthy of a 1950s submarine movie sound effect, the door opened, white fluorescent light flooding the corridor. Gray squinted on instinct—he'd thought ahead and put in his lenses—and stepped into the treasure trove.

To a surveillance geek like him, Paddy's storeroom was more enticing than a bank vault full of gold bullion. The room was stacked, floor to ceiling, with boxes and plastic crates overflowing with equipment, some of which he recognised as ex-SIU. Cables dangled from shelves; aerials poked out of the edges of split boxes; small black boxes were positioned at intervals around the perimeter of the room. Not surveillance equipment—rat poison. Gray shuddered, recalling a morning he'd arrived at Will's and bumped into Tie on his way out to release a rat from the humane trap they kept in the chicken coop. Gray couldn't imagine his newfound respect for animalkind would ever extend to rats. He shook off the shivers and returned to the task at hand.

Contrary to how it seemed, there was order to the chaos, and Paddy had already located the items Gray had requested.

"A couple of options for you, Mr. Fisher." He handed over a junction box similar to the one that had been on the front of the building on Gray's previous visit. "That's your best bet if you need to cover just the one property. Ninety-degree view angle, motion detection, about forty-eight hours' battery life—I've got others with higher spec if you can get them up on the streetlights."

"Best I don't upset the local council on our first job. Can I view remotely?"

"Via wi-fi only, but there's a memory card on-board."

Understandably, Rob didn't want to worry Zoë, so connecting it to their wi-fi was out of the question. Fitting it was the other challenge: the only time there was definitely nobody home was when Travis went to meet Lucas from school. It gave Gray about half an hour—hopefully long enough to screw a junction box to the front of the house.

"OK. I'll take one of those. What else?"

Paddy opened his hand, revealing a tiny black camera, less than two inches in diameter. "Line-of-sight transmission."

"No good," Gray said. He'd have to be sitting in a car outside Zoë's house—which he was going to do this evening—but he already had a camera for that, and with a more than decent zoom range. "I think one will be enough. What about the audio recorder?"

Paddy waved a brown-tipped finger in the air and held it there while he fished in his trouser pocket and extracted what looked like a pen drive. "Something like this? It's waterproof, so you can hide it in a plant pot or stick it under a windowsill."

"Perfect. How much?"

"Will you be needing a receipt?"

"No, I wouldn't think so."

"In that case, a hundred quid to you, Mr. Fisher."

Gray took out his wallet, thumbed the appropriate number of notes away from the rest, and the two men exchanged cash and goods. "Thanks, Paddy. Much appreciated."

"Always a pleasure, sir." He was already manoeuvring Gray towards the exit. The slam of the store's metal door and rattle of keys accompanied Gray along the dark corridor. He reached the end and peered back through the gloom while he waited for the aluminium roller to rise.

"See you, Paddy. Take care." Gray received no response as he stepped out into the blinding daylight and filled his lungs with the fresh March air, pollution and all.

***

As Rob had predicted, Travis—Gray assumed from the description 'a stocky Rio Ferdinand', although he'd had to look up who that was online first—left the house a few minutes after three. He was in running gear, which may or may not have been unusual, but Gray was taking no chances. As soon as Travis cleared the corner, Gray was out of his unremarkable hired hatchback—not his kind of car, but he was aiming for inconspicuous. The cordless drill dug into his chest as he strolled across the street, hi-viz vest over his jacket, defunct seven-inch touchscreen tablet in his hand. A man in a hi-viz jacket and carrying a tablet rarely roused neighbours' suspicions, and it gave Gray a buzz to find he still had the knack.

The house next door had a real junction box to the left of the window, with cables running up to the first floor. Next to it would have been perfect, rendered invisible by its symmetry, except the angle wasn't wide enough to take in the front door. Gray weighed up the space next to the gas meter under the bay window; it would be too low down to capture the face of anyone taller than about five and a half feet, but the rest of the front wall was a clear expanse of well-pointed brickwork. If the motion detection was sensitive, it might pick up visitors before they reached the house. That was the best Gray could do, because there was nowhere else for it to go. Checking he was still clear, he opened the gate and walked up to the house.

DIY had never been his forte, but he knew his way around a drill and it was only one hole. He positioned the end of the bit against a horizontal line of mortar, gave the trigger a gentle press to get a key, and then went full throttle. The bit cut straight into the mortar with virtually no resistance. Gray eased it out and affixed the back box, giving it a gentle tug to make sure it was secure before he attached the battery, switched on the camera and situated the front cover.

A quick check of the monitor app on his phone showed all was as well as he'd expected; he was five foot ten and appeared headless if he stood at the front door while all of him was visible at the gate but not clear enough for accurate identification of an unknown visitor. However, Rob had sent Gray photos of their targets, both of whom had obvious distinguishing features, and for one of them—the guy missing half an arm—didn't rely on a clear shot of his face.

Next, the sound recorder: there was a small gap between the top of the junction box and the bottom of the bay window casing, but as he took the recorder from his pocket, he caught movement in his peripheral vision. Travis was back, and alone. Gray stuffed the recorder and drill inside his jacket and blew the mortar dust on the ground to disperse it. He pushed against the front of the gas meter and turned towards the street.

"Afternoon, sir," he said with a nod, stepping past Travis. "Just taking a reading. All done."

"Again? It was only read a couple of weeks back."

Gray stopped at the gate. "Was it? I bet I've misread my jobs sheet again." He pressed the power button on his tablet and frowned. "Damn. Battery's dead. I'll check when I get back to the office. Sorry to bother you, sir."

"No problem." Travis jogged the rest of the way up the path and unlocked the front door without a second glance.

Given he'd returned without Lucas and he seemed to be in a rush, Gray predicted he'd be back out again in a couple of minutes, so he continued his meter-reader performance—checking house numbers, stopping at any with no cars outside and no visible signs of activity within. He was peeved he'd partly blown his cover, if not a little exhilarated by the near miss, but Travis didn't strike him as the suspicious sort. If it had been Rob, he'd have been demanding ID and making phone calls. Even so, Gray thought it best to steer clear of the car until he was confident Travis wouldn't see him getting into it.

Sure enough, Travis came out again a few minutes later, still in running gear, but this time with a gym bag over his shoulder. He set off in the same direction as last time and didn't even look Gray's way. Travis cleared the corner a second time, and Gray went back to the house. He pushed the voice recorder into the space above the junction box and checked it was out of sight but didn't hang around to test it; he'd used the same brand many times before, and it was highly reliable.

Back in the car, he stowed the drill and his hi-viz vest in the passenger foot well, sent Rob a text to confirm surveillance was in place, and started the engine.

He got the seat belt halfway across his chest before the realisation hit him of what he'd done. He'd been out of the police for almost a year, yet it had come so naturally to him, as if he'd never been away, and it was more than his actions. It was the mindset—the easy lies, the thrill of hiding in plain sight, and the mix of fear and excitement at being discovered. In less than fifteen minutes, he'd scrubbed out everything he'd achieved since leaving the SIU.

He stared across the street at the house he'd rigged. Zoë and Travis's house. He was spying on Rob's ex-wife with only Rob's say-so it was for Lucas's and her safety. No warrant, no consent. As for the information he'd planned to tap Dom for: once again, he was abusing his former position as Dom's superior, and worse, abusing their friendship.

He should've said no when Rob asked, and not only to spying on Zoë. No to the partnership. No to undercover work. He wasn't a detective anymore; he was a postgraduate student and an actor—precisely because living in the shadows had almost destroyed him once. He was a fool to have ever believed he could do it all over again with no fallout.

***

"Hey."

"Gray? Everything OK?"

"Yeah." He picked up a green bean from his discarded dinner and wrote his signature in the roux sauce. The skin wrapped around his bean pen and smeared everything. "Still at work?"

"Still at the office," Dom confirmed. "I'm not sure this constitutes work. We're investigating an online casino. They fix bets so new members have a sixty-percent win rate in the first twenty-four hours then refuse to pay out on a bonus play-through rule. I signed up last night—trying to spend two grand at five quid a pop is harder than you'd think."

"I can quite believe it." Harder still, Gray imagined, given Dom's recreation of choice was a night at the casino. "Are you having fun, though?"

"Oh, yeah," Dom said drolly. "It beats trawling double-entry books."

"Handwritten?"

"Yep. Thirty-seven years' worth."

Gray sighed. "If only I'd stayed a year longer." He was half serious about that; some of the accounts ledgers he'd analysed over the years were so rich he could've written a company profile based on that information alone.

"Do I sense regret?" Dom asked.

"A little," Gray answered honestly.

"Well, any time you're up for a consultancy..."

"Yeah, I'll keep it in mind." In the absence of something to say, Gray listened to the rapid click of Dom's mouse and tried to discern what he was playing. "Slots?" he guessed.

"Roulette."

"Ah, of course."

"Yeah. Time for a break." The clicking stopped, replaced by footsteps across carpet, a door opening, passing traffic... He was out on the fire escape. "So," Dom lit his cigarette, "what can I do for you?"

"Nothing."

"Nothing?"

"Social call."

Dom drew in deeply and talked through the exhale. "Bloody hell. I am honoured. Mind, I'd rather meet up for a pint. I should be out of here in the next hour."

"I'm tied up this evening..." Gray hesitated over saying more, but this was Dom, the closest thing he had to a best friend. "Rob asked me to keep an eye on his ex's place. A couple of old army buddies are giving them grief."

"What kind of grief?"

"I'm not sure. From what Rob said, it sounded fairly benign..."

"You think he's spying on her?"

"It crossed my mind, but for what reason? They're already divorced."

"Custody of Lucas?"

"I don't think so. Rob seems quite happy with the arrangement. Well, not happy, but you know what I mean."

"Yeah, I do. That's why you agreed, isn't it?"

"Agreed to what? The surveillance?"

"The surveillance, the PI agency..."

"What are you talking about?" Gray's arms erupted in goosebumps.

"You still feel responsible for Rob's marriage ending."

"I *was* responsible, Dom."

"No, you weren't. Even Rob said—"

"Rob let it go for his own peace of mind, but we both know the truth."

"Then you need to do the right thing."

"Which is?"

"Back out."

"I can't."

"Why? Because he'd never forgive you? It's the wrong reason, Gray."

"Story of my life." He laughed bitterly, too angry to defend his actions without resorting to snipes. He squashed the bean flat with his thumb and listened to Dom slowly killing himself. That was his fault too.

Eventually, Dom said, "Look, mate, you've got to do what feels right for you."

"I am—"

"*Whatever...*" Dom interrupted forcefully, "I'm here for you."

Gray released the rest of his protest as a breath. They were agreeing to disagree. "Thanks, I appreciate it." He meant every word. "And the same goes here. I'll leave you to get back to spinning the wheel."

"All right. Behave yourself, Gray."

"I'll try."

After he hung up, Gray cleared the table, symbolically clearing his mind. He and Dom had argued plenty of times before—about the job. It had never been personal, and it would be easy to blame it on the 'social call' when the truth was Dom had hit the nail on the head. Gray was trying to make amends, still trying to fix what he'd broken. And maybe it was the wrong reason—did that make it a bad one? He didn't think so.

In light of what was going on, Rob was curtailing his holiday. Once he was back, they could meet, thrash out a code of conduct, clarify data collection methods, learn some new techniques so they could stay above the law. Of course, all of that rested on Gray following through, and he needed to seriously consider, in the meantime, whether he had enough right reasons to do so.

At the very least, he'd see through the surveillance on Zoë's place. It wasn't illegal if they were preventing a crime from being committed, and he had reason to believe that was the case. Whatever doubts he had over his own motivations, the one thing Gray knew for sure was that he trusted Rob without reservation.

14: Baby

"Did you want a beer, Un…Rob? Is there beer in the fridge, Kyle? Excuse me, please, I need to get the lamb out of the oven."

Rob stepped aside, and Amber bustled past, pulling oven gloves onto her hands. She dropped the oven door and wafted the hot air away from her face. "*Kyle*?"

"What?" He appeared in the doorway, wailing baby in his arms. He shushed her, rocking from side to side; it was difficult to know whether it was to comfort the baby or himself. Rob's heart went out to him, and to Amber. Both parents had dark circles around their eyes and looked ready to flake at a moment's notice.

"Is there beer in the fridge?" Amber repeated. She poked the lamb joint with a fork. It spat at her.

"Well, I haven't drunk any in…let's see—" Kyle studied his daughter "—how old are you now? Eight weeks?"

"Oh my god." Amber threw a glance Rob's way. "There's beer if you want it."

"Err…thanks." He went over to the fridge. He didn't care one way or the other about beer, or roast lamb. "Anyone else want one while I'm here?"

"Breastfeeding," Amber muttered.

"Night duty," sighed Kyle.

Rob extracted a bottle from the four-pack, glad for the twist-off lid. He'd rather have been handed an armed grenade than ask for a bottle opener. "Can I get you anything while I'm here?"

"Please," Amber said. "Orange juice. In the door."

Kyle didn't answer—probably didn't hear the question.

"She's got a hell of a pair of lungs, eh?" Rob had to raise his voice.

"She never stops," Amber complained desperately. She tugged off the gloves and slapped them down on the counter on her way over to Kyle. "I'll take her to the bedroom." In one fluid movement, she extracted the baby from Kyle's arms and trudged out of the kitchen, disappearing through a doorway on the right.

Kyle shoved his hands in his pockets and gave Rob a watery smile. "Think I might have that beer after all." He collapsed onto a dining chair.

Rob collected a second bottle from the fridge and joined Kyle at the table. "There you go, mate."

"Thanks." He opened the bottle and tipped it to his mouth, holding it horizontal, his eyelids drooping further with each gulp. Finally, he put the bottle down and gave several exaggerated blinks. "She misses you."

Rob glanced towards the open door. "I miss her too." He could hear the baby's intermittent crying, so Amber would also be able to hear their conversation, but it was the truth. He'd seen more of her this evening than in the past three years, and he and Kyle—whom Amber had married the previous summer—were essentially strangers.

"Thanks for coming tonight. When Lois suggested I invite you, she said you might refuse."

"To be honest, I thought about it. I don't want to force her into seeing me if she doesn't want to."

"If she didn't want you here, you wouldn't have got through the door."

Rob smiled. "That's my girl." He could see her in his head, in her Spiderman outfit, leaning her full weight against her bedroom door to stop him going in because he didn't know the password. She'd have been about six years old at the time, and he'd had no idea what he'd done to upset her. He knew now, though.

The two men drank their beer companionably while Rob tried to figure out his best approach. He didn't want things to get heavy tonight. Amber was too tired to fight him; he was fairly certain he was in for an earful when she finally broke her silence. He'd take the blows, say sorry again for the pain he'd caused, but for tonight, all he wanted was a chance to get to know her again, and to meet Leila. If she was prepared to stretch to that, it would be more than enough.

A pan lid rattled on the stove, and Rob drew breath to ask if it needed turning down, but Kyle had nodded off, still upright with the bottle in his hand. Knowing there was a strong likelihood whatever he did would be wrong, Rob left the guy to doze and dealt with the pan. The potatoes inside were turning to mush, leaving him with no option but to drain off the water. He put the pan to one side and watched Kyle for a moment. The baby had stopped and all was quiet, but the dinner wouldn't survive without intervention.

As Rob was gearing up to giving Kyle a gentle prod, Amber slipped out of the bedroom and tiptoed back into the kitchen, closing the door behind her. When she saw Kyle, she gave a long sigh that seemed to drain her remaining energy.

"I can finish making the dinner if you like," Rob offered quietly.

"You're a guest." She plodded to the stove and lifted the pan lid. "Thanks."

"No worries. And I don't mind. Have a sit-down."

She swayed, and for a second or two, he thought she was going to take him up on it, but then she shook her head and pulled a drawer open. "I can't."

It was like an invisible force was moving her around, a puppet that would collapse in a heap on the floor if someone cut her strings. Stubborn, always so stubborn. Rob took some relief from recognising the family trait. They weren't so different, the two of them.

"Come on, turtle. Let me help." He edged closer to where she stood in front of the stove, staring in despair at the potatoes.

"But we invited you round for dinner."

"Yeah, and I really appreciate it, but I'm not royalty…or your nan."

She almost laughed at that. "Get the masher?" She thumbed at the rack of utensils behind Rob. He unhooked the potato masher and awaited further instruction. "If you can sort the spuds…"

"I can do that." He went over to the fridge for the milk and butter.

"I'll just do some peas and carrots from the freezer. I was going to do fresh veg, but…screamy baby." She shrugged.

Rob closed the fridge and smiled in sympathy. Lucas had been a little tyke, too, but he wouldn't share unless she asked. His sister had driven him mad with her knowledgeable parent quips—listening to her extol the benefits of demand feeding was at least as exhausting as putting it into operation—and she'd no doubt been handing out more of the same to Amber and Kyle. "Peas and carrots in here?" he asked, nodding at the freezer door.

"Yeah. Bottom shelf."

He dug out the two bags and took them over.

"Sorry. It's a bit crap." She tipped both bags into the same glass bowl and stuck it in the microwave on full power.

"Nah, it's great. You can't beat home-cooked food."

"Microwaved peas and instant gravy?"

"Beats chippy teas seven days a week," Rob said and then wished he hadn't, but apparently, his cholesterol levels were not a cause for concern. Arms folded, Amber leaned against the counter, chewing her lip. He kept mashing, adding more milk and butter, smoothing out the bumps and trying to ignore the eyes-burning-holes sensation.

"This PI thingy, what'll you be doing?"

"Investigating white-collar crime."

"Same as you did in the police?"

"Along the same lines, yeah."

"So it's still dangerous?"

"If we discover a crime's taken place, we'd have to advise the client to report it to the police—"

"That doesn't answer my question."

The mash was as smooth as it was going to get. Rob used a knife to scrape the masher clean; Amber took it from him and rinsed it under the tap, then she was back to watching him.

He exhaled through his nose and gave a reluctant nod of confirmation. "It won't be as dangerous as what I used to do for the police, but yeah, it might get dodgy sometimes. People don't like being caught out, and there's no telling how they'll react. But I can promise you, I won't intentionally put myself in harm's way. Well, unless it's to save Lu, or you or your sister...or Leila..."

She laughed, but there were tears too. "At least this time you didn't tell me you just fix bikes."

"It wasn't a lie."

"In a warzone," she pointed out. Her gaze drifted towards the bedroom. "I want you to meet her, for her to grow up with you in her life, like I did."

"Fun times," Rob said.

"Yeah, the best. But I can't cope with her asking all the time when Uncle Rob's coming to visit again, which she will. And I don't want to have to tell her one day that you're not..." There was no laughter now.

"Hey, come on." Rob took her in his arms, and she clung to him, sobbing—from exhaustion as much as anything. The microwave pinged to indicate it was done, and again a minute later. It woke Kyle, who squinted at them, trying to get his bearings. On the third ping, he got up and squeezed past to rescue the veg.

Still sniffling, Amber withdrew and muttered something about tissues as she left the kitchen.

Kyle watched her go and raised an eyebrow at Rob. "Is everything OK?"

"I hope so." Now he understood the cost of getting to know his great-niece.

By the time Amber returned, Kyle had made instant gravy and Rob had carved the lamb. Amber served up to save carrying everything to the table, and over dinner, they kept up neutral chatter about Kyle's nursing and Amber's plans to complete her dentist foundation training after her maternity leave. They were also hoping to sell the flat and buy a house, a point of conversation on which Rob could swap like for like and which inevitably veered into comparing house prices in the North and London.

"You must be a calming influence, Rob," Kyle said as they cleared the table afterwards. "This is the longest Leila's slept since she was born."

"Blimey. No wonder you're both shattered."

"Shattered doesn't come close."

"Night off tomorrow, hun," Amber said and explained for Rob's benefit, "Lois babysits for us on a Tuesday so I can go to salsa and Kyle can play squash with his dad. She's usually tearing her hair out when we get home."

"Yeah, she mentioned she looked after the baby for you." He still couldn't quite believe it, and it must've shown, because Amber grinned for the first time all evening—the first time in his presence for years. It sent warm tingly waves over him. He wanted to hold on to that feeling. "Listen, I'm gonna get going, let you two enjoy the peace while it lasts." He was already up and moving towards the hallway. Amber followed him out.

"OK. See you at Nan's on Wednesday?"

"Unfortunately not. Something's come up—I'm heading back first thing."

"Oh, that's a shame." She looked genuinely disappointed. She frowned; familiar thinking crinkles formed on the bridge of her nose. "Do you want to say good night to Leila?"

"And get blamed for disturbing her? Not likely."

Amber laughed. "If you're sure…"

"I'm sure. And anyway, I'm up again in a couple of weeks. I can meet her then. She might even be awake." He winked to emphasise he was kidding.

"Ha. She might," Amber said. She hugged him. "It's lovely to see you, Uncle Rob."

"For me too." He kissed her head and released her to put his helmet on even though he wouldn't usually do so until he reached the bike. He wasn't sure how much longer he could keep up the cheery façade. "You both take it easy, yeah?"

Kyle had joined them in the hall and stepped forward to shake Rob's hand. "Thanks for coming," he said. He held the door open for him. "See you soon."

"Count on it." Rob gave them a final nod and walked away. The quiet click of the door shutting behind him was like the inaugural tick of a stopwatch, a countdown until it would be too late to give Amber the assurances she needed and he missed the chance of ever knowing Leila.

***

"Rob, it's gone nine o'clock." His mum deposited a cup of coffee on the bedside table and left again.

"Ah, crap." Swinging his legs off the bed, he sat up and grabbed his phone. "I swear I set the alarm." If he'd been at home, his body clock would've beaten the alarm by a long shot. At his mum's, he slept like the dead. Too much stress or not enough? Either way, his plan to be on the road before seven had gone out the window.

"D'you want some breakfast before I go to work?"

"It's all right, Mum, cheers. I can make it myself or get something on the way."

"I'm leaving in ten minutes…"

That was code for 'I expect a kiss goodbye' and was enough to propel Rob from his pit to the bathroom for a quick shower. Even then, he had to race downstairs in a bath towel to catch her in time. His mum's coat was prickly against his bare chest and arms as he hugged her.

"Thanks for letting me stay, Mum."

"You didn't get to see your dad or JJ."

"I'll call them later and explain."

"OK, dear." She freed herself from his clutches. "You'll be careful, won't you?"

"I will, Mum," he promised.

She turned and picked up her bag. "And don't forget to phone me to say you're home."

"I won't."

Without looking, she cuffed him around the head.

"Ow!"

"That's for rolling your eyes."

He laughed but didn't deny it. "See you in a fortnight."

"A fortnight," she repeated with a nod. "I'll get a list from you of what Lucas is eating these days."

"Chips, crisps, chocolate—"

"He'll get no junk food here." With that declaration, she was out the door and off to work.

Rob went back up to his room to drink his coffee, in no rush to leave and stop-start his way through the tail end of school drop-off traffic, instead browsing social networks and reading random web pages—the kind of stuff he didn't normally have time for unless it was part of an investigation. Scrolling through seemingly endless ads, he quickly realised he wasn't actually interested in making time for it. He ditched his phone in favour of getting dressed, packed his panniers and carried them down to the hallway.

Linford opened one sleepy eye as Rob passed by on his way back from loading up the bike and followed him at a distance into the kitchen. Quarter to ten: a bowl of cereal, another coffee, and then he'd be on his way. Or that was the plan until his phone rang.

"Morning, Gray."

"Hey, Rob. Sorry for calling so early. I've downloaded the surveillance video from last night. We need to meet ASAP."

"OK. I'm heading back in about half an hour, so I can be with you by…two-thirty?"

"I'm working this morning, but I should be home by then. Want me to come to you?"

"Nah, I'll come to you. Is there anything I need to know now?" Gray would understand what he was really asking: were Zoë and Lucas in danger?

"Nothing that can't wait. I'll text you my address. Take it easy."

"You too, mate." The call ended. Rob chucked his phone aside and analysed the conversation. He'd already told Gray he was heading home today, so whatever the video had picked up was urgent enough for Gray to ensure Rob didn't change his mind.

Dispensing with the spoon, Rob tipped the bowl of cornflakes to his mouth. They hadn't even had time to go soggy, and he was still chewing as he cleaned up and pulled on his leathers. "In a bit, Linford." He patted the dog on his way out and fired up the bike, planning his route home on the move. The motorways were his quickest option, providing they were clear—he should've checked on his phone before he left.

"Phone. Shit."

Luckily, he'd only reached the end of his mum's road. He switched his indicator to turn left instead of right, raising a hand in apology to the driver of the car behind him, and rode around the block, leaving the bike at the kerb while he went back in. The dog watched in seeming bemusement but didn't bother getting up to greet him or see him off.

With a quick route check—contraflow between junctions five and six of the M6, otherwise clear roads all the way—Rob set off once more. He indicated right, checking his mirror as he moved towards the centre line and noting the car turning into the other end of the road, too far away to pose an immediate threat.

Rob pulled out and took the main drag into the town centre, taking a right at the crossroads, then right and right again, which brought him to an out-of-the-way petrol station which was nothing close to the cheapest, but that didn't concern him. He didn't need fuel; he'd filled up over the weekend. What did concern him was the blue Mondeo, presently idling in the supermarket car park across the street—the same car he'd cut up when he'd gone back for his phone; the same car he'd seen in his mirror, and in the pub car park on Sunday after the footy.

"Right, mate, let's see how well you can keep up."

15: Rescue

Gray was preoccupied with unsticking the zip on his rucksack and didn't see Will, in his postie uniform, complete with bulky post bag, until he was within a few feet of him. Will hadn't been looking either, his attention captured by whatever was in his hand—too small to be his phone—and they both back-stepped in surprise. Will shoved whatever it was in his pocket and smiled. "Hi."

"Hi." Gray smiled back, pleased to see him, if not a little curious. "How did you get in here? More to the point, why are you here and not at work?"

"Day off," Will said.

Gray bobbed his head in an exaggerated fashion, looking Will over. "And you love your uniform so much you wore it anyway?"

"OK, I'll confess." He held up his hands. "I had an appointment, and I'm done, so I thought I'd come and see you. I'm your number one fan—I've watched all your shows."

"Shopper in crowded marketplace, passenger in crowded train carriage…"

"I could pick you out of any crowd." Will grinned.

"Somehow I doubt that." Gray moved off, and Will fell in step alongside. "You didn't tell me how you got in here."

"Delivering mail."

"This isn't anywhere near where you deliver mail."

Will shrugged, tilting his head at the reception desk. "They don't know that."

"Someone needs to have a word about security."

Gray stopped to sign out, a simple task made complicated by being unable to keep his eyes off Will. He was rather partial to a man in uniform, cheesy as that was, but he'd seen him in his postie get-up plenty of times and that wasn't why he was watching him—as was the receptionist. In fact, she was watching them both, and no doubt wondering why Gray was escorting the postman from the building. Gray offered her a quick smile and ushered Will towards the door.

"Obviously, you weren't just passing by," he said once they were outside. Will unhooked his sunglasses from his hair and slid them down over his eyes. It was a pleasant spring morning—positively Mediterranean in contrast to the studio's communal dressing room, which had no windows and an enormous air-conditioning unit that turned the space into a walk-in refrigerator—but it was overcast and not that warm. In other words, not sunglasses weather.

"I kind of was, actually. I've got a couple of cats to pick up."

"Did you drive in?" Gray scanned the multistorey car park opposite the studio, on the lookout for Will's van.

"No, I caught the train."

"How are you going to transport them?"

Will tapped his post bag. "Foldaway carry boxes."

"On the train?"

"Cats aren't big or heavy, are they?"

"I suppose not." Now it dawned on Gray. "You need someone to help carry them home."

Will's lips pursed, but the taking of offence was fake, or that was Gray's impression. "That's a terrible thing to say. I knew you finished around twelve, and I thought it'd be nice to go for a coffee."

"Really?" Gray still wasn't convinced.

"Really." Will moved off slowly and glanced sideways over his glasses to make sure Gray was still with him, which he was. "Where to?"

"Chain store or independent?"

"Independent, preferably."

"OK. There's a place round the corner. Their almond-milk latte is excellent."

"Sounds good to me." Will was distracted, and fidgeting with whatever was in his pocket. As soon as he noticed Gray watching, he stopped and smiled innocently, or his mouth did. He could have been giving him evil glares behind those dark glasses. "Do you go to this place often?"

"Original. At least once a week. I keep thinking I might try somewhere different, but why bother when I've found something I like?"

"Not really into new experiences, are you?"

Gray laughed. "Not anymore. I mean, I love spontaneity—like having coffee with you on the spur of the moment—but that's about as adventurous as I want to get these days. Alas—" he turned his head so he could see Will's face "—adventure doesn't want to relinquish its hold on me, so if you do want a hand with those cats, we'll have to take them back to my place. Rob's coming over."

"Your surveillance paid off, I take it?" He was fiddling in his pocket again.

"It did," Gray answered distractedly. "What have you got in there?"

"In here? Oh, it's…a pager."

"A pager?"

"Old tech."

"I know what a pager is." They'd reached the café; Gray held the door open for Will to go in first. "Find us a table, I'll get the drinks."

"OK."

Will walked off, his lack of protest confirming he was up to no good. Gray ordered their drinks and joined him. He wasn't sure what he could safely say to break the uneasy silence that billowed between them, and was grateful for the intervention of the barista delivering their lattes a few minutes later. They both thanked her and picked up their cups at the same time; Will inhaled, sipped and sloshed his drink around his mouth. He swallowed and hummed his approval. Finally, the sunglasses came off.

"Do you really want to know?"

Gray shrugged. "Do I?"

With a sigh, Will leaned back, extracted the small, black gadget from his pocket and placed it next to Gray's drink. "It's—"

"A wireless jammer. Put it away." Will did so. "They're illegal."

"To use, not to own."

"You wouldn't have it if you didn't intend to use it." The penny dropped, although it felt more like a whole bagful had landed in his lap with no prior warning. "Tell me again about the cats."

"Gray…"

"Do you need my help?"

"Yes, but that's not why I'm here."

"Am I your alibi?"

Will's laughter camouflaged what he really thought of that question, and Gray couldn't figure it out. "The cats are strays, trapped in a building that's protected by a wireless security system. The woman who reported them thinks they've been in there since the building was vacated two weeks ago. I called the letting agency and asked if I could go in, but they've been locked down by the Inland Revenue. So…I'm going to break in and jam the alarm system."

"In broad daylight."

"Concealed entrance."

"You still need to shut it off first," Gray pointed out, which got him a smirk.

"Payback for my 'old tech' remark?"

"Something like that." He forgot…or intentionally overlooked that Will had the skill set of a cat burglar—a fitting pun on this occasion—and not that different from Gray's own talents. He also had some very clever friends who owed him. "Aaron?"

"Yep. He's going to shut the system down, but it's got a failsafe that sends a reboot signal. The jammer should give me enough time to find the cats before the alarm company turn up to do a manual reboot."

"How big's the building?"

"Not huge. Four storeys plus the basement. That's where I'll start—the cats must have a food source."

Basement...food source...rats... Gray shuddered, and yet... "What can I do?"

"Well, like I said, I came here to see you, but it would be a lot easier with the two of us, particularly if there are kittens to get out."

"It's almost as if you planned the rescue for when I had a car," Gray joked. He hadn't known himself that he'd have a car this week.

"You could keep watch, alert me when the alarm guys arrive."

"How? Exotic bird call?"

Will groaned. "Good point. We usually do these kinds of rescues as a two-man team, but it's outside of Tie's tag radius."

"How would Tie have alerted you?"

"He'd be inside the building."

"Ah." Gray picked up his cup. Filling his mouth with coffee might stop him volunteering.

"Never mind," Will said quickly. "If you're still up for being my getaway driver—"

"Gee, that sounds so much better..."

"Or I go with my original plan."

"Transport a family of wild cats on the Tube?"

"I've done it before."

"Wasn't that chickens?"

"Same difference," Will muttered obstinately.

Gray couldn't help it; he laughed. It was almost worth sustaining the argument to see Will riled, but he really did want to help. "OK, how about this: we'll park somewhere out of sight. I'll stay with the car, and as soon as you're clear, call me and I'll pick you up."

"If they report it to the police—"

"I was giving a friend a lift back from the vet's. I had no reason to suspect a crime had been committed."

"I've got previous."

"How would I know? I'm a civilian."

"What about Hedley?"

Gray thought back to Rob's leaving do, when Martina had failed to put two and two together, and not just because she'd been on the brandy. The night of Freddie Berringer's arrest, she'd assumed Gray was there on SIU business and gladly handed off the corporate investigation into the Berringers' business dealings. The Met Police were only interested in getting father and son on their respective murder charges, although, the chances were, Charles's would be reduced to involuntary manslaughter for putting a drunk Hector Laird-Browne behind the wheel and Freddie would get off on the grounds of self-defence.

"Gray?"

"Sorry, I was thinking. Where is it?"

"Acton."

"That's out of Hedley's area. Even if it wasn't, I'm not convinced she knows we're an item, and, you know…it's only been five months, and I'm a former police officer. You're worried that if I find out you have a criminal record, I won't want anything to do with you."

Will raised his eyebrows. "I am?"

"Stands to reason."

The familiar, warm smile returned. "You're good at this."

"Don't know what you mean." Gray hid behind his cup. Will laughed, but there was something more. Something else. Gray finished his coffee and put his cup back on its saucer. "OK, now you've convinced me you didn't come to talk me into doing what you talked me into doing, why are you here?"

"Headaches," Will answered without hesitation, following up with a hard swallow and the nodded equivalent of *there, I said it*. All the while, he held Gray's gaze. Gray tilted his head in query. "I've been getting them since just after Mum passed."

"How bad are they?"

"Bad enough for me to go to my doctor. She sent me to a specialist."

"That's where you've been this morning?"

"Yep. I had a scan while I was there."

"How long till you get the results?"

"Next week." Will didn't need to say anything else; his fear carved deep lines across his forehead, and Gray felt awful for not noticing before. Then again, Will would have distracted him any time he got close. No doubt, the stress was further exacerbating the headaches.

"OK. Let me know when your appointment is."

"You don't mind?"

Gray smiled and rested his hand on top of Will's. "Not at all."

"Thank you."

"No thanks needed. That's what friends…boyfriends…are for. And yes, you can tell Suzannah I used the B-word."

Will laughed. "You can tell her yourself."

No matter that Will's daughter had been calling Gray 'Dad's boyfriend' since she'd first known of his existence—understandably, given they'd been introduced at Will's mum's funeral. Gray had learned early on that whilst Will was sociable and outgoing, at times of emotional vulnerability he became insular and went off on his own—surfing or hill-walking or some other physical means of working through his feelings. It made it an even greater privilege for Gray to have been invited to the funeral, and for Will to have confided in him about the headaches.

"Deal," Gray said. "When shall we do it?"

"Well, I've got a week's leave before Easter. I was gonna pop up to see her."

"I could come with you."

"You want to visit Suzannah and Shelley?"

"We can make a holiday of it. It's time I got to know them better, but it's up to you—you don't have to tell me now, or tell me at all." He peered into Will's half-full cup. "We should make a move. I told Rob I'd be home by two-thirty."

"OK." Will finished his coffee as he got to his feet and walked ahead of Gray, looking back at him to say, "That was to both suggestions."

Outside, Will put on his sunglasses once more, and they walked back to the multistorey, where Gray had parked the tiny hire car that was costing him a not-tiny fortune in congestion charges and parking fees. From there, Will directed him through back streets to North Acton.

"That's the place." Will pointed as they passed a dilapidated 1970s prefab that looked like every local government building of the era.

Gray read the faded 'To Let' sign's boast of '100,000 sq ft of Office Space'. "Not huge, he says…"

"I'm pretty sure they'll be in the basement."

"I hope for your sake they are." Gray continued along the street, looking for a parking space or a side road, but there was nowhere.

"What about that pub?" Will suggested.

"It'll have to do, I guess." Gray indicated and turned into the technically full forecourt. There was a gap between the row of cars and an advertising board that he could just about squeeze the hatchback into. "You'd better get out now. I'll go in and buy an OJ or something."

Will got out and went around to the back of the car for his bag. "I'll be as quick as I can," he promised, slamming the boot shut. He sped off in the direction of the office building.

Gray parked up and eyed the pub in disappointment. It seemed to be a decent establishment, but he'd have stayed in the car if he thought he'd get away with it. Alas, the person watering the hanging baskets kept casting suspicious glances his way. Gray checked the time on his phone—12:56—and unmuted the ring tone, locked the car and went to join the other three punters enjoying an early afternoon pint.

"Alright?" the barman greeted him.

"Hello." Gray put on a show of inspecting the counter mounts before he ordered. "I'll have…a Coke, please."

"Not Newcastle Brown?" The barman collected a glass and filled it.

Gray smiled. "Later, maybe." The accent was only half-intentional, though he doubted the cloak-and-dagger routine was necessary.

"D'you live down here or…?"

"Just visiting a friend—he asked me to meet him here." Gray looked around him. "It's quiet, like."

"Always is weekday lunchtimes. Gets mad later."

"I bet."

The barman handed over Gray's drink. He paid and, seeing as he wasn't stopping long, decided to stay where he was. The other customers were dotted around the bar, all eyes trained on the large TV screen. Curling. Too sedentary, intriguing but not very interesting, other than the time in the corner of the screen that permitted Gray to subtly keep check—currently 13:04. In his experience, alarm companies' 'rapid response' would give Will around thirty minutes from when they noticed the system was offline. Was that long enough to catch a couple of stray cats? Gray had no idea, although the old adage about herding the wilful little monsters sprang to mind.

Meanwhile, the curlers bowled and brushed on. It wasn't quite as relaxed a sport as Gray had first thought, and he found himself wincing and puffing in frustration when a stone didn't quite go where it was meant to. Those shoes looked great, though. He hadn't been ice-skating since high school, and he wasn't awful, but curling shoes looked a lot easier to control than ice skates. Would they allow them at the rink?

Time check: 13:25. The alarm company might already be on the premises. Gray crossed his feet in an effort to stop his knee jigging, and timed his pulse between 13:26 and 13:27. Since knocking cocaine on the head, he was a steady 70 bpm guy, but it was up at 90+, and it was all about Will. If he got caught, he wouldn't implicate Gray; no-one would ever know he was the 'getaway driver'. If he stayed put. Which he should. Will could be on his way to the pub right now.

Right now being 13:29. He checked his phone in the impossibly unlikely event he hadn't heard the alert. The Norwegians won the curling match; the clock ticked over to 13:30. The last half inch of Coke slid from the glass onto Gray's tongue, and he endeavoured to savour the too sweet, no longer effervescent liquid before it drained away down his throat.

"Another?" the barman asked.

"No, thanks. I'm going to call my friend, see where he's got to. I might be back in a bit."

"See you."

Gray left the pub, looking towards the car, waiting until he was in the driver's seat before he chanced a glance along the street. He saw the security firm's van at the same time as his phone chimed.

Too many cats. Police on way. Call Tie. Sorry. x

16: Footage

The turn into the road was almost a hairpin, and Rob missed it on a first pass. He'd never been to Gray's house before and hadn't known what to expect—certainly *not* a two-bed mid-terrace with a front door that opened more or less onto the pavement. Gray had always struck Rob as more of a minimalist-loft kind of guy. However humble it looked, property in NW2 cost a packet, and if Rob was honest, his judgement was tainted by jealousy. He'd had a place better than this with Zoë and Lucas, although her parents had paid the deposit, so it was never really his, or even theirs, which meant Travis had no stake in it either. That didn't appease him as much as he'd thought it would.

The front door opened as Rob climbed off the bike. There was no cheery smile to greet him.

"Alright, mate?" He advanced, removing his helmet.

"Hey, Rob." Gray shook his hand. "How was your long weekend up north?"

"Not long enough, but I got to see both my nieces, so it wasn't a dead loss."

"That's good to hear. Come on in. Coffee? I've just made some."

"Yeah, cheers." Rob closed the door and waited for an indication of whether he should follow Gray into his kitchen, go find the living room or stay right where he was, admiring the décor. The hallway was spartan—bare wood floor, plain white walls—but for the poster-size silent movie stills following the rise of the stairs. A man smoking a pipe, a woman posed behind a microphone, and—the only actor Rob recognised—Charlie

Chaplin scowling face-to-face with another guy in a hat. It was like a movie studio reception, or how he imagined one would be.

Gray reappeared with two mugs. "Sorry, I'm a bit distracted this afternoon. We'll go in here." He nodded at the doorway on Rob's left, which turned out to be the living room and, thankfully, a bit more lived in than the hallway. It was still keeping with the black-and-white theme, other than the sofas, which were green, pink and cream—like weathered apples—and a blue envelope on the coffee table. The solitary picture on the chimney breast—there was no fireplace—was a splat from a giant fountain pen.

"Sit down, Rob," Gray invited, looking up and around as he sat himself. "The white walls aren't my doing."

Rob nodded. "I'm not judging. I know nothing about interior design."

"Same here. These—" Gray patted the sofa he was sitting on "—were Ade's idea. Kris Johansson's partner? He sketched the entire room for me, put together a swatch and everything, but I never seem to get around to it."

Rob knew Kris from high school, but not well, and he'd only met Ade in passing, so there was no further conversation to be had there. He leaned forward to pick up his coffee from the smear-free glass table, peering through it at the floor. "Oak?"

"Yes," Gray confirmed. "Now that *was* my doing. Two layers of carpet on top of lino on top of terrible floorboards. It all had to come out. The rest of the house was as it is now."

"It's got a lot of potential."

"I quite agree—in the right hands. I don't know...I spend so much time here—" he sighed as he looked around again "—but I can't muster the enthusiasm, and I don't get many visitors. Believe it or not, you're the first one this year. That's your leaving card, by the way." He gave the blue envelope a push, and it slid across the table. "I forgot to take it with me."

"Sixth sense." Rob picked it up and slit the top open with his key, laughing as he pulled out the card: *Good Luck – hope your new boss is less of a bastard.* "Depends who you ask," he said.

"Cheers, Gray." He stood the card on the table and picked up his coffee again. "It's still a bit unreal—I keep going to check what shift I'm on and then remember I'm not. How long does that last?"

Gray tapped his finger against his lips, thinking, and then gave a resigned nod. "At least eleven months," he admitted. "And we didn't even have a shift pattern."

"You mean aside from if it was a day ending in Y?"

Gray chuckled. "That's the one. OK, to business. I was at Zoë's until around nine last night, and there was nothing going on—it's a very quiet street."

"Yeah, it is." Rob had never been fond for that reason. Where he'd grown up, everyone knew everyone else and kept an eye out for each other's kids. The south-east was different, London especially, so it was only his northern roots showing.

"Typically, when I played back the video, I discovered if I'd stayed another ten minutes, I'd have got a good look at the van that stopped across the street—unless they were waiting for me to leave, of course—but it could've belonged to a resident."

"What kind of van?" Rob asked.

"A white transit." Gray picked up a remote control and pointed it at the TV.

"Sounds like Bish's van."

"One of the guys from your regiment?"

"Yeah. I was gonna tell you…never mind. It can wait." A fuzzy image filled the screen—a perspective that was unfamiliar to Rob but wouldn't be to Lucas. "Where did you put the camera?"

"Under the bay window, next to the gas meter."

"That explains the kneecap view." Rob was looking through the gate at the street, empty apart from an occasional flash of movement as a car drove past.

"I'll fast forward." Gray skipped the video to nine minutes and forty seconds, when a white van slowed to a stop opposite the house. If they'd been parked a few inches further back, the camera would've picked up the cab. As it was, Rob could see only the driver's right shoulder, along with the side of the van.

"That's not Bish's," he said.

"Are you sure?"

"Yep. For starters, that one's in better nick, and his has got a sliding door. I got shoved through it on Friday night."

"Was the side bump rail missing?" Gray asked.

"Yeah."

"And the nearside headlamp was dipped?"

"I wouldn't know about that. Why?"

"I saw it outside the restaurant. I assumed it was a delivery van of some sort." Gray increased the playback speed; they watched an hour of video footage in fifteen minutes, during which the van remained stationary, and then the screen went black. "No movement for the sensors to pick up," Gray explained.

"So they could've been there all night?"

"Possibly. Have you ever noticed a van there before?"

"Not that I recall, but I wasn't looking for one. People keep to themselves and have no time for nosey neighbours."

Gray hummed thoughtfully. "I hadn't realised how frustrating this PI business is. All that information we had at our fingertips in the SIU—I could've been straight into the DVLA database to check if one was registered locally."

"I was thinking the same this morning," Rob said. "A blue Mondeo tailed me from my mum's to the motorway."

"An unmarked car?"

"Yep. I got Aitch to run the plates to make sure."

"They might've been after a nick," Gray reasoned.

"If it had happened just the once, I'd agree. But I saw them on Sunday after footy too—actually, that's the other thing I want to ask you. The Strang case is still ongoing, yeah?"

"To my knowledge. Why?"

"Dan Jeffries mentioned an auction sting."

Gray nodded. "Comco Glass, yes. I'm not privy to the ins and outs of it, but it's part of the SIU investigation."

Rob drank his coffee while he absorbed the information. They'd known before they brought down the inheritance scam that it was only a tiny part of a massive operation, but Rob had left the SIU straight after. Even if Jess Lambert was the brains behind that part of it, once he had confirmation she hadn't been involved in anything worse, all he'd cared about was seeing Anders Folden put behind bars. He was devious and dangerous—the perfect hitman—and Rob regretted not killing him when he'd had the chance.

"What's on your mind, Rob?"

He looked up from his cup to find Gray watching him intently. "Do you think this could be anything to do with it?"

"I couldn't say no for sure, but I doubt it." Gray remained cool and passive, but he was well-practised in that regard, and it meant nothing.

"The Mondeo's registered to the Met," Rob said, holding eye contact, looking for a reaction.

"What was it doing two hundred miles north of London?"

Absolutely zip. "Well, unless it's one big coincidence that someone's watching Zoë's place and my mum's…"

"They're keeping an eye on you," Gray finished.

There went Rob's last futile hope he was being paranoid.

"We can come back to that. You were going to tell me the full story."

"Yeah, I was." Rob swallowed a mouthful of coffee for lubrication, aware that Gray had intentionally shut him down. "Right, from the beginning…I joined a REME unit in Germany as an apprentice, and when I qualified, I took over from the motor mechanic. There were five of us: Lieutenant Yvette Parker aka Tonka, Sergeant Ethan McGrath, Sergeant Olivia Simpson— she was the mechanic before me, they called her Lisa—Corporal Harry Wilson aka Jock, John Garvey aka Bish, and me."

"Aka…?"

Rob sighed. He'd thought he might get away with it. "Sharon."

"Sharon?"

"Sharon Stone. It was that or Bart, but we already had Lisa. Yeah, don't think I can't see you smirking."

Gray was doing a bit more than smirking. "How did I not know this? Sharon Stone…" It had really tickled him. "I always wondered where your…unconventional interrogation technique came from."

Rob would have been laughing too—if he hadn't heard it all before, and if he wasn't stressing about Zoë and Lucas. To be fair, stress was probably causing Gray's giggles, and he got them in check pretty quickly.

"Sorry," he said, dabbing his eyes. "Keep going."

It was hard in the face of Gray's mirth, but Rob forged on. "We were home on leave when Tonka got a call to say Ethan was in police custody. He'd caught his wife cheating on him and took a cricket bat to the pair of them, put his wife in hospital for six weeks. The bloke she was with…when the military police found him, he was naked, tied to a chair, and so badly battered they couldn't even identify him by his tattoos."

"Jesus."

"Yeah, it was bad. But it wasn't really a shock to any of us. Ethan got sent down for manslaughter on a defence of diminished responsibility due to PTSD, which is bollocks. I'm not disputing he's got PTSD—occupational hazard and all that—but he'd always been a liability. Him and Jock were at each other all the time, although Jock's a piece of work, so I could sort of understand why Ethan wanted to smash his face in."

"Where's Ethan now?"

"In Brookhurst secure hospital."

"So he's not the reason for the surveillance on Zoë and Lucas?"

"Indirectly. Last Friday, Tonka—" Rob spotted Gray's inquisitive frown and explained. "She grew up on a massive farm and is a bit nifty in a tractor."

"Fitting."

"Fits better than Yvette, that's for sure. Ethan didn't have a nickname—I don't know if that was his doing." Rob had never been interested enough to give it any thought. "Anyway, Tonka told me he was coming up for release and she knew someone who'd wipe his record for half a million quid. She asked me to contribute, and I told her I couldn't help. It would've cleaned me out, but even if I had that kind of money going spare, I wouldn't waste it on Ethan. As far as I'm concerned, he deserved everything he got and more, and Tonka knows that's how I feel."

"What did she do when you said no?"

"She got a bit shirty but let me leave without further argument. I should've realised something was off—now I think about it, she doesn't back down easily—but I just wanted to get out of there and back to the Quarterhouse."

"Did you get lost?" Gray asked dryly.

Rob managed a chuckle. "I couldn't be arsed, to tell the truth. They'd have taken the piss if I'd turned up, and I wasn't exactly in the mood for partying after I left Tonka's. Sorry."

"No, don't apologise. I understand. If I could've given Dom the slip, I wouldn't have gone to my leaving do either. Have you spoken to Hedley yet?"

"Yeah, on Saturday. She was all right—more worried than annoyed. I told her enough to reassure her I wasn't in trouble. I hope I didn't speak too soon. Did she enjoy herself?"

"I think so. She had a good drink, anyway. She'll miss you."

"Yeah." Rob would miss her too, but after seeing Lois and Amber over the weekend, he knew he'd made the right decision. "So, this investigation Bish and Jock want us to do…"

"They want us to find out what Tonka's up to, I assume?"

"That's what Jock said, but I don't buy it. The thing about him and Bish is they did twenty-two years, and they're unquestioningly loyal—I have enough of a problem disobeying Tonka myself, and I got out well before the rest of them. According to Jock, she did a bunk on Saturday morning, and it dawned on me on the way here. If she's under surveillance, I'd have been seen at her place on Friday night. The Met will suspect I'm involved."

Gray looked pained. "That's down to me. I hassled Petridis into sending out the troops. Traffic cameras picked up your bike on the M40."

"Shit. So they could've traced back to when I left Tonka's."

"It's possible. I'm really sorry, Rob."

"Nah, it's not your fault." His anger was surfacing, but Gray wasn't the target. "Right…let's think about this…" He needed to get it straight in his head. "After Jock told me about the investment Tonka tried to sell them, I thought the bit about Ethan had to be a red herring, which is why I asked you to keep an eye on Zoë and Lucas. We both know the lengths people will go to for money, and Bish and Jock would have no qualms about doing the necessary to help Tonka out. But with that van at the house and the Met tailing me…I'm not sure Tonka wanted money at all. I think she used me as a decoy."

"That's one interpretation," Gray said.

"You don't agree."

"I don't necessarily disagree." He leaned over the arm of the sofa, retrieved a folder from the floor and handed it to Rob. "After we spoke, I contacted a couple of brokers to see what I could find out about Eastern European property investment. It's a burgeoning market."

Rob flicked through the sheets inside, such good as it did him—the hard sell condensed down to numbers, graphs and stock-broker-code bullet points for busy investors. "This doesn't prove Jock was telling the truth."

"No, but…sorry if I'm speaking out of turn here. I get the feeling there's no love lost between the two of you."

"You could say that."

"And presumably, Tonka's aware, so she'd know she stands more chance of getting money out of you by asking directly than by getting Jock to do her dirty work."

"She did ask, and I said no."

"That's what I mean, because I think you were on the right lines. This isn't about money."

"Then they're both red herrings."

"Or red flags. If she's in the kind of trouble we're familiar with, she's going to be watching what she says."

Rob thought back to the conversation in Tonka's garage, trying to remember the exact words. "I'm shit at decryption."

"Aye, that's why we make such a smashing team." Out came the fake Geordie accent.

Rob had no comeback, seeing as it was the reason he'd asked Gray to come in on the PI business. "All right. I'll talk to Jock again, see if he's got any bumph on the investment."

"If you can get that information, I'll do the rest."

"Cheers." That saved Rob wading through reams of indecipherable financial jargon. "I'll see what else I can find out about Ethan's situation. What shall I tell Jock? Are we taking the case?"

"It's up to you. I can afford to keep us afloat for a while."

"You're already forking out for surveillance equipment," Rob argued.

"You paid for the website."

"Well...I paid for the domain name and bought Dan Jeffries a pint for setting it up."

"Right. So you saved us money."

"And now I'm going to earn us some. I'll just make sure Jock knows he's only the handbag and we're calling the shots."

"Tell you what, why don't you organise a formal meeting, and we'll both go?"

"Yeah, that might be better." Rob drained the last of his coffee and got up, ready to leave. "I'm going to pop over to Zoë and Lu's, make sure they're all right and see if there's any sign of that van."

Gray followed him to the front door. "Let me know how you get on. I'll leave the camera running for now, but I won't bother going over there, unless you want me to."

"Let's see how it goes. I'll alert Zoë and Travis to be on the lookout for anything suspicious, but if the police are keeping an eye, they don't need us amateurs to protect them."

"Amateurs? We're highly skilled, experienced private investigat—oh!"

Rob turned back to see why Gray had stopped and found him frowning at his phone. "What's up?"

"They've released him. Huh. I wasn't expecting that."

Rob raised an eyebrow rather than ask.

"Will got arrested earlier."

"What was it this time? Abandoned alpaca?"

Gray laughed. "He broke into a building to rescue some stray cats, and he had a wireless jammer on him. Or maybe not, if the police let him go."

"Didn't you give up the SIU for a quiet life?"

"That was the idea. Best-laid plans of… Alpaca?"

Rob shrugged. "First thing that came to mind."

"I'm sure they'll feature at some point."

"More than likely. I'll email you any info I get out of Jock and let you know about the meeting."

"OK. Take it easy, Rob."

"You too, mate."

Gray waited at the door and raised his hand as Rob rode off.

On to the next job, and not one he was looking forward to.

17: Due Care

After Rob left, Gray backed up the video footage to an encrypted external drive and then watched it again on his computer's high-res monitor, pausing and zooming in on the van and its occupant. Or occupants, as he discovered when he advanced, frame by frame, and a second head briefly popped into view. Neither was identifiable, not even by so much as gender or build; at a distance and in the dark, the picture quality was pretty awful.

For the time being, he concentrated on the van, comparing the shape of the side panel and door to images online. It didn't take him long to narrow down the make and model, and it was one used by the Met...and by thousands of UK businesses. Gray shut the browser window and returned to staring at the blurry still.

"This is so frustrating."

If he'd gone for the streetlamp-mounted camera, or stayed longer...but he hadn't, and there was nothing else he could glean from what he'd got. He'd review whatever footage he collected tonight and if need be, tomorrow, he'd go and see Paddy again.

***

"Rob. Hi."

"Alright, Zo?"

She was already eyeing him with suspicion—understandably when all he'd told her was he needed to speak to her and Travis together. First time for everything. As he stepped into the house, a door slammed upstairs, followed by the heavy, muted thud of a football bouncing on carpet and Lucas's appearance at the top of the stairs. He spotted Rob, yelled, "Dad!" ran halfway down and jumped the remaining steps, grabbing Rob around the middle while the football thunked its way to the bottom of the stairs.

"Alright, Lu? How you doing?"

"What did I say?" Zoë warned. Lucas peered up at Rob and slow-blinked.

"What's this? No football in the house?" Rob guessed. Lucas burrowed into his jacket. "Oy. Don't think I'm gonna take your side, mate." No response to that, Rob put his hands on Lucas's shoulders and took a step back. His son grinned sheepishly.

"Can you play in your room for a bit, Lu?" Zoë's tone turned the suggestion into an order.

"Why?"

"Your dad needs to talk to us."

"I'm us!"

"Travis and me," Zoë clarified, though Lucas understood perfectly the first time. He huffed about it, but he turned around and started back up the stairs. "Take the ball with you, please," Zoë said wearily and gave Rob a slow blink identical to their son's.

With another giant huff, Lucas collected his football and plodded, at a rate of a step every three seconds, back to his room.

"Kids," Zoë muttered.

"He's just going through a naughty phase," Rob defended with a wink.

"Yeah, it started seven years ago. I'm going to pour some wine. Do you want anything?" She was already moving towards the kitchen.

"I'm fine, cheers." Rob watched her a moment longer before entering the living room, where the low-volume TV was tuned to a news channel and Travis was working on his laptop, which he immediately abandoned.

"Alright? How's it going?" He half rose to shake Rob's hand.

"Not bad, mate," Rob said, as always distracted by the difference between his memory of this room and the reality. The big, cosy sofa he and Zoë had bought together was long gone, in its place an enormous leather L-shaped grey thing like the seating in a doctor's waiting room.

Zoë came in carrying a glass big enough to take a bottle of wine, and it was almost full. She kept hold of it as she sat next to Travis, leaving the shorter limb of the L to Rob. It was comfy enough, he supposed, and she'd given him first refusal on the old sofa, so he couldn't complain. Unfortunately, his flat was pre-furnished—cheaper rent—and he had nowhere to store a sofa until such point as he could afford a better place, so it had gone to a furniture recycling warehouse. At least somebody, somewhere was getting use out of it.

Travis kept shifting his eyes between Rob and Zoë. If he had one redeeming feature—well, he had quite a few, Rob was slowly beginning to accept—his politeness had stood out from the get-go. He was waiting for someone to speak, and Rob was still trying to come up with a way to explain without worrying them. There wasn't one. Rob opened his mouth at the same time Zoë did, but she got there first.

"Is everything all right with your mum?"

"Yeah." And now he felt like a thoughtless bastard. His mum and Zoë got along brilliantly, so of course she'd have thought he was here to deliver bad news. "Sorry. Mum's fine. Same as always, really. Tough as old boots. Harvey's not doing great, though."

"Oh?"

"Cancer of the prostate. He's starting treatment in a couple of weeks. The doctor's confident the radiotherapy will kick it into touch."

"Thank goodness." Zoë put her palm to her chest and exhaled heavily. It was a dramatic reaction, but Rob didn't think she was putting it on. He needed to tread lightly.

"What I came to talk to you about..." He sighed. "However I put this, you'll worry, but everything's OK."

Zoë lifted her wine glass to her lips, her eyes growing wide above it. She swallowed down a couple of large gulps, gripped Travis's hand and nodded for Rob to continue.

"Gray and I think the Met have surveillance on the house."

"Our house?"

"Yeah. That visit you got the other day from Jock?"

"He's the guy who came to the door on Saturday," Zoë explained to Travis.

"The geezer who looked like he'd had a frying pan in the face?"

Rob chuckled. "That's the one. As I told Zo, he's one of my old army mates. I say mates—we're not, but Jock and one of the other lads have hired Gray and me to look into our old CO." The events weren't quite in the right order, but it didn't sound as bad this way around. "They think she's in trouble of some sort, and it looks like the Met have already picked up on it."

"Why are they watching this place?" Zoë asked. "Are they expecting Jock to come back?"

"No. They're watching me."

"Oh, no. Don't tell me you're in trouble again."

"Again?"

"I'm joking, Rob."

He couldn't see the funny side, not after the con he'd had to pull on them all for their own safety. Zoë knew the truth now and said she'd accepted it, but joking or not, the accusation still stung.

With perfect timing, Lucas shouted from upstairs, "Are you finished yet, Dad? I wanna show you my new game."

"All right, Lu. Be up in a minute." Rob turned his attention back to Zoë and Travis. "I just wanted to give you both a heads up." He decided to skip 'there's a spy camera mounted on the front of the house'. "If you spot anything you're not happy about, let me know, OK? I'll have a chat with Hedley tomorrow, anyway, see if she can shed any light on what's going on. I also wanted to ask if you've got any plans over the spring break. I was thinking of taking Lu up to my mum's."

Zoë shook her head. "I don't think we have—Trav?"

"I might've looked for something last minute, but no. Nothing planned."

"Is that all right, then?" Rob asked them both.

Travis raised his hands. "It's between you two."

Zoë shrugged. "A week without 'Mum, can I have…', 'Mum, can we go…'? Sounds good to me."

Rob pushed up from the sofa, as did Travis. There were bum-shaped impressions where they'd been sitting.

"Memory foam," Travis said. "Comfy, eh?"

"Very." It wasn't a lie, but it had nothing on the old sofa.

"D'you want a drink, Rob? Beer?"

"No, I'm fine, honestly. I'm ready to flake out, but I'd best go have a look at this game first."

Travis nodded enthusiastically. "It's awesome."

"Yeah?"

Zoë tutted. "I knew it! You didn't buy it for Lu, you bought it for you."

Travis scowled. "Did not. I ain't got an Xbox."

"Aw, poor baby. Santa might bring you one if you're very, very good."

"Always," Travis replied with a grin.

Rob unclamped his teeth long enough to say, "See you in a bit," and made a swift retreat upstairs to Lucas's room. In fairness to Zoë, she usually avoided acting lovey-dovey in front of him. He kind of wished she wouldn't. He needed to get used to it.

"Oh, wow. Those graphics!"

Lucas was sitting on the floor, leaning his back against his bed, and didn't look away from the screen. His arms were up in the air, hard left, hard right, moving with the controller as he steered an unbelievably realistic Koenigsegg around a race track.

"You're good at that, Lu."

"Cheers." That was all Rob was getting out of him until the current race came to an end and Lucas sighed despondently. "Third again." He held up the controller. "Your turn."

"Can I?" Rob grabbed the controller before his son changed his mind and sat down next to him with knees bent; the gap between the bed and chest of drawers wasn't wide enough to accommodate his legs. "Right, what do I do?"

Lucas reached across and pressed buttons until he was back at the start screen. "Choose a car."

Rob scanned the list of supercars, his heart skipping a beat when he reached 'Lamborghini Aventador'. He hoped Tonka hadn't done anything silly.

"My other car's the Ferrari," Lucas said helpfully.

"Yeah? I wish mine was." Rob opted for the 1997 Lamborghini Diablo and ignored Lucas's disapproving 'huh'. "What do I do next? Choose a race? Is that Rio?"

"Yeah. That's the one I just did."

"That'll do me." Rob pressed what he thought was the start button, but nothing happened. Lucas came to his aid.

"D'you want me to teach you the controls?"

"Nah," Rob said bravely. He didn't mind making a fool of himself in front of Lucas, which was exactly how it panned out. It wasn't cool driving a Diablo at forty miles an hour, but once around the track and he thought he'd nailed it…until he got rammed from behind by a McLaren and was left wheel-spinning on the verge. Travis was right; it was an amazing game that made Rob's old favourite *Gran Turismo* look like a 1980s 8-bit video game. Eventually, the digital mechanics arrived to tow his Diablo off the track, and Lucas patted his thigh.

"Never mind, Dad. You'll be better next time. Want another go?"

"Tell you what, I'll watch you. Learn from the best."

Grinning, Lucas took back the controller and whizzed through the start-up screens, off to Monaco, his Koenigsegg in pole position. It was better than watching TV, but distracting— helicopters, passenger jets, camera flashes, skid marks appearing on the road—Rob was in awe of Lucas's ability to concentrate with all of that going on.

"So, d'you fancy going up to Nan and Grandad Harvey's?"

"Yeah! When? This weekend?"

"School holidays."

Another race finished in third place. "Are we going on the bike?"

Rob laughed. "Nope."

"Aw, Da-a-ad. But I'm nearly eight!"

"Nearly eight…" Rob tutted. Lucas had not long turned seven. "I told you. When you're big enough to ride a bike of your own…" With a struggle, Rob bent his legs so he could put his feet flat on the floor. He got up stiffly. "Right, I'm going."

"'Kay, Dad. Swimming on Saturday?"

"I'll check with your mum, but yeah, probably. Be good."

"I will. Bye, Dad."

"Laters, taters." He left Lucas to his racing and returned downstairs to the living room, where Travis was watching out of the front window and Zoë was pretending to watch TV. She was still worried about what he'd told them. "You OK, Zo?"

"I think so." She put her wine down and beckoned him close, holding up her arms for a hug. She always did it, and it had always felt awkward in front of Travis, but not so much this evening. Rob's animosity had taken a back seat; all that mattered was Lucas and Zoë's safety. How could he begrudge Travis when the guy cared for them as much as Rob did? He'd look out for them.

"See you Saturday?" Rob slowly eased out of the hug and braced for hearing they'd made other plans because he should've been at his mum's.

"Yeah," Zoë confirmed. "Please be careful."

"Promise."

Her eyebrow lift was as instinctual as the word tumbling from his tongue. Rob smiled to himself as he left the room. He wasn't the same guy anymore—the one who used the job as an excuse to break promises he should never have made in the first place.

As he neared the front door, he slowed for Travis to catch up. "Thanks for this."

"No problem." Travis opened the door and then followed Rob outside. "If there's anything I can do…"

"Cheers, but I don't think there is."

"If that changes…"

"I'll let you know."

"Alright, mate. See you." Travis went back inside.

Rob stopped at the gate, looking along the road: no white van, no blue Mondeo, as far as he could tell. Behind him, the key turned and the safety chain slid across. He glanced back at the house, scanning the vicinity of the gas meter until he located the camera. The relief that stole the last of his energy confirmed he'd done the right thing.

***

Rob's old army mates certainly put their money where their mouths were. An hour after Rob's text arrived confirming he'd arranged a meeting for the following morning, Gray received a second message notifying him of a deposit from 'Sequrco' into their business account. Gray stared at it until the pound sign morphed into a miniature dinosaur and chomped its way through the numbers. £5,000. It was enough to secure their services for at least the next two weeks—unless Jock was expecting twenty-four-hour surveillance.

It seemed they had their first clients, and it was, potentially, a much bigger and more interesting case than Gray had anticipated, which would have been more along the lines of spying on 'sick' employees or running background checks for investors.

But 'potentially' was key; Tonka might simply have cut Bish and Jock out of an investment opportunity, hoping to maximise her return. It didn't explain why she'd told Rob something else— strictly speaking, that had nothing to do with the investigation they were being paid to undertake—and Gray wondered whether their clients would expect a refund if it turned out to be a cut-and-run. He'd have to check the situation with Rob tomorrow morning, ideally before their breakfast meeting. He reloaded the text confirmation just so he could scowl at it.

Nine-thirty in Gatwick—'halfway' in terms of travelling time rather than distance. Much as Gray appreciated it was closer to them than it was to Bish and Jock, it still meant having to be out of the house by seven, and it was almost midnight. Sleepy or not, he needed to go to bed.

Up in his room, Gray undressed in the dark and sat in his boxers on the side of the bed. His mind kept flitting from the case to Will's arrest to Rob being tailed and back to the case. He couldn't see how the Met watching Rob—assuming they were—was linked to Tonka, and that worried him more, because he couldn't think of any other reason Rob would be under surveillance. Unless Zoë's new partner was shady? In which case, Rob's visit would've done more harm than good, although, given his feelings towards the guy, if Travis was involved in anything, Rob would've picked up on it a long time ago, and he wouldn't have kept it to himself.

"OK, not Travis, then," Gray confirmed aloud. He switched on the bedside lamp and just about got his pyjama top on before his thoughts wandered again.

The other possibility—which he wasn't going to mention until he knew more—was that Tonka had told Rob the truth, and the rest of it—Jock's investment story and hiring PIs—was a ruse. It would mean Rob was right about being used as a decoy. What Gray needed to establish was whether Bish and Jock's loyalty to their former CO extended to stitching up one of their own, and he could get a sense of that from how they operated their business. It gave him the impetus to finish putting on his PJs and get into bed. Pillows propped, he grabbed his laptop and opened the web browser.

Flash website, very healthy end-of-year accounts, dozens of positive reviews from staff and clients alike, Sequrco's clients were big, important companies—banks, pharmaceuticals and a couple of the cruise lines. They must have been raking it in, and while they stood to make a tidy sum out of investing in overseas property, it wasn't lucrative enough for them to go to the lengths of hiring PIs to track Tonka down. On Bish and Jock's part at least, Gray could safely conclude it wasn't about the money. He went back to the review site containing testimonials from their staff.

Excellent rates of pay, great working conditions, paid leave, health insurance, company vehicles, approachable bosses—give or take the occasional one star from 'dismissed and disgruntled', the comments were all much the same. Sequrco was good to its staff; it was a successful and well-respected company, all of which indicated Bish and Jock weren't in on Tonka's scheme, if indeed it was a scheme.

Whatever was going on, Gray had seen enough to be confident their clients were completely above board. He was ready for sleep, and sent a 'good night' message to Will, who would've been in bed for hours already, but apart from his text to say the police had released him, Gray hadn't heard from him all evening.

It was possible—probable—Will had gone back to the building after dark to collect the jammer from wherever he'd hidden it, or even to make a second attempt at rescuing the cats, hopefully not on his own. He and Tie were only two of a network of activists, some of whom came to the farmhouse when Gray was staying over. They all seemed decent people, even if a lot of them did look like ex-cons, stare at his boots—in judgement, not admiration—and ask too many questions about what he did for a living. He kept his answers current: *I'm a postgrad student, part-time lecturer and extra in a soap opera.*

That was usually sufficient to throw them off his ex-copper scent; somehow he didn't think Will would've shared that detail with them, if he talked to them about Gray at all. Animal libbers were a lot like undercover officers; they went by pseudonyms and used informal code when discussing cases. Unless their significant others were also 'in the job', at best they'd be the anonymous 'other half', 'the wife' or 'the husband'. Still, it was comforting to think that Will might've mentioned him in those terms.

18: Briefing

The buzz of Rob's phone vibrating wouldn't normally have woken him, but he'd slept lightly all night. He picked it up, opened his eyes long enough to confirm who was calling, hit the answer button and closed his eyes again. "Morning, Ma'am."

"Rob, is everything all right?"

"Yeah. Other than it's bloody early."

"I just picked up your voicemail from last night."

"It wasn't six a.m. urgent."

"It was eleven p.m. urgent…"

"Fair comment." Rob yawned and threw the duvet off. There was no point pretending he'd get any more sleep. He grabbed his bathrobe and talked as he walked to the bathroom. "Any idea why the Met are on my tail?"

"Are they? It's not our lot."

"I didn't think it was."

"Are you sure it's the Met?"

"Yep. Got the reg on a Mondeo up at my mum's. There's also been a van outside Zoë's—not sure on that one, though."

"That's…odd." She fell quiet for a moment. He could almost hear her mentally checking through the department's current case load. Apart from anything that had come in since Friday, which wouldn't have involved him anyway, Rob had already done that. "I wonder what the Berringers are up to."

"Why?"

"Well, I don't know that they're up to anything, but I got a call from the prison yesterday. Naomi Silvestri and Wilfred Richards planned to visit Berringer Junior next Monday."

"What the hell? Richards—"

"Is our lead witness. I know. And…I've just realised that's who Gray Fisher's seeing."

"Yeah, it is," Rob said, not that she'd asked for confirmation. "Can you order them not to visit?"

"I've spoken to the both of them and advised against it, but I can't stop them, not that I can think of any good reason why they'd want to visit Berringer."

"You think he's still pulling the strings from inside?"

"It wouldn't surprise me. When I get to the office, I'll have a look and see what I can find out. Text me that reg."

"Will do, Ma'am."

"Ahem."

"Martina."

"Better. Of course, if it is related to the Berringers, it'll be—"

"The SIU," Rob finished. He didn't try to hide his aggravation.

"At least they're looking after you."

"I guess." Small mercies. "I can't wait for the trials to be over."

"You and me both." She wanted it for his sake, not her own. After Rob had left the SIU, he'd told her as much as he could about what he'd had to do. She knew what it had cost him and how desperate he was to put that part of his life behind him once and for all.

"Can I ask you something, Rob?"

"Sure."

"Are you having a pee?"

Rob cleared his throat and flushed the loo. "No, Ma'am."

"Ugh. That's… Just go away."

Rob laughed. "Have a good one, Ma…mate."

"I'll take that over Ma'am every time. You too. Bye."

***

Gray had fallen asleep with the light on, and his laptop, which had been on his chest, was on its side next to him. He was lucky he hadn't flipped it off the bed in the night—luckier still he'd woken naturally at 6:30, seeing as he'd forgotten to set his alarm. He righted his laptop and reactivated it so he could shut it down. The screen brightened on the open message window; Will had read his 'good night' but hadn't replied, which wasn't like him. It usually produced at least a smiley, more often a comment of the 'don't you mean good morning?' variety. He'd be at work now, so calling him would have to wait until after the meeting.

In the shower, Gray contemplated the journey ahead. During peak times, there was little to choose between driving to Gatwick and taking public transport. Rush hour on the M25... But he had a car. Only a budget hatchback, admittedly, but still a car. And he loved driving. He didn't even mind sitting in traffic, although if he was going to do it, he'd need to leave within the next ten minutes.

"Who am I kidding? There is no if."

It was a little more than ten minutes later that he programmed the satnav with the postcode for the hotel and set off for their 'breakfast meeting'. The chain was listed on the clients page of Sequrco's website, which Gray took as further indication of the company's good standing. He usually avoided preconceptions, but on this occasion, he hoped they'd offer some much-needed balance. He'd experienced Rob's hostility firsthand and, irrespective of what had gone on between him and Jock in the past, the old wisdom applied: the customer was always right... until proven otherwise.

For the time of day—coming up on eight o'clock by that point—the motorways weren't too bad. He knew how to drive in heavy traffic; even at the busiest junctions, he mostly managed to keep moving, arriving at the hotel at 9:10—twenty minutes early, and time enough to squeeze in an espresso and the trip to the bathroom that would surely ensue.

The espresso was fast acting as well as excellent, and he was halfway through a second cup when Rob's bike pulled into the car park. It was one hell of a machine, and at 1000cc, not really a road bike, but Rob knew how to handle it. He stopped in a narrow space directly outside the window next to Gray's table and looked in, nodding an acknowledgement.

"You must be Rob's business partner."

So much for talking to Rob before their meeting. Gray turned to face the man who'd spoken and rose to shake his hand—the left one. "Mr. Garvey?"

"Yeah, well…I prefer Bish."

"Bish. And—"

"Jock to you." Jock leaned in as he gave Gray's hand a rough pump up and down. "Did he put up a fight?"

"Sorry?"

"Shaz, erm…Rob. About taking the job on."

"We haven't formally agreed yet that we will, Mr. Wilson."

Jock pulled his top lip between his teeth; the likeness to a British bulldog was uncanny. "You got the deposit, didn't you?"

"Yes, thanks, and we appreciate the prompt payment. Rest assured, if we can't help, you'll get it back in full." Gray was starting to understand Rob's reticence. Jock was the sort of guy who bullied to get his own way, but he was also an ex-squaddie with a long service record, used to following orders whether he agreed with them or not. "Let's get settled and order breakfast. I'm not a fan of doing business on an empty stomach."

"A man after my own heart," Jock said with a wide grin, less bulldog, more emoticon. He and Bish sat in the chairs on the other side of Gray's table. A moment later, Rob joined them.

"Sorry about that. I had to move the bike. Security kicked up a stink."

"Who was it?" Jock asked.

"Dunno. His badge was flipped. Five ten, light-brown hair, beer gut."

"Alan," Bish and Jock said together.

"He's a decent bloke," Bish defended, "just a bit of a jobsworth. D'you want me to have a word?"

"Nah. It's done now." Rob smiled quickly and picked up a menu. The other three men followed his lead. "How was the drive here?" he asked generally as he perused the selection.

"Clear for us," Bish answered.

"Yes, much the same," Gray said.

"Good stuff."

"Why do they have to do all this foreign muck?" Jock grumbled. "Continental breakfast…if I wanted a continental breakfast, I'd hop on a fucking ferry." He clapped the menu shut and sat back, arms folded. "Full English and a cuppa. That's proper breakfast."

Gray kept his eyes lowered and made a show of studying his menu, aware of Rob bristling on his left and the arrival of a member of wait staff on his right.

"Good morning. Are you ready to order?"

"I am," Bish answered. "A Full English and a pot of tea for me, please."

"Toast or fried bread with that?"

"Fried bread, please."

The waiter noted it down on their tablet and looked expectantly at Jock.

"Same here, ta."

That, too, was jotted down. Rob was next.

"Bacon toasted sandwich and coffee, please."

"Filter, cappuccino…"

"Filter, cheers."

"OK, and for you?" The waiter smiled at Gray. "Another espresso?"

"Lovely as they are, I'll be flying if I drink any more. Please can I have two croissants, butter and jam, and…a glass of orange juice?"

"Of course." The waiter scribbled once more and departed.

"What was *that*?" Jock watched the waiter leave and muttered something under his breath that sounded a lot like 'poofter'.

Gray decided to get the ball rolling rather than wait for their food to arrive. He wasn't sure how long he could tolerate Jock's bigotry without taking him to task. "OK, can we start from the beginning? Rob's given me all of the information he has, but I'd like to hear it from you two, if you don't mind?"

"Not at all," Bish said. From the way he adjusted in his seat, making himself comfortable, Gray got the feeling this was going to be a long story. "We all came out of the army at the same time—me, Jock and Tonka—five years ago, and until a month back, we hadn't seen her in a good while. What d'you reckon, Jock? Three years?"

"Yeah. She was down our way for her dad's funeral, wasn't she? We met up after."

"That's right," Bish confirmed.

"Did you stay in touch by other means?" Gray asked.

"We talked on the phone a few times—I couldn't give you dates and whatnot. She's not on social networks, so nothing like that."

"You said she got in touch last month. Was that by phone?"

"Yeah, she called Bish," Jock answered. "And—"

"Maybe Bish should explain," Rob cut in.

Jock did the lip-suck again but stayed quiet. He outsized Bish in all directions and, from what Rob had said, he'd been a higher rank than him in the army, yet Jock readily deferred and let Bish continue.

"She left a message on my mobile, short and sweet. How are ya, pop over next time you're up this way, et cetera. As it happened, we were up for a gala in Blackfriars the following weekend, so I called her back and we arranged to get together for Sunday lunch. We went to some pub not far from her gaff—three courses for twenty quid or whatever it is, you know how those places are. We were there an hour, if that, before we left and went back to the house. I was driving, but Jock and Tonka were on the beer. She gets all dewy-eyed when she's had a few, starts talking about how she's thinking of moving to Germany, how much she misses Siggy and all that jazz."

"Who's Siggy?" Gray queried.

"Her bird," Jock said.

"Not exactly," Rob argued and explained, for Gray's benefit, "They're romantically involved, but they've never officially been an item."

Jock scoffed. "They've been banging each other for twenty years. I'd say that's pretty fucking official."

"Let's leave that for now," Gray interjected before Rob could get another word out. Their breakfast also made a timely arrival, and the conversation was put on hold while they sorted out cutlery and poured tea, coffee and juice.

Jock nodded at Gray's plate. "How d'you keep going off a couple of airy bread rolls?"

Gray smiled disarmingly. "I don't, to be quite honest. I'll be starving by eleven."

"Should've gone with the Full English."

"I would've done if there'd been a vegetarian version."

"Ah. One of them salad tossers, are you?"

"I am," Gray confirmed. Beside him, Rob turned his angry growl into a clearing of the throat.

Jock picked up the HP Sauce bottle, shook it to within an inch of its life and liberally doused his breakfast. "It's meant to be healthier for you, that veggie malarkey. Low fat and all that."

"Very true." Croissants with butter and jam probably contained as much fat as the fry-up on Jock's plate, but nothing further was said about it. "So, you had drinks with Tonka," Gray prompted.

"Mmm." Bish had shoved a full rasher of bacon in his mouth and chewed at speed to get it down to an amount he could talk over. "She asked us how Ethan was doing—one of the lads who ended up in the nut house—and we didn't know." He swallowed, chasing it with a mouthful of tea and a satisfied sigh. "We hadn't visited him for ages, and she only said it to put us on a guilt trip. She'd seen him a couple of weeks before and knew good and well how he was doing."

"It worked, though," Jock said.

"Yeah, it did." Bish jabbed his fork into the other bacon rasher and lifted it from the plate. "We went to see him the week after. He'd just got out of the isolation unit, attacked one of the nurses." In went the bacon.

Jock gave Rob a supercilious nod. He'd already imparted that information, obviously. Gray heard the loud crunch of Rob tearing a chunk from his toastie. Keeping his mouth full—a wise move.

"The other thing Tonka wanted to know is if we'd seen Shaz… Rob. She'd heard you'd left the police a while ago and wondered if you'd gone back up north."

Rob swallowed in a hurry. "Where did she hear that?"

"Dunno. She didn't say."

Rob didn't do well at hiding how much that troubled him, but they could look into it later, once they'd got everything they could out of Bish and Jock.

Gray continued. "Tell me about the investment. When did she first mention that to you?"

"Beginning of last week. Her brother put her on to it—he's got money in land overseas—and said we needed to move fast. If we could buy while the price was still under ten euros, guaranteed we'd quadruple our investment."

"What's the name of the company?"

Bish shrugged, as did Jock.

"Yet you were prepared to risk a quarter of a million?"

"Tonka wouldn't screw us over," Bish said assuredly.

"No, she wouldn't," Rob agreed.

Gray turned and studied him in amazement. He'd thought Rob mistrusted everyone. "Is it an army thing?"

Rob laughed ruefully. "When it's life or death, you find out quickly who your friends are, and you stick together, come what may. There's no room for mistakes. Well, small ones…" He nodded at Bish, who wiggled his arm stump, funky-chicken style.

"I understand," Gray said.

Jock puffed air. "Don't let him fool you. He's no bloody hero. Just a cut, he said." He nudged Bish sharply with his elbow.

"It was just a cut!" Bish grumbled.

"What happened to it?" Gray asked, nodding at Bish's arm.

"Necrotising fasciitis and sepsis."

Gray grimaced without comment. Judging by the way Rob and Jock were acting, it was as gruesome as it sounded. He quickly moved on, or back, at least. "Did you give her blank cheques?"

"No, they were for a hundred and twenty-five grand each."

"Sorry. I meant was there a payee's name?"

"Ah. No. Tonka said she didn't know which of her brother's accounts it was going into. But she ripped them up—" Bish nodded at Rob "—right after you left."

"Right. So we need to look into her brother's business," Gray said.

"You're taking us on, then," Jock stated.

"Depends. What's the end goal? Find out what Tonka's up to, or find her?"

Bish shrugged; his stump bobbed and dunked into his egg yolk. He wiped it off with a napkin. "She'll have covered her tracks. You won't find out what she's up to until you find her."

"We don't investigate missing people," Gray said.

"She's not missing, she scarpered."

"Where do you think she's gone?"

"Germany—to Siggy's."

"Have you tried getting hold of Tonka? Or Siggy?"

Bish nodded. "Yep, both. Tonka's phone is out of service, Siggy says she's been in touch but she doesn't know where she is."

"Could she just be upset about the investment falling through?"

"If there was an investment to start with..." Bish replied cryptically.

"What makes you think there wasn't?"

"The way she ripped up our cheques, dramatic, like. That's not Tonka's style. If she was hacked off, she'd have told us so and sent us on our way, not put on a show."

"OK. What about her brother? Where can we get hold of him?"

"Not sure. He's away a lot on business. Try his secretary."

"And who's that?"

Bish's nose wrinkled. "Dunno that he's got one for sure, but he must have. So, are you gonna do this for us? We can pay you more if need be. Just name your price."

"That's a generous offer, Bish, but unnecessary at this stage." Gray glanced Rob's way. "Do you want to discuss it further in private?"

Rob shook his head but left it a good minute before he turned to Bish and Jock and said, "We'll take the case."

***

After they'd had another pot of tea each and availed themselves of the hotel's facilities, Bish and Jock departed, leaving Gray and Rob to discuss their next steps.

"I'm gonna have to go myself," Rob said. He was out of his seat and heading for the Gents' before Gray could confirm that was where he'd meant rather than home. With a few minutes to fill, Gray checked his phone for messages and tried to convince himself the absence of such from Will simply meant he was having a busy morning, not that he'd been arrested again. He didn't succeed and called Will's mobile.

It rang on but didn't go to voicemail, and reached the point where Gray thought he ought to hang up before Will answered with a neutral, "Hey."

"Hey, are you OK?" The question came out in a rush with the breath he'd been holding.

"Yeah, I'm fine." Will was distracted, offhand, probably in company. "What are you up to?" he asked.

"Just had a meeting with our first clients. How about you?"

"Stuck in traffic." Not in company, therefore. "How did it go?"

"Very well. It's an interesting one."

"Good. I'm glad it's working out for you and Rob."

"Thanks." Any less heartfelt congratulations Gray had yet to hear. "What's up?"

"Nothing. Why?"

"You sound...angry."

"Do I?"

"Are you angry?"

"Could be."

"Why?"

"No one reason. Crappy week, that's all."

"With work?"

"Work's fine."

"Headache?"

"It comes and goes. Nothing I can't handle. It's all the other stuff."

Gray floundered. He wanted to ask about the cats but wasn't sure if he was asking out of concern for their welfare or merely to avoid the patently obvious: Will's anger was directed at him, and he had no idea why. There was only one way to find out. "Does that other stuff include me?"

"You're a part of it, yep."

"What've I done?"

"You tell me."

"I genuinely don't know."

"Really? Then you'll be surprised to hear Detective Chief Inspector Hedley called yesterday and barred me from going to see Freddie."

"Did she?"

"Huh. OK, you do sound surprised."

"That's because I am. I haven't seen Hedley since last Friday."

"But you have seen Rob," Will pointed out.

"Yes. But I didn't tell him you were going to see Berringer."

"Come on! You two have been working closely all week."

"Rob only got back from his mum's yesterday. We met for an hour and then again today—with our clients. The only time you've come up in conversation was when I got your text about being released without charge."

"So how did Hedley know?"

"Maybe Aaron or Naomi told her?"

"They didn't. You realise they're gonna have to go on their own now?"

Gray was starting to lose his cool. "I didn't tell Rob, or Martina Hedley, or *anyone at all* that you were going to see Berringer. If I had, I'd have told you."

"OK," Will accepted but his tone made clear he still didn't believe Gray.

"What's happening with the cats?" It was a lousy attempt to change the subject.

"Long story. I'll tell you at the weekend…if you're still coming over."

"Fine. I'm going. I'm sorry you're upset, Will, but you're taking it out on the wrong person." Gray ended the call without waiting for a reply. He was angry too, although not so much that he couldn't see the situation from Will's point of view.

19: Aftermath

"I tell you what, you're lucky you didn't have the bacon." Rob resumed his seat and immediately chugged down a full glass of water.

"Salty?" Gray asked.

"Just a bit." Rob poured another glass and knocked back half of it. It had taken the edge off his thirst enough for him to notice Gray's mood had gone for a Burton. "You OK?"

"Yes, thanks." He covered whatever it was with a smile. "Productive meeting, I thought?"

None of Rob's business. "Definitely. So, plan of action?" He unlocked his phone and loaded the notes app.

"You still want me to look into the investment side?"

"If that's all right with you. I'm gonna get in touch with Siggy, see if Tonka will talk to me, assuming she's there and Siggy's not covering for her. I'll try and contact her brother as well. Their mum died a long time ago—I didn't know about their dad. Tonka was very close to him."

"That's sad," Gray said somewhat perfunctorily. "OK. While you're doing that, I'll see if I can find out what Tonka's brother's up to business-wise. Do you know his full name?"

"Philip Parker. Not sure on a middle name."

"That should be enough to pull him up on the national…" Gray sagged and stuck out his bottom lip. "Bugger."

Rob laughed. "Google?"

"I suppose it'll have to do. I'd say it's like losing an arm, but Bish manages all right. Aside from table manners."

"Ha, yeah. I almost offered to cut up his breakfast."

"I wish you had. He seems a nice guy, though."

"He is. And Jock's mellowed."

Gray raised an eyebrow. "He gave you hell, didn't he?"

"To be honest, he was no worse than anyone else—outside of our unit. The army's rife with racism, or it was when I joined up. It's better now, but Tonka never tolerated his bullshit. When it comes down to it, he's all mouth, and he stuck up for me when it mattered. By the way, have you always been veggie?"

"No."

"Thought not. Will's doing?"

"Hmm. There's only so long you can keep enjoying lamb chops and sirloin steak when you've heard enough about the inner workings of a slaughterhouse to write a thesis."

"I don't think I want to know."

"Neither did I," Gray said glibly. "Anyway, where were we?"

"Tonka's brother."

"Right. If he's actively trading, he shouldn't be too hard to track down. Even if he's not, he should show up in Companies House listings."

"I wonder if he took on the farm?" Rob thought aloud. "I know their parents weren't happy about Tonka joining the army, and I'm sure she said Phil was still involved in the family business."

"OK. I'll look into that too."

"And I suppose I'd better talk to Ethan," Rob said reluctantly. "If she really was planning to clear his record, I doubt he'd tell me, but she might've let something else slip."

"If it's easier for you, I could talk to him," Gray offered.

"Nah, it's all right. It's not like I've got to take the guy out for a pint and fake civility. And haven't you got enough to do already?"

Gray nodded in acquiescence. "We've got a couple of avenues each to explore. Any theories at this stage?"

"I dunno. It all feels like a bit of a wild goose chase, or is it just me?"

"No, I agree," Gray said. "Like you say, the investment and ID might only be to throw us off her scent."

"Or they're trails to our next set of clues," Rob suggested. "Nice hunting analogy, by the way."

Gray laughed. "The joys of having a hunt saboteur for a boyfriend."

"Yeah. You know, before dealing with the Berringers, I hadn't realised it still went on. I'm amazed Will didn't take them down a long time ago." Of course, Rob knew why Will had stayed quiet. Freddie Berringer claimed to have photos of Will leaving a lab seconds before it was destroyed by explosives, but the photos had 'mysteriously' vanished between Berringer's arrest and the full search of his apartment—Rob had an idea he knew where to. "I don't recall you referring to him as your boyfriend before."

"It's a recent development—on my part." Gray's eyes became distant, and for a while he was lost in thought. He shook himself out of it and smiled wistfully. "How is it that as soon as you acknowledge the emotional commitment, it all goes to pot?"

Rob nodded sagely. He knew that feeling.

"I called Will while you were visiting the loo. He..." Gray hesitated then raised his hands in a shrug. "You'll find out sooner or later, anyway. He was intending to accompany Aaron-Naomi to visit Freddie Berringer. Somehow, Hedley caught wind of it and ordered him not to. He accused me of ratting him out."

"Harsh."

"And false. I haven't said a word to anyone."

"The prison told Hedley," Rob said. "I spoke to her this morning."

"I thought that was the case, but Will wasn't listening to reason. The truth is, he's a bit of an anarchist—very anti-establishment. He forgets sometimes who he's talking to and goes on a full-scale rant about the extent of corruption within the criminal justice system."

"He's got a point."

"He has, but he also thinks we're all in cahoots. Since last weekend, he's shared his plans with me twice. Before that, he only told me what he'd been up to after the event, and idiot me thought it was because I'd finally made my commitment clear. Now I realise he was testing the waters to see if you and I could be trusted to not go running to the police."

"Sounds like it's me he doesn't trust, not you," Rob contended, although he was thinking Gray had been closer to the mark the first time.

"As that may be, you and I are working together. I'd like to think one day we'll be friends, if we're not already. I'm not seeking reassurance, just being honest. I consider you a friend. I trust and respect you, and it's important to me that Will does too."

It was as well Gray had added the part about not seeking reassurance; in all good conscience, Rob couldn't offer it. As a colleague, yes; the trust and respect was mutual. As a friend? That would take a bit longer. "Any idea why they were going to see Freddie?"

"Unfinished business, so Aaron said. Or so Will said Aaron said."

"You're second-guessing, Gray."

"It's hard not to. You saw the way he was at Berringer's apartment. Smooth, assertive, putting words in people's mouths—he's a con man."

"He's never used those skills to break the law."

"To our knowledge, but he uses them in court. I was at his friend's trial a couple of months back. They called Will as a witness, and he effectively lied through his teeth. Tie got community service—for a fourth offence—and Will's in exactly the same boat. He should've had at least one custodial sentence by now."

"It's all mind games, Gray. You really can't judge him badly for that. Lawyers do it and get paid handsomely for the privilege. You've got to admit, it bodes well for Berringer's trial."

"There is that, I suppose. Do you want me to see what else he knows?"

Rob eyed Gray, gauging his motive. "Are you intentionally trying to cause a rift?"

"Don't you mean widen it? I'm not, as it happens. I wasn't planning to coerce him. In fact, I'll tell him I'm asking on your behalf. How's that?"

Rob was no expert on relationships, but if he'd ever tried something like that on Zoë, he'd have been out the door carrying his balls in his helmet. "If he tells you anything else, and he's happy for you to pass it on…"

Gray grinned. "I'll see what I can do."

"Lunatic."

"In remission."

"Yeah, if you like," Rob said drolly. "Is there anything else we need to discuss?"

"No, we're done, I think." Gray unhooked his jacket from the back of his chair and shrugged into it. He left a tip on the table—Bish had paid the bill earlier—and the two of them walked out together. Gray pointed his key fob and clicked; the car closest to them beeped and flashed its lights.

Rob gave the car a brief once-over. "That's dinky…for you."

"For surveillance purposes—I was aiming to blend in. Where's your bike?"

Rob pointed to the far side of the car park. "I'm gonna catch up with Hedley on my way home. I'm not happy that Tonka and Jock were able to get hold of my info so easily. I don't mind either of them having it, but it needs to come from me."

"OK. I'll email you."

"Likewise. See you later." Rob moved off. "Oh, and Gray?"

"Yeah?"

"Don't do anything stupid."

Momentarily, Gray looked stunned, but then smiled. "I might be able to manage that."

***

"Here he is, the waster."

"They seek him here…"

"They seek him there…"

"Who is that helmeted man?"

"Yeah, yeah." Rob dismissed the jibes and asked generally, "How's it going?"

Tang nodded noncommittally as he wandered past, empty cup in one hand, scratching his backside with the other.

Miller lifted the topmost sheet on his desk, scowled at it, and slammed it back onto the pile. "Same as ever."

There were a few other officers about, but Tang, Miller and Hedley were the only ones left from 'the old days', before Rob had joined the SIU—almost five years ago. Times like this, bantering with his former colleagues, it was the same feeling as coming back from leave—the permanent stacks of long overdue paperwork on Miller's desk, the dead coffee machine shoved in the corner to make way for the all-new-and-unimproved coffee machine, Tang's Itchy and Scratchy performance—even the new faces bore some resemblance to the officers whose places they'd taken. Rob felt like he'd never been away.

Then he pictured the toddler who could barely string three words together yet almost every combination included 'Daddy', who became the five-year-old wary of the stranger who knew his name. Lucas had never forgotten him, not entirely, but schoolfriends, footy and hating homework had filled the hole his dad had left. Rob knew what it had to look like through his son's eyes: a short eternity.

"Are you hanging around a bit?"

It took a moment for Miller's question to filter through Rob's bleak reminiscence. "I popped in to see the DCI, but I will do if she's due back soon. Where is she? Do you know?"

"Interview suite, talking to that Naomi Tanner."

"Oh? What's she doing here?"

"You'd have to ask Hedley that. What d'you make of her?"

"Hedley?"

"No, Tanner, you balloon."

"I don't understand what you're asking." Rob understood *exactly* what Miller was asking, but hedged his bets in case he was wrong. No point kicking off without good reason.

"I mean her being a tranny. Well…him, I suppose. Like RuPaul. Mind, I won't deny he looks hot in a frock."

"Miller…" Rob wasn't sure how to handle the remark, but he couldn't let it pass. "You're out of order."

"Why? It's the truth."

"Apart from the fact it's a derogatory term—"

"Transvestite. That better?"

Rob sighed, his patience already depleted. "Just shut up, will you, Miller?"

"What's wrong with that?"

"If you're describing yourself, nothing. Otherwise? It's none of your business."

"He's not a transvestite," Tang said on his way back with two mugs of coffee. "He's like that officer with the two warrant cards." He handed one of the mugs to Rob, who did a quick recap to confirm he wasn't taking it from the hand Tang had been scratching with.

"Exactly. So he's one of those—" Miller started.

"With all due respect, Sarge, shut the fuck up." Tang turned his back on Miller and lowered his voice, addressing Rob. "We were talking about it, Aaron Tanner and me, when we were sat outside the court. He says that's what it's like for him and Naomi."

Rob's coffee was too hot and tasted like crap, but drinking it saved him from having to give a response. He'd had the same conversation with Naomi about the Met's first openly gender-fluid PC; Tang bringing it up outside the courtroom before Charles Berringer's remand hearing had given Aaron a panic attack. Freddie Berringer's hearing had been the following day, but it was Naomi in attendance and she brought it up with Rob, not the other way around. She was excited, knowing there was someone like her and Aaron, and impressed by the Met's support of the officer in question. It went without saying that the old guard blamed the public's lack of faith on what they saw as another crazy scheme of 'political correctness gone mad'. There again, they took issue with change of any kind, even when it was to their benefit.

Rob had to wonder if he hadn't met Aaron-Naomi whether he, too, would have considered the two separate warrant cards a step too far. It was hard to imagine a completely sane person having two entirely distinct personas, yet he'd seen it for himself. Aaron and Naomi had little in common beyond their height, build and complexion, and even those seemed to morph, retuning themselves to match the person inside. Beyond Aaron's social anxiety, they were both compos mentis.

"You can't keep away, can you?" Hedley murmured close to his right ear.

"Apparently not."

She sidled past him and propped on the corner of Miller's desk. "Social visit?"

Rob frowned, weighing up the value of an honest answer.

"No, then," Hedley concluded. "What's up?"

"My old army mates know stuff about me they shouldn't. I want to know how they found out."

"What sort of stuff?"

"My resignation...I think. It might've been when I was undercover. And one of them reckons someone at the station gave him my phone number."

"That's highly unlikely."

"I thought that."

"Any mutual acquaintances? Former REMEs in the job?"

"Not that I know of."

"OK. Well, we can check out his story." Hedley reached across the desk for Miller's phone, knocking his papers askew. He grunted. She flashed a not even a little bit apologetic smile and dialled an internal number. "When was it?" she asked Rob.

"Last week sometime. Friday, possibly. He phoned in."

She nodded, listening to whoever had answered her call. "Hi, it's DCI Hedley. Can you do me a favour? Check the incoming call record from last Friday to see if there were any relating to Rob Simpson-Stone?" She paused. "He's checking. I'm not sure about the resignation leak. Grapevine?"

"I'd only told family and friends up north."

"So it would've had to come from HR—hello, yes. Still here. ... OK, thanks. What about earlier in the week?" Hedley asked and then told Rob, "Not on Friday."

The pause that followed was worryingly long. Rob really hoped Jock hadn't lied to him. The implications for their investigation were enormous.

Finally, Hedley said, "And that was Thursday...1809. Got it. Thanks for your help." She hung up. "Miller?"

"Yes, Ma'am?"

"Did you phone last Thursday to get Rob's mobile number?"

"What do you think? I was sitting right here!"

"With the same paperwork in front of you, no doubt." Hedley shuffled around to face Rob. "Whoever took the call assumed it was Miller. Any thoughts?"

"Yeah," he confirmed with undisguised relief. "Jock and Miller sound pretty similar. It backs up what Jock said." It didn't answer the question of how Tonka had known about Rob's resignation or his undercover work—Bish had been vague—but it could've made it onto the gossip mill, he supposed. "Cheers for chasing it up for me."

"You're welcome. On the other one...you could see if HR have had any reference requests. That's the only way I can think an outside agency could leech info like that."

"I'll call them later," Rob said. "So, Naomi Silvestri's been in to see you, I hear?"

"Yeah. Just. Oh! That's what I needed to ask you. What name did she sign on her statements?"

"Naomi Silvestri, also known as Aaron Tanner, and vice versa on Aaron's."

"I thought so. The Berringers' lawyers are having a field day with them, as we expected. They're claiming Naomi's is a false statement intended to draw attention away from Tanner's misdemeanours."

"Is that why she's going to see Freddie?"

"She wouldn't divulge. I told her there's nothing he can do from where he is—I even threatened her with contempt of court. She didn't fall for it."

That made Rob smile. Aaron and Naomi were unbelievably intelligent, and savvy, and they were testifying against Charles, not Freddie. Thus, whilst there were plenty of common-sense reasons why they shouldn't visit Freddie, there was nothing legally stopping them.

"Right, I'll let you get on, Ma'am. Martina." Rob gave himself a smack on the head. "I'll get it eventually. See you, Miller."

"Detective Sergeant," Miller corrected with a cheesy grin.

"In your dreams. In a bit, Ste," Rob called to Tang, who waved without looking up from his sloth-like, one-finger typing.

"Don't forget you owe me a pint," Hedley called after Rob.

"At least," Rob agreed, ignoring the chorus of 'and me's as he disappeared through the door and went downstairs to sign out. He reached the bike, and looked back at the station; it was a much nicer place to visit than work. He flipped his helmet to put it on, and stopped.

"Naomi?" He hadn't meant to say it out loud until he was sure. His pulse quickened as he ran through the mental checklist—dark-brown straightened hair longer than the last time they'd seen each other; tall, slender; designer clothes cut to accentuate curves; skin like creamy caramel—to confirm it was her.

At first, it appeared she hadn't heard him. She glanced behind her and took a step or two more before she stopped and walked back, smiling all the while. He left his helmet on the bike seat and walked to meet her.

"Rob, hi! I thought it was your day off."

"Nope." He grinned, thinking he should say more but not quite sure of the order in which to say it. So he didn't look like a complete twerp, he asked, "How are you?"

"Very well, thanks." Her lightly glossed lips parted, deepest pink against whitest white teeth. He stared at her mouth; he couldn't help it. She noticed and laughed, then bashfully bit down on her bottom lip. "I just had them whitened."

"Sorry?"

"My teeth?"

Rob shook his head, bamboozled, catching on a second later. "Oh! They're...great. I mean, they look good on you." He squeezed the key in his fist until it hurt. "What are you doing here?" Tact of a brick through a plate-glass window.

Naomi's smile faded, her eyebrows drawing together in a sudden and surprisingly angry frown. "What is this? Some kind of good cop, bad cop routine to talk me out of it?"

"Talk you out of...going to see Berringer?" Rob guessed.

"So you do know."

"Well, yeah. I can't say I get why you're going, but I'm not here to stop you."

Naomi's breathing was fast and harsh, her folded arms tight against her chest. She'd been expecting a fight, and Rob wasn't sure why.

"What did the DCI have to say about it?" he asked.

"She suggested an officer escort me."

"Sounds like a decent compromise."

"I told her I'd only agree if it was you, and she told me you couldn't, so it looks like I'm going on my own." She smiled swiftly, sarcastically.

Rob mirrored her pose and shifted his weight to one foot, reducing his height by a couple of inches—enough to bring him down to Naomi's eye level. "I'm not happy about that," he said.

"So? What can you do?"

He shrugged. "Not a lot." She and Aaron had ignored his advice before—even when they'd asked for it—knowing full well he was trying to keep them safe. They were strong-willed and acted on impulse when under duress. It didn't bode well for a lone meeting with Freddie Berringer. "I could come with you. When are you going?"

"Next Monday. But...won't DCI Hedley have something to say about it?"

"More than likely." Hedley had something to say about everything, but he was on his own time now. She could like it or not. "Look...can we go for a coffee or something?"

"I'd love to, but I need to get home and change. Aaron has an online conference in an hour."

"Fair enough," Rob said cheerily to hide his disappointment. "Have you still got my number?"

"I have."

"Good stuff. And I've got yours. Give me a call or something and we'll sort out arrangements for Monday, yeah? If you want to. It's up to you."

Naomi studied him carefully, gauging his intent. "I'll give it some thought," she said, already turning away. "Speak soon."

"I look forward to it." Rob watched her hurry away towards the Underground station.

It was only when she disappeared into the crowd of other passengers that it dawned on him she didn't know he'd left the police. He took out his phone to text her, but changed his mind. It might influence her decision, and there was no predicting the direction. It could wait until Monday.

20: Intuition

Gray was making progress. Slowly. Less than snail pace. In the better part of two days, the only fact he'd established for certain was that Parker Farms was a remarkably successful company limited by guarantee, of which Tonka and her brother Philip were two of six guarantors, the rest extended family members, individually wealthy and more than capable of coming good on their financial commitments to the company should it ever go bust.

Not that it was likely. There were no shareholders and no debts; the accounts were up to date, and all reports had been submitted to Companies House. Indeed, Parker Farms was so squeaky clean, Gray was instantly and enduringly suspicious, in spite of having read through every report, every annual statement—every single last document he could find. No bad press, no unhappy customers or employees, no complaints from neighbours about noise or light pollution, the smell of cow muck, mud on roads, too many Land Rovers... Nothing.

That was two for two on the perfect business front, and Gray was beginning to wonder if he should be looking behind the scenes for a PR company working with both Sequrco and Parker Farms. It wasn't...*normal*, and not just by SIU standards, which, admittedly, negatively skewed his expectations. Every company had some financial skeletons in the boardroom closet.

As for Philip Parker's Eastern-European investments, Gray had found no evidence of investment activity, which begged the question of whether there was any credibility whatsoever to the yarn Tonka had spun Bish and Jock.

Something didn't fit. Two siblings running an honest-to-goodness family business worth £100m seemed an unlikely duo to be ripping off their friends for a relative pittance. That or it was a long con with thousands of victims, except Gray had seen the accounts, and there were no irregularities, as far as he could tell. Added to that, Rob had spoken with Philip and Tonka's neighbours, both in London and the Southwest, who had only good things to say about the Parkers.

With every last avenue exhausted, Gray quit all open windows, got up from his chair, sat down again and switched off his computer lest he was tempted to waste what was left of the evening looking over the same information duplicated elsewhere. It was Friday, almost seven p.m.; yesterday evening, he'd forgotten to eat—no surprise there. The argument with Will had played on his mind every time he stopped thinking about the investigation, and his appetite was non-existent.

He wouldn't have cared to estimate the number of times he'd almost called Will, only to abandon the idea at the last second. It would be better to wait and talk face-to-face—less chance of misunderstanding—or that was the theory at war with his desire to resolve their differences posthaste.

Now to while away the hours until bedtime; he had essays to grade, but he was mentally exhausted. He could visit the local pub, but that didn't appeal, so he made a cup of tea and sat down to watch TV. After ten minutes of flicking through the schedule and finding nothing that took his fancy, he relented and went to bed. It wasn't even nine o'clock and had to be his earliest night since his teens.

Alas, early to bed went hand in hand with early to rise, and with his brain replenished, his thoughts raced ahead of him, from the shower back to the bedroom and downstairs to the kitchen for coffee, forming new questions he could've answered in a jiffy if he'd still had access to the SIU's resources.

He supposed, in a way, it was more fun doing it without those tools at his disposal—more of a treasure hunt, a mystery to be solved. Or, at least, it would be if Gray had half a clue what he was doing. He thought back to his final SIU investigation, and how Josh—almost to spite Gray's refusal to give him access—had uncovered so many facts from so little information.

It was the complete opposite to Gray's established method of gathering every piece of information at his disposal and trawling through, discarding the irrelevant until he'd narrowed it down to a set of testable possibilities. In contrast, Josh dug into the minutiae, sifting out the smallest, inconsequential snippets and turning them over and over like a competitive gardener preparing his seedbeds. He cross-checked, trawled for more to corroborate, and re-examined his evidence, from which he conjured a conclusion.

Perhaps 'conjured' was the wrong word; Josh was no sorcerer, but from Gray's vantage point it looked like advanced magic, and he needed to know how Josh did it. Was it something he could learn? Would Josh be prepared to give away his secrets? There was one sure way to find out.

"Graham! I was just thinking about you."

"Should I be worried?"

"Potentially. How is everything?"

"Yes, good," Gray answered straight away, knowing even the slightest hesitation would be subjected to rigorous analysis. "And with you?"

"As well as one can hope. So…what do you want?"

"Charming! I could have just called to see how you are."

"At seven o'clock on a Saturday morning?"

"It's possible."

"You didn't."

"No, you're quite right. I want to tap into your expertise, if I may?"

"Aren't you still having therapy with Sean?"

"Your other area of expertise."

"Profiling?"

Gray laughed. "The *other* other one."

"You've lost me."

"Research."

"Ah. See, it would've been much easier if you'd been less... elusive."

"Sorry, but you will have such a wealth of skills."

"Flattery will get you nowhere, or no further than simply asking outright. What do you want to know?"

"Rob and I have our first case, and I'm struggling to isolate the finer details. I want to know how you do it."

"You're a former police officer and a postgrad student. You know how."

"I read old books, analyse and critique. You're a social scientist."

"The principles are the same. If not in your literary work, then your detective work."

"And herein lies the problem. I'm so used to having the info at my fingertips, I've forgotten how to detect."

"I see. Well, contrary to where you began this conversation, I'm no expert, but I can tell you how I do it if you feel it would help."

"It's not a trade secret?"

"Hardly. I teach a simplified version to my students to help them elaborate their arguments."

"What's the process?"

"I begin by assigning every piece of information its own cube."

"Cube?"

"Six-sided, three-dimensional—"

"You can skip the geometry lesson."

"Testy this morning, aren't we?" Josh tormented. "Are you having trouble sleeping?"

"Josh, please?"

"You can tell me afterwards. My technique will make perfect sense if you allow me to explain." Josh paused, expecting an interruption, but Gray had his lips tightly sealed. Josh continued. "I visualise writing each piece of information—established facts, theories, intuitive feelings—onto the front faces of blank cubes, or, rather, a mental representation. Any new information is added to the relevant cube or allocated a new one."

"Wouldn't Post-its do the same job?"

"Not exactly, although they might work better for you."

"As a novice, you mean?"

"Your words, Graham, not mine. The benefit of cubes is they can be shaken and thrown like dice, which randomly brings up different combinations. Of course, it's not actually random at all; it's a mental representation governed by unconscious choice."

"I don't think I've got the right kind of brain for this."

"Perhaps not. Do you possess any Post-its?"

"I believe so." He knew so. "Hold on." Gray went up to his office, to his 'teacher's bag'—a thing he'd hoped never to own—and rifled through the dry-wipe markers and other sundries until he found a dog-eared slab of Post-its. "OK. Got them."

"Different colours, perchance?"

"Stock yellow."

"How about coloured pens or pencils?"

He only had the dry-wipe markers. "Will red, green, black and blue do?"

"Perfectly. Now, write down one piece of concrete information about the case."

"Colour?"

"Pick one."

"OK. I'll go with…blue. The pens are quite thick."

"Use shorthand."

Gray stared at the blank yellow square and tried to think. He had the gist of Josh's method already and would have been happy to have a go at flying solo but played along and wrote *Parker Farms – wealthy, solvent.*

"Have you ever used a memory palace?" he asked, pulling off the top sheet and sticking it to the desk so he could write on the next: *shell company?*

"Method of loci—yes, and this isn't the same. Repeat the process until you've recorded all of the established facts."

Gray screwed up *shell company?*—very much not an 'established fact' when it had just popped into his head—and thought back over his research of the past two days. What else did he know for sure?

Bish and Jock are loyal, he wrote and then screwed that up too. He only had Rob's word for it, plus his perception—nothing more than a strong inkling. Or was it? They'd been prepared to go in blind on Tonka's say-so; that struck him as very loyal. Or gullible. He switched the blue pen for the green and jotted it down again to come back to later. On the next sheet, he wrote: *Overseas property investment – money laundering?* He wasn't sure where that had come from. It certainly hadn't occurred to him until that moment.

"Are you done?" Josh asked.

"Hold on." His thoughts were tumbling out faster than he could write, resulting in barely legible scribble of the highlights from the meeting with Bish and Jock until his entire desk was covered in yellow paper squares. "I'm done."

"OK. Next, jot down what you think you know—any theories or ideas for which you have no evidence yet."

"Done that already."

"In a different colour?"

"Yes."

"Excellent." Josh's praise always sounded condescending, though Gray liked to think it was genuine. "Is there anything you've put down that, at first glance, seems irrelevant?"

"All of it?"

Josh laughed. "Come on, Graham. This isn't hard."

"It'd be a walk in the park if I had access to the PNC."

"But you haven't. Don't think about it, just pick one."

Gray sighed and scanned the notes, homing in on *Overseas property investment – money laundering?* "OK."

"Put a tick next to it."

"Why?"

"Because it means something."

"This is getting ridiculous."

"You asked me to show you how I do it…"

"Fine, fine. What's next?"

"Focus on that note."

"Focusing…" Gray didn't mean to be flippant, but he couldn't see the point. "I don't hold much stock in intuition."

"What about policeman's intuition?"

"Application of stereotypes—not the same, but equally unreliable."

"Ah, he sees!"

"I don't."

"That's precisely the point. The key is to examine the root and establish whether it's reliable. If it isn't, you can discard the information. Probably."

"Probably? That doesn't sound very scientific."

"Something gave this particular note primacy."

"Or I'm hankering after my old job."

"It's a possibility. What does it say?"

"Overseas property investment as money laundering."

"Why did you write it?"

"The majority of money laundering cases I worked involved funds crossing national borders. But there's no evidence the target is investing in anything outside of their legitimate business. Although…" He hit the power button on his computer.

"You've thought of something," Josh said.

"It's a long shot. They used the same firm of accountants for twenty-five years, and then switched to another company a few months into the last recession. Before that, the estates expenditure consisted of multiple entries. The more recent accounts record it as one lump sum, and I didn't check if it was in line with previous years. I'm just waiting for the computer to start up."

"While we wait, you can tell me about your argument with Will."

"My…" The word fell away with the chin drop. "What makes you think we've had an argument?"

"We've been on the phone for half an hour and you haven't so much as uttered his name."

"Because we've been otherwise occupied."

"Am I wrong?"

"I didn't say that." When Josh didn't quip back at him, Gray relented with a sigh. "Yes, we kind of had an argument. I told you about the murder trial, didn't I?"

"The toff who killed a hunt saboteur?"

"That's the one. Will had plans to visit him in prison but the police intervened. He accused me of telling them."

"And did you?" Josh asked.

Gray bristled. "Thanks for the vote of confidence."

"OK, so, you didn't."

"No, I didn't, and I'm hurt he doesn't trust me."

"Do you trust him?"

"Of course I do!" Gray winced at how defensive he sounded, but it was true. Mostly true. His computer was up and running, giving him a chance to cool down. He opened the folder containing the downloaded spreadsheets of Parker Farms' accounts. "We're still getting to know each other," he reasoned.

Josh didn't say anything—not that he needed to when Gray could see for himself.

"I'm going to talk to him about it later."

"Good."

"OK, these figures…" Eager to move on, Gray ran a few quick calculations and scratched his head. "It's not a significant change. Twenty-five thousand—a five percent increase, on average. That's not enough to purchase real estate."

"Do you think you can safely discard that information?"

"It looks like it." He felt quite despondent, but he had a whole desk full of Post-its to work through yet, and there was still something niggling him about that change from multiple to single entries. "I think I've got this now," he said.

"Are you sure?"

"Yeah. I hit a mental block. Thanks for helping me push it out of the way."

"Any time, Graham. I hope you fix things with Will."

"I'm sure we'll be fine. I'll see you…soon, hopefully."

"How soon?" Josh asked suspiciously.

He'd had a brainwave about popping across the Pennines to visit Josh, George and Libby while they were up that way for Will's daughter, which rolled into *I should ask Will first*, and from there into wondering if Will was really OK with Gray's admission of his feelings towards Josh. "Summer, perhaps?" he bluffed.

"Hmm. Until the next time…" Josh hung up.

Gray stared at the monitor, or through it. If they were still off with each other in a fortnight, Will would be visiting Suzannah alone. Better to take it day by day and then decide. He refocused on the document and scanned the figures again, absently running the cursor back and forth over each spreadsheet entry. As he did so, it changed from an arrow to a pointing finger. Gray clicked, and his email programme opened. He broke into a grin.

"Well, hello, Hilary Gelling. What are you doing here?" It was too easy, but at least he had a jumping-off point.

***

"Anyone home?" Gray closed the door and took a couple of steps into the kitchen. "What on earth…?" There was an enormous glass tank, complete with sand, rocks and a chunk of tree, taking up most of the kitchen table.

"Tie?" Will appeared in the hallway. "Early fin— Oh, hey." He continued into the kitchen with his head down. "I didn't expect to see you today."

"It's Saturday. Haven't you been to work?"

"Called in sick."

"Headache?"

"Yep."

Ah." Gray pointed at the glass tank. "What's that?"

"Bearded dragon."

"A *dragon*, did you say?"

"Yeah. It's a kind of lizard. Holly found it in the woods earlier in the week. Turns out she's a terrific little terrier."

"Not the fire-spitting creature of myth and legend, then?"

"Nope, she's definitely a dog." In spite of his joke, Will remained solemn.

Gray took a cautious step closer and peered through the glass, though he couldn't see much. "Is it injured?"

"No. I don't think so." Will frowned and came over to look for himself.

"Where is it?"

"Behind the rock."

Gray squinted and thought he saw movement, but it could have been his eyelashes. "Are you going to release it?"

"Release it?" Will clearly thought Gray's suggestion was absurd, but then something must have clicked and he *almost* smiled. "No, it's not a native species. I put a call out online to see if one had escaped from anywhere nearby. No-one's claimed it—they probably turned it out on purpose when it got too big."

"A dragon is for life…" Gray mused. He'd yet to lay eyes on it but imagined he'd only be disappointed when he did. "You're still sulking about Monday, aren't you?"

"A little bit. I'll get over it." Will sighed and rubbed his temples. "My head's banging."

"Have you taken anything?"

He laughed ruefully, wincing with the motion.

"Would a massage help?"

"It can't make it any worse."

Gray pulled out a dining chair, and Will sighed again as he sat. Freeing his hair from its ponytail, he flicked it back over his shoulders. Gray caught a whiff of lavender. "You'd rather smell like my gran's wardrobe than take paracetamol?"

Will's answering chuckle was little more than a deep hum in his throat.

"OK, let's see what's going on here…" With his palms on either side of Will's neck, Gray pressed his thumbs lightly against Will's nape and alternated between circling and smoothing upwards along the tight muscles.

"That feels good."

"Does it?"

"Yeah. It's um…" He breathed out heavily. "It's starting to get me down."

"Are they always this bad?"

"The past couple of weeks, they have been. Usually, they come and go, but this has been more or less constant for days."

"The muscles are very tight."

Will's shoulders tensed, and Gray eased off a little.

"Sorry," Gray said.

"I'm sorry too."

"Don't be. To tell you the truth, I've been so caught up in the case, I completely forgot about you going to see Freddie or I would've mentioned it to Rob—not to tattle." Gray worked his fingers into Will's hair, slowly travelling up his scalp to his crown and around to his temples.

Will leaned back with his eyes closed and a contented half-smile. "Because you trust him."

"Yeah, but if I'd told him, he'd likely have told Hedley, so your assumption was reasonable."

Will slid down the chair. "Don't stop, will you?"

"Is it helping?"

"I don't care. It's nice."

Gray laughed. "Then I'll keep going." He worked his way back down to Will's neck to give his arms a rest. "Have you spoken to Naomi?"

"Yep. I asked her not to go and see Freddie on her own. She made no promises." Will's neck muscles tightened again. Gray went back to circling and smoothing.

"What do you think this business is between them?"

"I'm not sure there is any—well, other than that they're still in love with each other."

"Wasn't Freddie and…I can't remember her name…"

"Carrie."

"That's it. Weren't they getting married?"

"Until he got locked up. Carrie's family won't want anything to do with the Berringers now, but she's always known about Freddie and Naomi….ouch!"

"Hmm…perhaps we should change the subject."

"Yeah. How's the case going?"

"Not well. What do you know about property prices in Eastern Europe?"

"Very low before the banking crisis, though it varies by country. Some have lost value, some have gained."

"What would twenty-five thousand get you?"

"Stirling or euros?"

"Stirling."

"Are you looking to buy a holiday home?" Will turned to grin. Gray pushed his cheek to get him to face front again.

"Is it enough to buy a house?"

"At a push, but it's not a good investment. You'd make very little from reselling, and timeshare is dead. Agricultural land is where the money's at. It's dirt cheap. A lot of Western-European farmers upped sticks before Bulgaria, Slovakia, Lithuania and a few others imposed legal restrictions. The EU have threatened sanctions."

"Agricultural land…" Gray echoed. "That's it!" He leaned down and planted a firm kiss on Will's forehead that made him flinch. "You are brilliant."

21: Out of Water

"Hang on," Rob called as Lucas made for the stairs to the bus's top deck, but he was already out of sight. Rob waited in line to board, flashed their travel passes at the driver and set off after his son. The bus from the swimming pool back to the house was almost always a double-decker, yet Lucas acted as if it were a novelty every time. Rob couldn't really complain when he'd been exactly the same himself as a kid.

With his shifts over recent weeks and being at his mum's the previous weekend, it was a month since they'd been swimming—longer since he'd been to the gym—and he was feeling it. Funny how the football match hadn't been a stretch, yet climbing those steep, narrow stairs to the top deck was like hiking up Hay Bluff.

By the time he made it to the seat—at the front of the bus, naturally—Lucas had already scoffed his half of the KitKat from the vending machine. He handed over the remaining two fingers, part-melted, and declared, "I'm starving."

"Are you?" Rob knew what was coming next.

"Can we go to McDonald's?" Rob opened his mouth to reply, but Lucas followed straight up with a whiny, "Pleeeease, Dad."

"You don't like cheeseburgers."

"What? I do!"

Rob ruffled Lucas's hair and grinned. He was pretty sure if Lucas had to choose one food at the expense of all others for the rest of his life, it would be cheeseburgers. He'd probably choose them over contact with other human beings, parents included, especially if they came with gallons of tomato ketchup. "Yeah, OK. Seeing as you said *pleeeease.*"

"Yesss!" Lucas turned to watch out of the front window, clinging to the safety bar as if it steered the bus. "Was it about my Christmas present?" he asked.

"Was what about your Christmas present?"

"When you came to see Mum and Travis the other day."

"It's April, Lu. It's another eight months till Christmas."

"So?"

"So we're not going to be discussing your presents yet."

"Oh." Lucas frowned in deep concentration—long enough for Rob to finish the KitKat—and then grinned victoriously. "Have you got a new girlfriend?"

"Nope."

He sagged. "Boyfriend?"

"Nope." They'd had a conversation some time ago—along the lines of some people liked girls, some liked boys, some liked neither, some liked both—and Rob had said he was in the 'liked girls' category. He'd been figuring out how to explain that some people were neither girls nor boys—something he'd never really considered before meeting Aaron-Naomi—when Lucas beat him to it. His school had toilets—not boys' or girls' toilets, just toilets—because, 'Not everyone is a boy or a girl, Dad.'

"What were you talking about, then? Grown-up stuff?"

"Serious stuff, yeah." Rob nipped that one right in the bud. He'd really hated it as a kid when adults dismissed him from discussions that had something to do with him by saying it was 'grown-up stuff', and he wasn't about to pay the same discourtesy to his son. "I was telling your mum and Travis about someone I used to be in the army with. I think she's in trouble."

Lucas gasped. "With the police?"

"She might be. Not sure."

"Did she ask you and Fish to help her?"

Rob chuckled. "Gray, you mean."

Lucas narrowed his eyes. "You called him Fish."

"You misheard, mate. I called him Gray Fisher, because that's his name."

"No, you never." Lucas adamantly shook his head.

"Yeah, I did."

"Did not."

Rob refused to argue with a seven-year-old who was stubborn and…correct, although the actual phrase was 'slippery fish'. Rob figured it would work in his favour to *not* remind Lucas of that. He had a knack for serving up honesty at the optimum moment, and never forgot things he shouldn't have heard to start with.

"Are you going to have a girlfriend one day, Dad?"

"One day…" Rob joined his son in staring out the window to distract from the image of Naomi that popped into his head. Even after the Berringers' trials were out of the way, he'd be on dodgy ground pursuing anything more than friendship. It didn't matter that he was out of the police; threats of disciplinary action or dismissal had nothing to do with it. As lead officer of an investigation for which she was a key witness, he'd held a position of power over her, and that power wasn't readily neutralised by his resignation. Maybe he'd feel less uneasy if she made the first move. He had mixed feelings about whether he wanted to be put in a position to find out.

Lucas stood up, bringing Rob to his senses. He almost told him to sit down again before he realised they were back in Kilburn and nearing the stop outside their local McDonald's. Sliding his legs around to the end of the seat, he let Lucas out so he could ring the bell and then followed him downstairs. The bus stopped, the doors opened, and Lucas jumped down to the pavement.

"They were at the pool," he said.

Rob looked around to see who he was talking about. A few other people had got off the bus with them, none of whom looked like they'd been swimming.

"In that 508 GT." As Lucas pointed, the car signalled, pulled out and sped past the bus. "Aw…they could've given us a lift—they live in our road. You would've, wouldn't you, Dad?"

"Guess so." Rob's chest tightened; the half a KitKat threatened a repeat appearance. He took out his phone and acted as if he were casually checking for messages. "What number do they live at?"

"Dunno. Think they just moved in."

"Gotcha." Rob typed the Peugeot's registration number into a text message, along with 'reg check pls', and sent it to Gray. He put his phone back in his pocket and held out his hand. "Come on, then, mate. Let's get those cheeseburgers."

Lucas pushed Rob's hand out of the way and marched off towards McDonald's. Still reeling, Rob followed him in and joined the queue. It took ten minutes to reach the counter, which was long enough for Rob's heart to slow to something closer to normal, and for Lucas to decide on which half of the menu he was ordering. Rob didn't usually let him get away with it, but it was a good distraction tactic.

It proved both expensive and unnecessary. Cars in general were Lucas's current obsession, and he swiftly moved on from the Peugeot to a long list of his favourite supercars, as test-driven in his racing game.

Rob struggled to keep up with the high-speed gabble as Lucas barely paused to shove food in his mouth and swallowed without chewing. It was astounding how much he knew, most of it stuff Rob wouldn't have had a clue about at that age. He hoped it would be enough to steer Lucas's interest away from bikes and didn't care if that made him a hypocrite. Much as Rob wouldn't be without his, the idea of his son riding one terrified him, so much so that when Lucas pointed out Bugatti rhymed with Ducati, Rob told him about Tonka's Lamborghini just to keep him talking about cars.

"Wow! Does she let you drive it?"

"I wish!"

"Is she rich?"

"Not, like, mega-rich." Meeting the Berringers, Sharstons and Strangs of this world had given Rob new insights into what real wealth looked like, and Tonka wasn't even close to owning that kind of fortune. More likely, the half-a-million car was why she lived with her brother instead of buying a place of her own. Rob wasn't criticising; one night at Siggy's, when they'd all been a bit the worse for wear, they'd shared their 'when I leave the army...' wish lists.

Top of Rob's had been the bike he now owned—a crazy expensive wedding present from Zoë that he wouldn't have bought for himself and never got the chance to reciprocate. Jock's was a Honda GoldWing, predictably—cumbersome, expensive, might as well own a car, but it attracted attention. A Lamborghini had been at the top of Tonka's, and Bish...

Bish was driving a van that looked like it had never seen better days.

"Will you be all right there a minute, Lu?" Rob asked, already on his feet.

"Are you going for a crap?"

"Excuse me? Language?"

Lucas lowered his eyes and mumbled an apology around the last of his fries.

"I'm just going out to make a phone call."

"Please can I get an ice cream?"

Rob fished some change out of his pocket. "I dunno how you've got room." He slapped the coins down next to the heap of scrunched-up wrappers and blobs of ketchup. "I'll be right outside that door, OK?"

"'Kay." Lucas had darted off to order his ice cream before Rob made it out of the building.

Rob placed the call and turned back so he could keep an eye on his hollow-legged son. "Alright, Gray?"

"Hey. I was about to call you. That reg number. Were you expecting it to belong to a van?"

"Ah, no. Sorry. I didn't have time to explain. It's off a Peugeot 508."

"Yes, it is—one of the Met's."

"Crap. I asked Hedley to chase up the Mondeo. It's used by a specialist unit, but she couldn't find out which one."

"Are we thinking the same thing?" Gray asked.

"SIU?" The possibility didn't bother Rob so much now he'd reasoned it through. "Can we get it confirmed?"

The silence betrayed Gray's reluctance to agree, but he relented. "I'll give Dom Hooper a call."

"Cheers. And sorry." Rob didn't like putting him under pressure, but for his own peace of mind, he needed to know.

"Don't worry. It's disappointing when I've done everything by the book so far. It's not easy, but the sense of achievement is tremendous. How are you getting on?"

"Not well. I've got two numbers for Philip Parker. One's unrecognised, the other goes through to Parker Farms' voicemail."

"That doesn't surprise me. Based on the company profile, I doubt they have a staffed office. I did, however, manage to trace Philip Parker's overseas investments."

"Nice one."

There was a mumble in the background at Gray's end of the line, followed by, "Yeah, OK, Will helped me. Accordingly, Parker Farms financed the purchase of thirty hectares of agricultural land in Bulgaria, bought for cash in eight separate lots over several years."

"Blimey. When Tonka said it was a big farm, I didn't realise it was that big."

"It's a lot of land, but relatively cheap—well within the company's budget—which is why I didn't notice it on a first pass. I was looking for larger transfers of funds when it's less than they spend per year on maintaining the boundaries on their UK land."

"Any dodgy business going on?"

"Clean as a whistle so far. They're limited by guarantee, so there's no share trading, and the guarantors are all minted. Parker Farms is, essentially, a hundred-million-pound leviathan steered by half a dozen well-to-do Lilliputians."

The analogy mostly went over Rob's head but the value didn't. "You know, Tonka and her brother aren't exactly living the high life. D'you reckon they're being extorted?"

"It's possible, I suppose, although there's nothing in their company accounts to indicate that's the case, or not that I could find. Will's helping me crunch the numbers."

"See, now, *that's* commitment," Rob teased. Gray laughed. "We could afford to pay him."

"We could. Have you arranged to visit Ethan yet?"

The change of subject was subtle as a well-aimed axe, and Rob couldn't really throw it back when he wasn't pulling his weight. "I'll sort it after the weekend," he promised. "I also had a thought about Bish's van. Why's he driving a clapped-out old heap when he could afford a decent motor?"

"I assume that question's rhetorical, although I can think of a couple of reasons."

"Go for it."

"It could be adapted for his arm."

"He just sticks it between the steering wheel spokes."

"OK, in that case, personal experience would have me believe he's emotionally attached to it."

"Yeah? What did you have?"

"Ford Fiesta, one-litre, went through a gallon of oil a month and the driver's side window dropped if I went over thirty."

Rob chuckled. "Mine was a Honda c50 and the throttle used to stick."

"My sister had one of those for a few months. She gave it up for a boyfriend with a big, warm car."

"I don't blame her."

"Nor did I, even if he was a bit of a poser. The van could be Bish's runaround—a case of 'my other car's a Jaguar'. He strikes me as a Jag kind of guy."

"That's not a compliment, is it?"

"No comment," Gray said, opting for diplomacy.

"I'll give him a call after I drop Lu home so I'll let you know." Rob hadn't been watching as closely as he'd meant to, but all was well—for now. Lucas was scraping the last dregs out of his McFlurry pot and probably working up to asking for a cookie to take with him. "I can't shake the feeling there's something Bish and Jock aren't telling us—if I can catch one of them on their own, I could push them a bit harder."

"Give it a go," Gray encouraged, which was also Rob's cue to wind up the conversation.

"OK. I'll catch you later, mate." Rob moved his phone away from his ear and eyed the 'call ended' notification in amusement. Gray obviously had better things to do with his Saturday afternoon. Rob put his phone away and went back inside. Had he not just looked at the time, he'd still have known it was half past one from Lucas's sprint for the toilets; the kid's bowel movements were regular as an atomic clock.

While he was waiting, Rob cleared the rubbish from the table and drank the last of his Coke with a grimace. The ice had melted, and the only thing going for the flat, tasteless liquid was that it was wet. He threw the cup in the bin and moved closer to where the toilets were, hoping if he could collar Lu on the way out, they'd avoid spending yet more money Rob didn't have to spare on junk food.

His mind returned to his conversation with Gray. It looked like he and Will had sorted out whatever was going on earlier in the week, and Rob was pleased for them. No two ways about it, Gray was more laid-back these days—a change that could mostly be attributed to getting rid of the stress of heading up the SIU, but Will must've played his part. Rob had only met the guy a handful of times and couldn't say he knew him that well; however, his judgement of 'smooth-talking slacker' was corroborated by Gray's snipe about him being a con man, albeit in a strictly legal sense. Freddie Berringer and Aaron Tanner were both also of the opinion that Will could've made a killing in investment banking if he'd wanted to, and neither could understand why he'd bowed out for a simple life with his family and other animals.

Rob got it, though. If he had the choice, he'd set up a bike workshop for the sole purpose of tinkering. He'd buy up old Harleys and the like so he and Lu could spend hours taking them apart and putting them back together again, sell them to collectors or even start their own collection, go to rallies, live in their overalls. Nearly all of Rob's happiest moments saw him covered in oil, and not always of the engine variety, although those were *not* the kind of memories he wanted to build with his son, who appeared directly with a 'just had the best poo ever' grin on his face and a tp streamer stuck to his shoe.

"Lu?" Rob pointed to alert him. With a huff, Lucas stamped on the toilet paper with his other foot, net result: it was now stuck to both shoes. Laughing, Rob beckoned him closer and gave him a hand. He chucked the paper in the next bin they passed and put his arm around Lucas's shoulders, guiding him towards the exit.

"Can I have—"

"I'm spent up, mate. Sorry."

"Ohhh." Lucas plodded sulkily at Rob's side.

"Don't you think you've had enough?"

"No." That was the last Rob heard from him until they reached the corner of their road, at which point he asked, "Can I go and call for Adil?"

"See what your mum thinks."

"'Kay." Lucas shoved his swimming bag at Rob and ran ahead. It was easier to let him, plus it gave Rob a chance to case the street. There were lots of cars and no way of knowing which belonged to residents. Lucas had been right, though; one of the cars was a Peugeot 508 in the same flint grey, but it wasn't the one that had overtaken the bus. Nor was it the GT model, but with all the raving about cars Lucas had been doing, Rob couldn't imagine he'd get a detail like that wrong.

Still contemplating cars as he opened the gate—Lu dodged past him on his way out—Rob turned towards the house at the last second and startled. "Alright, Zo?" She was standing in the doorway, frowning and looking where he'd been looking a second ago. She smiled swiftly.

"Travis has got something to tell you. He's upstairs."

Rob followed her in, and she gestured for him to go up ahead of her, which he did, dragging his feet and dreading he might be about to enter Zoë and Travis's bedroom for the first time. It was one thing to accept they were a couple, another entirely to have their intimacy shoved in his face. At the top of the stairs, he vented a sigh of relief.

Travis was a few feet along the landing, on his hands and knees, and peering into the gap left by a raised floorboard. He glanced up long enough to notice Rob's arrival. "Alright?"

"Yeah. What you up to?"

"Installing an alarm. If...I...can...jussst—" There was a heavy, metallic *thunk* below, followed by Travis's hiss of, "Shit." He sat back on his haunches. "I need to feed the cable back to the fuse box." He scowled at Zoë.

"Ah, that scary magic called electricity," Rob said knowingly. Zoë punched him in the arm. "Ouch!"

"Don't you *dare* make fun!" If looks could kill... Luckily for Rob, they couldn't, but electricity could, and Zoë was legitimately terrified of it.

He ducked his head contritely. "Sorry. That was out of order."

She glared at him until he had to break eye contact, returning his attention to Travis. "You've got something to tell me, Zoë said?"

"I have. It might be nothing, but when we got back from school yesterday, there was a silver van stopped across the road."

"What time was that? About half-three?"

"Yeah, it would've been. My mate was here before that, and he'd been parked where the van was. I wouldn't have thought anything of it, but the driver and passenger—such as I could see them, it had dark windows—were just sitting there, not talking to each other or getting out. I stuck my iPad on the windowsill with the camera running—they drove off about ten minutes later."

"And it was silver, you say?" Rob asked. "Not white?"

"It was silver, definitely. A Mercedes. I could only see one end of the reg, but it was this year's plates."

"Right." Rob automatically went to his pocket for his notebook and then closed his eyes, laughing at himself. "I'll stick the info on my phone in a bit. D'you want a hand?"

"I wouldn't say no."

"What d'you need?"

"If you can go down to the fuse box and pull the cable through…"

"Sure." Rob edged past Zoë—still glaring—and went back downstairs. He knew why they were installing an alarm, and he wanted to tell them it was unnecessary but wasn't sure it was true. Besides, he'd sleep better himself for knowing they had an extra layer of security between them and whoever it was who'd taken an interest in all of their lives.

22: Worms

Dom wasn't answering his phone. The first attempt, it rang before it went to voicemail; the second, it didn't ring at all. Gray left it for the time being and reopened his browser, wishing he'd brought his tablet or laptop with him—either would have been an improvement—but he hadn't come to Will's with the intention to work. Alas, he'd got them both at it, and so far, Will was in the lead. They now knew the exact location of Parker Farms' overseas acquisitions, and that their accountant—Hilary Gelling, retired—undertook pro-bono work for non-profits, which was interesting but not especially helpful.

As for Gray's progress: he'd made none.

"I bet you're playing FreeCell," he muttered enviously at Will, across the table. Only Will's eyes were visible above his laptop screen, and the corners crinkled in amusement.

"I haven't played that since uni. It's boring."

"Yes, I can see how winning all the time would be a terrible bind."

Will chuckled without taking his eyes off the screen. The tensing of the tendons in his forearm and the dull click of the trackpad gave away that he was still doing...whatever he was doing. "I was no Hector," he said. "He could deduce from the opening deal whether it was possible to win—the same strategy he used with the Alternative Investment Market." Will sighed wistfully. "If only he could've applied his skills to reading people..."

He'd still be alive, Gray finished in his head. He hadn't had the privilege of meeting Hector Laird-Browne, and what he knew of the guy was what Will and Rob had told him. Accordingly, Hector had been a profoundly gifted mathematician, autistic, and naïve in his professional dealings with the Berringers. He'd also been in a relationship with Naomi, and asking how she was coping with her loss was a pertinent in-road, but Gray was reluctant to take it. No matter how hard he'd tried to convince himself he'd be asking on Rob's behalf, his desire to know more about Will and Aaron-Naomi was driven by curiosity, and it was his alone.

"Got 'em!" Will spun his laptop around.

"Who?" Gray didn't like the victorious smile beaming his way. He coolly pulled the laptop closer and read the answer onscreen. "GP Investments. The G is Gelling, I presume?"

"Yeah. Want to know how I found them?" Will was evidently going to tell him anyway.

"Only if you can multitask." Gray tilted his head in the direction of the kettle.

"*More* coffee?" Will teased but got up and switched on the kettle, talking as he prepared two mugs. "To be fair, I wouldn't have made the connection if we hadn't started out with the accountant's pro-bono work. There are very few truly benevolent individuals and corporations these days." He leaned back against the counter, ankles crossed casually. "My undergrad diss was on the history of friendly societies in the UK since 1875. That's when the legislation came in, but the big changes came with the introduction of state welfare in the mid-twentieth century. Most of the friendly societies still in existence are in the insurance sector, and hardly any operate on a purely non-profit basis—even fewer in the finance sector."

Gray pointed at the screen. "Am I correct in thinking GP Investments is a friendly society?"

"Yep."

"That's interesting." Gray scanned their scant homepage—no reference to the names of individual associates. "It doesn't explain how you made the connection."

"I'm getting to that." The kettle switched itself off, and Will paused to make their drinks. He was deliberately stringing out his explanation.

While Gray waited, he watched the glass tank for its alleged occupant. His eyes were accustomed to the light now, but he still couldn't see anything other than a big dead log.

Will put the mugs on the table. "You don't believe it's in there, do you? Want me to get it out?" He reached for the lid of the tank.

"No!" Gray shoved his chair away, ready to flee if it proved necessary.

Will resumed his seat, laughing. "It's—" he measured about twelve inches with his hands "—including its tail, and cute in a reptilian kind of way."

"I'm happy to take your word for it—unless my compliance is required in order to get an answer out of you."

"Not at all. Is there another tab still open?" Will nodded at his laptop.

Gray checked the screen and clicked on the tab in question. The result was a mess of form fields, most empty, some unlabelled, black Verdana text on a pale-grey background. "It's like Web 1.0 all over again."

"Yeah. Aaron doesn't exactly have an eye for design. Function all the way."

"This is Aaron's work?" Gray leaned closer and tried to extrapolate from the acronyms. "What does it do?"

"In simple terms, it's a search engine. You give it some parameters to work within—keywords, databases to search, Boolean operators—and it does the rest."

Gray scrolled through the endless list of checkboxes. "IR? DWP? Are those what I think they are?"

Will coughed and picked up his coffee.

"Search engine, you say…" Gray scrolled back up until the list was no longer in view. "You hacked a government database."

"I cross-referenced Companies House and the Charity Commission—both public listings, no hacking required."

"Truthfully?"

Will looked Gray dead in the eye. "Truthfully. I heard what you said to Rob, about doing everything by the book, and I respect that. It was something that never sat easy with me in the banks, and not just Berringer's."

"An honest con man," Gray mused.

"Ha. I'm not sure about honest." Will directed Gray's attention back to the screen. "You can see what Aaron's algorithm is capable of, but I assure you, on this occasion, I only used it to make our search more intuitive. I'll show you." Will waited for Gray to turn the laptop so they could both see it. "This box, where I typed 'Hilary Gelling', searches for exact and partial matches. I check this box to tell it to also match company names by their initials, and the checklist identifies which sources to search. There are other variables we could provide, such as annual turnover, trading partners, and so on. I left those empty, hit submit and…"

"GP Investments," Gray read off the screen again. "Only one match?"

"The only 100% match. Closest after that is 92%. You'd have to ask Aaron how that bit works."

Gray stared at the company names until they blurred to a dark smudge. He blinked and refocused, and opened a new tab. "What about the 'P'? Can we extrapolate outwards?"

"Why don't you have a go? Ace is really easy to use."

"Ace?"

"Aaron's Search Engine."

"That's clever." But nowhere near as clever as the engine itself. "This would've taken us days, you know, in the SIU." He clicked in a field near the top, but had no idea where to start, not with Will watching. He relinquished control of the laptop and picked up his coffee. "Thanks for this."

"Not a problem," Will answered vaguely. He typed and clicked, and typed and clicked, inhaled, exhaled…

"Can I ask you about…the cats?" Not the question Gray had intended to ask, but a better one, although Will was only half listening so he could probably have got away with asking anything. "Where are they?"

"RSPCA."

"Oh. Is that good?"

Will peered through his eyebrows at him. "What do you think?"

Gray shrugged. "I thought they might still be stuck in the building."

"The police went in with an inspector and got them out. Three litters, at least four adults—they had to euthanise most of the kittens, *apparently*." Will's voice strained; there was a lot of anger and sadness there.

"I'm sorry."

"Thanks." Will smiled and shrugged philosophically. "That's how it goes sometimes. We did what we could." He continued clicking and typing. "One positive, though: when the inspector called to update me, I told her about my most recent house guest, and she offered to take it in."

Gray looked around the room at the various pets in residence. "I'm surprised you're willing to let it go to a new home at all, let alone with an RSPCA inspector."

"She's already got a beardy...and doesn't have an issue feeding it live insects."

"Ah." That explained it. "Still, how many live insects can an invisible dragon eat?"

Will cracked a smile. "In all honesty, I won't be sorry to see it go. And the inspector seems to be one of the good ones."

"Well, when it comes down to it, you are both fighting for the same cause."

"Like Germany and Japan."

Gray laughed. "More the Allied Forces and the Resistance." A movement from within the tank startled him.

"Told you it was in there," Will said.

Gray didn't answer, dumbfounded by the creature now perched regally on top of the log. He'd expected it to be duller, not the shimmering pale gold it was. With the mass of soft-looking pointed scales covering its chin and neck, the name made perfect sense. "It's beautiful," he uttered.

"Do you think so?" Will asked doubtfully.

"You don't?"

Will eyed Gray suspiciously and leaned his chair back on two legs, reaching for a plastic box from the dresser behind him. He tilted forward again and set the box down next to Gray's mug.

"What's this?"

"Worms."

"*Live* worms?" Gray peeled back one corner of the lid and peered inside. "Oh." He nodded. "Live worms."

"Drop a couple in the tank," Will instructed with his eyes closed.

Unperturbed, Gray pulled the lid off the box and picked out two of the short, fat worms. He rose slowly and stepped towards the tank, all the while watching the bearded dragon, which scurried to the closest end of the log and was, in turn, watching him as he lifted the mesh to drop the worms in. The dragon snapped the first one out of the air, and within seconds had gulped down both of them. "Can it have more?"

"Yeah, but not too many. They're a treat." Will's voice was thick and muffled by tight lips.

Gray glanced over and stifled his laughter. "You really can't deal with this, can you?"

"I'm horrified you can."

"I used to go fishing when I was younger," Gray said, quickly adding, "before I knew any better." He dropped a few more worms into the tank and put the mesh back in place. The dragon devoured the lot. "Fascinating."

Will grunted.

Gray closed the tub and pushed it back across the table; Will returned it to the dresser. He looked like he might cry or vomit, or both. "What else does it eat?" Gray asked.

"Veggies. Food pellets. And crickets. Moving swiftly on…I haven't found out who the 'P' is yet, but I have found GP's portfolio."

Gray went and stood next to Will, reading over his shoulder. "Wow, that's quite a list of clients." He recognised a few of the names onscreen. "Scroll down—oh, hold on." His phone vibrated across the table. "Can you copy and paste that into a document, please?"

"Sure."

"Thanks." Gray answered the call. "Dom, you busy, busy man."

"I was driving. Is everything all right?"

"I was hoping you might be able to tell me. Rob's picked up a couple of followers."

"Right?"

"Unmarked, registered to a Met specialist unit."

"And?"

"Any idea why?"

"If I have, I can't tell you. But you already knew that."

Gray's scalp prickled. He tried to contain his irritation, reminding himself that if their positions were reversed, he wouldn't have told Dom, either.

"OK," Gray accepted finally. "Forget I asked."

"Asked what?" Dom replied.

"Yeah, yeah. Talk to you soon."

"Be safe, Gray."

"Dom—" He'd already ended the call.

Gray stared at his phone screen for a long time after it had gone dark and only looked up because several sheets of printer paper fluttered down in front of him.

"That didn't sound like a particularly illuminating conversation," Will said.

"It wasn't." Gray's agitation was mounting rapidly, not entirely under his control. "My old unit's watching Rob. I'm sure of it."

"To do with the Berringers?"

"I think it's bigger than that." He scanned the printout, but he'd lost his focus and switched to watching Will, back on Aaron's search engine.

"I'm going to add a few more options, if that's OK with you."

"Yeah, fine," Gray answered vaguely. He was pissed off with Dom and for no good reason. Trust—or lack of—had nothing to do with it. Keep it simple and on a need-to-know basis was how the SIU operated; not even those involved in an investigation had access to all of the information. That was the privilege—and burden—of the unit leader.

"Yes!" Will punched the air and startled Gray yet again. He wasn't usually so jumpy.

"What've you got?"

"The 'P' of GP Investments."

"Nice work!" That broke Gray out of his trance—briefly, until he saw the name. The familiar itch in his brain started up, impossible to ignore, making his pulse race. He had to think to breathe normally. The craving, stronger than he'd felt in months, threatened to overthrow his resolve as his worst fears rose to the fore.

"Gray?" Will was suddenly in his space, observing, frowning... worried.

"I need to go." Gray bolted from the room. He was in his jacket and halfway to the door before Will intercepted.

"Whoa! Go where?"

"Home. I'll call you, OK?"

Will spread his arms, barring the exit and cranking Gray's urgency up to desperation. "What's going on? Who's Raymond Perlett?"

Gray moved to push him aside, but thought better of it and instead attempted to stare him down. "Will, I *need* to go."

Will lowered his arms but maintained steady eye contact. "I understand, but there's no immediate rush. You won't make the next train, so take a few minutes, put a plan together—"

"Excuse me, please."

Will rubbed his chin, slowly, thoughtfully—or faking it to hold Gray long enough that he had no chance of getting that train. "If you really have to go, fine. I won't stop you." He spoke quietly, without challenge—the voice of reason. The voice of a negotiator. "I'd rather you stayed, even if you can't tell me what that name means. This is our time together, and I'd like for us to make the most of it. But it's up to you. All I'm asking is you consider before you do anything rash."

"Tell me about Naomi and Freddie."

"I beg your pardon?"

Gray tried to cajole the words into the right order. The pain registered—his fist bashing against his forehead. He stopped. "I messed up, Will. Big time."

"How?"

"With the SIU. My recklessness has put Rob in danger."

"Did Dom tell you that?"

"He told me nothing."

"Then you can't be sure what's happening has anything to do with whatever you did."

"I *know* it does, Will. That name...I can't explain, and I can't do anything to jeopardise..." He bit his fist to stop himself from saying more.

Will continued observing him. "You want me to tell you about Naomi and Freddie?"

"Yeah, I do," Gray said obstinately.

"What do you want to know?"

"Why you always shut down the conversation when they come up. Is it jealousy?"

"Absolutely not." There was no defensiveness in Will's answer, just a statement of fact.

"OK. Is he abusive?" Gray shook his head. "Scratch that. I know he is. I mean, is he abusive to Naomi?"

"No...well...kind of."

"Meaning?"

"More so to Aaron. Ironically, it's one thing I can say in Freddie's favour. He accepts the dichotomy between Aaron and Naomi. What he can't accept is their co-existence. Aaron comes between him and Naomi."

Briefly, Gray forgot about cocaine and Raymond Perlett. It was for no more than a second or two, but the distraction seemed to be working, so he stayed with it. "It sounds like Freddie sees Aaron as a love rival."

"That's exactly it."

"Did Freddie feel the same way about you?"

"Far from it. He told Naomi I was using her to get at him, and he honestly thought that's what I was doing. She asked me if it was true." Will chewed his lip, guilt creasing his brow. "I told her it was, hoping it would make the decision easier for her... It would've been a safer lie to say I wanted a serious relationship. It might've kept them apart."

"Instead you pushed them together."

"Yes, but it's not as callous as it seems. When I said they're in love with each other, I was simplifying, and it's not how you think. Freddie's besotted—has been since uni. And Naomi...she's a wily one. She knows how to play him, giving him just enough to get what she wants. Money, cars, clothes, sex—the house. Were it not for Aaron, I'd say she and Freddie deserve each other."

"But they're the same person," Gray argued.

"Spend any amount of time with them, and you'll see how wrong you are, which is why I offered to go to see Freddie with them. Naomi can handle him, no problem at all. Aaron is a different matter. Is that enough distraction? Or do you have further questions, Mr. Fisher?"

"Do you feel interrogated?"

"Not really." Will smiled and held out his hand. "Come and sit with me?"

Gray glanced behind him at the door, and then at the clock. If he didn't leave in the next couple of minutes, another train would have come and gone. But really, there was nothing he could do. He had to trust the SIU had his and Rob's backs.

"I'll let you feed the beardy more worms," Will offered.

Gray's eyes flitted to the tank. His newfound friend was still perched on the log, and still watching him…he liked to think. "OK." He took Will's hand and permitted him to lead them back to the table.

"Do you want another coffee?"

"No, thank you. And thank you for sharing."

"Thanks for listening, and staying. I'm not deliberately hiding anything, Gray. You only have to ask. You know that, don't you?"

"I'm getting there." He was trying, but not being able to reciprocate Will's honesty reminded him how much he missed being with someone in the job—how much he missed Jean. "Can we just sit and watch TV, forget about all of this?" He indicated the laptop and printout. It would drive him crazy if he let it.

"Sure," Will agreed. "We should eat too. Are you hungry?"

"I could eat, as they say."

"What d'you fancy?"

"Hummus?" Gray suggested and even managed a grin.

"Huh. I should've let you catch that train after all."

23: Networking

After watching Travis's footage of the silver van, which told Rob no more than Travis had already told him, he connected wirelessly to Gray's camera. It turned out to be even less use, but at least meant he could come clean about the surveillance. He wasn't comfortable spying on Zoë, and could understand why she was upset he hadn't said anything—even if he did have Lu's and her best interests at heart.

It made for a tense atmosphere, and as soon as he'd finished helping Travis with the alarm, Rob gave his excuses and got his leathers on to leave, though he had nowhere better to be. Unexpectedly, Travis was on his side, which only served to aggravate Zoë further, and as the door closed behind him, Rob heard her say, "Why do all men think we need looking after?" If she thought he was doing it simply because she was a woman, she was sorely mistaken.

"Dad!" Lucas came tearing up the street to intercept. Rob quickly pulled his visor over his face and pretended he hadn't seen his son slump, dejected. "I thought you were staying for dinner."

"No, mate. I don't want to get under your mum's feet, and I've got work."

"But you're not a policeman anymore."

"I still have to work."

Lucas sighed heavily. "'Kay." He turned around and plodded back the way he'd come.

"Laters...taters." The words fizzled out pointlessly. Rob glanced back at the house, wondering if he could stand to swallow down a slice of humble pie for Lucas's sake. Zoë was watching from the front window, arms crossed, chin jutting defiantly. Lu would pick up on the bad feeling between them, and Rob had already said he was going. He straddled the bike, took a last look along the street, and took off.

Back home, he put his phone on charge and called Bish, who stammered some bullshit about his car being in for a service, laughed way too enthusiastically when Rob asked if his other car was a Jag, and then claimed he owned a Prius, which was about as likely as Rob swapping his two wheels for four. Due credit to the guy, no matter how much Rob probed, he didn't change his story, but it was a puzzle for another time.

Next, Rob called Martina, first and foremost to ask if she fancied going for that pint, but she was away with Erica for the weekend. Even so, she got Miller to check the partial plate from the silver van; Miller called back, confirming it was a possible match for a couple of Met Police vehicles, but without the full reg, there was no way of knowing for sure.

Best guess: each time a search registered on the system, the unit in question switched vehicles, but Rob couldn't see why they'd go to the trouble when he'd sussed he was being tailed a week ago. If it was to prevent potential retaliation from the Berringers, it wouldn't matter if he knew they were watching, and if they thought he was involved in whatever Tonka was up to, their surveillance was a bust. It made no sense, and Rob was sick of thinking about it. He'd cut his holiday short, missed out on dinner with Lois and catching up with the rest of his family to spend half a week chasing a seemingly non-existent threat. Now it was the weekend again, and he was still working.

Hypocrite much? Remembering Lois's comment raised a smile, at least. Surely, Bish and Jock wouldn't begrudge him a night off…if he could think of something to do with it.

In spite of his post-swimming weariness, Rob put on his running gear and headed out to pound the streets. The evening was cool but dry, the daylight dimming as he found his groove.

He wasn't a regular runner; he normally only ran to the gym for a workout and then back again, and in retrospect, running hadn't been the best choice. With no phone, he couldn't listen to music, and the area was too familiar to offer up any distractions.

His mind kept turning over the unanswered questions. Was he barking up completely the wrong tree in thinking it was to do with Tonka? Had something happened to her? In his first stint under Hedley, there'd been two attacks on young women, and they'd kept a lid on it, knowing the attacker would strike again if he thought he was getting away with it. They'd caught him as he moved in on his third victim. If something had happened to Tonka... Except her neighbours had seen her leave home the previous weekend, the house was secure with no signs of a struggle, and Siggy claimed she'd heard from her. It all pointed to Tonka being alive and well. Besides, he was certain—almost certain—Hedley would've told him if there was an investigation underway.

Twenty minutes of churning thoughts later, Rob decided to cut his losses and go back to the flat. He nodded an acknowledgement at his upstairs neighbour, who was putting his rubbish out. Rob had an open invitation to go up and share a spliff—a particularly tempting prospect this evening—but it had the potential to put him on a major downer, and he'd delayed dealing with Ethan long enough.

A quick shower first, order in a takeaway, check out Brookhurst's visiting protocol—Rob was starting to question his decision to leave the police. He could've just turned up and demanded Ethan talk to him. Instead, he was still working antisocial hours and with none of the benefits of instant access to witnesses. He could only hope the PI business would get easier with practice.

He emerged from the bathroom to the ringing of his landline phone and the thought that he needed to set some boundaries on his working hours because his mobile was also vibrating. He answered it and let the landline go to messages.

"Alright…Naomi?" Calling from that number, it usually was.

"Yes," she confirmed. "Good evening, Rob. I hope I haven't caught you at a bad time."

"Not at all. How are things?"

"Oh, everything's fine. I've been thinking about your offer to accompany me to see Freddie. Does it still stand?"

"It does. What time do you need me?"

"Visiting is from nine-thirty. Connections allowing, it should take less than an hour to get there. Aaron's around, though, so we may need to ditch public transport at the last minute."

"I'll sort something out," Rob offered. "About eight-fifteen?"

"Perfect. Thanks so much for this. I really appreciate it. And perhaps we might get a chance to—oh, there's your phone. I'll talk to you on Monday."

*A chance to…*what? "OK, mate. Take care." Rob quickly ended the call, at the same time picking up the landline cordless. He didn't recognise the number, but it was a Watford code, most likely Gray calling from Will's place. "Hello?"

"Rob?" And that was definitely a sigh of relief. "Is everything all right?"

"Yeah. Everything's fine. Why wouldn't it be?"

"No reason. Just…I've been trying to get hold of you. I wanted to give you an update."

"I've not long got back from a run, and my phone was charging. What's up?"

"OK, firstly…the Mondeo and Peugeot are SIU."

"You've spoken to Dom, I take it?"

"I have. He more or less confirmed it."

"More or less?"

"By omission."

"Gotcha." Rob recalled Gray being much the same when he was unit leader. It was a case of asking the right questions and reading between the lines. "And the bad news?"

Gray gave a hollow laugh. "Still as astute as ever. How d'you fancy a working lunch tomorrow?"

"Sure. At your place?"

"We've come up with a way to shift our investigation along without stepping on SIU toes."

"Who's their targ…never mind." Rob knew better than to ask questions like that over the phone. It could only be Tonka or her brother if it was related to their investigation. "What time?"

"Sigma-SMS."

That was the secure service they'd used in the SIU, and Rob hadn't re-installed the app on his new phone—it was something else to fill his empty evening. Gray's precautions seemed a bit over the top, but he'd have his reasons. "I'll keep an eye out for it. See you tomorrow." He hung up and started the app download then switched to the browser to search for a number to call to request a visit with Ethan, thinking he'd be able to delay making that call until Monday. Instead, the hospital website had a form: seventy-two hours notice, and it had to be approved by the patient. It was over to Ethan now.

Soon after, Rob's takeaway arrived, followed by Gray's message confirming their lunch arrangements—midday at Will's house—along with instructions to turn off his phone's GPS and leave his bike at Croxley station. Gray had usefully—or pointlessly, Rob was undecided—included directions to get him from the station to Will's house on foot. Rob saved the message without any further thought, more than ready for some downtime. Grabbing a beer from the fridge, he stuck on the first movie that took his fancy and settled in for a couple of hours of escapism.

***

"I should've checked—are you OK with veggie?" Gray asked, inviting Rob to step into the warm, herby kitchen.

"Yeah, I'll eat pretty much anything." He was about to acknowledge Will—back turned, hard at work at the stove—but got distracted by the cacophony of barking from beyond the door Gray opened. Rob had met Will's dogs before, and they seemed a friendly bunch, but he was on their patch so he kept his head up and ignored them as far as was possible when they were running circles around him and bumping his legs.

Will glanced away from the pan he was stirring and gave a short, rising whistle. The dogs turned and dashed over—all except one.

"Alright, mate?" Rob peered down his nose at the big dog intent on sniffing every inch of his jeans—it seemed respectful to leave his leathers off for today.

"Jesus, Kenny, where are your manners? Give the man some space." Will clicked his tongue, and the dog slithered—there was no other word for it—away.

"He's paralysed," Gray explained. Rob hadn't planned on asking.

"And he's a tart for a good-looking copper," Will added.

Rob raised an eyebrow; Gray's pink-cheeked smirk was a sight to behold. He cleared his throat and indicated the old pine table tucked into a wide alcove. "Have a seat. Would you like a drink?"

"Please, if it's not too much trouble."

"Tea, coffee, squash…or there's some beer?"

"Coffee, cheers." Rob pulled out a chair as much as he could when there was a large glass tank on the floor behind him. He sat and peered in. "Is that a bearded dragon?"

"Yep," Gray confirmed without looking. "Will hates it."

"He doesn't," Will said.

Gray's blush had subsided, and his smirk became a grin. "I stand corrected. He hates feeding it."

"Two more hours…"

"It's going to a new home."

Rob nodded, entertained by Gray and Will's domestic bliss routine. He'd never seen Gray fully off-duty, padding around in socked feet, so completely at ease. And this felt nothing like a working lunch.

The back door opened, and another man walked in, also shoeless—and sockless—wearing board shorts, sweatshirt and a head of messy blonde dreadlocks. He acknowledged Rob with a nod and sniffed. "Is that roast dinner?"

"Yep," Will confirmed. "You staying?"

Gray delivered Rob's coffee and tilted his head towards the newcomer. "This is Tie—Will's lodger. Tie, this is Rob, my business partner."

Rob made it part way to his feet before Tie lurched across the room, extending a hefty arm. "Alright, mate?"

"Alright? Good to meet you."

"You too. Another copper, then?"

"Former copper."

"Right." Tie stepped back and scratched his head. "If you're here on business, I won't impose."

"Actually, it would be a good idea for you to stay," Gray said, warily meeting Rob's gaze. "There's a chance what's going on will affect you."

"Fair enough. I'll just go feed Benj and get some feet on. Won't be a mo." Tie went to the fridge, grabbed a handful of leaves and left the same way he'd come. A chilly rain-damped draught wafted across to the table, but it wasn't the cause of Rob's goosebumps.

Gray edged past to reach a Welsh dresser and retrieved a wad of A4 paper, which he handed to Rob.

"What's this?" He glanced over the first page. "GP Investments?"

"Philip Parker's broker." Gray was watching him carefully.

"I thought you said Parker was legit." Rob flipped the page, and then again, not sure what Gray was expecting of him. He skimmed over the lines of text—arrangement fees, transfer of money for purchases on behalf of Parker Farms, confirmations of purchases. "What am I..." Rob flipped the page and froze. "Shit." He re-read the name to check he wasn't seeing things. "That's not a coincidence, is it?"

"Unfortunately, no. He was on the hit list at the start of the Strang investigation, but he wasn't involved, so I took him off."

"You think—"

"Lunch is ready," Will said, cutting off Rob's question. "Let's eat and talk." He set down a glass dish in the middle of the table. "Gray, can you get the plates, please?"

"Certainly." Gray edged past Rob again and collected plates and cutlery from the dresser while Tie returned and gave Will a hand with bringing over the rest of the food—roast potatoes, courgettes, orange and purple carrots, red peppers—as colourful as Rob's mum's dinners, and it smelled fantastic.

"Help yourselves," Will invited once everyone was seated; Tie sat opposite Rob, Gray sat to his right, opposite Will. Tie offered Rob the serving tongs, but Rob gestured for him to sort himself out first.

"You should've made a bigger loaf," Tie said, transferring two steaming slices from the glass dish to his plate. "You a meat-eater, Rob?"

"Err...sometimes." In the present company, he didn't want to admit that pretty much his every meal included meat of some sort.

"You're not missing out with Will's nut loaf, I tell you. It's the dog's..." Tie broke off with a laugh. Will shook his head, laughing too.

"It's definitely not the dog's bollocks. But it is tasty. My mum's recipe."

"Yeah?" Rob accepted the serving tongs and helped himself to a couple of slices. It looked a bit like fruit cake, but once he'd loaded his plate with roasties and veg, topped off with a good dollop of thick, dark gravy, there was no distinguishing it from a traditional roast dinner. For the most part, it tasted like one. Will was right, the nut loaf was good—a cross between sage and onion stuffing and date and walnut bread—but a bit odd to Rob's meat-eater taste buds.

Were it not for the discussion looming on the horizon, lunch would've been a very chilled affair. Will's house had a great atmosphere; Rob had picked up on it on his last visit, and he tried to soak it in, watching the activities of the kitchen's various non-human inhabitants. His mum would go nuts if she were here now. *What are all these dogs doing in the kitchen? It's unhygienic!* But sooner or later, they needed to get down to business.

"So, what's going on, Gray?"

Gray put his fork on his plate and finished his mouthful of food before he began. Rob prayed it wouldn't be a Windbag Fisher Special.

"Briefly, for your benefit, Tie, and you need to keep this to yourself…"

"Of course," Tie agreed—too easily for Rob's liking. Will must've noticed his caginess.

"Before you continue, Gray, can I just assure you, Rob, that Tie's involved in the same…undercover work I am."

Rob chuckled at Will's choice of description, as did Gray.

"If it was still my unit, I'd have had them both working for us months ago."

"That good, eh?"

Will grinned broadly at the compliment.

"You were saying," Tie prompted Gray to continue.

"Yes. A couple of years ago, Rob and I investigated a group of lawyers who were defrauding their terminally ill clients by amending wills so they named deceased or contested beneficiaries, which put them intestate. We knew our targets were working with corrupt court officials in order to push the wills through. What we hadn't realised was the extent of that corruption.

"The lawyers involved in the inheritance scam are either dead or in prison, but what they were doing is part of a much bigger scheme that's the subject of an ongoing investigation, the details of which we're not privy to. I left the unit running the investigation last year, and Rob left the year before that. However, in light of recent events, it would appear that we have attracted the attention of associates of the criminals we put away, and our old unit is also aware of that."

"Hang on," Rob said. He couldn't fault Gray for his brevity on this occasion, but either he'd missed a few steps along the way or he was jumping to conclusions. Rob seriously hoped it was the latter. "The Mondeo and Peugeot 508—"

"Are SIU. The vans outside Zoë's…" Gray shrugged.

Rob sighed rather than swearing. "What's Tonka got to do with it? And Jock and Bish, for that matter."

"You're not going to like it, Rob. I'm sorry."

"Why?"

"Because…as far as I can tell, they're using Tonka to get to you. Raymond Perlett's got to be involved somehow."

"I'm lost," Tie said. "Who's Tonka?"

"My old CO," Rob answered.

"Oh, really? Regiment?"

"REME."

"Fusiliers. Four years."

"Same." Rob was mildly surprised that the vegan animal-libber new-age-traveller type sitting across the table from him was ever a squaddie. The bloke clearly hadn't had a haircut since he came out.

"And Raymond Perlett?" Tie asked.

"Tonka's brother's investment broker," Gray said.

"Raymond is Michelle's brother?" Rob guessed. Tie mouthed *who?*

"Father," Gray corrected. "Michelle was one of the lawyers we put in prison."

Tie nodded in understanding. "And you reckon her dad… what? Made the connection between Tonka's brother and the copper who put his daughter away?" He thumbed in Rob's direction as he said it.

"That's the bit I'm not sure about. My guess is serendipity had a hand. Parker Farms took their business to GP Investments, and Perlett made the connection during their background checks."

"It's a bloody long shot, Gray," Rob said.

"I know. It's a gut feeling, but we need confirmation. Which is where Will's plan comes in."

Rob was uneasy with the entire setup, and he wanted to discuss it with Gray in private, but short of kicking Will and Tie out of their own kitchen, he couldn't see a way to make it happen.

"May I make a suggestion?" Will asked. Gray shrugged his consent. "After we've eaten, Tie and I will take the dogs out so you can fill Rob in."

For a moment, Gray looked like he was going to refuse, but conceded with a reluctant nod, after which they resorted to small talk, or Rob and Tie did. It was the same old, same old—where they'd been based, tours of duty, bland brushing over of the grimmer details, especially in Tie's case; he'd served in Afghanistan, whereas Rob had come out a few months before the first troops were sent over. He'd been lucky; Bosnia was bad enough, but 'keeping equipment serviceable for peace implementation' was an all-inclusive holiday by comparison to what the lads endured in Afghanistan and Iraq.

That conversation took them through to the end of lunch, which Rob enjoyed, though perhaps not enough to consider giving up his mum's curry chicken or the medium-rare T-bones he treated himself to when he had time and remembered to buy one. While they'd been eating, the dogs had quietly stayed out of the way, but they must've picked up on what was happening because as soon as Will set down his knife and fork, they started pacing between him and the back door.

Rob watched, fascinated, as Will affixed wheels to the big dog whose back legs didn't work while the other five milled around with none of Linford's lunacy at walkies time, although it got a bit raucous when Tie opened the door and they all tried simultaneously to charge out into the rain. Sadly, they seemed to have taken the relaxed atmosphere with them, leaving only tense silence.

Gray cleared the serving dishes from the table. "Want a coffee?"

"Sure. I'll give you a hand." Rob stacked the plates and carried them across to the sink, not sure where to start with either the washing up or his questions. He didn't want to throw accusations around.

"Leave those." Gray advanced with the kettle, and Rob stepped aside. "I'll wash them later." He filled the kettle and returned it to its base. "What's on your mind?"

"How much did you tell Will?"

"Everything."

Rob frowned, processing the meaning of 'everything'. Before today, and in spite of knowing far more about each other's private lives than either would've voluntarily shared, Gray had always been a little remote, maintaining a distance congruent with his former role as Rob's superior. The difference was palpable, leading Rob to conclude Gray really did mean everything. "I don't know if I'm impressed or pissed off."

"Understandably. I was thinking over what you said, among other things. Is coffee OK? Or would you rather have tea?"

"Coffee's fine, cheers." Rob wasn't much of a tea drinker.

Gray set out two mugs. "May I ask you a personal question? It's about you and Zoë."

Rob shrugged his assent to the question, not to answering it. He'd decide once he knew what it was.

"Did you ever confide in her?"

"Confide...about work?"

"Yeah."

"The bare bones. How long I expected to be away, whether I'd be able to keep in touch..."

"And after you'd finished a job?"

"I'd give her the general gist, not the ins and outs. If the case was in the news, maybe I'd mention that was what I'd been working on, but she didn't ask, so it didn't come up. It was the same with the army. If my mum or dad asked what I'd been up to, I'd give them the sanitised version, but otherwise?" Rob shook his head.

"See, I think that's the difference, and it's key." Gray finished making their coffees, and they took them back to the table. "With

Jean being in the job too, we talked about work all the time. I'm not sure we talked about much else, to tell you the truth. Even my friends, family—those I'm still in contact with—are either in the police or involved in police work in some way."

"I didn't realise your sister was."

"Yeah. Well, sort of. Part-time special constable. Obviously, George isn't, and I doubt we'll ever be close, for lots of reasons, not just that. But it's part of what got me thinking. Up until last year, I lived to work, and I loved it. I really did. I hated going on leave, I worked all the overtime I could get. I went for promotions to sink my teeth into something new, not for salary or status. My job was my life, and it was great. Then Jean died, and I couldn't find my footing again. People kept telling me I needed to take a break, give myself time to recover, and I believed them.

"I didn't follow their advice, as you know. I kept going, and with hindsight, I admit there were times I wasn't up to the job. But I wasn't wrong to keep working. I was wrong to not ask for help. I should've delegated more, stuck to admin for a while... Anyway, I'm not intending to do a full post-mortem. I fucked up, and that's why we're in this situation now.

"The bottom line is, I can't have a proper relationship with Will unless I trust him with my work, because it's me. It's integral to who I am, and Will's work—not the delivering post bit, that's a means to an end, but his activism—is integral to who he is." Gray picked up his cup, smiling as he lifted it to his lips. "I think we've cracked it, Rob."

On the balance of what he'd seen and heard, Rob was inclined to agree. "OK. I wouldn't have done the same, but like you say, that's how we're different, and if it's working, fair play to you. So, what's this plan you mentioned?"

"GP Investments—we need to confirm whether they're involved. However, if they are, they'll know who you are, and possibly who I am too. I've exhausted all avenues, and...we need inside information."

"Are you talking about sending Will in undercover?"

"Only as a prospective client. He's meeting with Perlett tomorrow afternoon—subject to your approval."

Rob's mind reeled. That was a whole new level of Gray trusting Will with his work. And risky. "Surely if they've connected Tonka to me—"

"They'll have connected Will to me? It's possible..." Gray paused as the back door opened to admit five wet, muddy dogs, followed by Tie, then the dog on wheels, and finally Will.

"What if they have?" Rob asked.

"I doubt they'll recognise him," Gray said, far too casually, but he went on before Rob could call bullshit. "At your leaving do, Martina asked me if I was involved with anyone. She didn't even make the connection when I mentioned him by name."

"That's...interesting." And extraordinary, though it explained her remark about Gray and Will being an item. Martina was a damned good detective; not much got past her. "Have you ever considered becoming a spy, Will?" Rob asked, tongue-in-cheek.

Will laughed but didn't pass comment. He kicked his wellies off and left the room.

"OK. What's this plan?" Rob still needed convincing.

"Will's going to pose as an investor working on behalf of Berringer's bank. He's got a documented track record, which should be enough to get him through the door."

"If we discount the fact that Berringer's is defunct," Rob pointed out.

"Ah, well..." Gray fidgeted cagily.

"They're still operating?" Rob asked even though the answer was right there on Gray's face. "They liquidated their assets."

"And both Berringers are in prison, yes," Gray stated. "But you know as well as I do, they won't be there for long."

"And in the meantime, their lackeys are holding the fort so they can pick up where they left—" The pieces all fell into place at once. Rob put down his coffee lest he was tempted to launch it. "That's why Naomi's going to see Freddie."

"I doubt it," Will called from just outside the door. He reappeared, half in and half out of his sweater. He tugged it over his head and chucked it on the back of a chair to re-tie his hair. "But you're on the right lines. Freddie only needs one person on the outside to facilitate running his business from where he is."

"Aaron, you bloody..." Rob stopped short of calling him an idiot; Aaron was far from it, but the Berringers were bullies. Rob had hoped, with Freddie in prison, Aaron and Naomi would be safe from his constant threats to expose Aaron as a hacker. All it had done was lengthen the puppet strings. Of course, it would help if they kept their distance instead of running to Freddie on a whim.

Will patted Rob's shoulder. "Thanks, by the way, for offering to accompany them tomorrow."

"No worries." He was disgruntled Will had followed his train of thought; Rob was doing it for Naomi's benefit, and his own, if he was truthful, but Will obviously felt guilty for letting Naomi down. He'd put his neck on the line to protect her and Aaron, and he was about to do it again for Gray and Rob. The risks were tremendous, unacceptable. These people were ruthless; Rob had seen it for himself. They weren't just fraudsters and embezzlers; they were murderers. "Wouldn't we be better leaving this to the SIU?" he said. It was a last-ditch attempt at persuading Gray, and utterly pointless, knowing the man as he did, but he had to try.

"I get where you're coming from," Gray said amenably. "And I'm sure Dom's doing what he can to protect us, but if it comes to the crunch and it's us or jeopardise the whole operation..."

"We're on our own," Rob finished. He'd witnessed Gray do exactly the same 'for the greater good' on more than one occasion and dismiss the risks as collateral damage. "All right. What d'you need from me?"

"Did you manage to arrange a visit with Ethan McGrath?"

"I put in a request. There's no guarantee he'll accept."

"If he doesn't, see if Martina can get you in."

"I'm not happy—"

"I understand, but Tonka gave us two trails to follow."

"I could go back to Bish and Jock…" But then, Bish wouldn't even come clean about his clapped-out van. "Fine. I'll give it another twenty-four hours."

"OK," Gray accepted. "One last thing… You need to prime Freddie in the event that Perlett goes digging."

"You think Berringer's going to corroborate Will's story?"

"If it's in his interests." Gray looked Rob dead in the eye until it sank in.

"Oh, for fu… You've got to be joking. You're not really going to let him get away with murder. Will?"

"From what Gray's told me, we don't have much choice."

"We don't have *any* choice," Gray said. "This is war, Rob, and I put you in the enemy's sights. I'm sorry."

Rob breathed through his nose, slow and steady, working to keep his cool. He didn't like it—any of it—but Gray was right. This *was* war, and they were outside of the system that had once protected them. They were going to need all the allies they could get. "OK. I'll talk to Berringer."

24: Journeys

Gray came to with a half-conscious remnant of his ring tone decaying in his ear and an arm that felt like it belonged to someone else. The arm flopped off the edge of the bed as he rolled and squinted at the clock.

"Ah, hell." He threw the duvet aside, got one leg out, his sleep-deprived brain clutching at reason—*7:15, alarm not set, not a work day, no need to rush or panic*—and quickly shut his eyes against the sudden illumination of his phone screen. Grappling blindly, he picked it up and chanced a painful glimpse at the caller before he answered.

"Good morning, Dom." Those were not the words in his head. His previously dead, now pain-spiked hand instinctively curled into a fist.

"Morning, Gray. Apologies for the early hour. I hoped to catch you before you left for the day."

He hadn't planned on going anywhere until he'd heard from Rob, which would be another three hours at the soonest. Now fully alert with no chance of going back to sleep, he contemplated letting Dom know precisely how unimpressed he was with his rude awakening and Dom's attitude in general. Instead of any of that, he offered a heavily self-censored, "I'm not at home. It sounds urgent."

"It is. After you called on Saturday, I got in touch with the superintendent—you know O'Rourke retired?"

"I do." At least, he'd known O'Rourke planned to retire; he'd said as much when he'd visited Gray in rehab the previous spring and advised him to resign.

"Well, the new guy's a jobsworth, but he has his moments. I explained the situation to him and he arranged an emergency meeting with the assistant commissioner—that happened yesterday."

On a Sunday... It was some consolation to know the high-ups were taking the matter seriously. "Still AC Jackson?" Gray asked. It was irrelevant and he wasn't interested. He knew where the conversation was going. Delaying the outcome wasn't going to change it.

"Yeah," Dom confirmed. "I formally requested permission to share sensitive information with select non-police personnel, i.e. you and Rob. Jackson wanted to know the ins and outs of a duck's arse, as per. I told her as much as was needed for her to understand the necessity. She agreed to my request, but she's bringing in one of her trusted minions to keep her apprised."

"Good," Gray said neutrally though his heart was in overdrive and he was sweating like he had a fever. He was angry, beyond the point of being able to express it in any coherent form. Dom was brandishing his professionalism, telling Gray by omission that the mess he'd left behind had finally caught up with him when he was already acutely aware. "What's next?"

"We need to meet. I'd suggest we come to you..."

"No, it's fine. Do you need me to get in touch with Rob? He was heading down to Sussex first thing, but I could ask him to come back." It would mean abandoning Naomi, unless Will could ditch work and revert to Plan A.

"Visiting's at nine-thirty, isn't it?"

"As far as I know," Gray confirmed curtly. He hadn't said where Rob was going, but Dom's question confirmed what they'd both suspected; the SIU were doing more than tailing Rob if they had that kind of information.

"You can feed back to him later."

"That urgent, is it?" Gray left a pause which Dom didn't fill. "OK. I'll come on my own."

"I'm here all morning. See you when you get here." A lighter clicked a split second before the beep of the call ending.

With the greatest of care, Gray put his phone on the bedside table and covered his face with both hands, rubbing hard at his eyes until yellow dots appeared in the darkness.

***

Leaning against the wall next to the ill-fitting door, Rob held his phone higher than necessary so he could watch Naomi buzz around the room without her realising. It was a tiny studio flat—about 10x12 feet—with a sofa bed in one corner and Aaron's desk and computer diagonally opposite. A narrow combined wardrobe/drawers took up most of one wall, the counter at the end holding a kettle and toaster wasn't even enough to call a kitchenette, and the small, off-centre window in the other wall, had it not been covered by a closed blind, would have offered a view of the side of the run-down B&B next door.

The bathroom—shared with the other first-floor tenants—was at the end of a grim corridor that stank of something as unpleasant as it was unidentifiable, and the carpets—where they existed—were stretched, crumpled and scarred by the tongue-and-groove joints beneath. Rob wasn't one to judge—he'd lived on a shoestring himself—but this was a very steep drop from the lifestyle to which Aaron and Naomi had been accustomed when Aaron worked for Berringer's. The fact he was *still* working for Berringer's made it even more wrong. They deserved so much better.

"I'm ready," Naomi said brightly with a smile to match as she turned away from the mirror.

Rob locked and lowered his phone, pressing his lips together to cover his reaction.

Her smile faltered. "Do I look OK?"

"Yeah, totally." With the pale-cream short blazer held together by one button over a plain white shirt, café-au-lait straight pants and mid-heel shoes that put her close to Rob's height, she could've stepped straight off a catwalk. She was absolutely stunning—too stunning for a prison visit, or was that the point? Rob had no idea why she was visiting Freddie Berringer. He supposed he'd find out soon enough.

"Rob, you're staring."

"Sorry." He scratched his nose, his hand covering his smile, though there was little point. She'd caught him out good and proper. "You look great, Naomi."

She bowed her head demurely. "Thank you. Shall we get going?"

"Let's do that." Rob stepped back to give her access to the door and quietly vented a breath, glad she hadn't taken offence. The attraction was still there, as undeniable as his loathing of the Berringers for making it possible for him to meet this incredible woman and impossible for him to do anything about it.

Once they were outside, Naomi double-locked the Yale, affixed a padlock to a hasp and then turned a deadlock, pulling the door tight into the frame.

"Aaron," she said, by way of explanation.

Rob nodded his approval. Regardless of Aaron's anxiety, there was a lot of valuable equipment—and clothing—in that room, and most of the tenants were the type who would help themselves if they got the chance. Not that they saw any of them on the way downstairs; it would've been nice to imagine he was stereotyping and they were all out at work, but behind those closed doors, with TVs constantly rumbling, were spaced-out junkies and prostitutes on downtime.

When they reached the street, Naomi stopped and leaned out into the road. "No bike?"

"I didn't think you'd be up for that, so I borrowed a car." Rob pointed a key fob at Martina's Renault.

"That's not a CID car, is it?"

"No. Actually, I need to tell you something."

"You've left the police?"

"Yeah. How did you know?"

"Just a feeling I got when we were in court. I thought you'd see through Freddie's and Charles's hearings first, though."

"Are you disappointed?"

"About you leaving the police?" He couldn't decipher the look she gave him but bottled out of probing further.

"That I borrowed a car for today," he blagged. That raised a knowing smile. She had him well sussed.

"A little. I've never ridden a bike."

"We can rectify that at some point if you fancy it?" Rob unlocked the car and held open the passenger door. Naomi smiled in thanks, her shoulder brushing his chest as she slid past him and into the seat. It didn't strike him as accidental.

***

Gray emerged from the Underground station and strolled casually, taking in the splendour of the old buildings. Redbrick, art deco, and an inordinate quantity of sandstone. He'd rarely had the luxury to pause and consider the beauty of this part of the city; the times he'd worked 'at the office' had been few and far between, and always hurried in-and-outs to present cases, pick up briefs, attend disciplinary meetings or, on the last occasion, to officially hand over his department to Dom Hooper.

Dom Hooper, his oldest friend, the one colleague with whom he'd stayed in touch throughout his career. The only people Gray had known longer were his mother and sister, and they knew less about him. His work had been his life, and Dom his right-hand man. Yet, in the face of Dom's secrecy over the ongoing SIU investigation—one which Gray had set in motion—he was questioning the extent of his trust.

The reason: Gray had trained him, and if Dom was doing the job right, a couple of civilians, irrespective of their personal importance, would be far down his list of priorities. Nevertheless, he was going out of his way to give them a head start, and it was more than a gesture. Just how much he'd told the new superintendent was unclear, and Gray knew nothing about the guy. John O'Rourke—his predecessor—had left Gray to run the SIU as he saw fit. While on the one hand, he'd enjoyed that level of autonomy, on the other, nobody stepped in when his decision-making went awry.

He assumed that was why the assistant commissioner was keeping tabs this time, and it bothered him, but not for that reason. The more non-SIU personnel involved, the greater the chance they'd be silenced, shut down before they reached the source of the corruption. Gray had sacrificed everything for this operation, his sanity and Rob's safety included. If bringing it to a conclusion required lying down with dogs, so be it.

The SIU was housed on the second floor of an ordinary commercial building with signage indicating it was a Metropolitan Police administrative base, which was mostly the case. The constant drone of air-conditioning, computer fans and polite murmurs of conversation filled the cool, modern offices on the upper floors in stark contrast to the familiar sights and smells that greeted Gray as he stepped out of the century-old, well-oiled revolving door. Originally a bank, the lobby still presented an expanse of gleaming-white marble floor and the unguarded oak counters from the 1920s, along which, interspersed at wide, regular intervals, were three receptionists. All three looked up when Gray was still several feet away and on a trajectory for the smiling woman to his left.

"Good morning, Mr. Fisher."

"Good morning, Belinda. How are you? You're looking very well."

"Thank you." She asked no questions, simply handing him a pen to sign in and watching him the entire time. His face burned under her scrutiny, but he couldn't help smiling at her customary appraisal. He handed the pen back. "Do I pass muster?"

She chuckled but gave no answer as she reached under the counter to collect his visitor's pass from the printer, expertly feeding it into a holder. "DCI Hooper is in conference room two." She held out the pass; he took it and clipped it to his shirt pocket.

"Thanks. See you shortly," he said and set off for the lift up to the third floor.

***

"How's Lucas getting on?" Naomi asked. They were fifteen minutes into their journey, and the roads were quiet for the time of day. There was a possibility they'd reach the prison early enough to stop for a coffee somewhere nearby. "Have I got that right?"

"Yeah," Rob confirmed. Perhaps he shouldn't have told her about Zoë and Lucas—they'd engaged in small talk to pass the time spent sitting around in waiting rooms at the station and in the courts—but with Naomi, conversation came easy. Too easy. "He's doing great. He had me playing this racing game last week. The graphics were out of this world."

"Which one was it?"

"Haven't a clue, mate. It was all the supercars and Grand Prix tracks—he kicked my arse."

"You're not a car man, are you?" Naomi's voice had the thickness that came with a smile. Rob chanced a glance her way. She still hadn't responded to his offer of a bike ride, but maybe it was better this way.

"My driving's that bad, is it?"

She laughed. "Not at all. I feel very safe in your capable hands." She reached over and lightly squeezed his arm. The contact lasted a second at most, but the tingles it sent through his entire body took a good minute to dissipate. "I loved those racing games when I was a kid."

"Did you?" Rob concentrated on the road ahead—and keeping his capable hands firmly on the wheel. He was picking up the signals. That or it was wishful thinking.

"Before Aaron and I parted company. Even back then, he was far more interested in the workings of these things. That was how he got into programming—decompiling software. He can't enjoy something for what it is. It's a man thing, isn't it?"

"I dunno about that. Computers have never interested me."

"But I bet you spend a lot of time fine-tuning your bike."

"Err…" Rob laughed. "You might have a point there."

"And you enjoy your sports."

"Not as much as I want to, but yeah. I love a good game of footy. I wouldn't say it's a man thing, though. My mate captains a Sunday league team, and their striker's a woman. She used to play for England."

"Oh, wow! I'd ask who, but there'd be little point."

"Charlie Davenport," Rob told her anyway. "She still coaches for them."

The conversation reached a natural lull, and he thought about putting on the radio, for Naomi rather than himself; he preferred to hear what was going on around him, even if it was only the quiet hum of the blowers. He stopped at a red light and watched his passenger. She, in turn, was watching out the side window, unaware, giving him the first proper chance he'd had to look at her since Berringer's remand hearing. She hooked her hair behind her ear revealing a delicate, bare shell, no earrings. No jewellery at all, in fact, and he couldn't recall if she normally wore any, although she was beautiful with or without. The spring morning sun cast a pale glow across her cheek and chin, accentuating her smooth creamy caramel complexion. He wanted to reach out, feel her soft skin under his fingertips, an urge that became stronger each time he was in her company.

She turned and met his gaze, her expression questioning, concerned, but then her cheeks lifted and dimpled with her smile. A car horn sounded, and Rob startled back to the reality of the green light ahead. He moved off, blinking in an attempt to clear the dizziness from holding his breath, getting a little hotter under the collar at Naomi's quiet laughter.

"You're still searching for Aaron," she said.

"Sorry?"

"When you look at me like that."

Rob chuckled self-consciously. "That's definitely not what I'm doing."

"It's perfectly fine. I'm used to it." She said it so carelessly, he almost believed her, but she was wrong—about him, at any rate.

"Can I be honest with you, Naomi?"

"Always."

"I never see Aaron when I look at you, though I do sometimes see you in him."

"You mean when you met at the Science Museum? Those under-table lights…"

Rob nodded. "That's what Aaron said. But…you know that."

Naomi shifted in her seat to face him. "You really do see us as different people, don't you?"

"Yeah. Because you are."

"Most people can't. Even Will struggles at times."

"I noticed that the night we arrested Freddie. Will didn't realise it was you."

"Yet you did."

"Yeah. About two seconds before I decked Berringer, when Carrie admitted Charles killed…" Rob grimaced. "Shit. Naomi, I'm sorry." He should've stopped at decking Berringer.

The journey continued in silence long enough to get them out of the city, broken by a message alert on Naomi's phone. She sighed as she took it out of her bag, her actions indicating she was typing a reply. Rob waited until she was done before he asked, "Are you OK?"

She nodded. "I think so. You're right, though. I hadn't planned to be at that meeting at all. It was the shock, I think. Aaron wanted to face Freddie, negotiate terms, and he was doing so well until..."

"Until we arrived," Rob finished for her.

"Yes. Don't get me wrong, I'm glad you were there. We got the answers we needed, about Hector's death, and Carrie double-crossing Freddie."

Rob suspected the 'we' incorporated Freddie, and that the terms Aaron had negotiated that night were for the deal currently in place. At some point in the next couple of hours, he'd be able to confirm if he was right.

***

Never had a three-storey ascent seemed so rapid. Gray had been fine until the lift doors had closed with him on the inside, but in the few seconds it took to reach the third floor, he successfully worked himself to the brink of a panic attack. Every sensation—the inertia, the smell, the slight flicker of the dull light, the scratch on the control panel—rammed home that he was here again, in this place that had almost destroyed him once. With hands gripped tightly together, he stayed absolutely still as the lift eased to a stop and the doors opened.

"Hey, Dom." One foot in front of the other, controlled, measured steps, hand out...

"Gray." Dom shook his hand, brow furrowed, the combined aromas of cigarette smoke and mint gum ratcheting Gray's physiological arousal to nausea. "You all right?"

Gray shook his head slowly, yet perceived it as a rushed, jerky side-to-side that tilted every flat surface in sight before catapulting them upwards and outwards as if the entire corridor had quadrupled in size.

"Here. Sit a minute," Dom instructed, pushing Gray into a chair next to a vacant desk and then perching on the edge of said desk with arms folded. He looked past Gray, into the distance of the ogre-capacity corridor. "Did you see Belinda downstairs?"

"I did."

"Chatty as ever?"

Gray managed a smile. "Couldn't get a word in edgeways." Belinda only ever said what was required to do her job—in words. She could hold an entire conversation in facial expressions.

"Better?"

"Getting there." The corridor had shrunk back to almost normal size.

"You can take another minute—you might need it when I tell you who the AC's sent."

Gray chanced lifting his head so he could see Dom's face. "Who?"

"Assistant Chief Constable Martin Winstanley."

It was the mental equivalent of a hard shove in the chest, and the impact jolted Gray back in his seat. "He's not internal affairs anymore. He has no jurisdiction here." Gray's protest was feeble, and pointless.

"Joint ops. I didn't even know myself until he showed up this morning. Eight o'clock, sharp. You know how he is."

"Yeah, don't I?" Gray muttered. If he had a nemesis, Martin Winstanley was it. Before Winstanley made assistant chief constable, he'd been part of internal investigations and had outed more corrupt officers than Gray had had hot dinners—or certainly vegetarian ones. He was a stickler, even more so than Rob, and he'd been there, loitering in Gray's peripheral vision throughout his career, waiting for that one moment to occasion when Gray screwed up.

He'd been in for a long wait. Until the Strang case, Gray's record had been exemplary, but Winstanley was tenacious. He'd begrudged Gray's every promotion, even if he had admitted—after Gray had tendered his resignation—that he respected him. It had been a vendetta motivated by jealousy and a rightful sense of injustice. Winstanley had been passed over for promotions that should've been his, but he was far too good at what he did.

Ultimately, that was how Gray had attracted his attention when he'd needed his help to bring down a senior officer in his very last case with the SIU. Martin Winstanley had a nose for corruption, and had no doubt been sniffing around the SIU's operation since the very beginning. He was going to be a major nuisance and would try to block Gray and Rob's investigation. Even so, Gray couldn't think of anyone else he'd rather have on their side. Because if there was one officer he knew for sure wasn't corrupt, it was Martin Winstanley.

25: Pay The Reaper

Two and a half years ago

"What are you doing here?"

He'd expected a door slammed in his face. This was marginally better—last he knew, looks couldn't kill.

She spun sharply and marched away. He pushed the door to, not quite closed, and pursued at a distance.

"Jess—" And stopped when she whirled around.

"How dare you! After everything we had, you..."

In two steps, she closed the space between them, her glare impaling him like cold steel rods, pinned to the spot, frozen to the core. The pain was physical, a clenching in his chest that cruelly mimicked his deception. In another life, he had loved her. In this life too.

"We were friends." She spoke in a desperate whisper of disbelief, and he fell for it again—the lie that it was he, not she, who was the betrayer. "Whatever else happened between us, we were friends." Her eyes shone with hatred, with anger, with the threat of tears.

He nodded, in thought. In deed, his body failed. "That's why I'm here. I need—"

"You set me up."

He couldn't dispute it. He had set her up, and for that, he was sorry. For that, he hated himself more than she ever could.

"The bullshit heart condition, the shitty fake reunion... Why, Rob? Why didn't you just ask if you needed money? I'd have given it to you without a thought. I wouldn't even have expected it back."

"There's more to it than needing money. I'm sorry."

Her shrill laughter rang in his ears long after it had ceased, echoes of this new Jess, the one he'd refused to believe existed until he'd seen and couldn't deny it.

"You're sorry? For…what? Lying to me? Or screwing me first? What was that? Something to remind me after you'd gone?"

"Don't be—" Her slap stopped him from finishing, and perhaps it was as well. *Don't be like this.* Why was he pleading for her forgiveness when she'd set this in motion? His cheek stung, his vision blurred, and he remembered then; she'd slapped him once before, back in sixth form. No recollection of his crime on that occasion, perhaps the same as on this—that he had loved her. "Yeah, I lied to you," he admitted. "But what I say now—what I need to tell you—is the absolute truth. You're in danger, Jess. Your life—"

"No!" Her hand shot up again, and Rob braced for another slap, but she reared, shaking her head, as beautiful in fury as in passion. "I don't believe you. I can't, after…" She gripped her hair as she turned away, moaning like the bereft she had left penniless, blonde silk tangled in her fists. When she turned back, the glisten had become fully fledged tears, tiny glass beads cascading over pale-pink cheeks. Still beautiful in sorrow and disappointment. "Have you any idea what you made me do? I neglected Ellie for you." She was his ten-year-old desk mate again. *You didn't put the lids back on properly and now her felt-tip pens are ruined—because of you.* "Her hen night, her wedding, her fucking honeymoon… I fucked it all up for you, because I thought you were going to die!"

Still beautiful in her lies.

"I know about the wills," Rob said. Her shocked gasp was so well covered he'd have missed it if he hadn't seen it in their love-making more often than he wished to admit. He could tell when she was faking, when she wasn't. But she was proud, and she cared. She faked to protect his feelings, when he got carried away and didn't care enough. She still cared. He had to believe that. She'd never intentionally cause harm. Not his Jess.

He couldn't stand the deception, on either part. Say his piece and leave as quickly as possible. Never come back.

When his thoughts released him again, he found she'd moved away and was leaning against her desk, arms folded, expression hard, unreadable. "What are you talking about?"

Not a wrinkle, nor a twitch. No tells to give her away as she lied through her teeth.

"Fraud, forgery..." he began.

"Just go."

Her words crossed with his, and once she processed what he'd said, she laughed as if it were a ridiculous notion, but he'd unnerved her. He wasn't done yet.

"Biddiscombe, Campion..." There were dozens more names going back four years, possibly longer, but those were the most recent, the ones that would bring her down. The ones that gave him hope she wasn't as evil as the others. She was still the Jess he had crushed on since high school. "I know about all of it."

She swallowed, lost it a little, recomposed, smiled in an attempt to disarm him, but there was no need. He was shooting to incapacitate, not kill.

"How?" she asked.

"I needed a job. You know how things are at home..."

"No. You told me how they allegedly are. I don't trust a word you say. Not anymore."

"It's true, I swear. Zoë and I separated. She's petitioning for a divorce."

Jess's right eyebrow arched and returned to resting. She refused to release him from her gaze, pushing him to continue his explanation, but he was giving it willingly; lying to save her.

"I decided to look for a job that'd get me out of the way for a while, give us a fighting chance. There was an ad for a bike courier, carrying legal documents between London and Newcastle."

"You're working for a law firm?"

"You know which one."

"Newcastle, did you say?" Her eyes became distant in thought—more faking. "I haven't worked with any—"

"Don't you think I can recognise counterfeit IDs? I saw Jennifer Campion's passport." Or it had borne Jennifer Campion's details...along with Jess's photo.

"Right. At least I know where we stand. You've turned grass and you're giving me a chance to run. Is that it?"

She'd admitted it too easily, but then, who was there to hear? It was her word against his—respected family lawyer versus lowly document courier.

"I haven't told them, and I'm not going to." There was every possibility someone had ears on this conversation, and not those of her co-conspirators. Sharston Strang's offices were bugged; Yarrow and Perlett's too. What he was doing now was the reason he'd been kept in the dark. He was 'too close to the target', and he couldn't walk away without warning her. "I'm not in as deep as you, but I've done enough to go down."

"Your fake reunion..."

"I had to prove my worth."

"Well, I was impressed," she spat. "You didn't have to come back to gloat. To remind me what an idiot I was, trusting an old boyfriend."

Old boyfriend? He was never that. She'd never permitted him to be. "I'm not here to gloat. I'm here to warn you about Simon Yarrow. Or, should I say, Anders Folden."

"I can handle him, don't you worry."

Perhaps she hadn't seen what Folden was capable of, but Rob had. "They're suspicious, Jess. Someone tipped off the police about Campion's inheritance."

"We don't know for sure anyone did tip them off."

"*Your colleagues* don't. Not yet. But *you* do."

Jess's eyes narrowed dangerously. "And you're going to be the one to tell them it was me."

Now Rob laughed. His anger would've got the better of him if he hadn't been so close to breaking down. "You don't know me at all, do you?" He lifted his helmet, studying the lining, preparing to say goodbye for the last time. "I still love you, Jess. In spite of everything." Her eyes were on him, imploring him to look at her, and he fought against it. "It doesn't matter what you've done, I don't want you to get hurt, and right now, the safest place for you is in police custody. You could turn queen's evidence—"

"Are you insane? I'm not handing myself in!"

He lost the fight and met her gaze, less cold but still hard as steel. Resolved. "Then walk away while you can."

She held him there a moment longer then turned and went around to the other side of her desk, picked up a file and flicked through the sheets within. "Goodbye, Rob."

***

"Naomi. So glad you could make it."

She rose to her feet as Berringer approached them in the visiting area, and they embraced like lovers reuniting after a lifetime apart. Over Naomi's shoulder, Berringer locked eyes with Rob and sneered. Rob looked away, studying the low tabletop, permitting their murmured conversation without eavesdropping. They weren't the only ones who had yet to sit down, a requirement of which a guard imminently reminded them. Berringer and Naomi released each other and joined Rob in the blue and yellow plastic seats around the small Formica table.

"Well, well, Mr. Simpson-Stone. Fancy seeing you here."

"Freddie. How are you?"

"I've been better."

The niceties weren't reciprocated, and that suited Rob just fine. He wouldn't have engaged Freddie at all if he'd had a choice. Watching him caress Naomi's hand made Rob uncomfortable, like he was watching something far more intimate.

"Are you keeping well?" Freddie talked as if he and Naomi were alone. "You look…beautiful, as always."

"Thank you. Yes, I am quite well."

"Have you been to Roger lately?"

"Last week. He sends his regards."

Freddie leaned forward to cup her chin in his hand, looking into her eyes like a vet examining a much-loved pet. "And was everything all right?"

"Everything's fine, Freddie. Please don't fuss."

"Of course I must fuss, sweetcheeks." He let his hand drop, trailing his fingers over the line of small round buttons fastening Naomi's shirt. "There's little else to occupy my time. Do you miss me? I miss you."

Naomi nodded but otherwise didn't answer. She broke away from Freddie's gaze and looked down to where he was once again toying with her hand.

"This is new." He spun the ring, easing it past her knuckle and sliding it back into place. The weight of it made it twist to the side. He straightened it and did it again, and again...

Rob averted his eyes, and not out of courtesy. The sexual overtone made him want to knock Berringer out cold, more because it wasn't entirely for show. So there was still something between Naomi and Freddie, at least on his part, or Rob had misread how she'd been with him in the car, but he hadn't been wrong about the lack of jewellery. The ring was too big to miss— big enough to conceal tech of some sort—and when Rob looked again, his suspicions were confirmed. Naomi's fingers were bare once more, and Freddie was sitting back, smiling at Rob like the proverbial cat that had got the cream.

"Will's newest beau talked some sense into him, I presume?" His lazy drawl was like the sensation of walking through spider webs, and apparently the question wasn't rhetorical.

"Sorry?"

"Why are *you* here?" he asked slowly, accompanied by that smarmy half-smile, as if Rob were an idiot, but it was water off a duck's back. Rob had heard the same and worse from the lawyers to whom he'd played courier, with the exception of Folden, who'd had no need to belittle people to maintain the upper hand, which was why he was their hitman. He could murder in cold blood over and over without breaking a sweat while Rob stood by unable to intervene, sickened to the core by those dead eyes that lit up only when Folden snuffed out the life of another.

"Or was it Martina who sent you? She's such a doll. My father and hers are well acquainted."

"Small world," Rob remarked coolly. It was the same flashback he'd experienced on the night they'd raided Berringer's apartment, the hint of Folden in Freddie's absolute belief he was in control, the lack of regard for those he'd hurt. Yet watching him now, clutching around for bargaining chips, Rob realised he'd been wrong. Berringer was nothing more than a spoilt brat who stamped his feet until he got his own way.

As for Martina and her dad...they were close enough for their relationship to be usurped by privileged arseholes like the Berringers, but any sway Charles had over Hedley Senior would be rendered unnecessary in the next five minutes.

"Have you spoken to Will recently?" Rob asked.

"He writes to me on a daily basis." Freddie gave a short, false laugh and then cut it dead. "Why? Does he have something to say to me?"

"You'd have to ask him that."

"The chance would be superb."

"It might come sooner than you think."

"Oh?" Freddie sat up straight again. "Do tell."

"I'm afraid I can't."

"Robert, you're such a tease." It was a flippant comment, flamboyant even, but Rob had Freddie's full attention—and Naomi's. "My lawyer hasn't mentioned the hearing being brought forward."

"It's got nothing to do with the hearing. It's about—" Rob shifted his eyes in Naomi's direction "—the bank." Barely a flinch; she was good.

"Which bank?" Freddie asked innocently—another flawless performance.

For a second, Rob wondered if Will had merely been speculating and their entire plan was about to go west. "Yours."

Freddie crossed his legs and straightened his prison-issue trousers as if they were tailor-made—a force of habit that gave away his ill-ease. "If you're after a loan, you've come to the wrong place. As you may recall, we went bust—thanks to your old cronies."

"I know you're still in business, Freddie, but I don't need your charity."

"What *do* you need?"

"If anyone asks, Will Richards still works for you."

"Anyone being…?"

"I can't tell you." Rob maintained eye contact, hating himself for what he was about to do.

Freddie's expression rolled through disbelief, cajoling, infuriation and finally acceptance. He gave a wide shrug, like he didn't care. "What's in it for me?"

"Will thinks he may have omitted a few details from his statement."

Naomi whirled in her seat, eyes blazing. The colour had drained from her face, leaving stark flashes of rouge on suddenly sharp cheekbones. "What?"

He'd wanted to warn her. The second she'd opened the door and invited him to step in while she finished getting ready, it had been there, like over-chewed, tasteless gum that he needed to spit out and instead swallowed down. Seeing her reaction now… She wasn't afraid, she was outraged, and Rob was pleased. It suggested whatever was going on between Naomi and Freddie, the feelings were one-way. Freddie still loved her, but she didn't love him.

Freddie clicked his fingers a couple of times, and Rob snapped to attention, his face heating at Freddie's knowing sneer. "I'll take it under advisement. If my barrister agrees, we have a deal. But tell Wilfred Richards if he thinks he can double-cross me…"

"It's time to go." Naomi brusquely rose from her chair, as did Freddie, stepping around the table to block her exit route. This time, when he embraced her, she remained rigid and refused to look at him. He kissed her cheek and murmured into her ear. Whatever he said, Naomi didn't react; he released her and she marched to the door where she waited with her back turned, her shoulders narrowed and tense.

Freddie watched on like a groom jilted at the altar but quickly covered up and looked Rob in the eye, extending his arm. "I'm relying on you to take good care of her...until I get out of here."

Rob almost shunned the handshake—Naomi's business was her own—but he couldn't risk Berringer changing his mind. Reluctantly, he shook Freddie's hand and went after Naomi.

26: Defiance

Gray handed the form back to Dom—the third non-disclosure he'd signed in the past five minutes. His phone was in a locker in a room along the corridor, and he'd been body-scanned before being allowed through the biometrically protected portal to the 'inner sanctum' of the SIU—where the case files were kept.

"Like I say, it's procedure," Dom explained again as if Gray were a first-time visitor. He countersigned all three agreements and put them back in the folder. "As Rob isn't here, there's only limited information we can permit you to share with him—the rest is at your discretion."

Gray nodded, distracted by ACC Winstanley's antics. A catering assistant had delivered a tray with a coffee pot, cups and associated sundries, and Winstanley had insisted on 'being mother'. With a swift, nervous, "If you're sure, Sir?" the bamboozled catering assistant had taken him at his word and darted from the room, leaving her trolley over which the ACC loomed, weeping-willow-like.

"Are you listening?" Dom asked.

"Hmm?" Gray endeavoured to concentrate. "Sorry. Yes. Selected information at my discretion." Winstanley stalked over with a first cup and saucer—like doll's house crockery in his spidery hand—and set it down next to Dom.

"Thanks, Sir." He waited for line of sight before he continued. "I presume you've figured out this relates to Operation Tabula Rasa?"

Gray nodded again, which was to say he'd figured out it was to do with *an* operation.

"A clean slate, Mr. Fisher," Winstanley explained loftily as he swayed back to the trolley, collected a second cup and delivered it to Gray.

"Yes, thank you, Martin, I'm well aware of the meaning of that particular phrase. As for the operation to which it applies…"

"The can of worms you upended when you went after Strang and Folden," Dom muttered and shot Gray a warning glare over the top of the cup, but Gray wasn't deliberately playing silly buggers. When he'd resigned, that 'can of worms' was still known as the SAP case—based on the initial targets and the filename suffix. Given Strang and Partners were but few of many involved, the acronym had ceased to be accurate almost as soon as it came into being, but Gray had seen no reason to complicate matters by changing it; they all knew what they were talking about. Evidently, on that score, Dom didn't agree, and it was of no concern to Gray, or it shouldn't have been.

Winstanley finally made it to the table with his own coffee and folded his elongated self into a chair. "I took the liberty of reading the files on Strang et al. while I was engaged in your disciplinary investigation. Impressive work, Mr. Fisher. Very thorough indeed."

"Thanks," Gray graciously accepted Winstanley's backhanded praise. The man never could deliver a compliment without a criticism, as if it were crucial to keeping the balance of the universe, and the supercilious expression that went with it was laughable. Or perhaps it was the gravity of the situation. Either way, Gray shifted in his chair so he was facing Dom more than Winstanley. "You were saying…"

Dom exchanged his coffee cup for a pen to fiddle with, which predictably he held like a cigarette. "Without giving you a full blow-by-blow of the last eleven months, all you need to know is the operation has expanded significantly. Our initial focus on legal and financial firms was the tip of the iceberg, and we're now working in partnership with colleagues in multiple departments, including the Ministry of Defence and the Home Office.

"We have operatives in strategic locations—some SIU, some insiders. We're looking at corruption on a massive scale, Gray, and at every level all the way to the top. They've attempted to shut us down twice. Officially, Rasa ended six months ago when MI5 took it off our hands. They reviewed our evidence and concluded it was too costly to pursue further. Then our funding was cut. However—"

"Mr. Hooper..." Winstanley warned.

Dom exhaled heavily, eyes rolling as he rephrased on the hop. He tried again. "In short, our funding was reinstated, and we were instructed to continue our investigation—unofficially." He was clearly itching to give Gray the full story, but there was no way Winstanley would stand for it. Frustrating. Someone high up—Cabinet or judiciary, maybe—had a vested interest in the SIU and the investigation, and Gray would have loved to know who, but he didn't need to.

"Perhaps, Mr. Hooper, you could skip forward to the details most salient to Mr. Fisher?"

"Of course, Sir," Dom accepted with a forced smile. "One of our operatives in the MoD alerted us to a situation concerning Yvette and Philip Parker. Rob's told you who they are, I take it?"

"He has," Gray confirmed. "MoD...this is about Yvette rather than her brother?"

"In a roundabout fashion. The system logs all searches of personnel data—where they originate, what they search for—"

"They were looking for Rob," Gray said, hoping he managed to conceal the sudden spike of anxiety.

Dom nodded. "Predictably, when we tracked down the login ID, the person in question was on annual leave, but we know it came from within the Inland Revenue..." Dom glanced Winstanley's way, as did Gray. He'd procured a clipboard from somewhere—perhaps one of his colossal jacket pockets—and was scribbling furiously with a scratchy pencil. He paused without looking up and flicked his fingers at them to continue.

Dom's surprise at the lack of objection matched Gray's own, but he eventually picked up where he'd left off. "They searched Rob's contact info and hopped from his record to Yvette Parker's—she's listed as his last commanding officer. He's still on the electoral roll at his old address, which is also what's on his army record, so we assumed they were trying to get a current address for him. We checked other government agencies and made two discoveries: one, he hasn't updated his address anywhere, which means they haven't found him yet; and two, there have been multiple searches on both Rob's and the Parkers' records going back several months." Dom paused, eyes narrowed beneath his deeply lined forehead as he studied Gray. "What's on your mind?"

Gray had only been half listening; there was a lot on his mind, at the forefront a burning and seemingly obvious question. "I'll wait to hear what you think first."

"Well, with all Rob's previous undercover stints and the high profile Met cases he's worked, he's got a fair few potential enemies—"

"You don't need to soft-soap me," Gray cut in. It earned him a derisory sniff from Winstanley, and it riled him. The trail Gray had left was entire bread slices, never mind crumbs, and he'd come clean, put it all on record and accepted the consequences, because there had been more at stake than his reputation. Besides, Winstanley got a promotion out of it, so he had absolutely no right to be up there on his very high horse.

Nevertheless, this time they were on the same side and a spat would be counter-productive, so Gray gave himself a minute before he said, "I appreciate that you're trying to protect my feelings, Dom, but we all know how badly I screwed up. It's why I'm wearing this." He flicked his visitor's badge in disappointment. Strangely, it hadn't bothered him until now, when he realised he regretted his actions—not just for what it had done to Rob, but to his own career.

"Dom, you asked me why I agreed to go in with Rob on his private investigation venture, and I've given it a lot of thought. Was it guilt? At first, yes. But I think what it comes down to is this. I asked for Rob's help. He knew what it would cost him yet he still gave it. When he asked for mine, I reciprocated, because it's the right thing to do, and because this is who I am. A former police officer with years of specialist training and experience.

"After rehab, I made a conscious effort to box it away, leave it in the past, but I couldn't. I knew, as soon as Rob came to me about the Berringers. Too much of me still resides here." Gray looked around the room they were in; he'd rarely used it, preferring to meet his team 'in the field', but the ambience, the décor, the heavy scent of ancient teak—there was no ignoring where he was. "More to the point, I no longer want to put it behind me, and I can't come back, which means sticking with the private sector, and I can deal with that.

"Rob and I work well together, but we're still building trust. I threw him under the bus, for which I accept full responsibility, but it'll be a sight easier to live with if I know all I need to in order to make sure it doesn't get a second chance to flatten him."

Dom sucked hard on his pen and slowly withdrew it from his lips. "All right, Gray, I'll cut to the chase. We believe what's going on with Rob and the Parkers is related to Rasa. Someone's trying to get to Rob via the Parkers—who, and for what purpose? We don't know, but we're doing everything we can to find out."

"And if he gets in the way of the operation?" Gray asked. Dom steadily held his gaze. No false assurances. "Thank you for your honesty."

"It's all I've got, Gray." Dom peered past him to Winstanley; still scribbling. "I'll give you a brief overview of recent events so you've got a better sense of what's going on." Winstanley flipped to a clean page and continued. Dom mouthed, "Catching up on paperwork."

Gray had to agree. They hadn't said enough to fill one sheet, let alone the three dangling over the top of the clipboard. "Should I take notes?" Gray asked, straight-faced.

Dom chuckled silently and cleared his throat. "Not a good idea, but I don't envisage you'll need to. Our first task was to establish whether the Parkers were unwitting victims or willing accomplices. We received that confirmation three weeks ago when Philip Parker checked in for an investors' meeting at the Royal Chester Hotel and didn't check out."

"Interesting." Gray had cottoned on now. This wasn't Dom briefing him; it was an exchange of information. "According to his sister, he's away on business."

"But you haven't been able to get hold of either of them," Dom pointed out.

Gray bristled. "Are we bugged?"

"Do you honestly want me to answer that?"

Gray didn't care for Dom's sarcasm, although he deserved it for asking a daft question. "Go on."

"We couldn't get past hotel security. UAE royalty, diplomatic envoys—it was tight. Parker attended the first hour of the presentation, went to the lounge for coffee, and vanished."

"Yet you're still sure he's above board?"

Dom shrugged. "Your guess is as good as mine. Better, I imagine."

"Now why would you imagine that?" Gray was starting to get a very clear sense of what it was like to wear the boot on the other foot. It wasn't the violation Josh and others had reported when he'd informed them they'd been subjects of surveillance. More like being a rookie again, with someone constantly looking over his shoulder.

Dom wagged his pen in Gray's direction. "If you haven't already trawled through every bit of Parker's paperwork you can lay your hands on, I'll be a monkey's uncle."

"I knew there was a reason I recommended you, suck-up."

Dom dipped his head demurely, and Gray laughed. The more they got out in the open, the less tense they both became.

Dom continued, "As far as we can tell—you'll correct me if I'm wrong, I'm sure—both Parkers and their corporate interests are legitimate and fully above board. They even pay their taxes."

"I concur..." Distracted by the grating sound, Gray caught a jerky arm movement out of the corner of his eye. Winstanley made a few more brisk turns of his pencil and withdrew it from the self-contained sharpener, which he returned to his pocket. He offered Gray a grim smile and went back to his scribbling.

Gray ignored Winstanley's oddity and asked, "Do you think Parker's dead?"

"No," Dom said. "We know he's still alive and, as far as we can tell, so is his sister. We switched all surveillance to Yvette, yet somehow she's managed to disappear too."

"If you know Parker's still alive…what are we talking about here? A kidnapping?"

"Yes," Dom confirmed.

"Right. That explains why his sister was trying to get a large sum of cash together."

"No, it doesn't."

"Oh…hell." On impulse, Gray picked up his coffee but was struck motionless before it reached his mouth. He clung to the cup, focusing on the feel of it in his hands, its shape, its size, and begging internally for Dom to tell him he was wrong. An impossibly long time passed before Dom said anything at all, and it wasn't what Gray wanted to hear.

"The exchange was supposed to happen on the night of Rob's leaving do. Parker's sister turned up with a couple of heavies and bundled him into a van, as per her arrangement with the kidnappers."

"I didn't see any of you lot lurking outside the restaurant."

"Not knowingly," Dom said. "But you spoke to one of us."

Gray shook his head, dismayed. All those months of constant self-chastisement for his hyper-vigilance and the one night he'd needed it, it had failed him. "I'm losing my touch."

"No, mate. I'm just an expert at dodging you."

"Is that right?"

"I've had a lot of practice." Dom winked. Winstanley sniffed. Dom got back to it. "Needless to say, she didn't deliver him but took him to her dead aunt's place in Hampstead Heath instead— we discovered later. We lost her en route. Next thing, we were getting Traffic reports that Rob was headed up north. Then you called asking me to look into his phone…"

Gray absently sipped his coffee as he merged the various accounts of the evening together in his mind. Either Bish and Jock were damn good liars or Tonka hadn't told them about the hostage exchange. Given their conversation the other day about loyalty, Gray was inclined to think they were in on her plans, but something had gone wrong and now the kidnappers had two hostages. The question was, had Bish and Jock hired Rob to find Tonka because they were worried about her, or were they intending to make the exchange themselves?

"What do you know about John Garvey and Harry Wilson?" Gray asked.

Dom shrugged. "Not a lot. Stationed with Yvette Parker and Rob in Germany, now run a security firm...that's about it."

So much for his honesty. If Dom hadn't known who they were before they'd abducted Rob, he'd have done a full workup on them since, never mind that he kept glancing towards the door, desperate for a smoke, to escape, or both. He settled for taking his empty cup over to the coffee pot and refilling it.

Gray turned his attention on Winstanley, who was no longer scribbling; he was watching Dom with interest. A blink and his eyes were on Gray's, where they lingered briefly, narrow and perceptive. Another blink and they were back on Dom.

"We should take a break soon," Dom suggested and resumed his seat, acting as if he wasn't aware of Winstanley following his every move. When he could pretend no more, he said, "Sorry. Does anyone else want a top-up?"

Winstanley waved his hand, dismissing the offer. Gray watched him for a few more seconds before turning back to Dom.

"No, thanks." He weighed up the prospects of a straight answer in return for a straight question. Minimal, he envisaged, and headed around the houses. "So you followed Rob up to his mum's and you've had surveillance on him ever since."

"That's right," Dom confirmed. He was still on edge, aware he wasn't off the hook. "We wiped next of kin off his records when he was with the unit, and he's bloody nippy on that bike. We only caught up with him because we knew where he was going."

"OK." Gray smoothed his palm down over his mouth and chin. However 'nippy' Rob's bike was, it was conspicuous, which meant the SIU had intercepted their targets' attempts to pursue him, but if they'd had line of sight… "Why haven't they just taken him out?"

"If I was a gambling man, which I am, I'd lay my money on Rob having information they need, or at least, they think he does."

It was a reasonable theory. Rob had played courier for three years, during which he'd transported millions of pounds' worth of counterfeit documents around the country. He'd likely been privy to all kinds of meetings, just a lowly grunt awaiting his next order, until the final few weeks when he'd stuck to Folden like glue. When the SIU brought in Folden, Perlett, Sharston and Strang, Rob should've been fully debriefed, and the reason he hadn't been was Gray's reluctance to put him under further strain. If he had, they wouldn't be in their current predicament, because whatever Rob knew—assuming he knew anything at all—would be as valuable to the SIU as it was to their targets.

"Are you sure this has nothing to do with the Berringers?" Gray asked. "We did royally piss Freddie off."

Winstanley snuffed air out of his nose, and Gray fought the urge to smile. It was an intentionally ludicrous question. True, the SIU romping around Berringer's bank had curtailed trading for a few days, but the damage had already been done—by Freddie's father—and it was old news. But Dom answered anyway.

"Put it this way, Gray. If it did, I wouldn't have allowed Rob to visit Berringer Junior this morning."

"You're talking about dodgy investors, the Berringers were investment bankers…"

"Oh, they move in the same business circles, I grant you, but by comparison, the Berringers are good, honest businessmen. Decent sorts, as they say."

"Aside from the murder of innocent men."

"I'm not so sure they murdered anyone. The guy in the Merc, for instance—the Berringers get chauffeured everywhere. I doubt it would've even crossed Berringer Senior's mind that Laird-Browne would get behind the wheel drunk. As for the hunt sab, I haven't seen the video, but…well, let's just say that boyfriend of yours is no Saint Francis of Assisi."

Dom's analogy was flawed, but Gray got the gist and let it pass. "This investors' meeting Philip attended…"

"Yeah, money laundering. They're using their spoils to make legitimate overseas property purchases on behalf of investors. The purchase goes through, they bill their investors, et voilà! Clean money with a track record. We've managed to shut down several firms—there are others. Unfortunately, we lost our source."

Gray was torn. He'd been intent on withholding what they'd discovered, at the very least until he'd heard from Will, but it was currency, and they were, allegedly, all on the same side.

"GP Investments," he said quickly before he changed his mind.

Dom shook his head. "Never heard of them." He was telling the truth.

"The G is Hilary Gelling—Philip Parker's accountant. The P is Raymond Perlett."

"Michelle's father?"

"The very fellow."

"Wasn't he on our original SAP list?"

"Yes, and he was clean, so it might be a dead end."

"I'll get someone on it." Dom moved to stand.

"If you can wait a couple of hours, I should have the answer for you."

Dom sat again, his knee jigging. Gray recognised the symptoms, the withdrawal kicking in.

"I think it might be time for that break, Sir," he said.

Winstanley set his clipboard on the table and checked his watch. Dom was already at the door.

"Just one more thing." Gray casually rose to his feet and straightened his shirt, drawing out the motion before he glanced up at Dom. "How long have Garvey and Wilson been reporting to the SIU?"

Dom turned puce. He looked from Winstanley to Gray and back again. The silence loomed large; Dom was waiting for Winstanley's permission. It took a while—at least a minute—before he nodded once to give it.

"Since we confirmed someone was going after the Parkers," Dom said.

"And you instructed them to hire Rob and me...why? To send us on a wild goose chase?"

"Not at all." Dom pulled out his cigarettes. "I did it because I needed extra eyes on Rob...and your help."

"You could've just asked. Did you think I'd refuse?"

"No. I was confident you'd agree. This way, you don't have to lie to Rob."

"But you don't want me to tell him about Bish and Jock—sorry, Garvey and Wilson."

"I'm familiar with their nicknames. I see no problem with you telling Rob now. Even if he pulls out of the investigation..."

"I can't," Gray finished, as impressed with Dom's cunning as he was infuriated by his solipsism. "You're a devious sod, Hooper."

Dom shrugged nonchalantly. "I'm merely following the rule book written by my predecessor. See you in twenty." The door closed.

Gray stared after him, no idea what to do next. Now he knew for sure there was a target on Rob's back, he wanted as much information as he could get his hands on, but he doubted Winstanley would permit him access to the case files.

"If I may offer a word to the wise, Graham..."

He still had his back to Winstanley but noted the change of address along with what sounded suspiciously like empathy or concern. Gray gave him the go-ahead.

"There's nothing to be gained from bringing Simpson-Stone up to speed on Garvey and Wilson."

Gray had been thinking the same. There was no telling how Rob would take the news that his old army mates had lied to him by omission. It may even hinder their efforts to keep him safe, but Gray had to go back with something or Rob would seek his own answers.

At such times, and in the present company, humility was his friend. Of course, Winstanley would see straight through it, but he might play along if Gray buttered him up enough.

"Thanks, Martin. I appreciate the advice. It's been good to see you again."

"Likewise."

"I had my reservations when Dom told me our meeting would be supervised."

"Quite," Winstanley said, his attention seemingly back on his note-taking. He knew what Gray was playing for, and he was making him work for it.

"Yes, I was relieved to discover it would be you."

"I'm sure."

"Of all the officers I've come into contact with in my career, and it runs into the hundreds, you're the only one I trust."

That stopped him, albeit for only a few seconds. Nor was he entirely successful in hiding his pleasure at Gray's admission. "All right," he said, "let's have it, Fisher."

"I want access to the Tabula Rasa files. No notes, no copies, I'll read them here, today, under your eagle-eyed supervision."

"That's all you want?"

"Yes, Sir."

Winstanley slowly inhaled, the air whistling its way up his nostrils. Gray waited with breath held for as long as he could, but the man had the lung capacity of an ox, and Gray had to give up before he passed out.

"That seems acceptable." Discarding his clipboard, Winstanley rose from his seat. "More coffee?"

"Yes...please. And thanks."

And *still* he didn't exhale.

27: Double Crossing

Rob slowed and dropped a gear as they passed a pub with 'food served all day' signs. "How about there?"

"Fine by me," Naomi replied in the same couldn't-care-less tone she'd used since they'd left the prison, such as either of them had said much at all, which was why Rob had suggested stopping somewhere for lunch to clear the bad air between them. Understandably, she was angry. The Met had put serious pressure on her and Aaron to testify against the Berringers, but it only worked because they'd wanted to be free of Freddie. That or they'd just wanted to bring him down a peg or two.

Either way, Rob was still confident Naomi didn't want Freddie out on the prowl again. Beyond that, he had no idea what she wanted, not when she'd flirted with him and then let Freddie fawn all over her. He was jealous, and aware of the parallels to the accusation he'd levelled at Jess all those years ago—*you led me on*—the difference being Jess *had* led him on, for sex, not the relationship he'd craved. With Naomi, he couldn't even be sure she was flirting. It wasn't the first time, but it hadn't mattered before Gray suggested brokering a deal with Berringer. It had been clear-cut, or clearer than the muddy mess it was now. Whether the trial went ahead or not, Rob was still a former police officer, and he'd met Naomi while on the job.

The pub's wait staff must have assumed they were a couple and showed them to a secluded table in a dark corner screened off from the rest of the dining room. Menus appeared in front of them, from which they both made an arbitrary choice and ordered soft drinks. The waiter took back the menus, returned briefly to deliver their drinks, and then left them to their silence.

Rob wanted to know about the ring Naomi had smuggled to Freddie. He could ask straight up—that was what he'd normally have done—but the last thing he wanted was for her to think he was accusing her of wrongdoing. She'd broken the prison's rules, which could have a bearing on her reliability as a witness if Berringer still went to trial *and* it came out, but Rob was increasingly apathetic towards the whole situation.

He'd done his job thoroughly, knowing the Berringers' QC would trawl every document and analyse every word for any means to have the case dismissed, and it had all been for nothing, so what did it matter if Naomi had broken a couple of petty prison rules? Freddie had wielded power over Aaron too long to uphold the illusion that Naomi was acting of her own volition, although the longer Rob spent in her company, the less certain he became that it was an illusion.

They sipped their drinks; their meals arrived. The silence continued, finally broken by Naomi's request for ketchup and Rob's unchecked reaction.

"What?" She was immediately defensive. "I like ketchup."

"I didn't say a word."

"You didn't need to. Your face said it for you." She deposited a large dollop on the side of her plate, clicked the lid shut and set the bottle down. There was a smile lurking behind that moody scowl.

Shaking his head, Rob tucked into his gammon and chips. "You and Lu would get on like a house on fire."

"How so?"

"United in your love of ketchup. The kid puts it on everything—chips…"

"What are chips without ketchup?"

"Fry-ups…"

"The perfect accompaniment."

"Carbonara." Rob nodded at Naomi's plate. Almost to spite him, she swirled her pasta-loaded fork in the ketchup, covering it completely. Rob laughed, relieved the ice was starting to melt. "I'm sorry," he said. "I should've warned you."

"Was it an option?"

"Yeah. I bottled out."

"Were you worried I'd jeopardise your success in talking Freddie round?"

"No, nothing like that. I didn't want to upset you. And for the record, it wasn't my idea."

"I'd gathered as much." Naomi exchanged her fork for her glass. "It has Will Richards written all over it."

"Does it?" Rob thought it had come from Gray—contrary to his claim it was Will's scheme—because it was a DCI Fisher tactic too. Clearly, they were well suited.

"What's it about, or can't you tell me?"

"I can't say much as it relates to an ongoing investigation."

"The PI business?" Naomi guessed.

"Yep."

"Mmm." She wanted to say more, and Rob wanted to tell her more. In spite of what he'd witnessed at the prison, he trusted her to keep it to herself, but it wasn't solely his decision.

"You've got ketchup..." He subtly indicated her chin. She wiped with her napkin, but the ketchup stayed put. She tried again. Rob shook his head. She gave her chin one more broad wipe, to no avail. It was the tiniest spot and he'd only used it to redirect both of their attention, but this was possibly worse. "So what have you been up to?" he asked, attempting to move the conversation on again.

"Are you really going to let me go through the rest of lunch with ketchup on my chin?" She held out her napkin and leaned forward. "No spit," she warned.

With a smile, Rob took the napkin and rubbed at the offending spot, but the ketchup was stubborn as anything.

"Everything all right with your meals?" A waiter stopped at their table.

Naomi quickly leaned her chin on her hand. "Yes, thanks."

"Great, cheers," Rob said. "Could I trouble you for a glass of water?"

"No trouble," the waiter said and left, soon returning with the water. Rob offered thanks and waited for them to move on before he dipped a corner of the napkin into the glass and used it to successfully clean the ketchup away. The cool wetness amplified the heat radiating from Naomi's skin, and Rob was once again fighting the urge to touch. Carefully withdrawing, he dropped the napkin onto the table and sat back in his chair, fingers locked and steepled above his plate.

Naomi frowned in concern. "What's wrong?"

"Nothing." Rob clasped his hands tighter together, not yet safe from temptation. "Can I be honest, Naomi?"

"Twice in one day?"

"Actually, it was the same point, but I got sidetracked."

"Oh, now I'm intrigued." That smile...if that didn't mean what Rob thought it meant...

"All right. Cards on the table. I'm very attracted to you. I have been since I met you."

"When you thought I was Aaron's wife," she said. Her smile faltered, and there was a hint of worry there, but it made her no less beautiful. "He told you we were separated."

"Yep." Rob briefly got lost in reminiscing the night she'd called him over to her mother's flat. He'd thought back on it a few times and couldn't recall if she'd claimed to be Aaron's wife, although Aaron had referred to her as such, probably because Rob had put him on the spot. If he'd known about Aaron's anxiety, he'd have taken a gentler approach. "The thing is...there was this girl back in high school I fancied like mad, and we ended up going out a couple of times, slept together quite a few more over the years... I thought she wanted what I did." He hid behind his hand and laughed at himself. "Turns out I'm really shit at interpreting signals." He peered over his fingers. Naomi smiled back at him. "Am I way off, or...?"

"No, but I have to ask. How on earth did you get with Zoë?" She was tormenting, Rob thought, but also interested to know.

"She's pretty blatant about what she wants." She hadn't changed in that regard, which was how Rob had known he was ready to move on. He was OK with Zoë loving Travis. "Anyway, it's all academic. I can't do anything about it."

"Because I was a suspect?"

"Suspect, witness, makes no odds. My hands are tied—at least until the Berringers' trials are over, maybe even beyond."

"But those won't go ahead if your plan comes to fruition," Naomi argued.

"Freddie's won't. However, we're both prosecution witnesses against Charles. That aside, seeing you and Freddie together today—"

Naomi held up her hand, no trace of the smile now. "OK, I need to explain."

"You don't."

"I do, Rob. Because if the only obstacle to our friendship becoming something more meaningful is Freddie's and my little game…"

"It's not a game to Freddie."

"Oh, it is. I know how it looks, but you have to get into his mindset. Freddie's all about acquisitions, trophies." She tapped her finger to her chest. "That's what I am to him. I'm not saying he's lying when he claims he's in love with me. I'm quite sure he believes it's true. But if he did *acquire* me, then what?"

She paused. Rob couldn't decide if it was for effect or if she was expecting him to respond, but he had nothing to say so was relieved when she answered her own question.

"It would be over, and that's the last thing Freddie wants."

"It's the chase," Rob said.

"More…a Victorian collector of exotic species. Freddie naively imagines I could survive in captivity, but he'd soon tire of me and grow neglectful. Roger—a doctor friend of his—insists Aaron and I will converge if we submit to gender alignment and psychotherapy when, in truth, Freddie will either lose me—his *exotic bird*—or he'll lose Aaron."

Rob nodded slowly. He sort of understood what she was saying. "That's who Freddie mentioned earlier—Roger?"

"Yes. He's an endocrinologist—prescribes my HRT and gives me a check-up every once in a while."

"HRT?" Rob's mum had been on it during her menopause, and if he'd given himself a minute to reason it through, he wouldn't have repeated it aloud. "You agreed to the treatment? I thought Aaron said—"

"He doesn't want it? You're quite right, but we compromised. Freddie and me, that is. You might have noticed Aaron has little regard for his appearance." Naomi smiled and bit her lip. "I must tell you about the time Aaron went clothes shopping. It wasn't long after I'd come out to our friends—Will, Hector, Carrie and a few others—not Freddie at that point. The first time Freddie met me, he didn't know who I was, other than Will's girlfriend, but that's another story."

"Touchy subject?" Rob asked. It wasn't news. Will had mentioned he and Naomi were an item back in university, but she hadn't spoken about it before. Again, Rob was struck by a touch of jealousy—mixed in with his desire to know everything there was to know about Naomi Silvestri.

"A little," she confirmed, and then, responding to whatever signal he was giving off—he hoped it was curiosity—added, "Nothing sinister. I'll tell you sometime. So, this one morning, Aaron got up and immediately flew into a fury because I'd spent all his—our—student grant on clothes, mostly for me, although I did buy him a suit, shirt and tie. He'd rather slouch around in jeans and t-shirts, and they were tatty and old, so…"

"You threw his clothes out, didn't you?" Rob guessed.

She laughed. "Yes, I did. Not all of them, mind you. I saved a couple of the less faded t-shirts and—don't you shake your head at me."

Rob *was* shaking his head, but he was laughing too. "Zoë did that to me a couple of times. They're only faded because we love them and want to get our money's worth."

"Aaron got more than his money's worth out of that lot. Some of those t-shirts went back to his high school days. Anyway, to cut a long, arduous story short, he asked Freddie to pay some of what he owed him and replenished his wardrobe. Bear in mind this was eighteen years ago, and he's still wearing those same jeans and t-shirts now."

"They're timeless," Rob reasoned, which earned him a light smack on the arm. "That was the last time he went clothes shopping?"

"Sadly, yes."

"Good for him."

Naomi narrowed her eyes. "I was starting to rather like you."

Rob laughed. He didn't actually mind buying new clothes and always tried to dress well, but it was fun winding Naomi up. Fun spending time with her, full stop. He was losing his resolve, and they'd both finished eating some time ago. "Do you want to stay for dessert?" he asked.

"Are you in a rush to get back?" she countered.

"Not especially, but there're things I could be doing, and Hedley will expect her car back at some point."

"Then we should make a move." Naomi waved to catch the waiter's attention. "Bill, please?"

The waiter acknowledged the request with a nod and left to get it.

"My shout," Rob said, pulling his wallet from his pocket. Before he could open it, Naomi's hand landed on top of his.

"Why?"

"Why not? I suggested we stop for lunch. It's only fair I pay."

"Consider it a thank-you for accompanying me to the prison."

The plate with the bill appeared on the table between them; Naomi got to it first.

"I'm not happy about this," Rob grumbled. Still intent on at least paying his share, he pulled a twenty-pound note from his wallet and dropped it onto the plate.

"Rob, you really don't have to. Aaron's bringing in a regular income." She sifted through a stack of cards and withdrew a gold one.

"From Freddie?"

She hesitated—very briefly—as she put the card down on top of his note. No denial, but he'd let her play ignorant so far; now he needed to know if she trusted him with the truth.

The waiter returned with a card reader, and Naomi paid the bill, leaving the twenty-pound note on the table. Rob exchanged it for a more sensible tip, and then they were in the car again, heading for home. They were almost outside Naomi's place before she broke her silence.

"Will you come up for a coffee? I'll tell you everything."

"What did you give to Freddie?"

He heard her draw breath as if to answer and then release it.

"Please, Naomi." Her response—or lack of—would decide where they went next, and Rob couldn't force it.

She fidgeted with her seat belt, tugging it away from her neck. "Are you obligated to report back?"

"To who? Gray?"

"Your former boss."

"You mean Hedley? No." He indicated and pulled into a space outside Naomi's building, watching her and waiting.

"An encryption algorithm."

"He's not planning to break out, is he?"

"No, nothing like that. He has restricted internet access, and it's monitored. The algorithm bypasses the restrictions and encrypts Freddie's data. He's not using it for criminal purposes, only bank business."

"How do you know?"

Naomi smiled. "The prison might not be able to monitor what he's up to…"

"But Aaron can," Rob finished.

Naomi unfastened her seat belt. "So, about that coffee..."

It was too tempting. "Some other time, yeah?"

She studied him for several seconds and then nodded. "Some other time," she said and leaned across to kiss his cheek. "Take care, Rob."

"You too," he replied, still facing forward and refusing to look as she got out and shut the door behind her.

***

"Rob. I left you a voicemail."

He startled. He'd been checking the car to make sure it was clean and tidy and hadn't heard Martina come up behind him.

"Did you?" He handed her keys over and took out his phone, tutting at himself as he turned it back on. He'd switched it off at the prison. "What's up?"

"The Quarterhouse sent us their security camera footage from the week of your leaving do."

"I know who abducted me."

"This is from earlier in the week." She moved off, expecting him to follow, which he did, into the station, pausing to sign in, and up to her office, where she logged in to her computer while he checked his other messages. All junk other than one from Brookhurst hospital to say Ethan had approved his visit—tomorrow at 1800—although Rob wasn't sure it was necessary anymore.

"Ready?" Martina asked.

"Hmm? Sorry. Yeah."

She pressed play and stepped back to give him an unobstructed view.

The footage was a wide shot of the restaurant's interior which also took in the front entrance and half of the window next to it. Rob watched the staff going about their preparations—vacuuming floors, laying tables. "What am I looking for?" he asked.

"Keep your eye on the window."

Rob shifted focus, glancing at the date and time in the top-left corner of the screen—Tuesday afternoon, three days before his leaving do—and then he saw it. A white van, sliding door on the nearside, a line of rusty holes where the rubber bump rail should've been. "What the hell? How long was it there?"

"Only a few minutes," Martina said as the time changed again and the van magically disappeared.

"The bastards. They knew I'd be there. The whole setup was bullshit. Any idea what they were up to?"

"I was hoping you might be able to shed some light."

"Nope. I haven't the foggiest, but I'm gonna bloody well find out." He was tempted to get straight on the bike and head down to Brighton. He could be there in an hour.

"How did it go with Berringer?" Martina asked. He wouldn't have put it past her to have caught on to what he was thinking and delay him on purpose, although it was a reasonable question.

"All right," he said neutrally, hoping to shut down further enquiry. No such luck.

"Nothing untoward?"

"Apart from the two of them getting all lovey-dovey?"

"Ah. Sorry to hear that."

Rob frowned. "Why?"

"I know you've got a soft spot for Naomi."

By the time he'd got over his shock, it was too late for him to convincingly deny it, although there was no reason for him to do so. As Martina kept reminding him, she was no longer his boss, and they were still friends…for the time being. "Yeah, well, even if there was nothing between them, I can't act on it."

"Not at the moment. Once the Berringers' trials are over, there's nothing to stop you pursuing something more."

Rob's pulse rate shot up, and he was glad he had the cover of his crush on Naomi because when Martina found out what he'd done, she'd be gunning for him.

28: Answers

The conference room table should have been bowing under the weight of the multiple stacks of files over which ACC Martin Winstanley presided like a praying mantis.

"Reference number?" He licked the tip of his pencil and poised it above the clipboard balanced on one spindly arm, waiting to record the requested information as he had done for every file Gray had touched so far.

Gray suppressed a sigh and flipped the cover shut. "It's—"

There was a knock at the door. Martin held up his hand as if Gray were still talking. "Come!"

The door eased open, and another stack of files appeared, followed by a female officer.

"Well blow me down," Gray muttered and laughed at how obvious it was—now he knew. It was the woman he'd seen in the metro supermarket on the night of Rob's leaving do. "You were tailing me."

The female officer set down the files and brushed her palms together before offering her hand. "Dee Knight. Good to meet you, Mr. Fisher."

Gray shook Dee's hand. "And you. So that spiel about the missing partner…"

She grinned sheepishly. "DCI Hooper told me to draw attention to myself or you'd get suspicious."

"Ah, he knows me too well. You did an excellent job, incidentally, although a few times I've wondered if you ever managed to track him down."

"Yeah, sorry."

"No problem. You do what's necessary to get the job done. So, how long have you—"

"Mr. Fisher? If we may continue?" Winstanley rapped his pencil against his clipboard.

Seeing as he had his back to Winstanley, Gray took the opportunity to pull a face before he answered, "Of course, Sir. My apologies."

"That's the last of the files, Sir," Dee said, grinning at Gray's antics. He approved of Dom's decision. He liked her.

Winstanley nodded and flicked his fingers to send her on her way. "Reference number?" he repeated once the door had closed.

Gray pursed his lips but then decided to just come out and say it. "I thought promotion might make you less bitter."

"I'm not bitter, Graham."

"That's not quite the right word. Resentful?"

Winstanley placed his clipboard on top of the new stack of files and pulled out a chair but didn't sit. "Yes," he said, exaggerating the 'e' and keeping the 's' short and sharp. His focus was on the files, not Gray. "I resent having to play over-attentive nanny to an impetuous child."

"Then leave me to it. I can't go anywhere without you or Dom letting me out."

"That's precisely my point. You shouldn't even be here."

"Fine, I'll go." Gray unclipped his visitor's badge and started towards the door.

"Don't act the fool, Graham."

"I've taken up enough of your precious time. Can you let Dom know—"

"Stop!"

The hairs on the back of Gray's neck prickled. It was never wise to take on Martin Winstanley, but he was tired of hearing it—same overture, different movement. Still, he couldn't walk away; there was too much at stake. Taking a couple of slow, deep breaths, he turned around and retraced his steps until he was only a foot from Winstanley, whose face was thunder. "Look,

Martin, it's done. If I could go back and fix it, I would, but I can't. The sooner you and Dom accept—"

"For God's sake, man, this is no longer about your misconduct, nor even the devastation you left in your wake. My resentment for your involvement now is that it's come too late. Have you any idea how much evidence I've gathered in the past ten years on the very people you threatened to expose?"

"You're telling me there was already an internal investigation underway?"

"I'm telling you I've known for a long time both who they are and what they're capable of, but, as the old adage goes, fools rush in..."

"If I'd had access to that information two years ago—"

"I could not have given you that information two years ago nor at any point prior, and my personal feelings toward you had nothing to do with it. We may have had our differences in the past—" Winstanley's vacuous nostrils flared wider still at Gray's disbelieving 'ha'. He inhaled—slowly, steadily—and started again. "We may have had our differences in the past, however, I would suffer your company for all eternity before I let my *resentment* stop me from doing my job."

"Suffer my company? I didn't choose to be here, nor did I request your presence."

"No. I volunteered."

"Why? Because you don't trust me?"

"Quite the contrary, Graham." Winstanley's right nostril twitched so violently it mobilised his cheek and ear, yet his tone remained as droll and irritatingly nasal as ever. "I volunteered because I cannot watch from afar when your life, and Simpson-Stone's, is in danger."

***

It wasn't often Rob was too hyped to focus on his riding, but he'd arrived home on autopilot. Still livid, he slammed his front door and didn't bother taking off his leathers before he called

Bish. No answer, he tried Jock instead. He got no answer there either, and dug out Bish's business card, calling their office number.

"Sequrco, Mr. Garvey's office."

"Hello. Put me through to Mr. Garvey, please."

"May I ask who's calling?"

"Rob Simpson-Stone."

"One moment, sir."

The line went quiet. Rob used the time to unzip his jacket and walked through to the kitchen, absently checking the fridge for beer.

"Mr. Garvey's not here at present."

"Bullshit." No beer. He kicked the fridge shut.

"Excuse—"

"Sorry, I know you're only following orders, but I need to speak with him right now."

"Please hold the line, sir." She was curt to the point of rudeness—no less than he deserved.

Rob switched his phone to speaker and left it on the counter so he could get out of his jacket. He'd walk to the off-licence once he was done with this phone call.

"Shaz, mate…"

Not Bish. "What the fuck's going on, Jock?"

"I dunno what—"

"You knew I was leaving the police."

"Yeah. You told me." He sounded suitably puzzled by the accusation, but Rob was having none of it.

"You acted ignorant about my leaving do even though Bish's van was parked outside the restaurant three days before. You *know* what's going on."

"I swear—"

"Cut the crap, Jock. Now's your chance to talk, because if you don't, I'm gonna come down there and beat it out of you."

"For fuck's sake. We're trying to save your neck here."

"Who's 'we'?"

"I can't tell you."

Rob balled his fist but stopped short of hitting anything. He was still in half a mind to get back on the bike. "Where's Tonka?"

No answer.

"Where is she, Jock?"

"I can't tell you."

"But she's safe?"

"For now, yeah. It's not her you need to worry about."

"Her brother?"

"It's—"

Rob heard Bish going nuts in the background. The bloke could swear for England when he was on one. He snatched the phone from Jock. "Rob, alright?"

"Far from it."

"What's up?"

"You and Jock are in on whatever Tonka's up to."

"Need to know." Bish wasn't kidding around, but Rob wasn't taking any more crap.

"*I* need to know," he said.

"It's better you don't."

"You're not gonna deny it?"

"There's not much point when you're right. But it's not what you think."

"No? Why don't you put me straight, Bish?"

No quick-fire response this time, Bish's noisy nose-breathing crackled against the mic until, finally, he relented. "OK. But not over the phone."

"Fair enough. Where d'you want to meet?"

"Tonka's gaff. Two hours. Bring your partner with you."

***

Gray was much more comfortable with the abundance of information heaped all around him—albeit largely irrelevant— than he'd been with Josh's approach of picking through sparse facts and following gut feelings. Nonetheless, it would've been far easier to find what he was looking for if the evidence had still been computerised, but the SIU had been ordered to destroy all files associated with Tabula Rasa after MI5's review, so he was stuck with archive copies—which included the evidence he'd collected during the SAP investigation—and handwritten records of everything since the review.

As Dom returned from his fourth smoke break of the afternoon—just after two o'clock, which Gray only noticed because it was also the time of Will's appointment with GP Investments—Gray finally found the file on Michelle Perlett and her law partner Simon Yarrow. It dated back to the beginning of the investigation, when the two first set up shop in Newcastle. Before that, Yarrow had been operating in London; the Met Police alerted the SIU when they received a complaint about Yarrow's conduct and discovered the real Simon Yarrow was dead.

For a long time, Gray was unable to identify the imposter, largely because his attention was on an insider-trading scheme that had coincidentally led him to a company in George's hometown. The coincidences didn't stop there; Yarrow's former partner in London was Terence Strang, the brother of a named partner in the law firm representing Campion Holdings—the company Gray had been investigating.

Campion's was a well-respected, benevolent firm which offered community service placements to young offenders. While Alistair Campion—founder and CEO—had been a great believer in criminal rehabilitation, Gray's experience didn't afford him the same faith in people's capacity to turn over a new leaf, so when the CEO turned up dead, rather than waste time going after Campion's competitors, Gray dug deeper into their personnel records and, by chance, discovered Simon Yarrow's real identity.

From that point on, the investigation only got stranger, and there were times Gray had wondered if he was seeing connections that simply weren't there. After all, his decision to pursue Campion's had been an excuse to get closer to George— on a conscious level, at least.

Unconsciously? Perhaps Josh's point about intuition was valid because, with the full body of evidence stacked before him, Gray was back in his SIU mindset—with a new twist. He saw...not cubes, but a map like the London Underground, and there, amid the tangle of links and terminals, one line stood bright and stark against the rest.

***

Rob had a sharp sense of foreboding about this meeting with Bish and Jock, so much so he decided to use the time before he'd need to leave for Tonka's to pick Lucas up from school. And then immediately changed his mind. Taking Lu out of class before the end of the school day would get Rob in hot water with both the headteacher and Zoë, not to mention that Jock's warning—'it's not Tonka you need to worry about'—on top of Gray's theory that someone was after them, had Rob's imagination working overtime, and he was no longer sure whose side Bish and Jock were on. Paranoia or justifiable caution?

If he'd believed it was all hot air, he'd have refused outright to go along with Will's scheme. Giving Freddie a get-out-of-jail-free card went against everything Rob believed in—same for Gray, for that matter—yet here they were, descending the rabbit hole with no idea where they'd land. To add to that, it was looking increasingly likely that Rob would have to go it alone at this meeting—Gray must still have been with Dom as his phone was going to voicemail—and he couldn't shake the feeling he was being set up.

At two-thirty, he tried Gray one last time—still voicemail—before he got on the bike and headed for Hampstead Heath and Tonka's place, keeping a close eye on his mirrors, but if he had a tail, it was someone who knew what they were doing. Once he was off the main road, he pulled over next to one of the bathing ponds, powered down the bike, removed his helmet and took out his phone.

For several minutes, he stared at the screen, re-activating it each time it went dark. His decision was already made, but putting it into effect felt like sealing his fate. In the near distance, he heard the rev of a diesel engine. A second later, a van rounded the corner—a mint silver Mercedes with dark-tinted windows. The driver's window lowered, and Bish and Jock visually acknowledged Rob as they passed him on the way up to Tonka's. Time was up; he hit the call button.

"Hello?"

"Travis? It's Rob."

"Oh, alright, mate?"

"Yeah. Well, no, actually. Listen, I need to tell you something, but you'll have to keep it under your hat for the time being. Can you do that for me?"

"OK."

"There's something going down this afternoon. I'm not sure what it is, but if it comes to the worst, there's a guy lives upstairs from me—Shammy, an old Rasta, decent bloke. He's got my spare key, and Lois, my niece, is my executor. She's got a copy of my will."

"Whoa. This is some serious shit, Rob."

"I know, and I might be way off, but if I'm not…"

"Yeah, I'll sort it, mate. Don't you worry."

"Cheers, Travis."

"Be careful."

"I will. You…too." He stopped short of saying 'look after them for me'—he knew Travis would—and ended the call, sending Martina a quick message along the same lines before he tucked his phone away and put his helmet back on.

Eyes on the road ahead, he restarted the bike and set off, prepared for the worst. Anything else would be a bonus.

29: Up The Junction

"Dom, remember the inquest into Biddiscombe's death?" Gray was already thumbing through the file.

"Bits and pieces."

"You said you saw... This is it." Gray read from the page in front of him. "Perlett and Folden left in the same car—a BMW 535."

"That's right," Dom confirmed. "It was registered to Perlett's father."

"Who was driving, do you recall?"

"Folden."

"You sound sure."

"Yeah. They had a hoo-ha over him moving the seat back. I thought they were acting up because they'd seen me, but they drove off soon after and went back to their offices."

"So Perlett must've driven them to the coroner's hearing." Gray continued reading to himself. Patricia Biddiscombe had been Folden's—or, rather, Yarrow's—client. Her doctor had ignored an advance directive and resuscitated her because her relatives noticed her will had been changed. Folden deflected the accusation back at the doctor, whose medical licence was suspended as a consequence, and in the midst of the General Medical Council's investigation, Folden had managed to disappear—temporarily—but all the SIU had to do was wait for the will to be held intestate and they'd have their lead on which court officials were also involved in the scam.

Fortunately for the SIU—but not for the woman's relatives, who never received their inheritance—Perlett and 'Yarrow' moved to pastures new, separately, which was when Gray ordered Rob to infiltrate deeper and gain Folden's trust, believing it was only a matter of time before Folden's greed got the better of him. He'd been right.

"Perlett and Folden were having a relationship," he said and continued in response to Dom's predictable 'where did you conjure that from?' frown. "He used her to infiltrate the fraud ring and ditched her once he was in. He did the same with Terence Strang and Angela Sharston."

"Didn't we establish Folden was just their puppet?"

"That's what he wanted them—and us—to think." Gray was up on his feet and moving around the conference table, sifting at speed through the stacks of files. He glanced up at Winstanley, who was twitching like he had his fingers in a power socket. "I'll give you all the references once I'm done, Martin." That seemed to satisfy him for the time being, but Gray was on a deadline. If Winstanley cottoned on to what Will and Rob were up to today, he'd immediately rescind Gray's access to the evidence.

"OK." Gray held up the half-dozen files. "This is where it gets interesting."

Dom raised an eyebrow.

"Shut it, Hooper."

"Didn't say a word," Dom muttered.

"Your briefings are a laugh a minute, I bet."

Dom folded his arms and held his smirk while Gray cleared a space at one end of the table and laid out the files he'd selected, one by one, in a line, identifying each in turn.

"Clarkson, Biddiscombe, Campion, Black Hole, R v Hogarth, and the Parkers. What have they all got in common?"

"Well, the first four were the SAP case," Dom said. "Hogarth..." He thought about it but then shook his head. "I'm not seeing a connection, or nothing that makes those specific files stand out from all the rest."

That surprised Gray; Dom was sharp as they came. But that was the problem with working in a close-knit unit and constantly sifting through the same evidence; a theory rose to the surface and there it stayed, blocking all other potential explanations. With the benefit of a year's distance, Gray could see it clear as day. "I haven't looked in the file, but I read the newspaper reports. Hogarth's husband was a senior civil servant shot dead by her lover, I believe."

"Correct."

"Was he one of yours?"

Dom waited for the nod from Winstanley before he answered. "Yes. Stephen Hogarth was a section manager in Revenue and Customs. All the overseas investment intel came from him. That's why we don't know which firms are involved currently."

"And the lover?"

"Never found. Victoria Hogarth's looking at ten years, secondary liability."

Gray studied the files again, giving himself a moment to get his narrative in order. "There are points of commonality in these six files. Mind if I share them with you?"

"Fill your boots," Dom invited.

"OK. So, first we've got Clarkson's forged will, the complaint that kicked it off. Somehow, Strang and Folden got wind of the Met's investigation and moved on before their offices were raided. Then we've got Biddiscombe, same offence, but this time, Folden slipped through the net during the GMC inquiry, ditching Perlett somewhere along the way. Similarly, with Campion's murder, Folden framed Callaghan, and by the time we'd figured out how he'd done it, the CPS had already prosecuted.

"Next was the Black Hole hostage situation, which concluded the SAP investigation. All living suspects were successfully arrested, tried and convicted—"

"Eventually," Dom interjected. "Folden's trial was adjourned twice."

"Hold that thought," Gray said. "These two cases are key. Hogarth's murder and last, but by no means least, the abduction of the Parkers, both within two days—"

A knock at the door interrupted his presentation, and Dee Knight poked her head into the room.

"Sorry to disturb you, Sir," she addressed Dom and then looked at Gray. "Mr. Fisher, I'm just letting you know your phone keeps vibrating."

"Thanks. I'll come and deal with it in a moment." It would be Will or Rob calling to update him.

Dee backed out of the room. The door clicked shut, but before Gray could continue, Winstanley cleared his throat with a loud, fake 'ahem'. Gray gestured for him to speak, though he'd have done so with or without the invitation.

"Mr. Fisher, every file you see before you—" he swept his arm over the entire conference table "—shares *commonalities*, as you call them."

"Yes, Sir, they do." Gray figured he'd wound the man up enough for one afternoon, but patience was running low on both sides. "I don't have time to go through every file, and it may well be I'm seeing a connection that isn't there."

"Which is?"

"Has anyone checked in on Folden recently?"

"He's not the only assassin on their books, Graham. Folden's of no consequence to us."

Winstanley's attitude was starting to piss Gray off, the way he spoke to him as if he were a little boy telling tales to teacher. It was nothing new; indeed, it was why Gray had never had any qualms about shoving Winstanley aside on his way up the career ladder. They had no time to waste on another round of tit-for-tat, however, so Gray battened down the urge to retaliate and smiled amenably.

"Just humour me, Martin, OK? You're both right, of course. To a network of this size with this much power, Folden's kind are ten a penny, but I've seen how he operates. He infiltrates, gets close to his target. He doesn't do it for the money. He does it because he enjoys watching people suffer and die at his hands. Now, you know I'm not a gambler, Dom, but I would bet everything I own that Victoria Hogarth's lover—the man who shot her husband— is Anders Folden."

"He's still locked up," Dom said with a confidence that implied he received regular updates on Folden's status, but Gray had to ask anyway.

"You're absolutely sure?"

"We'd have heard about it if he wasn't. A patient on the run from Brookhurst would've been all over the news."

"Brookhurst?" Gray slapped his forehead as if his oversight was a matter of stupidity rather than a consequence of only having half of the riddle until that moment. "When was he transferred to Brookhurst?"

"About six months ago. Looks like his lawyer finally found someone who believed that bullshit about a personality disorder."

It was the reason Folden's hearing had been adjourned—first to await his diagnosis, then to bring in psychiatric expert witnesses to testify—but the court ruled his actions were premeditated, and he had full mental capacity. Personality disorder or no, Folden should've been serving three consecutive life sentences. There was no reason for him to be transferred to a hospital.

"That's what Tonka was trying to tell Rob," Gray realised.

"Who?"

"Yvette Parker. The night she picked Rob up, she asked for his help..." Gray hadn't met the woman and was reluctant to incriminate her, but one way or another, she'd led them to Folden. "There's a former REME in Brookhurst. Yvette asked Rob for a financial contribution towards a new ID for the guy, claiming he's up for release soon. Tonka knows Folden's in there."

"Or it's a coincidence," Dom reasoned. "Brookhurst is the only high security hospital in the south-east."

"True, and it's plausible it could have been the only one with a bed available. Even so—"

Again, Gray was cut off by Dee's knock at the door. "Sorry about this. Mr. Fisher, there's a call for you, on our system this time. He said it's urgent."

"Who is it?"

"He didn't give his name."

It had to be Rob. Will didn't have the SIU's number. "Excuse me a moment." Gray followed Dee out and across the corridor to Dom's office—what had once been Gray's office.

"I transferred the call here to give you some privacy."

"Thanks." Gray entered and paused to take in the familiarity—same desk, same computer, same tower in the in-tray. And it was a lot tidier than he'd expected. Dee's doing, because Dom was a messy—

The door closed behind him, setting him back on track. He went over to the desk and picked up the phone. "DCI Fisher. How can I…" He sighed, exasperated at the instant slip, and started over. "Gray here, although you knew that already."

"Gray, it's Tie."

"Oh! I was expecting Rob."

"He gave me this number. I think Will might be in trouble."

"Why? What happened?"

"We got here early and I hung back at the train station just in case. He sent me a text once he was in, and I walked down—I've been watching from the park across the street. The place looks dead from the outside. Blinds down, nobody coming in or out until a couple of minutes ago when an older guy came out, locked up the building and drove off. I did a quick internet search, and I'm pretty sure it was Perlett."

Gray glanced up at the clock: 3:20. "Could Will have left another way?"

"Not that I can see. It's one of those one-storey buildings that looks like a glorified Portakabin. I could always jemmy the door."

"Yeah, don't. If you get caught, you'll go to prison. You're already out of your tag radius."

"Well, I figured the police turning up wouldn't be such a bad thing."

"I'm not so sure of that." There had always been corruption, but if it was endemic—and the way Winstanley talked, it sounded like there were only one or two decent officers left—there was no predicting how it would turn out. But doing nothing wasn't an option when Will might be in danger. If Gray got a cab, he could be at GP Investments within half an hour, but he didn't know what he'd be facing when he got there. Another hostage situation?

"I'm going to request backup," he said. "Can you stay put for now?"

"No problem."

"Thanks, Tie. Update me if anything changes. I'll be with you as soon as I can."

"OK, mate. See you shortly."

***

"Did she ever live here?" Rob asked as he returned to the living room, having completed a search of the house that confirmed the car was gone, as were Tonka's clothes and, of course, Tonka herself.

Neither man answered; Bish kept his back turned, labouring over making three mugs of tea, while Jock loitered and snarled like a steroid-enhanced bodyguard.

"You know what? I am so done with this bullshit. One of you needs to start talking, and soon, or—"

"Or what, Shaz?" Jock side-stepped to block Rob as he moved towards Bish, getting right in his face. It was the same old trick; he was too close for Rob to take a swing at him without backing up first, and it was tempting. So very tempting.

"Pack it in!" Bish growled and slammed a mug down on the counter closest to Rob. "Punching each other's lights out will solve nothing."

Rob was still staring Jock down, waiting for him to back off. It took a smack on the arm from Bish before he did.

"You didn't answer my question."

"Yeah, she lives here," Bish confirmed. "Temporary arrangement. Phil was trying to raise the capital to buy her out of the family business so she could move to Germany."

"To be with Siggy," Jock added.

"I gathered," Rob said. He really wanted to knock that smarmy smirk off Jock's face.

"As you were, lads." Bish glared at them and took a slurp of his tea. "Yeah, so, Tonka and Phil discussed selling the business years back. They were only waiting for their dad to die."

"That's morbid," Rob remarked.

"They expected him to go a lot sooner. After their mum died, he sort of gave up, which was when the rest of the family stepped in. They wouldn't let them sell, and all the capital's tied up in land, so Phil had to look elsewhere. His accountant put him on to the overseas investment, and it was a good move to start with. He was buying thousands of acres of Bulgarian agricultural land for next to nothing and selling them a few months later for four times what he'd paid."

"You weren't spinning me a yarn, then, about the Eastern European investment?"

"Half a yarn," Bish said with a shrug. "We weren't going in on it, but we wanted to give you and your partner enough that you'd figure out what was going on."

"I knew it was bollocks. Why didn't you just tell us?"

"We couldn't, but if you'd shut up…"

Rob raised his hands and let Bish continue.

"The last lot of land Phil acquired was just before they changed the law in Bulgaria, restricting the sale to nationals only, and Phil's broker couldn't get shot. A massive firm had been buying up from Parker Farms and the like, and they'd taken the matter to the EU. Apparently, what Bulgaria are doing is illegal, but Phil wanted out anyway.

"Some farmers' collective had been in touch wanting to buy the land from him for half of what he'd paid. Well, we know what it's like in the old Eastern bloc. They had nothing to start with. With all this going on, they've got less than fuck all. But Phil wasn't aware, and I think the collective must've hit him with a few home truths because he accepted their offer.

"Then, a few weeks ago, there was this investors' meeting where they were reporting back on what happened with the EU, and Phil had only gone to inform the broker of his decision. He called Tonka from the hotel to tell her it was all sorted, and that was the last she heard from him."

Bish stopped talking and started rooting through cupboards. "Why does she never have biscuits in? I blame you, you fat bastard." He tossed an empty Jaffa cake box at Jock.

"Oy! You ate them all last time we were here, you cheeky c—"

"Enough!" Rob barked, instantly silencing both men. "What the fuck are you doing, looking for biscuits? What happened to Tonka's brother?"

"He was kidnapped," Bish said, no messing about this time.

"Who by? The Bulgarian farmers?"

Jock laughed. "You're bloody hilarious, Shaz."

Rob turned his back on him and addressed Bish. "It was a serious question."

"Not the farmers. We don't know who's got him."

"What do they want?"

"They want..." Bish swallowed hard. "You, Rob. They want you."

Rob shook his head, muttered, "What?" then, "I mean, why? Are they expecting me to do something in return for Phil's release?"

"I dunno, mate. It was meant to be an exchange, the night of your leaving do. Tonka was told to pick you up and take you to the drop-off location."

"But she brought me back here instead."

"Yeah. There's not many people know Tonka and Phil live here. It belonged to their mum's sister, and she was a bit of a black sheep. We figured it was the safest place to bring you while the police were tracking down Phil's kidnappers."

"They didn't find them."

Bish shook his head.

"Why the hell didn't you tell me any of this?"

"Like I said, we couldn't, not without disobeying a direct order."

"She's not your superior officer anymore." The irony was laughable when Rob was experiencing the same struggle with Hedley.

"If we'd told you, what would you have done? Gone after them yourself."

"With backup, yeah." No way would he have gone it alone. "It doesn't make sense. Why didn't they just pick me up?"

"Maybe they couldn't get close enough?" Bish suggested, and Rob got the feeling it was more than mere speculation.

"Who are you working for?"

"We don't work for no-one, Shaz," Jock said.

"No. You said it yourself, Jock. You're trying to save my neck. Someone's paying your firm to keep tabs on me or else it'd be me sitting wherever Phil is. Do you know where?"

"No," Bish answered. "But Tonka does."

"Then you'd better get in touch with her, right now." Rob downed his tea and dumped his cup in the sink on his way past.

Jock stepped in front of him. "Where d'you think you're going?"

"To call Gray, bring him up to speed. Not that it's any of your business."

Jock moved aside. "Off you go, then."

With fists clenched to his sides, Rob dodged around Jock and went to the garage where he took his rage out on the stack of tyres in the corner before he placed the call.

30: Jammy

"Anything?" Gray asked when he finally found Tie in his hideout: a wooden igloo-shaped hut in the kids' playground.

Tie shook his head without taking his eyes off the GP Investments building across the street. "I thought you were bringing backup."

"I wanted to see how the land lay first." It was an outright lie. He'd told Dom and Winstanley he needed fresh air and then grabbed the first cab that passed. Thanks to a nifty cabbie who assumed he was with the Met, he'd been whizzed through back streets and reached Tie in well under twenty minutes. "Are you sure Will's still in there?"

"Unless he's burrowed his way out…" Tie muttered sarcastically. "You didn't report it, did you?"

Gray drew breath but thought better of continuing the deception. "No. We're already jeopardising the SIU's investigation."

"And you care more about that than Will's safety?"

To his shame, Gray had no immediate answer. The situation was too complex for a simple 'no' to suffice, because it wasn't just Will's safety here and now at stake, but it *was* Gray's current priority. He ducked inside the igloo and scrunched down next to Tie on the narrow curved seat, trying—and failing—to contain his anxiety under the constant bombardment of second thoughts. He should've talked Will out of coming here, shouldn't have made a deal with Freddie Berringer. If anything happened to Will, or Rob, or Naomi—

Tie's hand landed heavily on Gray's and squeezed. "He'll be all right."

Gray panned up to Tie's face, surprised by his sudden tenderness. He'd expected the guy to give him hell for putting the operation before Will, knowing how close the two of them were. They shared a long history, at some point lovers, but, more importantly, friends who fought for the same cause. Tie knew Will better than anyone, and Gray really hoped his faith in Will was justified, and contagious. They were sitting close enough for him to catch it—also close enough for them both to startle when Gray's phone vibrated against the plywood seat. He took it out and checked the screen before answering. "Looks like we might have backup after all... Yes, Dom?"

"Where are you?"

"Play igloo." Gray ducked to peer out of the opening as a black Transit van turned the corner, slowly drove past and parked twenty yards or so along the street.

Dom jumped out, rotating on the spot until he found his target and strode in their direction. "Bloody hell. How did you fit in there?"

"Found a bottle labelled 'drink me'."

"You'll never learn, will you?" he joked and hung up. It was a little close to the bone and the situation was as serious as they came, but Gray still managed a chuckle.

Dom arrived at their hut and leaned on the top, talking through the little round window. "Cosy in there?"

"Never been cosier," Gray deadpanned. There was no point asking how Dom knew where he'd gone.

"Seeing as you're sitting comfortably... The good news—I've spoken to one of the nursing managers at Brookhurst. Folden's accounted for."

"Thank God." Gray would've sagged in relief if there'd been space to do so, even though it meant he'd been way off with his analysis of the files. "And the bad?"

"We'll deal with that later. Including Winstanley."

"Threat or promise?"

"Devil and deep-blue sea, mate."

Only ninety-nine other problems to worry about, then. "This is Tie, by the way. Will's lodger."

Dom nodded. "Brian McIntyre..."

"That's right, sir," Tie confirmed. It wasn't the first time Gray had seen him defer to authority. In court, he'd been a model citizen—polite and well-spoken, hair tied back, clean suit, shiny shoes—nothing like the dreadlocked anarchist animal-libber who bunked in a damp caravan in Will's backyard.

"So you say Richards is in that building?" Dom tilted his head to indicate GP Investments.

"Yes, sir."

"Are you sure it's locked?"

"No, sir. I didn't try the door. I thought it would be better to keep my distance, but I saw a man leave and lock up on his way out."

"How long ago was that?"

"About two minutes before I called Gray, so...twenty-five minutes ago?" Tie turned to Gray to check.

"It would have been, yeah."

Dom straightened up and scanned the vicinity, chewing his bottom lip in thought. If it had been Gray's call, he'd have sat tight and waited to see if Perlett came back. Or that was what he'd have done as head of the SIU. Right now, he was hoping promotion hadn't destroyed Dom's gung-ho streak. Either way, Dom had come up with something. "We're gonna try and keep this on the down-low. You two stay put."

"Yes, boss," Gray said.

Dom patted the roof of the igloo and strode back to the van.

"He's the guy who took over your unit?" Tie asked once he was out of earshot.

"Yeah."

"Seems to know what he's doing."

"He does. I hope he's quick, though. I've got more cramps than a marathon runner at the finish line."

"Surely that should be the Great North Run?"

Gray smiled self-consciously. The Geordie accent… Every time he went incognito, it resurfaced. He wouldn't have minded if he did it on purpose.

On the plus side, the weather was lousy, so they had the tiny hut to themselves with an unobstructed view of the officers getting into position—all three of them. One entered the park and crouched behind bushes a few feet from Gray and Tie's location. Another—Dee Knight—rounded the corner on foot, carrying a briefcase. She crossed the road to GP Investments, tried opening the door—Tie muttered a choice word or two when the door stayed shut—and then knocked. She gave it another thirty seconds before she continued along the street towards the van.

"He's armed," Tie murmured.

Gray shifted his gaze to the guy hidden in the shadows, the butt of an MP5 just visible against his dark jacket. Tie had gone still, his breaths coming short and fast. "Are you all right?"

He nodded. "Yeah, but this is mental. He only went in there to ask some questions. How the fuck did it turn into an armed siege?"

"It's precautionary," Gray said, fairly sure he was right but aware it could all change in the blink of an eye, particularly as a second van had arrived, and this one wasn't SIU. It stopped outside GP Investments, blocking their view of the building, and two burly guys in security-guard uniforms climbed out. Judging by the lumpy bulk of their gilets, they were both armed too. Tie moved fast, but Gray was faster and threw his arm out, shoving Tie back down. His head thudded loudly against the igloo's curved wall. "Stay," Gray commanded.

"Those guards—"

"Have got guns. I know. Dom's got it under control." Gray's confidence was absolute. The officer in the park had changed position, giving him a clear shot if he needed it. Dom and Dee were also on the move, now both in uniform.

"Keep it on the down-low?" Tie said, incredulous.

"They're covering their tracks—called out to a burglary…"

"So much bullshit. You need to be straight with Will, if he gets out in one piece—" Tie began, but Gray cut him off.

"You changed your tune."

"Yeah? That was before all the fucking guns. He thinks you've got a future together."

"As do I."

"No. This, happening now, is your future. Catching the bad guys. You're not bothered who gets hurt in the process."

"It's no different than you, Will and the rest in your cell." It was a low blow, but Tie had hit the raw nerve Winstanley had been twanging all day.

"Of course. We're terrorists…according to you lot."

"Take a look where I'm sitting, Tie," Gray hissed, but their argument was brought to an abrupt end by the crack of a door giving way, immediately followed by the wail of GP Investments' alarm. Dom and Dee broke into a run and disappeared behind the security van.

Minutes passed. Gray watched the armed officer, who, in turn, was watching whatever was happening across the road through his gun sight. Other than the constant, ear-splitting warble of the alarm, there was nothing to hear or see until, finally, someone stumbled into view: Will—uninjured as far as Gray could tell, and cuffed—with Dee right behind him. She walked Will to the SIU van while Dom dealt with the security guards. There was a lot of posturing and gesticulating on their part, but whatever Dom said appeared to do the trick as he gave the nod to the officer in the park, and the two of them returned to the SIU van, which took off soon after. It was several minutes more before the alarm fell silent. Tie moved to get up again, and once again, Gray stopped him.

"Did they just arrest him?"

"Yeah, or made it look that way. We need to wait for the all-clear." Gray's phone was already vibrating. He took it out and hit answer.

"You're a mercenary son of a bitch, Fisher."

"Why, thank you," Gray replied drolly. "Is he all right?"

"Ask him yourself." Dom's phone crackled and then Will's voice came on the line.

"Hey."

"Hey, are you OK?"

"I'm fine. Is Tie with you?"

"Yeah, he's fine too. What happened?"

"Perlett got a phone call, cut our meeting short, but he wasn't saying anything useful. He saw me out, and I dodged back in, stayed out of sight while he set the alarm and locked up, then I called Naomi and got her to shut it off."

"The jammer…"

"Don't know what you're talking about," Will lied. "Anyway, I thought she'd have to hack into Perlett's computer, but he hadn't logged out. I managed to copy most of the hard drive before your mates arrived."

"Nice work." Gray was grinning with pride and had a shocking urge to brag. *Have you met my boyfriend?*

"I'll hand you back," Will said. The phone crackled again. This time, Gray didn't wait for Dom to speak first.

"Can we get out of here yet?"

"Yeah, but one at a time. We'll be at the gate on the other side of the park."

"OK." Gray hung up and relayed the instructions to Tie, letting him leave first and wincing along with him as he straightened up and hobbled away. Once he was clear, Gray followed in much the same fashion, checking his phone rather than returning it to his pocket. It was as well he did; he'd missed an encrypted message from Rob:

*En route with Bish and Jock. Tonka's staying in a
B&B 2 miles from Brookhurst hospital. She knows
where her brother is – will call when I know more.*

***

No satnav necessary, Bish was evidently familiar with the
locale and barely slowed to turn off the road onto the gravel
driveway leading to the hotel—a moderately large Edwardian
detached property with gable-end thatched roofs and modern
double-glazing. Bish reversed into the space between a hefty SUV
and a four-by-four—the only two vehicles in the hotel's car park.

"Where's the Aventador?" Rob asked.

"She sold it." Bish got out, slamming the door behind him.

"She what?"

"You heard," Jock said and got out of the other side. He
stomped away, leaving the door open.

Rob slid across the seat and jumped down, sinking an inch or
more into the gravel and rocking on his heels, a little off-balance.
It had been a crazy day—prison visit, lunch, emergency meeting,
and now this—with no sign of it letting up anytime soon. He
pushed the van door shut and followed Bish and Jock towards the
building. He needed coffee. That or to pay for a room so he could
get his head down for a couple of hours.

"Afternoon, gentlemen," a woman greeted them the second
they stepped through the door. The place was much as Rob had
expected: cream walls, thick red carpets, a staircase directly
ahead, dining room to his left, small bar room and lounge to his
right, a muted TV playing within.

Bish approached the woman at the reception. "Good
afternoon. We're friends of Yvette Parker's."

"What's your name?"

"Garvey."

The receptionist smiled and walked around to their side of the
counter. "This way, please." She led them down a passage that ran
alongside and under the stairs, slowing as she reached the door

at the end. She knocked and turned the handle; the door dragged on the carpet as it opened. "Ms. Parker…"

Bish and Jock marched in without hesitation; Rob held back a moment to get a sense of what he was walking into—a small function room by the looks of it, but set out for a conference with tables in a U, around which five people were seated, all in combats.

"Are you OK for refreshments?" the receptionist asked.

"For now, yes, thanks," Tonka replied, although Rob couldn't see a coffee pot or even jugs of water. Nor had he yet set eyes on Tonka; Bish and Jock were in the way. "Let the dog see the rabbit, eh, lads?" she said. The two men did as they were told and went to sit with the others.

Tonka rose to her feet, holding Rob's gaze as she advanced on him, faltered briefly, and then hugged him. He reciprocated, perplexed—or, at least, he had a good idea what was taking place, but he was having a problem believing she'd do something this risky.

"Ma'am? What's going on?"

She didn't answer him, but instead withdrew with a smile that fooled no-one. Murmured conversations started up around the room as she put her hand on his arm, guiding him to one side. "It's good to see you."

"And you." Still no explanation forthcoming. "Tonka, talk to me."

"They've got Phil," she said.

"I know. Bish told me about the investors' meeting and the exchange. Who are 'they'?"

"I don't know."

"Surely you must've spoken to them."

"They call from Phil's phone and use a voice synthesiser."

"Did you record the calls?"

"A couple." She already had her phone in her hand and swiped the screen a few times before she gave it to Rob. "The top one is from the night of your leaving do. It came just after you left my aunt's house. Did you ever find your phone?"

"A colleague did, but I'd already ordered a replacement."

"I'm sorry, Rob. I should've told you what was going on."

"Yeah, you should, but it's done now." He hit play and listened: *It's not too late. No more games.* "Did they set up a new time and place?" Tonka shook her head. "It's been two weeks," he said, but he wasn't going to spell it out. The chances of a hostage still being alive after that long, and with no further demands, were slim to none.

"To be honest, Rob, I accepted it as inevitable, but I've spoken to him. He's drugged up, but he's alive."

"When?"

"In the last seventy-two hours."

"Bish told me the family stopped you and Phil selling the business."

Tonka frowned. She'd already cottoned on to his line of inquiry. "That was a few months after we lost Mum, and she's been dead eleven years."

"What about the land Phil bought? How much did he have tied up in that?"

"He had a buyer lined up. Rob..." She sighed in exasperation. "There's absolutely no reason Phil would voluntarily disappear. Listen to the other message. If you don't believe me after that, well..." She was angry and upset, and Rob's low-level interrogation was making it worse.

"I'm sorry, but I had to ask."

"I know." She shifted her eyes to her phone. Rob played the second message.

Why are soldiers so stupid? Why haven't you delivered Simpson-Stone? Time's almost up.

The message sent a chill down his spine. Not the demand itself, something about the tone, and he couldn't figure out what it was. "When did you get...never mind." The date was on the recording; it was two days old.

"They called again a few hours later, but I didn't realise who it was until after I'd answered. They said the deal was off and they'd collect you in person."

Yet they hadn't…so far. Rob would've preferred to believe it was because the kidnappers were inept rather than the truth that kept smacking him around the head. Between SIU tails, Sequrco and the squaddies in this room, the kidnappers hadn't been able to get near. "And Phil?" he asked.

"All I had to do was find him. We need to get on." She turned away, blocking any further questions. "I believe you know Olivia Simpson?" She gestured to the only other woman in the room.

Rob nodded and grinned in spite of himself. "Alright, Lisa?"

She rolled her eyes and laughed. "Nobody called me that in years until a fortnight ago. Now this lot have picked it up. How are you doing, Rob?"

"Not bad, cheers. You?"

"Much the same."

"This is Olivia's unit," Tonka explained. "Private military contractors."

"Gotcha." Now he knew why she'd sold her car, and, presumably, why she'd asked him for money. Of the three options—overseas investment, hiring a private army or buying Ethan a new ID—the latter was the one he was least likely to say no to. In fact, if she'd told him what she'd planned, he'd have gone straight to Martina. "Is this a rescue mission, Ma'am?"

"Phase two. Phase one is still ongoing. It's been a success so far." She squeezed his arm.

"Yeah." Rob glanced over at Bish and Jock, both with their heads bowed in contrition. To give them their due, they'd convincingly kept their cover, but there were discrepancies, too many things they knew that they shouldn't. By now, they'd have updated their 'boss', and Rob really needed to pay Gray the same courtesy, but he was prepared to hold off a little longer and hear what Tonka had to say first.

31: Decoy

Gray couldn't get hold of Rob. He wasn't answering his phone, and he'd turned off GPS, so they couldn't get a fix on his location either. Working only with his message that he was heading for a B&B in the vicinity of Brookhurst hospital, Dom made a quick stop at SIU HQ to arrange transport home for Will and Tie but was unsuccessful in his endeavour to persuade Gray to go with them. Bizarrely, Winstanley sided against Dom and suggested Gray's understanding of the operation made him a valuable asset, along with a reminder that he was there in a consultative capacity and he'd have to remain in the van for the duration.

Winstanley agreed to stay back and coordinate with the team going through what Will had copied from Perlett's hard drive, while Gray joined Dom, Dee, Tarquin—the firearms officer from the park—and Isobel—who had been part of Gray's old team—for the forty-minute drive out to Berkshire.

Dom had sacrificed riding shotgun to Isobel and joined Tarquin and Gray in the back. Once they were underway, he called his contact at Brookhurst to warn them to be on the lookout for suspicious activity. It was a precautionary measure; the hospital was near a large military base with a forest and an abundance of varied sports and leisure clubs between. Philip Parker could be virtually anywhere, yet the closer they got to Brookhurst, the more certain Gray became that he'd been right in the first place. It was giving him stomach cramp, not helped by sitting sideways on a none too comfortable bench seat, on top of a wheel arch and sandwiched between Dom and a tower of equipment crates.

"She's taking Rob to Folden."

His statement drew everyone's attention, including Dee's via the rear-view mirror. They were all looking at him like he'd lost the plot.

"Folden's in isolation," Dom said. "No visitors. No contact with other patients."

"You think he can't manipulate the staff to do his bidding?"

"They're trained professionals. They're used to dealing with the likes of Folden."

"I don't mean directly. He knows a lot of powerful people."

"I'm sorry, Gray, you're wrong, and not just about Folden. If Yvette Parker intended to hand Rob over, she'd have made the exchange on the night of his leaving do."

"Unless she'd discovered Garvey and Wilson were working for you, in which case, the story about McGrath's new ID was her second attempt—a ruse to get Rob to Brookhurst."

Dom sighed and rubbed his temples as if staving off a headache. Only he was paying attention; everyone else had gone back to whatever they'd been doing prior to the conversation. "Look." He leaned in close and spoke so quietly Gray could barely hear him over the road noise. "When we're done with this, do me a favour? Talk to someone, I don't care who—Sean Tierney or Josh Sandison-Morley if you like—"

"Yes. Fine," Gray agreed to shut Dom up. There was no point arguing with him or showing his anger. Had anyone else dared to dismiss Gray's concerns as some kind of post-traumatic paranoia, he'd have given them hell—if they'd been anywhere but the back of an SIU van, he'd have given Dom hell too. He was prepared to concede Folden might not be the man at the top, but it didn't make him any less dangerous nor alter the fact that sixteen months ago, Rob had put Folden behind bars. Their proximity *could not be* coincidence.

Whoever wanted Rob wanted him alive, and if it *was* Folden…well, they might as well ditch the entire operation right now because once he'd broken Rob, he wouldn't stop until he'd squeezed every last bit of information from him—about the fraud ring, his police work, his colleagues past and present.

And when he was done with Rob, he'd come after the rest of them.

"Update from Garvey," Dom announced. "How close are we?"

"Five minutes, Sir," Dee said.

"Pull over the next chance you get. We need to put together a plan of action."

"Will do, Sir." Dee indicated and dropped a gear.

In his peripheral vision, Gray saw Dom watching him. His pulse went into overdrive. He hadn't been wrong.

***

Rob sat through the briefing in a half-dazed state he blamed on lack of caffeine and the increasing surrealness of his day. Olivia detailed the plan and doled out tasks; her team asked questions—good questions—and came up with strategies for multiple scenarios. None wore rank insignia yet Rob felt like a fly on the wall of the officers' mess, although the situation was more reminiscent of the police briefings he'd attended—bar the fact they were acting illegally. Granted, working undercover, Rob had crossed more than a few lines himself, but never outside the confines of an investigation.

Tonka had given him the option to join the mission, which he'd flat out refused while also aware his continued presence signified his tacit agreement to keep schtum. No problem on that score; Bish and Jock looked as shocked as Rob felt, and perhaps it was cowardice on his part, but there was no need for him to further dirty his hands when the details would already have been relayed to the SIU.

In spite of everything that had gone before, he empathised with Bish and Jock. Whether it was for the greater good or to save a life, betraying someone you loved and respected terminally damaged something inside. Every lie uttered was like watching them swallow down another mouthful of poison, and it hurt almost as much as losing them through death.

Needless to say, Bish and Jock willingly agreed to play their part in the mission. Jock didn't even kick off when Olivia assigned them to a lookout post half a mile from the target—Bish's van would serve as a secondary escape vehicle should Tonka's four-by-four be compromised—and Rob's impression was they were being kept out of the way. After all, if he'd sussed them, Tonka would be on to them too.

He didn't blame her for taking the matter into her own hands. She'd been a brilliant CO, although he'd always been lucky in that regard. Martina Hedley was easily up there, and even Gray had had his moments, but with Tonka, the one strength that stood above all the rest was her sheer grit. The phrase 'it can't be done' wasn't in her repertoire, and from what she'd told them today, she'd tried going through official channels, but either the powers-that-be were rotten through and through, or whoever was behind Phil's disappearance had them by the balls.

On the balance of probability, Rob thought it was a combination of the two, and it put him in a major quandary. On the one hand, the SIU and Tonka's private army were on the same side, up to a point. On the other hand, the mission to rescue Phil Parker could screw up the entire SIU operation.

There was a reason they'd left Rob to fend for himself. Dom was deploying the same strategy as the Black Hole heist, when Rob had warned Gray in advance of Folden's plan to take hostages—and that there would be fatalities—but Gray had let it run its course, confident it would lure the rest of the fraud ring out into the open. That he'd been dead right was small consolation when Rob was a sitting duck.

With the briefing over, they all began to move out, and Rob went to the hotel bar, watching through the front window as the rest of them climbed into their vehicles. He was safe here, or no less safe than he'd be anywhere else, but once again, he was caught in the middle, under pressure to pick a side. Did his loyalty lie with his old army mates or with his former SIU colleagues, by default, because that was where Gray's lay? Their first case, farce that it was, was solved. They'd found Tonka and knew what had happened to her brother. By rights, he could go home and crack open that beer he'd been craving earlier. Or he could if his bike wasn't locked in Tonka's garage.

"What can I get you, sir?" the bartender asked.

"Never mind," Rob said and sprinted out to the car park, shouting, "Ma'am!" as Tonka shut her car door. She heard him and rolled down the window. "Mind if I join you?"

She studied him intently, considering his request for several seconds before she nodded and said, "Go with Jock and Bish."

"I'm in the doghouse too, am I?"

A half-smirk, half-smile was her answer as she started the four-by-four and reversed out onto the road. Bish had also fired up the van, and Rob quickly jogged around to the passenger side and hauled the door open.

"Budge up, Jock. I'm coming with."

Grunting, Jock shuffled along the seat. Rob climbed in and fastened his seat belt.

"We need to hang back for five," Bish said.

Rob nodded and took out his phone. It was the first chance he'd had to check it since he'd texted Gray. Still no reply to that, but there was a message from Martina Hedley—*stop being so bloody morose*—which made him laugh. Maybe he had jumped the gun a little with the text he'd sent her and the call to Travis. His part in the rescue mission should be danger free. Just sit tight and leave Tonka, Olivia and her unit to break Phil Parker out of a high security hospital. Piece of cake.

***

Gray stared over Isobel's shoulder at the stationary dot marking Bish's GPS tracker on the onscreen map, as he'd been doing for almost all of the ten minutes since they'd pulled into a lay-by on the main route between the hotel and the hospital so they could intercept Tonka and crew. While they were waiting, Dom and Tarquin had popped outside for some 'fresh air'. Gray could've done with stretching his legs and a warm-up—the air con was brutal—but he was doing as he'd been told…for now.

"Are you all right, Sir?" Isobel asked without taking her eyes off the screen.

"Yeah, thanks. You?"

She nodded but didn't continue the small talk, and Gray realised he was drumming on the back of her chair. He stopped.

"Sorry, Iz."

"No problem, Sir. I get a bit restless in here myself."

He'd have been a lot less so if he could've forewarned Rob. He resumed his spot on the bench seat, making a concerted effort not to fidget, and then startled when, a moment later, Isobel bolted from her chair and opened the van's side door.

"They're on the move, Sir. Heading for the ring road."

Dom followed her back in, along with the stink of smoke. He checked the screen. "Right. Let's see which way...yep. Dee?" She'd already started the engine and waited just long enough for Tarquin to get back in before she put her foot down. Dom jammed his hand against the roof. "Iz, have you managed to find out anything about these private soldiers?"

"Only Olivia Simpson, Sir. Former REME, served with Parker, Wilson and Garvey in Germany before she transferred to a specialist unit in Kuwait. Rob was her replacement. Garvey didn't recognise any of the others."

"Ah, well. I don't suppose it matters. Soldiers are soldiers, and we know they're aiming for a quick in and out. I'm inclined to leave them to it." Dom was watching Gray, like he was waiting for him to say something.

"It's your decision, Dom."

"I've told Garvey he's to keep Rob away from Brookhurst by all means necessary."

"And?"

"It's no great loss, is it? If they take a pop at Folden."

So that was what he was waiting for. While none of them would shed a tear for Folden, if they didn't intercept Tonka's team before they reached the hospital, there would be other casualties. The alternative, or the one that didn't involve saving Folden, required overt intervention from the SIU. If Gray's interpretation was correct, Dom was prepared to blow up Tabula Rasa on his say-so.

"I'm as sure as I can be," he said.

Dom nodded. "That'll do for me." He made the call. "It's Hooper. Evacuate your staff from the isolation unit and tell security to stand down. There's a BMW SUV and a Jeep in convoy about five minutes away. You need to let them through—we'll be right behind them. Understood?"

***

"Can't see fuck all from here." Jock hoisted his foot up on top of the dashboard, knee stuck out and encroaching into Rob's space. On the plus side, he didn't fart, and he wasn't wrong. Tall trees lined the road—more a dirt track—on either side, and the view was much the same across the T-junction ahead. In short, it was picturesque, but useless as a lookout point, not that it mattered with the hospital's twelve-foot-high perimeter wall. As long as at least one of them was in contact—the signal was lousy, which was how they'd ended up on a dirt track—they could be at the hospital's east service entrance in under two minutes.

Aside from having Jock's knee in his face, Rob was fairly chilled out. He'd seen the black van tailing them through the town centre. Even if he hadn't recognised it, he'd have known from Bish and Jock's shifty looks at each other that it belonged to the SIU, although they played ignorant admirably when he asked whether Gray had talked Dom into letting him come along for the ride. His gut said the answer was yes, but it was by the by. When Bish had turned off to head around the back of the hospital, the van had gone straight on, following Tonka and Olivia to the front entrance. If the combined expertise of six soldiers and however many SIU officers couldn't break Phil Parker out of Brookhurst, no-one could.

Jock dropped his foot to the floor and put the other one up, earning him a noisy backhander on the thigh from Bish. This time, Jock pushed out a retaliative fart and laughed like a loon. Bish wound down the window and let rip with an equally offensive stream of insults, and Rob tuned them out. Lucas could've taught them a thing or two about appropriate behaviour, like he'd done with Rob and his attitude towards Travis. He was a good kid with a sensible head on his shoulders, albeit one preoccupied with cars and junk food.

And ketchup. Rob's thoughts drifted to Naomi and their talk over lunch. Even though she hadn't said straight up she was interested in him, the lengths to which she'd gone to dismiss her relationship with Freddie spoke volumes. He'd wanted so much to stay for that coffee, and that was before Martina gave him her blessing, so to speak. If he'd accepted Naomi's invitation, it would have been a very different day, that was for sure.

"…fantasising about what he's gonna do to Lisa this evening. What d'you reckon?"

"Oh, shut up, Jock."

Rob sighed and turned away from his travel companions, staring out the side window. Up close, the trees were much more sparse and deadly still. *Could be an omen…* He should have been more worked up about what was going on. Now he thought about it, he hadn't heard from Tie since he'd called for the SIU's number, although, with the change in Gray over the past few weeks, he'd have been over to GP Investments like a shot. Will would be fine. They'd all be fine.

"Shaz, mate. You're off with the fairies."

Rob blinked and stretched his eyes wide open. "Sorry. Knackered." He felt stoned. "What's up?"

Bish released the handbrake and put his foot down. The wheels spun against the loose road surface as the van took off, flinging Rob's head back sharply and jolting his neck. He muttered a muted, "Fuck," and straightened up, supporting his neck with his palm.

"We're needed on-site," Jock said. "They've cleared the service entrance."

"What's happened to Tonka and Olivia?"

"I don't fucking know! I'm just following orders."

Rob leaned across Jock to reach the air-conditioning dial, turning it up to full and opening the vent on his side, angling it towards his face. He needed to clear his woolly head before they reached the hospital.

***

There wasn't a lot of room for pacing in the back of a fully loaded surveillance van. Gray realised he was doing it again and stopped, quite sure he was getting on Isobel's nerves. She'd stayed behind to monitor the team's activity, and to keep an eye on Gray even though he'd sworn, hand on heart, short of earthquake or nuclear explosion, he wouldn't leave the van.

"Where are they now?" he asked, squinting at the map from afar rather than moving closer and getting in her way.

Isobel pointed at the dots onscreen. "Tarq's in an office building opposite the main entrance to the isolation unit. The DCI is…on the move. He's just gone in. And—"

"Gone into the isolation unit?"

"Yes, Sir."

Dom was deviating from his plan. "Something's not right. Where's Dee?"

"Also on the move, heading towards us."

Gray moved to the front of the van and saw Dee sprint around the end of a building. She made it back to them, clambered behind the wheel and started the engine. The door slammed shut as they moved off.

"Folden's on the loose," she explained breathlessly. "The DCI needs us around the back. Get a vest on, Sir."

Gray looked behind him at the crate of vests. He'd fall flat on his face if he tried to reach it before they stopped. Isobel gasped and blanched.

"Garvey's just come through the service entrance."

Gray flung himself a few feet along the van and grasped the computer bench before he flew right past. Bish's dot jumped a few millimetres closer to their location. "We need to stop him."

"But the DCI—" Dee began.

"I know!" And Gray was a civilian. Irrespective of their acknowledgement of his former rank, they had to follow Dom's orders. Luckily, Dee had done exactly that and screeched to a halt on the other side of the building. Gray made it the rest of the way to the crate and fought his shaking hands to get a vest on and fastened. "Do we know where Folden is?"

"No, Sir. Just that his room's empty."

"Where's Parker's lot?"

"All over the place. Yvette's on the first floor with Philip. He's not mobile and the lifts are locked. They're having to carry him down."

At least they'd have one success today. "OK. What are our orders?" Gray asked.

"Watch the back doors in case Folden comes this way."

There was only one way to stop him getting to Rob now. Paying no heed to the voice in his head reminding him his firearms licence was no longer valid, Gray loaded the Glock from Tarquin's AFO kit, ready to do what he should have done two years ago.

***

"Where am I going?" Bish asked as he took another speed bump at 40 mph and all three of their heads hit the roof. A swerve to the right and Jock crushed Rob against the passenger door, a lecherous grin on his stupid moon face as he hoisted himself upright again. "Jock! Where the fuck am I going?"

Jock got his shit together and refocused on the road ahead. "Next right."

"Fuck's sake." The van took the corner on two wheels and ran straight over a tulip-covered roundabout. "Flowerbeds in a prison hospital. Whatever next?"

"Good to know our taxes are being well spent, eh, Shaz?"

Rob ignored them, his attention on the view ahead: a box-grid-covered access area, and the SIU van.

"Cavalry's here," Jock spat. Bish slammed on and reversed back, having another go at the tulips.

"What are you doing?" Rob asked. "That's the isolation unit."

"Wrong side," Bish said, spinning the wheel hard right. As they took off, Rob caught sight of one of the SIU waving both arms, Semaphore-style.

"They're trying to get our attention. We need to go back," he said, turning in his seat to look behind them. "Bish—"

"There they are," Jock said.

Bish hit the brakes before Rob had a chance to turn around, and his seat belt almost decapitated him. He unclipped it, but Jock didn't wait and instead clambered over the console and followed Bish out of the driver's side. They made it over to the small group struggling from the building just as the siren went off, and suddenly there were people everywhere. Rob got out and stood, leaning on the door, watching security staff armed with batons jog past as if they weren't there, all heading into the building.

"Rob! Get back in the van!"

He spun in the direction of the voice. "Gray—"

"Get back in the van. Folden's out."

"Folden...what?" Rob replayed Gray's garbled statement, but it still made no sense.

"He was transferred to Brookhurst six months ago."

"Shit."

"They brought you here on purpose."

"No. Bish and Jock are undercover."

"I know. Dom can deal with them later. You need to get in the back and keep your head down, all right?"

"Yes, Sir," Rob answered automatically, only realising because Gray smiled and patted his arm.

"Stay safe, Rob. I'm going to bring this bastard down if it's the last thing I do." With that, Gray sped off towards the building and Rob went around the back of the van, but neither reached his destination.

At some point, Dom had arrived on the scene and was walking and talking with Tonka behind two of Olivia's team who were carrying Phil over to Bish's van. Without looking away—and with no sense of urgency whatsoever—Dom waved his arm, flagging Gray down, and then stopped next to Rob, who stepped aside and held one of the van doors open while they lifted Tonka's brother in. Phil was doped up to the eyeballs but otherwise looked fine. As the soldiers pulled the door shut, Rob noticed a stretcher and other medical equipment in the back of Bish's van. It had been part of their plan from the beginning.

"Dom, with all due respect..." Gray marched over, red-faced and looking ready to thump him. Dom raised his hands in surrender.

"Cool it a minute, all right? Folden's long gone."

"What?" Gray glared at Dom and then Tonka. She nodded, and Dom gestured for her to explain.

"The ward plan—you know, the chart of which patient is in which bed, who their doctor is, and so forth? The room they had Phil in was listed as Anders Folden."

"Jesus." Gray clamped his hand over his mouth, inhaling through his fingers. His horror was genuine, and Rob shared it.

"So...he's been out for three weeks?" Rob asked.

Dom nodded. "Looks that way. We've requested access to all security footage to see if we can pinpoint exactly when it happened and how. Obviously, we'll question the staff in the isolation unit over the next couple of days, and the hospital's press officer's going to inform the media ASAP. I'm sorry, Rob, but as of now, you're a protected person."

32: Interim

"I'm not putting him back in hospital," Tonka snapped when Dom asked, again, if she was sure she could cope with looking after her brother. "Someone making tea?" she threw over her shoulder on her way up the spiral stairs. Getting Phil up those when he could barely stand had been an absolute bugger.

Bish obediently refilled the kettle. They'd been stuck at Brookhurst for a further hour while security confirmed Folden wasn't on-site, during which Dom had spoken briefly to several of the senior staff before they convened an emergency meeting to try to establish how Folden had escaped and what they were going to do about it. When they were finally allowed to leave, Olivia had taken her team back to the hotel, and the SIU, plus Rob and Gray, had followed Bish's van back to the Parkers' aunt's place so they could check it was secure.

With Tonka's insistence that she'd nurse Phil at home, Bish and Jock had agreed to hang around for the next forty-eight hours, more for the Parkers' peace of mind than anything. Dom and Gray were in agreement that Folden was done with them; Dom had told Dee, Tarquin and Isobel to return the van to HQ and go get some shut-eye—"Full team briefing, 0800."

It was while they were waiting for Phil's GP to arrive, and Gray had gone outside to call Will, that Dom broached the subject of protection again, but Rob was as adamant as Tonka; he wasn't moving to a 'safe house'. Too long spent in bedsits up and down the country and living out of his panniers had taught him the value of privacy, of having a base. His flat was small, basic, not in a great area, expensive for what it was, but it was his own space where he could come and go as he pleased and do whatever the hell he liked.

"To be honest, I'm glad," Dom said, nodding thanks at Bish for the fresh cups of tea that appeared in front of them. "It's a pain in the arse to set up, and your flat should be safe enough, seeing as you haven't even told the council you're living there."

"I wasn't banking on staying more than a few months," Rob justified.

"Well, we'll keep an eye on you, obviously…" Dom paused to take a drink. "My bigger concern is Zoë and Lucas."

"Yeah. Mine too." It was all Rob had thought about for the past two weeks, and that was before he knew Folden was at large.

"We could get them into the women's refuge until we sort out something more long-term."

"What about Travis?"

"Ah, yeah, that's a point." Dom rubbed his eyes and yawned. He'd aged considerably in the past sixteen months. He was a couple of years younger than Rob, and smoking wasn't doing him any favours, but he looked bone-tired, like he might keel over at any second.

"Hey, Bish, what the hell's in this tea?"

"You what?"

"I've been spaced out all afternoon and poor Dom's nearly in a coma."

Bish looked at the kettle, then at his own cup, then shrugged. "It's just ordinary tea, isn't it?"

"Passion flower," Tonka said. Rob hadn't noticed her come down. She walked over to the window and peered out into the almost-darkness.

"Everything OK?" he asked.

She nodded but kept her back turned. "He's only half with it. Says he can't remember much, other than arguing with the staff over his name. How do you convince doctors you're sane when they think you're delusional? You could rot away in a place like that."

She fell quiet, and Rob wondered if she'd been talking about Phil or Ethan—or both. The story about getting Ethan a new identity might have been bull, but her fears for his future were genuine and, after what Rob had witnessed today, with good reason. Every building inside those high walls had been windowless, the atmosphere eerily oppressive, and then chaotic and dangerous.

Rob assumed secure hospitals, like prisons, locked down after an incident, so his visitor's pass probably wasn't valid anymore. Nor did returning to Brookhurst appeal to him, particularly as he didn't *have to* visit Ethan now. But still, he was considering it.

"What are you doing?" Tonka's question jolted Rob out of his thoughts and he opened his mouth to answer, but she wasn't asking him. He followed her bemused gaze across the room to the kitchen area.

"Is it an aphrodisiac?" Jock asked, peering into his cup.

Tonka laughed. "You wish! Passion flower aids relaxation and eases anxiety. I've needed it of late, but there's ordinary tea in there as well." To prove it, she went over and took a box of Tetley out of the cupboard. "Try these next time, lads."

"An aphrodisiac?" Bish repeated and slapped Jock upside the head.

"Passion...passion flower...should do what it says on the tin."

"Idiot."

"Fuck off."

Dom turned away and mouthed at Rob, "They'd drive me round the bend."

Been there, done that.

The front door opened, and Gray came in—Rob had almost forgotten he was out there—along with Phil's GP; Tonka went to greet her and took her up to Phil while Gray joined Rob and Dom on the sofas.

"Will and Tie are both fine," he said before either could ask. "At the pub."

"All right for some," Dom grumbled.

Rob nodded in sympathy, knowing Dom still had a good few hours of work ahead of him, although Rob was well past his beer craving. He just wanted to go home and watch crap telly in bed, but he had a few things to sort out first. "What shall I tell Zoë and Travis? The refuge would be OK. Travis'll do whatever's best for Zo and Lu."

"Leave it with me. I'll have a chat with witness protection. We should be able to sort something for tomorrow. In the meantime, the surveillance is still in place." Dom yawned again and stood up. "Right. I need to head back, get the paperwork done, for what it's worth."

"You won't lose your job," Gray asserted. Rob hadn't been aware it was a possibility; Gray had yet to brief him on what he'd found out earlier. "Not with Martin Winstanley in your corner."

"We'll see," Dom said, sounding far less confident than usual. "Rob, I'll be in touch."

Rob got up and shook his hand. "All right, mate. Thanks for everything."

Dom forced out a smile and moved on to Gray. No handshake for him; they hugged, and it wasn't a short one.

Rob switched his attention to Bish and Jock, sitting at the kitchen counter and figuring out their duty rota. However much they got on his nerves, Rob was grateful for all they'd done and no doubt would continue to do until this was over. They were good people to have onside, and he knew he could count on them, one hundred percent. Even Jock.

***

Gray handed the debit card reader back to the driver and chastised himself for once again wasting a small fortune on a cab. He'd got in it with the intention of going home to pack a few things and then driving the hire car—which he should have returned a week ago—to Croxley. But when the driver had asked 'where to?' he'd made a split-second decision. Surely he'd left enough items of clothes at Will's over the past few months to have a full change. If not, he'd stick the same ones back on in the morning.

Either way, there he was, standing outside Will's local, as were Will and Tie but on the other side of the building, evidenced by the sound of Will's hot-chocolate laughter drifting on the cool breeze that blew across the waterways and golf course beyond the pub, bringing with it the distinctive aroma of cannabis and tobacco.

Gray sighed. Not the welcome he'd hoped for, but it was his own fault for not sharing his plans. He entered the pub, muttering, "They're shitfaced," to himself and preparing to find out exactly how shitfaced they were.

Not very, it turned out. As he came through the front entrance, they walked in the back and, in spite of the sizeable mid-evening crowd, Will saw Gray at once. His face broke into a broad, definitely pleased smile. "Hey. I didn't know you were coming over."

"Surprise?" Gray smiled back coyly, and Will laughed.

"BRB," Tie said and set off in the direction of the Gents'.

"Wheat beer?" Will suggested, already moving towards the bar.

"Need you ask?" Gray followed him over and stood next to him, leaning heavily on the counter as the tension of the day seeped away. It wasn't over yet, not by any stretch, but he had to keep it in perspective. They were in a better position than eighteen hours ago; Phil Parker was safe and well, and there was an entire force of police and ex-army personnel making sure he—and Rob—stayed that way.

"How's everyone doing?" Will asked, sliding Gray's pint to him. He picked it up and drank thirstily, half-emptying the glass before he found the wherewithal to move it away from his lips. He glanced around him before he answered. No-one was close enough to overhear.

"OK. Rob's gone to see Zoë and Travis. Dom's arranging a safe house."

"For all of them together?"

Gray raised an eyebrow. "Much as Rob seems to be getting along with Travis these days, they're far from best mates. No, Rob's staying in the flat." Gray wasn't sure how Rob had talked Dom into agreeing and couldn't say he was happy with the arrangement, but it wasn't his call. "Dom's worried about his job."

"Really? After what he did today, he should be up for a medal or promotion."

"I couldn't agree more." Gray nodded an acknowledgement at Tie, who joined them at the bar and tapped his pint glass to Gray's in a silent toast. "I can't say much, but the long and short of it is he disobeyed orders from on high."

"Will he lose his job?"

"Honestly, I don't know, but he'll almost certainly be suspended." Someone on the Tabula Rasa roster would have the authority to make Dom pay for his insubordination, but at least he had Winstanley on his side.

"What happened with that Perlett guy?" Tie asked.

Gray had been hoping—unrealistically—they wouldn't bring it up. "Believe it or not, he's innocent, but you still both did great work this afternoon."

"In other words, it was a waste of time." Will winked at Tie.

"Not at all. Perlett recognised Rob's name from his daughter's trial when he was doing the background checks on Parker Farms, and he told her when he visited her in prison. She passed it on to Folden. All her dad did was break a few data protection laws, and not on purpose."

"Doesn't surprise me," Will said. "His computer was wide open. And a mess. Worksheet one, worksheet two...worksheet five thousand, four hundred and sixty-one..."

"That's what my hell will be like," Gray said.

Tie was listening to them and grinning into his beer. Will pointedly ignored him. "He seemed a nice old guy."

"He was very cooperative, apparently, and a great believer in the justice system." He'd also said Michelle deserved to be in prison, which was probably why Winstanley had gone lightly on him.

"Well, I'm glad he's in the clear," Will said. "We need to look after companies like GP Investments."

Gray picked up his pint and drank to hide his smirk, noticed Tie doing the same and laughed, spurting beer all over his face.

"What?" Will protested. "Friendly societies are an endangered species."

"Only a merchant banker..." Tie muttered.

"Did you want another beer or a smack in the teeth?" Will threatened.

"My round," Gray said. "Then I'm going home to bed."

"I thought you were staying over."

"Well, when I say home..." Gray left it open for Will to interpret however he saw fit.

The conversation moved on, or, rather, Tie chatted away to another guy who came in with a German shepherd while Will fussed over the dog. He was too quiet—he usually talked to them—and Gray was beginning to wish he'd dismissed his error with 'you know what I mean' or blatantly stated that what he was really saying was he wouldn't mind taking their relationship to the next level.

The guy with the dog moved away to sit at a table, and Will straightened up, lifting his glass to his lips as he said, with no more than a glance Gray's way, "Whenever you like."

***

"Hello?" The crackle of the intercom made it impossible to distinguish who had answered.

"Hey, it's Rob."

The external door buzzed, and he stepped in, trudged across the scruffy foyer and up the creaking stairs to the first floor, just as he had fourteen hours ago. It felt like days, and he was dead on his feet, but his heart put on a final sprint when he reached their room. *Still Naomi.*

She smiled and beckoned him inside. "I wasn't expecting to see you again so soon."

"I hadn't planned on stopping by..." He didn't know what else to say and it left him dumbstruck and defenceless. The way she was watching him... He saw the moment she registered something was wrong, a flicker of fear across her face, a fleeting glimpse of Aaron, and then she smiled. Confident, flirty Naomi was back.

"How about that coffee?" she suggested.

"I'd like that." He chanced moving further into the room, drifting closer as she filled the kettle and switched it on, slid two mugs in front of it...

"Instant OK? I can make filter if you..." She turned, her gaze holding his briefly as he took the final step and their torsos made contact.

He leaned in, murmured, "Instant's fine," against her cheek, traced her jaw with parted lips. A remnant of his resistance whispered *stop* then was silenced by the warm pressure of Naomi's palm on his back. She rolled her head to the side, a soft sigh escaping in response to the kisses he scattered over her neck, slowly working his way to her mouth.

"Are you sure you want this, Rob?" she asked, closing her eyes as he mirrored her, pressing his palm to her back and pulling her body tight against his.

"Do you?" he countered. Their lips bumped with his words, then met in mutual response.

They kissed deeply, passionately, continuing long after the kettle had clicked off, neither willing to stop. It would've been easy to take it further—the bed was just across the room—but for now, the kiss was enough.

When they finally eased apart, breathless and giddy, still in each other's arms, Naomi said, "I've wanted this for so long."

"Me too," Rob admitted. No point denying it anymore.

The intensity of the moment had passed, and he released her. She switched the kettle back on and resumed making the coffee.

"What made you change your mind?" she asked.

"The shit that's happened today." He wasn't sure how much he should tell her, or what effect it would have on Aaron.

"You're in danger, aren't you?"

Rob stared at the floor, suddenly ashamed of his selfishness in coming here, driven only by his need to see her before he was forced into hiding, or worse.

"Talk to me. Please, Rob?"

He nodded. "Yeah. I'm in danger."

"I'm so sorry." She reached for his hand, weaving her fingers with his. She understood his fear. She'd been there too. "Can I do anything? Or Aaron?"

"I don't think so." Rob lifted his head so he could see her, acknowledging the sincerity of her offer with as much of a smile as he could muster before he pulled her to him again, needing someone to hold him, someone to hold. "I just had to see you tonight. I hope you don't mind."

"Of course not."

"I can't stay, though."

"I know. You need to check in with Lucas and Zoë." She kissed him gently, squeezed his hand. "Do what you have to, Rob. I'm not going anywhere."

***

The safety chain rattled, keys jangled, and the door swung open on Zoë in pyjamas. "Rob," she said, stony-faced, making sure he wouldn't miss her displeasure.

"Hey. Sorry. I thought I'd be here sooner. Were you in bed?"

"No." She plodded back along the hall, leaving him to shut and re-lock the door. "Lu is, though," she warned and disappeared into the living room.

Rob followed her in, and he and Travis gave each other a nod in both greeting and confirmation that it hadn't 'come to the worst'. Not yet.

"I need to talk to Lu too."

Zoë reached the sofa and about-turned, muttering, "I'll go make coffee," as she dodged past him and back out to the hallway, where she shouted upstairs, "You still awake, Lu?"

The answer came in the form of a heavy thud and the scrabble of bare feet overhead, down the stairs...

"Dad!" Lucas tumbled to a halt in front of him. "What're you doing here? Is it to do with the police?" He looked towards the window. The curtains were drawn, but Rob had seen the car outside.

"Yeah, mate, it is."

Lucas's mouth opened in a big, wide 'o'. "Why are they watching us?"

"I'll explain when your mum comes back."

"I'm back." Zoë stepped past again with three mugs. She deposited one on the table at the free end of the sofa and the other two on the table at 'her' end. "D'you want a drink, Lu?"

He shook his head without taking his eyes off Rob.

"Are you going to sit?" Zoë asked, more prompt than question.

He didn't want to—he'd been sitting for most of the day—but reality kicked his feet from under him. This was what nightmares were made of. A real-life bogeyman was out there. He was coming after them all, and he'd take Lucas first just to watch Rob suffer. That twisted smile, that singsong snide tone, it was a game, a sick game, and Rob could've stopped him, could've—

"Rob?"

Zoë's voice shoved the image of Folden's face aside, in its place the sight of Lucas, staring up at him, frowning, puzzled, not yet afraid. Rob smiled and ruffled his son's hair, but he couldn't stretch to the lie that it would be OK.

"You need something a bit stronger than coffee," Travis said. He left the room before Rob could reply.

"Sit down," Zoë commanded. He did as he was told.

Travis returned with a tumbler of Scotch. "Here you go, mate."

"I'm on the bike," Rob protested but took the glass anyway and gulped down a mouthful, relishing the unfamiliar burn in his throat.

"Leave the bike here. We'll call you a cab, or you can kip on the couch." Travis looked to Zoë for support, which she gave without hesitation.

"You can use Lu's sleeping bag," she said. "I've never seen you this shaken up."

There was no point playing it down, but he'd keep it to the bare bones for Lucas's sake. He was sitting so close he was almost on Rob's knee. "Have you seen the news this evening?"

"Local or national?" Zoë asked.

"Either. The patient who escaped from Brookhurst?"

"Yeah," Travis confirmed. "It was on the radio. Someone you know?"

"I put him in prison."

"Ah. D'you think he'll come after you?"

"He might." Rob held eye contact until he was sure Travis understood there was no 'might' about it.

Travis nodded. "What do you need from us?"

"The head of my old unit is arranging temporary accommodation for the three of you, just in case the escapee gets hold of this address."

"Is that really necessary?" Zoë asked and then glowered when Travis interjected before Rob could answer.

"Tonight?"

"Tomorrow," Rob said. "Not sure what time it'll be."

"No problem. We can pack a few things before we go to bed so we're ready."

"Hold on!" Zoë held up her hand. "What about Lu and school?"

"Isn't spring break next week?"

"Yep," Travis confirmed.

"It'll be sorted before they go back."

Lucas groaned.

"It better had be," Zoë warned. "He's already behind with his work."

"Can we still go to Nan and Grandad Harvey's, Dad?"

With everything else going on, their trip had slipped Rob's mind.

"Pleeease, Dad?"

Lucas was doing it again, the big wide pleading eyes, and Rob didn't know how to answer. He looked to Zoë and Travis for guidance; they both shrugged.

"I think we'll have to leave it till the next holiday, Lu."

Lucas slumped in disappointment but said, "OK. Can I go back to bed?"

"Course you can."

He got up, calling, "Night!" as he hurried from the room, on the brink of tears.

"Laters, taters." Rob's heart was breaking. He couldn't let his son down. Not again. He glugged the rest of the Scotch and accepted a top-up, waiting until the thumps overhead ceased, signifying Lucas had made it to his bed. "I'm gonna get a car," he said, then clarified, "I'm not selling the bike, but it's noticeable."

"If you need somewhere to store it, you can leave it in my warehouse," Travis offered.

"Cheers, but I should be OK." He'd already arranged to leave it in Tonka's garage, but he appreciated the offer. "And if it's all right with you both, I'm still gonna take Lu up to Mum's next week."

Travis thumbed at Zoë. "It's the boss's decision."

She locked eyes with Rob. "No, it's your decision. I trust you."

"Thank you," he said. He vented a long, exhausted breath and downed the second glass of Scotch. "Right, where's that sleeping bag?"

Epilogue

"I'm still blown away they didn't notice their patient had changed identity." Gray had said the same thing, with minor variations, at least a dozen times in the week that had lapsed since they'd discovered Anders Folden's body-swap trick. Theorising how he'd conned an entire team of medical professionals was an excellent and necessary distraction from the horrifying reality of Folden being out there, somewhere, enacting the next stage of his plan.

A doctor emerged from one of the two doors on the other side of the waiting room and strolled over to the admin desk. He looked so confident, so sure of his abilities, Gray wondered if he'd have fallen for Folden's ploy. What would it say of his competence in treating the sick?

The doctor picked up a patient's file from the desk and called, "Joan Ogilvy?" The woman sitting in front of them gathered her belongings and hurried after the doctor, already back in his room. The door closed.

"Why would they question it?" Will asked rhetorically, which was a new development. Every time Gray had brought it up, Will had listened but made no comment, and that was fine. Gray was only thinking aloud. But they both needed the distraction today.

"Why wouldn't they? Parker's twenty years older than Folden, and completely grey."

"Ah, but there was that psychological study, wasn't there?" Will said.

"Was there?"

"Yep." He was on his phone, playing a game that consisted of repeatedly poking the screen to land a blob of bright-green jelly with eyes on a tower of neon-pink blocks. He mistimed a poke, and the blob splatted against the side of the screen. Will locked his phone and put it in his pocket. "The participants thought it was a job interview. Halfway through, the interviewer left, and a different person came back in. Most of the participants didn't notice. It's called change blindness or something."

"After months, though?"

"They could all have been in on it."

"They weren't," Gray said.

Will shrugged. "Why don't you ask Josh? He'll know."

Gray felt his face warm and glanced sideways, spotting the wicked glint in Will's eyes. He bumped Will's thigh with his own. "How's your head?"

"Fine today, typically." He took a breath to say more but didn't—another instance of the unspoken fear rising almost to the surface.

Will didn't talk about his mum's illness, only her life before diagnosis—the protest marches and sit-ins, her amazing vegan meals, all the skills she'd taught him, the knowledge she'd imparted, her unconditional love—so Gray didn't know if genetics had ever been mentioned. Whatever the outcome of today's appointment, he was sticking around for as long as Will would have him.

"Wilfred Richards?" It was a different doctor, but she made the same slow scan of those waiting. Will got up, and the doctor gave a polite almost-smile, directing him towards her consultation room. As he reached the door, Will glanced back, his chilled confidence supplanted by nerves and panic. Gray was right behind him and met his gaze, transmitting good thoughts and reassurances that Will wasn't doing this alone.

"Mr. Richards, I'm Miss Crawford, consultant orthopaedic surgeon. Please, have a seat." She indicated the plastic chair closest to her desk for Will and then the one next to it, casting a cursory glance at Gray before she seated herself in a comfy-looking swivel chair and opened Will's file. "You've been having headaches?"

"Yes."

"For how long?"

"About six months."

She hummed, her eyes still on his notes. "Debilitating... No blurred vision... No dizziness..."

"No," Will confirmed.

"What do they feel like? Are they in one particular place, or...?"

"Mostly here." Will touched the area behind his right ear, holding position until she looked his way. "It feels like something's squeezing my skull."

"All of it, or just that region?"

"Just that bit."

Wheeling her chair closer to Will, the doctor leaned forward and cupped the side of his head, pressing her thumb and fingers into his hair and working her way down and around to his nape. "Any pain in your neck at all?"

"Sometimes, maybe? It's hard to tell."

She rolled her chair back and flicked through the rest of the pages in Will's file. "You came for an MRI scan two weeks ago?" Will nodded. "It's clear." She must've heard him exhale—she'd have needed to be in a different room to miss it—because she asked, "What did you think it was?"

"I hoped it was migraines, but...my mum died last year. She had a glioblastoma."

"Ah, I see. Well, glioblastomas are not inherited, unless they're a secondary symptom of something else, and even then, it's rare. I think what's happening here is what's called a cervicogenic headache, caused by an impinged nerve in your cervical spine. The nerve pathways are very close and they interact. The brain can't discriminate, so it makes a best guess. The pain in your head is referred pain—the problem is in your neck. Before the headaches started, were you in an accident of any kind, or did you change your lifestyle?"

"Yeah." Will laughed and rolled his eyes. "It was when I started working for Royal Mail."

"Lots of lifting?" the doctor guessed.

"Yep, and getting in and out of the van."

"OK." She put the file on the desk and focused on Will, properly, for the first time. "I can give you an injection now that will see off the headache, possibly for good. I also want you to attend physiotherapy for a few weeks and sort out your posture, get some pointers on how to lift without injury. The important thing is there's no underlying medical cause."

Will sighed and reached for Gray's hand, squeezing it hard. "Thank you. That is a huge relief."

"For both of us," Gray said.

The doctor's smile was more convincing this time. "I'll get that injection for you now. It—"

Will gave a tentative cough. "Sorry to interrupt, but I don't want the injection."

"It's very quick and no more painful than a tetanus jab."

"I'm OK with needles, but I don't take medication."

She leaned back in her chair, her eyes coolly judgemental. "It's your choice, Mr. Richards…"

"I appreciate you taking the time to see me, Miss Crawford. You've lifted a massive weight from my mind. I can handle the pain myself, now I know it's nothing serious, but I would like to take up your offer of physio."

"I'll make the referral today—you'll get a letter within a couple of weeks with a number to call to arrange an appointment."

"Thank you."

"Any further questions?"

Will shook his head. "Gray?"

"None from me."

"All right. I'll see you for a follow-up in three months." Miss Crawford picked up a pen and started writing, offering another almost-smile to send them on their way.

***

"How long now, Dad?"

"About quarter of an hour."

"You said that last time."

"Because you only asked two minutes ago."

Lucas huffed, jiggling in his seat. "Are we stopping at the services?"

"Not unless you're gonna pee your pants." Rob indicated to overtake a truck. The drive up north had been uneventful—no hold-ups, normal traffic—but five hours on the road had him fidgety too, and he resisted the temptation to put his foot down, indicating to pull back into the inside lane. The motorhome drifted in behind him and flashed its lights twice. Rob watched the speedometer, laying off the gas until the needle returned to hovering on sixty.

Lucas twisted in his seat to look out the back window. "Does Nan know they're coming?"

"Yeah." He'd had to tell her—the same version he'd told Lucas—seeing as she'd be stuck with that motorhome in the drive for the next week. "Sit properly, Lu."

That earned Rob another huff, but Lucas turned to face the front again and started fiddling with the blowers. "Are you keeping this, Dad? Once the crazy man's back in hospital?"

"I dunno. D'you want me to?"

"If you like."

Lucas fell silent, and Rob briefly glanced over, laughing when he saw his pinched-lipped expression. "What car d'you reckon I should get?"

"An Agera."

"How much are they?"

"Two million."

"That all? I could get you one while I'm at it."

"Will you, yeah?"

"Oh, yeah," Rob said, nodding solemnly.

"Or a Veyron. They're not as much."

"We don't want to cheapen our image, Lu."

"True, that. What about a Veneno?"

"I thought you didn't like Lamborghinis."

"The new ones are all right, I s'pose. Will your mate get hers back?"

"I hope so." Now the Parkers' relatives had agreed to sell the company, there was no reason why Tonka couldn't buy back her Aventador, or a Veneno even.

"How about a Lykan Hypersport?" Lucas suggested.

"How much are they?"

"Guess."

"Hmm...two million?"

"Nope. More."

"Two and a half?"

"More."

"Blimey. Three?"

"Nope..."

***

"I think I'm going to buy another car."

A catering porter stopped next to their table and held open a rubbish bag. Will dumped their empty cups in it and smiled in thanks. "The journey's been all right," he said.

"Yeah, it has," Gray agreed. "But the cost of train tickets...I could lease a car for that. Actually, I might look at leasing instead."

"Just a little runaround?"

"I was thinking more along the lines of an Audi. Something with a bit of oomph."

"You're a speed demon," Will teased.

Gray weighed it up. "I don't push the engine beyond its limits, but—" He paused to listen to the announcement that they were arriving at Leeds. Other passengers were already out of their seats and moving along the carriage. In the next gap, Will stood to get their bags down from the overhead lockers, and he and Gray joined the slow flow towards the doors.

"But?" Will prompted, glancing back.

"Yes. I'm a speed demon," Gray admitted. Will laughed. "I'm nervous."

"You'll be fine."

The train stopped, and the queue edged forward. Will stepped down onto the platform, waiting for Gray to clear the door before they moved off again, side by side, close enough they could've held hands but settled for the safer contact of knuckles brushing together, parting briefly to pass through the ticket barrier.

"It bothers me," Gray said.

"Seeing Suzannah again?"

"Not exactly. How reckless I was. Sometimes I almost forget, but then we do something like this, and my thoughts immediately default to the worst-case scenario."

"Everything in life carries risks, Gray. It's unreasonable to believe you can mitigate all of them."

"I know, but I have to exercise more caution." Gray spotted Suzannah up ahead, waving frantically. He waved back, even more astounded by her and Will's alikeness than the last time he'd seen her. She was a beautiful young woman and, judging by her smile, as happy to see Gray as he was her. "Especially now I have responsibilities."

***

"You all right, Mum?"

She was standing, arms crossed, staring out of her living room window at the motorhome taking up all but an eighteen-inch-wide strip of driveway and blocking most of the daylight, leaving the front of the house unusually dark.

Rob drew up next to her. "Mum?"

"Yes, dear. Just daydreaming." She nodded at the motorhome. "Does it have all the mod cons?"

"You mean a fridge and cooker and stuff? Yeah. It's even got a shower."

"A toilet?"

"Yep."

"Mmm." She nodded thoughtfully. "Would your friends like to come in for a coffee?"

They were there as a deterrent, a show of force, so it wasn't as if they were aiming to stay hidden.

"I'll ask them," Rob said. With a quick check what Lucas was up to—playing with Linford in the back garden, under Grandad Harvey's supervision—he opened the front door and almost walked into Dee Knight. He startled and stepped back.

"Sorry!" Dee grimaced.

"No worries. Everything all right?"

"Yes, thanks. And in here?"

"Same," Rob confirmed.

"Great. I just came to let you know I'm heading out to the local supermarket. We forgot sugar."

"Ah, OK. My mum'll have some, I'm sure, unless you needed to pick up other things? I was actually coming to invite you both in for coffee."

"Oh, fab! We don't want to impose, though. Are you sure your mum won't mind?"

"It was her idea. Believe me, she wouldn't have invited you if she minded."

"OK. I'll go get Tarq and we'll be right in."

"See you in a minute." Rob left the door on the latch for them and went upstairs to use the bathroom before he joined everyone in the garden.

It had been a hell of a week. Between getting Zoë, Travis and Lucas settled in their temporary home—a ground-floor flat in St. John's Wood—and telling Dom Hooper and Martin Winstanley everything he could remember from his work on the SAP case,

Rob had barely had a minute to himself. His flat was full of surveillance equipment, and the car he was driving—not his choice—was a basic Ford Fiesta bought by the SIU and registered under the pseudonym 'Steven Radley'.

The rest of his paperwork was being processed and would be ready by the time he and Lu got back to London, which would be about when the Freddie Berringer shit hit the fan. Not that Rob had anything to do with the case anymore; with no leads on Folden, Rob was out of circulation indefinitely, but he was also out of the loop.

Not surprisingly, Hedley hadn't been in touch since Will amended his definitive statement that 'Berringer attacked the victim without provocation', which would have resulted in a murder conviction, to 'the victim had a hammer in his hand when Berringer attacked', which would more than likely lead to a complete acquittal. Rob felt terrible for his part in sabotaging the case, but it was all horses for courses at this point, and he had bigger things to worry about than Freddie Berringer getting away with murder, or whether Martina ever spoke to him again.

He finished up in the bathroom and walked along the landing, pausing at the window that overlooked the back garden. Lucas and Linford had stopped chasing around in circles and were crashed together on a picnic blanket while Harvey was giving Dee and Tarquin the guided tour, which made Rob chuckle. Either they were really into their bedding plants or they were great actors. Fortunately for them, it wasn't a big garden, and in any case, Rob's mum imminently came to the rescue with a coffee pot and mugs.

Turning from the window, Rob took his phone from his pocket and checked it, purely out of habit; he wasn't expecting any calls. Just one notification: he opened the message on his way downstairs, smiling at the caption 'your gorgeous nieces xx' accompanying the photo of Lois and Amber enjoying a rare night out together. By the looks of it, they were in the wine bar in the town centre; too much black and white, too many lights, it attracted the younger, trendy crowd and was not somewhere he'd choose to go. There again, they didn't like his choice of social venue much, either.

He re-locked his phone and made a mental note to give them a call later, see if they fancied having a pint with their Uncle Rob. He'd even put up with the wine bar if they insisted; the 'where' didn't matter, only the 'who'.

Rob almost made it to the garden before it hit him, stopping him dead in his tracks and turning his blood to ice. The image of Lois and Amber, smiling into the camera...

It wasn't a selfie.

About the Author

Debbie McGowan is an author and publisher based in a semi-rural corner of Lancashire, England. She writes character-driven, realist fiction, celebrating life, love and relationships. A working class girl, she 'ran away' to London at seventeen, was homeless, unemployed and then homeless again, interspersed with animal rights activism (all legal, honest ;)) and volunteer work as a mental health advocate. At twenty-five, she went back to college to study social science—tough with two toddlers, but they had a 'stay at home' dad, so it worked itself out. These days, the toddlers are young women (much to their chagrin), and Debbie teaches undergraduate students, writes novels and runs an independent publishing company, occasionally grabbing an hour of sleep where she can.

Social Media Links

Website: debbiemcgowan.co.uk
Newsletter Signup: eepurl.com/b8emHL
Blog: deb248211.blogspot.com
Facebook: facebook.com/DebbieMcGowanAuthor and facebook.com/beatentrackpublishing
Twitter: @writerdebmcg
YouTube: youtube.com/deb248211
Instagram: instagram/writerdebmcg
Google+: plus.google.com/+DebbieMcGowan
Tumblr: writerdebmcg.tumblr.com
LinkedIn: uk.linkedin.com/in/writerdebmcg
Goodreads: goodreads.com/DebbieMcGowan

By the Author

Checking Him Out Series
Checking Him Out (Book One)
Checking Him Out For the Holidays (Novella)
Hiding Out (Novella – Noah and Matty – HBTC Crossover)
Taking Him On (Book Two – Noah and Matty)
Checking In (Book Three)
The Making of Us (Book Four – Jesse and Leigh)

Seeds of Tyrone Series
~ co-written with Raine O'Tierney
Leaving Flowers (Book One)
Where the Grass is Greener (Book Two)
Christmas Craic and Mistletoe (Book Three)

Hiding Behind The Couch Series
The ongoing story of 'The Circle'…
Nine friends from high school;
Nine friends for life.

The Story So Far…
in chronological order:
novellas and short novels are 'stand-alone' stories, but tie in with the
series. Think Middle Earth—well, more Middle England, but with a
social conscience!

Beginnings (Novella)
Ruminations (Novel)
Class-A (Short Story)
Hiding Behind The Couch (Season One)
No Time Like The Present (Season Two)
The Harder They Fall (Season Three)

Crying in the Rain (Novel)
First Christmas (Novella)
In The Stars Part I: Capricorn–Gemini (Season Four)
Breaking Waves (Novella)
In The Stars Part II: Cancer–Sagittarius (Season Five)
A Midnight Clear (Novella)
Red Hot Christmas (Novella)
Two By Two (Season Six)
Hiding Out (Novella – CHO Crossover)
Breakfast at Cordelia's Aquarium (Short Story)
Chain of Secrets (Novella)
Those Jeffries Boys (Novel)
The WAG and The Scoundrel (Gray Fisher #1)
Reunions (Season Seven)
To Be Sure (Novella)
Tabula Rasa (Gray Fisher #2)
What A Scorcher! (Short Story)
Goth of Christmas Past (Novel)

Stand-Alone Stories
Champagne (LGBT Historical Novel)
'Time to Go' in *Story Salon Big Book of Stories (Contemporary Short Story)*
And The Walls Came Tumbling Down (Sci-fi Novel)
No Dice (Sci-fi Novel)
Double Six (Sci-fi Novel)
Sugar and Sawdust (M/M Romance Short Story)
Cherry Pop Valentine (M/M Romance Short Story)
Coming Up ~ co-written with Al Stewart (LGBT Short Story)
Of the Bauble (LGBT Fantasy Romance Novella)
So Long, Little Black Diamonds (Short (True) Story)
The Pastor's Last Drop (Historical Novel (Ongoing) – Wattpad)
When Skies Have Fallen (LGBT Historical Romance Novel)
A Snowy Ball (When Skies Have Fallen #1.5)
The Great Village Bun Fight

www.hidingbehindthecouch.com
www.debbiemcgowan.co.uk

Beaten Track Publishing

For more titles from Beaten Track Publishing,
please visit our website:

http://www.beatentrackpublishing.com

Thanks for reading!